ETCHED ON MY HEART

SAMANTHA YOUNG

Etched On My Heart

By Samantha Young

Edited by Jennifer Sommersby Young
Cover Design by Samantha Young

ALSO BY SAMANTHA YOUNG

Acknowledgments

I was writing Jane and Jamie's story just as the coronavirus was beginning to spread around the world. It's a true testament to how enraptured I was by these characters that it wasn't until the book was finished that I really began to feel the emotional impact of the pandemic. I'll be forever grateful to this story for providing me with that escape. There were a lot of important subjects to tackle in this novel, and because of my sincere desire to handle them with sensitivity, this book has probably been one of the most difficult of mine to write. I gave it everything I had. And I hope readers felt my total immersion in *Etched On My Heart* through the bond between Jane and Jamie.

First, I must thank the Goldbrickers for keeping me sane when I "went with my gut" a number of times writing this book. And by going "with my gut" I mean cutting chapters, rearranging narrative, and rewriting until I told the story I needed to tell. Goldbrickers, your support meant so much to me. Thank you!

For the most part writing is a solitary endeavor but publishing most certainly is not. I have to thank my wonderful editor Jennifer Sommersby Young. Thank you for believing in this story too!

And thank you to my bestie and PA extraordinaire, Ashleen Walker, for handling all the little things and supporting me through everything. I appreciate you so much. Love you lots!

The life of a writer doesn't stop with the book. Our job

expands beyond the written word to marketing, advertising, graphic design, social media management and more. Help from those in the know goes a long way. A huge thank you to Nina Grinstead at Valentine PR for brainstorming with me, for your encouragement, your insight and for going above and beyond. You're amazing and I'm so grateful for you.

Thank you to Liz Berry and Jillian Stein for giving me the encouragement and advice I needed in deciding to relaunch a story I love so much!

Thank you to every single blogger, instagrammer and book lover who has helped spread the word about my books. You all are appreciated so much! On that note, a massive thank you to all the fantastic readers in my private Facebook group *Sam's Clan McBookish*. You make me smile every day!

As always, thank you to my agent Lauren Abramo for making it possible for readers all over the world to find my words. I feel privileged to have you as my agent and friend.

I have to say thank you to my family and friends who were particularly patient and supportive with me as I worked on this book. Thank you for loving me and for getting it.

Finally, to you my reader, the biggest thank you of all. I hope you're all safe and well. And I hope you enjoyed this small piece of escapism.

When you embark on a journey of revenge, dig two graves.
Confucius

PART ONE
THE PAST

CHAPTER ONE

JANE
Thirteen years old

THE SMOG WAS A PAIN. Willa sometimes let me go with her when she drove into the city, but it was a bad smog day, which meant we were staying at our apartment in the nice complex in Glendale. I was bored. Willa was too busy with my younger foster siblings to care about my boredom. Flo was eighteen months old and fascinated by sockets and switches. Tarin was three and interested in destroying everything in sight.

His screaming and Flo's yelling was not fun.

"Can I help?" I asked from the hallway.

Willa waved me away as she lifted Flo up into her high chair. "It's the summer, kid. Go be with your friends."

Willa and Nicholas Green were the nicest foster parents I'd had. I'd been with them for over two years, and I hoped I'd get to stay with them until I was eighteen. That was five years away, so I knew I should get used to the constant nerves in my belly, waiting for my social worker to turn up and tell me I was being moved again.

Hoping Willa and Nick would keep me around, I tried to be as helpful as possible.

They were kind of busy with the younger kids, which was why Willa still hadn't realized I didn't have any friends. But they didn't drink, they didn't cuss at me, and they'd never hit me.

"Are you sure?"

My foster mom shot me a flustered smile. "You're not hired help, Jane. It's summer vacation. Go be a kid."

Nodding, I turned toward the small bedroom at the back of the apartment. Nicholas worked as a production manager for one of the big film studios, which was why we lived in a nice apartment. It was one of the bigger three-bedroom units. The little ones shared a room and I had the smallest room.

Willa and Nick might not give me a lot of their time, but they buy me books and art supplies. Grabbing my sketch pad and a tin of charcoals, I swiped a bottle of water from the refrigerator and stepped outside. It was like walking into a bubble of heat, the air sticking to my skin as I wandered along the balcony. It overlooked the pool, and I saw a few neighbors on loungers while some kids from school splashed around in the water.

Those kids weren't my friends. I'd never been very good at making friends.

As I passed my neighbors' apartments, I could hear loud voices coming from the last unit by the staircase. They had interesting accents, like they might be from Boston, and they were shouting to be heard over their music playing.

I noted their door was wide open.

"Lorna, we haven't finished unpacking. Get up, Lor. I want this finished by dinner. You can park your butt on the couch for the rest of the evening once it's all done."

I slowed. She said "park" like "pahk," which was definitely Bostonian, right?

"I'm bored unpacking," a girl replied in the same accent. "Can we take a break?"

"But once it's done, it's done. Your brother has already unpacked all his stuff."

They continued to argue while I sat down on the first step and opened my sketch pad. Their conversation became background noise as I sketched my neighbors at the pool.

Like always, I zoned out. Sketching made everything else go away. The loneliness. My fears. The separation I felt from almost everyone else. Drawing was my way to connect, but from a safe distance. I liked the rasp of the charcoal against the vellum, the way it smudged my hands. The freedom of using the smudge to create interesting shadows and curves. It gave life to the kids splashing around in the pool. Movement. Energy. Made me feel as if I were a part of them.

So lost in creating, I didn't hear her approach until she was sitting down beside me on the step.

"You're wicked talented."

I jumped, startled, and a charcoal line scored through my drawing.

"Sorry about that."

I looked at the girl, who wore an apologetic wince. She had eyes the color of the ocean and short, light brown hair.

"Your drawing." She pointed to it. "It's wicked good."

"It was okay," I murmured as I tried unsuccessfully to rub out the charcoal line.

"Where did you learn to draw like that?"

I shrugged because, truthfully, I didn't learn. I just ... drew.

"What's your name?"

"Jane."

"Jane. I'm Lorna McKenna." A hand appeared above my sketch.

The small hand had stubby fingernails painted with a bright pink, glittery polish. I smiled and looked up at Lorna. She seemed determined to get to know me. Usually my shyness pushed would-be friends away.

I showed her my charcoal-covered palm and fingers.

She shrugged, her chin jutting out with determination. "Then shake it with your other hand."

I did. Her hand was cool, as if she'd been sitting beneath the AC inside her apartment.

She broke into a wide grin as we shook hands, and I couldn't help but return her smile. Her gaze dropped to my left cheek. "You have a dimple!" Lorna exclaimed, as if this was the most impressive thing she'd ever encountered.

I automatically touched the dimple with my charcoal-covered fingertips.

"It's cute. I wish I had a dimple. How old are you?"

"Thirteen."

She nodded like she'd expected that. "I'll be thirteen in three weeks."

"Where are you from?" My curiosity got the better of my usual timidity. I had to know if I was right about Boston.

"The Dot."

I frowned.

Lorna smirked. "Dorchester. That's in Boston."

Ah. I *was* right. I'd seen the movie *Good Will Hunting* a lot because Willa had a thing for Matt Damon.

"Is it nice there?" I asked.

Lorna wrinkled her nose. "Boston is. Not the area of Dorchester we lived in. It was a shitty neighborhood. A guy got shot outside our apartment a few months ago." She shrugged like it was no big deal.

I was pretty sure my mouth was hanging open.

"So, how come you're not playing with those kids down by the pool?" she asked.

I followed her curious gaze to the two girls and two boys squealing and splashing around. The girls were neighbors; the boys lived on our block. And I knew because we were in the same class at middle school. "That's Summer and Greta. They're the most popular girls in my class."

"Yeah, so?"

I blushed, knowing what I was about to say would probably push Lorna away. "I'm not exactly popular."

Lorna nudged me with her shoulder, giving me a conspiratorial nod. The action was familiar. Like we'd been friends for ages. It was nice. "Popular and not-so-popular kids? Like on TV, huh? Back at my school, we didn't have cliques like that. You had the kids who were just trying to lie low and get through the year and the kids who were shiesty—already into bad shit and to be avoided at all costs."

"Did you live in the ghetto?"

She laughed. "The ghetto? Really? Noooo." She nudged me again as if she thought I was cute. "We were poor, though. Everyone we knew was. Mom said people do stupid shit to forget the crappiness of their life or even stupider shit to cheat their way out of poverty."

I didn't know a lot about money, but I knew our apartment complex wasn't cheap as far as rent costs went because Willa was always complaining about it.

Seeming to read my thoughts, Lorna told me, "We moved in here with our big sister, Skye."

As if on cue, a woman's voice rang out from the apartment. "Lorna! The Waterboys!"

Her face lit up. "Come on." Lorna grabbed my hand, pulling me to my feet, so I had no choice but to follow. I dropped my sketch pad on the top step and let her lead me into the apartment. When was the last time someone held my hand?

A thrill thrummed beneath my skin.

The apartment was the same size as Willa and Nick's, and there were packing boxes everywhere.

A tall, stunning young woman was swaying with her hands in the air as an unfamiliar song played from the TV. She broke into a gorgeous smile at the sight of us. "Who's this?"

"This is Jane!" Lorna called over the music. "Jane, this is my big sister, Skye."

"Nice to meet you," she said, and seemed to mean it. I waved shyly. Then she leaned over, picked up a remote and pointed it at the TV, and the volume increased.

I watched as Lorna let go of my hand and joined her sister in the middle of the room. It occurred to me that Lorna was tall for her age too, ably spinning her big sister as they shouted lyrics at the top of their lungs about how the other saw the whole of the moon while they only saw the crescent. As unfamiliar as the song was, I immediately liked it.

Realizing I was just watching, Lorna waved me over.

Too timid to join them, I stayed put.

It was Skye who broke away from her little sister and pulled me into the center of the room with them. "Just let go!" she yelled. "You'll love it!"

And to my surprise, my feet moved, my hips too. Lorna grabbed one hand, Skye the other, and we made a circle, lifting our clasped hands in the air. I laughed as the siblings continued to shout the lyrics at the top of their lungs. It was the most bizarre and wonderful moment, feeling a part of something with these two strangers.

When the song ended, I giggled with them, feeling high on the connection—and the feeling of being *seen*.

"I've never heard that song before," I confessed as Skye lowered the volume.

"It's called 'The Whole of the Moon' by The Waterboys," Lorna informed me. "They're an eighties band. It was our mom's favorite song."

"Now it's our song." Skye reached out to wrap an arm around her sister, pulling her into her side. Lorna giggled and playfully pushed her away.

Her big sister turned to me. "Lemonade?"

I nodded, thirsty after all the dancing.

The sitting room and kitchen were all one room. She moved into the kitchen while Lorna gestured for me to take a seat on the sofa, the only piece of furniture not covered in stuff.

I relaxed, surprised how quickly I'd become comfortable around the sisters. Lorna threw herself energetically down beside me. We both wore shorts and T-shirts, but where my legs barely touched the floor, hers sprawled out on it. She was paler than me and Skye, but winters in California versus Massachusetts would fix that.

"When did you move in?"

"Last night. You're the first person we've met."

Skye returned with the lemonade, a glass for each of us. She pushed aside items on the coffee table and sat on it to face us while we sipped the cool drink.

"You live here, Jane?" she asked.

At Skye's stillness, I was once again struck by her beauty. I really wanted to draw her. She and Lorna shared the same ocean eyes and light brown hair. Except Skye's reached the middle of her back in soft waves, and she had golden highlights. While Lorna had a strong nose, Skye's was daintier. A little button. The resemblance between them was undeniable, but it was as if Skye's features had been perfected, while Lorna's had quirks and imperfections that made them even more interesting. I thought they both had wonderful faces— great for sketching.

"I do," I answered Skye's question. "I live a few doors down."

"With your parents?"

"Foster parents."

Her expression softened in sympathy.

"It's just me, Jamie, and Skye now," Lorna stated.

I looked at her, my brow furrowed in confusion. "Who's Jamie?"

"My big brother. He'll be fifteen this September. Our mom died three months ago. And our dad took off when I was young." Lorna's mouth twisted in a bitter sneer. "He never liked me."

Uncomfortable, I didn't know what to say.

Skye apparently sensed this and reached to pat Lorna's knee. "Sweetie, you know that's not true." She flicked me a look. "I'm sorry, Jane. Things are a little difficult at the moment."

"No, they're not." Lorna pushed her sister's hand away. "They're the best they've ever been."

My eyes widened. Her mom died, and this was the best things had ever been?

"What is Jane going to think?" Skye huffed in exasperation.

"The truth." Lorna gave me that stubbornly determined look I'd already come to suspect was a common expression for her. "Jane's going to be my new best friend, and best friends tell each other everything."

While Skye chuckled at this, I felt my heart lurch in my chest.

I hadn't had a best friend since second grade.

"Skye moved to LA a few years ago to become an actress, and she just won this amazing role on the show, *The Sorcerer*."

My eyes widened. There were a lot of wannabe actors in

LA, but that didn't mean I'd met anyone from a show as big as *The Sorcerer*. "I love that show."

Skye beamed. Like Lorna, she had the kind of smile that prodded your own lips to mirror the action. While Lorna's ocean eyes were flinty and a little too hardened for a thirteen-year-old, Skye's were warm and sparkled like waves beneath the sun. "Great! A fan! I'm a new major character."

I noted then that Skye's accent was more diluted than her sister's.

"That's amazing." I was totally impressed.

"You want to be an actor?" Lorna misunderstood my awe.

I shook my head adamantly. *No way. Cameras in my face, pretending to be someone I wasn't. People watching my every move. My face plastered across tabloids. Ugh, I would rather eat slugs.*

"Let me guess ... an artist?"

I blushed at Lorna's guess and shrugged. Which meant yes.

"Do *you* want to act?" I asked Lorna.

"Nope. The money is too uncertain." Lorna straightened her spine. "I'm going to go to college and become a fancy litigator. That's a kind of lawyer. They make a ton of money."

"And she'll do it too." Skye grinned affectionately at her sister before turning to me. "Your new best friend is the most ambitious person you'll ever meet."

"Well, it makes up for having an actress and a moody writer in the family."

Lorna's sister scowled. "Stop teasing Jamie about his writing. You know it sets him off."

The brother was a writer. How cool. "I love books."

"Yeah, see?" Skye gestured to me as she stood. "If Jamie finds out you're telling everyone about his writing, this place will turn into World War III, and I don't have time for that."

"Jane can keep a secret. Can't you, Jane?"

I nodded vehemently.

"Told you."

Skye offered me her kind smile. "Jane, I love my sister, but try not to let her bulldoze you into agreeing to everything she wants you to agree to. Or doing stuff during this burgeoning best friendship of yours that you're not comfortable with."

Lorna huffed. "I wouldn't do that."

Her sister rolled her eyes. "I have to get to work. There's money on the counter for pizza and Jane is welcome to join you. I'll tell Jamie to order more than one pizza, so there's enough for everyone. That boy could eat through a house."

Skye disappeared down the hall, and I could hear her talking to someone.

Obviously, Jamie. Despite my shyness, I was curious to meet him. If he was anything like his sisters, I'd probably fall in love with him immediately.

After Skye left, Lorna turned toward me on the sofa, tucking her knees to her chest. "Skye has been living in LA for a couple years, but her new job means we can afford to move here instead of the crappy apartment she was sharing with a buddy. She said there's a big shopping area here. Is that true?"

I nodded and told Lorna about Brand Boulevard, a stretch filled with shops and restaurants, a movie theater, and how there were plans in development for an outdoor shopping mall. I told her how Glendale was the one place you could get authentic and great Armenian food. We didn't eat out a lot, but we'd eaten enough takeout I could recommend my favorite places. I also offered to take Lorna to my favorite bakery.

After listening intently, Lorna cocked her head to the side and studied me. "You seem way older than thirteen. I know why *I'm* wicked mature." She gestured dramatically to her chest. "But why are you?"

I was a little thrown by the change of subject. I considered it, though, and remembered the time I'd overheard Willa and

Nick talking about me. It was not long after I'd arrived to stay with them.

"She's like a little grown-up," Willa whispered to Nick. *They were in the kitchen; I was in the hall, having gotten out of bed for a glass of water.*

"I know. That's what growing up in the foster system does to you."

"Yeah, knock every ounce of childhood out of you. This is why I prefer fostering younger kids. If we're lucky, we can keep them long enough to give them a proper childhood."

"Do you wish we hadn't agreed to take Jane?"

"No, I'm glad. She's been through a lot. At least we know she's safe here."

Overhearing that hadn't eased my worries. What if one day, Willa decided they couldn't handle a teenager on top of two young kids?

It occurred to me that all the worrying was probably one of the reasons I came off twenty years older than my actual age.

"Foster kid," I replied to Lorna. "Seen a lot too, I guess."

Lorna considered this and nodded. "I knew from the moment we met, we were kindred spirits. Do you know what that means?"

I nodded. I read a lot.

"So, you agree?"

I nodded again.

She smiled. "Do you want to see my room?"

I followed her down the hall, but as she marched ahead, I slowed to a stop at the first open doorway. It belonged to the smallest room where a boy, several years older than me by the look of his long legs, laid on a single bed pressed up against the wall under the window. He'd unpacked his room quite neatly for a teenage boy. A poster of the album cover for Eminem's record, *The Marshall Mathers LP*, hung on the wall above his headboard. On the opposite wall was a scary-looking poster with blurred faces and a fanged skull. The name Richard Matheson was typed along the top of the image and above that were the words *I Am Legend*.

Was that a book?

My gaze swung back to the boy, and I felt goose bumps prickle all over my skin.

His light brown hair hung over his forehead in disarray, earbuds visible in his ears, an audible low hum of music playing through them. He had a strong profile, a slight cut to his cheekbones, and an angular jaw. One jean-clad knee was bent, his arm resting on it and in his hand, a worn paperback. His lips were pursed, as if in concentration.

A flutter made itself known in my belly.

A flutter that intensified when I watched him slowly turn his head toward me.

Stormy ocean eyes glared at me from beneath a moody brow.

We stared at each other a moment. A moment that felt like forever. My skin flushed.

The boy suddenly dropped the book and swung his legs off the bed.

His black T-shirt had the words "The Black Keys" on it. My heart skipped a little beat. We liked the same band. The T-shirt was paired with jeans that might have been dark denim once but had been washed within an inch of their life. He pulled out his earbuds.

"Who are you?" he bit out, just before his eyes flicked to my left.

Lorna had returned to my side.

"What are you doing?"

She shrugged. "Showing Jane around. She's my new best friend. Jane, this is my big brother, Jamie."

Jamie McKenna transferred his glower from Lorna to me. "God help you."

"Hey!" Lorna cried, indignant.

"I don't need your friends poking around my room."

I blushed. Hard. Mortified.

"Ugh, you're embarrassing Jane with your moodiness," Lorna huffed. "It's not cool to be a broody bastard, Jamie, no matter what those books you're reading tell you. It's very nineties, and if you hadn't noticed, that decade is way over."

"Oh, I'm so sorry I embarrassed your nosy little friend here," he scoffed, before marching across his room to the door. "And stop cussing, you little brat. You don't sound smart— you sound like you're trying too hard to be cool." With that, he slammed his bedroom door in our faces.

Oh, I'm so sorry I embarrassed your nosy little friend here.

My cheeks burned even hotter.

"Don't mind him." Lorna grabbed my arm and hauled me down the hall to her room. "He loves me really."

Lorna's room was the same size as the room that Tarin and Flo shared back in Willa and Nick's apartment. I tried to throw Jamie out of my head and concentrate on the surrounding space. Lorna's room was bigger than Jamie's, which I thought was odd since he was older.

There were a few boxes piled in the room, but she didn't seem to have a lot of belongings. As if she'd read my mind, she put her hands on her hips and announced, "Skye has promised to take me shopping before school starts. I'll need new things. Lots of them. And she can afford it now." Her expression turned mischievous. "I'll buy cute posters, too, for my room. Unlike Jamie's. Did you see the skull thing?"

I nodded.

"Creepy, right? It's his favorite book."

I mentally added *I Am Legend* to my to-be-read pile.

I'd noted there were stacks of books organized along one wall in his room, all in need of a bookcase. He was a fellow bookworm. That fluttering in my stomach wouldn't go away. It was so weird!

"I bet he's hidden his writing in his room somewhere." She smirked, like she was thinking of breaking in to find it. "He writes by hand because we can't afford a laptop. Or we *couldn't*. I bet Skye will buy him one now. Did you see his books? Back home, he'd never have left those out."

"Why?"

She shrugged, turning to me. "If his friends knew he liked to read books and write stories, they'd have kicked the shit out of him."

"They don't sound like very nice friends."

Lorna snorted. "Right? I don't understand why he's so pissed we moved when he can, like, be himself here. So, this is my room. Nothing special. Yet." She grabbed my hand again and led me back out to the living room, where she gestured for me to sit on the sofa. She plopped down beside me, turning her knees toward mine.

"Okay, we're going to be best friends, agreed?"

I nodded, getting the feeling I might not have a choice in the matter.

"There are rules in friendship. Rule number one: Always have each other's back."

I could do that.

"Rule number two: Don't give each other shit about the things that we like or don't like. For instance, you enjoy drawing and art and stuff, and I enjoy shopping. At least I think I'll like it."

I grinned at that.

"Rule number three: No liking the same boys. Friendship is more important than boys. That's if you like boys?"

Considering my crush on Zion Reynolds in the sixth grade, and the way my heart still raced after the run-in with Jamie, I'd say so. I nodded.

"Cool. Though it would have been cool with me if you didn't."

I liked rule number three. Loyalty was important to me. I didn't have a lot of experience with it, but I'd like the chance to prove I was capable of it.

"Rule number four." Her eyes narrowed on me, as if she could see right into my soul. "And this is the big one because I've lost friends to this shit."

"Okay?"

"You can't crush on Jamie like every single one of my other friends, and you can't become best friends with Skye. You're *my* friend."

I blushed. Could she see I thought Jamie was cute? Not that her fifteen-year-old brother would ever pay attention to me. As for Skye ... I liked Skye, but she was older. I doubted she wanted to become best friends with her little sister's best friend.

"Okay."

Lorna grinned and clapped her hands together. "Sick!"

I smiled, feeling another flutter of nerves. This time I realized these were butterflies of nervous anticipation. Maybe my final year at middle school wouldn't be so bad now that I had a best friend. And not just any best friend—a tough-talking Bostonian who seemed as fierce as she was determined.

CHAPTER TWO
EIGHTEEN MONTHS LATER

JAMIE
Sixteen years old

MY PHONE BUZZED, interrupting the Silverchair track I was listening to. Probably one of the guys. Pulling my cell out, I discovered I was wrong.

The text was from a girl.

> Hey, Jamie, it's Julie. Trewitt. Wht r u up 2 2nite? Xx

The plans I had for finding a girl to hook up with that night came to fruition in one text. Julie was a senior, and she'd been checking me out lately. Who she got my number from, I didn't know. And I didn't care. Everyone knew Julie was a sure thing, and she wasn't interested in a relationship. The girl just wanted to have fun—who was I to stop her?

My fingers hovered over the keypad, about to tell her where to meet me, when something whacked softly against the back of my head. A cushion.

I spun around, ready to chew out Lorna, and instead found Skye standing in my doorway.

She mimed pulling earbuds out of her ears and I did as she asked, "Ana's Song" fading into a murmur.

"What's up?" I didn't have much patience for my annoying little sister, but I had all the time in the world for my big one.

At first, it pissed me off to leave Boston. I was pissed about everything. My mom being selfish and bitter her whole life, my dad taking off because he couldn't stand being around her anymore, my mom dying when I never got a chance to stop being mad at her, and then having to leave behind what I knew for California, of all places. LA couldn't be more different from Boston.

However, the last year and a half in LA hadn't been so bad. I joined the track-and-field team, something the guys back in Boston would've ripped me apart for. But my new buddies on the team were cool. Not cool enough to tell them I was a writer, but safer than the friends I grew up with who were already getting into seriously shiesty shit back in Dorchester. A couple guys back home had been good friends; the rest, not so much. All of them, however, were heading down a dark path toward prison.

I was glad to be away from all that.

Skye did that for me and Lorna. Gave us a safer place to live. Only a few years ago, I was so pissed at her for leaving us behind, but when Mom died, Skye stepped up.

Now she was doing so well as an actress, she'd moved us from the apartment into a three-bedroom house in Glendale, close to the apartment we first moved into.

A house.

None of us had ever lived in a house.

And this one had a pool and views of the Verdugo Mountains from the back deck.

"I hope you don't have plans for tonight." Skye looked apologetic.

Any hopes of finding satisfaction between Julie Trewitt's gorgeous thighs hovered precariously out of reach. "Why?"

"I have a meeting."

I frowned. "It's Saturday night."

"I know, but I can't skip this meeting. It's with a very important guy who could do amazing things for my career. Amazing things." She stepped farther into my room. "Which would mean having the financial freedom to give you and Lorna whatever future you dream of."

Shit.

Why couldn't Skye be even a little like my mom and Lorna? Selfish to the core. Instead, she genuinely cared about making life better for us.

I tried to argue anyway. "She's fourteen."

Skye gave me a look that pricked my guilt. "If something happened to Lorna while she was alone, neither of us would forgive ourselves."

"Fuck." I slumped down onto the bed. "I had plans tonight."

"I'm sorry. I know babysitting your little sister and her best friend is not what you had in mind, but it's just one night."

That meant I was babysitting Jane too.

Shit, I could deal with Jane over Lorna anytime. "She's such a brat when you're not here, Skye."

"Uh, she's a brat when I *am* here. But she's our sister and we love her."

"She's Mom." I gave Skye a concerned look. "She's Mom through and through."

Skye sighed heavily. She knew I was right. My little sister was selfish and self-involved and intensely focused on money because until last year, she'd never had it. She was also exhausting. No one ever loved her enough. Cared enough. Paid her enough attention.

Mom through and through.

"I'm not sure that's true. I think she's fourteen, and fourteen-year-old girls can be hard work." She shrugged. "You weren't exactly a picnic a year ago."

I grunted.

"And Mom didn't have Jane Doe in her life. Jane's a good influence on Lorna."

I snorted. Jane was a pushover. That kid was so desperate for someone to care about her, she let Lorna bulldoze her. I felt a little guilty thinking that, knowing what I knew about the kid. As bad as we'd had it in the parental department, we hadn't been left outside a police station as a baby.

I'd never met anyone who was a real-life Jane Doe before.

Skye smiled, her eyes flicking to the hall. "I love that kid," she confessed. "I love that *our* kid is hanging out with a great kid like Jane."

I already knew that. Skye didn't hide her affection for the little orphan. I sighed. I guessed if anyone could temper Lorna, it would be Jane.

There went my night. "Do I have to be in the same room as them?"

My big sister chuckled. "No, drama king. But I want you in the living room and not hiding out in here. They could sneak out if you do that."

"Sneak out where?"

"This is Lorna we're talking about. She's unpredictable."

That was true. "Fine." I pushed up from the bed and kicked off my shoes. Grabbing my copy of *The Stand* by Stephen King from my bedside table, I followed Skye out of my room. Down the hall came the sound of giggling beneath the strains of Kings of Leon's "On Call." I smirked. Another point in Jane's favor was that when she was around, she improved my little sister's taste in music.

As we made our way downstairs, I texted Julie back that I was babysitting, but we should catch up tomorrow night. Passing the coffee table, I saw the open sketch pad sprawled across it and stopped to look. I turned the pad by the corner so I wouldn't smudge the drawing. It was a sketch of Skye. She was staring off into the distance, fingering a strand of hair, wearing a thoughtful expression.

Jane drew it.

I felt Skye's chin rest on my shoulder. "I love how that kid sees me."

I smiled.

"She's so freaking talented, it's unreal." Skye moved away. "That sketch is just the tip of the iceberg." She returned to my side and pushed her phone in my face. "Her freshman art project."

I blinked in surprise at the structure of 3D wooden boxes of various size. They created what appeared to be a city skyline. On every single box was a sketch of a different face. Familiar faces. They wore a variety of expressions, together conveying a plethora of emotions.

"It's a cityscape of comedians and comedy actors, and then actors and writers famous for playing more serious roles. She's drawn them wearing expressions opposite to what they're known for. The comedians are sad and reflective. The writers are laughing or in love. It's supposed to be an artistic discussion about how faces get lost in a city, and because of that, we don't know who people really are until we take time to actually *look*."

My eyebrows hit my hairline and Skye grinned. "She's fourteen," she reminded me.

Sometimes I couldn't work out Lorna and Jane's friendship. Jane was mature and introspective for her age. Lorna was ambitious and smart, sure, but she was also more than a little shallow.

My phone buzzed, drawing my attention from Jane's artwork. I slumped on the large sectional in the open-plan living room/kitchen and opened the text.

That's so cute xx

I sighed.

Was that a no to tomorrow, then?

My phone buzzed again.

I can't 2morro. Dinner with parents' friends, ugh. Meet me @ school 1 hr early Mon? I'll make it worth it ;) xx

Heat flooded my groin at her meaning.

You got it.

I threw my phone on the couch, feeling a little better about missing out on getting laid tonight. By all accounts, Julie would be worth the wait.

Still, I wondered if Bethany was free tomorrow night? I reached for my phone to text her.

"Texting all your ladies?" Skye teased as she pulled on a light sweater.

I shrugged.

She sighed. "Just don't break any hearts, Jamie. Believe me, you don't want to be that guy."

Annoyed by the insinuation I was that guy, I scowled. "They know the score. I never make any promises."

As she grabbed her purse and keys off the coffee table, she

eyeballed me in that big-sister way of hers. "I know you're only sixteen and I don't want you getting too serious with anyone when you're this young ... but can I ask if there's a reason you're not interested in dating just one girl?"

I did not want to have this conversation.

Sisters were a killer.

"Skye," I groaned.

"It's just a question."

"Yeah, it's the kind of question sisters ask each other ... not ... Guys don't talk like this." I gestured between us in aggravation.

She laughed. "Some guys do. It doesn't make you less of a guy to have feelings. Or are you just typing random words on that laptop of yours at night?"

I squirmed at her dig.

So, okay, I had plenty of fucking feelings that I put into my stories. That was different. Hoping if I answered, she'd go away, I bit out the words, "It's not that I'm not interested in dating one girl."

"Really?"

"Oh, Jesus," I huffed. "Is that not enough?"

"Nope."

"I'm sixteen." I gestured again, the paperback in my hand flapping around so I lost my place. "I haven't met her yet. End of story."

"Met who yet?"

Sororicide was a crime, right? "The girl that makes me want to stop screwing around with other girls. Now can we please be done with this conversation?"

She looked smug. "I knew a writer had to be a secret romantic. But remember, there's no need to settle down too soon. Keep playing the field for as long as you can, but do it *safely*. Use protection and don't be an asshole." On that annoying note, she sauntered toward the door. "Call for take-out. Remember to ask the girls what they want first."

"Yeah, whatever."

"And thank you."

"You owe me."

"I know."

I looked up from my book. "And good luck with the meeting tonight."

My big sister grinned, gave me a little wave, and breezed out the door.

Sometimes it was difficult to have a big sister your friends all wanted to have sex with, a big sister who was always in my business, and a big sister who didn't know when to leave well enough alone.

But secretly, I wouldn't trade Skye for any other sister in the world.

Snorting and shaking my head at her, I cracked open my book and tried to forget that she'd cock-blocked me tonight.

A little while later, my belly grumbled. It was tempting to just order a pizza without asking Lorna and Jane what they wanted, but Lorna would complain all night if I did. It would be worth the effort to climb the stairs and ask them just to avoid her whining.

I couldn't hear the music anymore, not until I had almost reached Lorna's bedroom door. They'd turned it down so they could talk. Knowing how much talking Lorna and Jane did was one reason I didn't want a girlfriend. I wasn't sure I was the kind of guy who could put up with someone chattering at me nonstop.

"It's rule number two," I heard Lorna snap.

Her bitchy tone made me halt. I didn't want to talk to her when she was in a mood. I loved my little sister, but most days, I did not like her. I didn't care if that made me an asshole. Skye told me repeatedly that Lorna would grow out of her bratty shit and turn into a cool person I might one day call friend. *Yeah, right.*

"That's not rule number two," Jane replied in her quiet voice, steel in her words. Her tone surprised me.

"It is so," Lorna argued. "We're supposed to support what the other likes and have each other's back."

"We're also supposed to support what the other doesn't like. I don't like Greta. She's a bully. I don't have time for bullies." Jane didn't raise her voice, but there was that steel again.

About to knock and interrupt, I stopped when Lorna snapped, "It's just a party. And I'm sick of not being included in anything because you're a baby!"

I scowled. Jesus, my little sister was a pill.

"I'm not a baby." I heard a tremor in Jane's voice. "I just don't need to befriend the kind of people who bitch about each other behind their backs and wouldn't know what the word *loyalty* meant, even if Gucci brought out a bag with the word printed on it. I don't need to be popular to be happy. I'm not a sheep."

My eyebrows rose. Who was this kid?

"Are you calling me a sheep?"

"If the shoe fits."

I kind of wanted to high-five Jane Doe right then.

"At least I'm not an orphan loser! No one but me wants you, Jane. Think about that before you say anything else you might regret."

Anger churned in my gut. Lorna McKenna, mistress of manipulation. And she was only fourteen.

A creak of the floorboards alerted me too late and the door flew open. Jane charged out, almost colliding with me. I reached out to steady her and felt my annoyance with my sister grow tenfold. There were tears on Jane's flushed cheeks.

Great.

A crying teenage girl. Let me count the ways I loathed being in this kind of situation.

Jane swiped at the tear tracks and then jerked out of my hold, hurrying past and down the hall.

It occurred to me that her apartment complex was a half-hour walk from here. Skye would kill me if I let the kid walk home alone.

I could kill Lorna.

With an aggravated sigh, I stuck my head into Lorna's room and saw her sitting on her bed, glaring at the wall, two bright red spots of anger on her cheeks.

She had the bigger of the smaller two bedrooms after throwing a fit when Skye wouldn't let her have the master suite. Skye was paying the rent. The master bedroom was hers. Made sense to me. Try telling Lorna that. How a kid who grew up like we did could be so spoiled, I had no idea. I just gave in and took the smallest room in the house. Even though Skye was happy to fight for me to have the larger one since I was older.

"I'm going to see that Jane gets home okay."

Her gaze flew to me. "What?"

I seethed. "I'm walking Jane home. You leave this house while I'm gone, and I'll make your life a fucking misery until I go to college." I reached in and slammed her door shut.

Hurrying down the stairs after Jane, I thought about grabbing my car keys and giving the kid a ride home, but I needed the walk to cool off before I returned to my little sister.

Outside, I found Jane hurrying down our sidewalk.

"Jane, wait up," I called after her.

She whirled in surprise, her long, dark hair flaring around her shoulders. She waited for me.

As I approached her, the last of the sun caught in her hazel-green eyes, and it hit me out of nowhere—like a lightning bolt or a Mack Truck or some other cliché—Lorna's best friend was kind of beautiful.

The thought caught me off guard as I drew to a halt in front of her.

Only a year ago, Jane Doe had been an awkward little thing. Big eyes, big ears, big mouth. She'd looked like a cartoon character.

But now, I saw she'd lost the roundness of youth in the angles of her cheeks and jaw, and she'd grown into her features.

She'd really, *really* grown into herself.

Jane Doe was on her way to being a knockout.

Huh.

I shook myself out of the stupor this revelation caused.

"I'm walking you home." I touched Jane's elbow and began to walk.

Thankfully, she fell into step beside me without argument —I didn't want to spend half an hour convincing her she needed me to walk her home.

I slowed my long strides when I realized she was struggling to keep up.

A cool breeze caused goose bumps to sprinkle across my arms. I should have brought a hoodie with me. Mid-October in LA was still warm, but the evenings were cool. Not cold, just enough where jeans were better than shorts, hoodies were better than T-shirts. Still, Jane didn't shiver in her summer dress, so if a fourteen-year-old Californian could hack the breeze, so could a guy who grew up on the East Coast.

Glancing down at the top of her dark head, I took in her downcast expression and once again cursed my little sister. I sighed. "Don't listen to Lorna, okay. She just doesn't like to not get her own way."

Frankly, I didn't know Jane had it in her to stand up to Lorna.

"I know." Jane looked up at me with those pretty eyes. "But she's been mean a lot lately, and there's only so much a person can take."

Now, I was a guy, and guys liked to think we were above petty shit, but I'd seen enough jealousy between my friends, even between the ones I'd grown up with in Boston, to know what could sour a friendship. Maybe Lorna wasn't happy her shy, awkward little friend was growing into a cute, talented artist that boys would start noticing soon. If they hadn't already.

"Good for you. Sticking up for yourself." I felt awkward saying it. But I didn't know what else to say. Jane and I had exchanged perhaps twenty words between us in the last year.

"Everyone thinks I'm a pushover. Even Lorna." She looked up at me and then glanced away as soon as our eyes met. "I'm not."

I realized a while ago that I made the kid nervous. She rarely met my eyes if we were in the same room.

There wasn't a lot I could do about that.

We walked down the gentle slope of the quiet street on clean sidewalks, passing Spanish Revival homes with palm trees in nearly every garden. It was a world away from Dorchester.

"Are you writing anything new?" Jane suddenly blurted out.

I almost stumbled.

My eyes narrowed.

Lorna, I'm going to kill you.

"Um ... not that ... I mean, I didn't know ..." Jane squeezed her eyes closed and some of my anger dissipated at her cute floundering.

Aggravated, but not at her, I waved her off. "It's fine."

"I won't tell anyone."

I shrugged, like I didn't care when I goddamn did.

We continued in silence.

Until ...

"I read that book. The Richard Matheson one. *I Am Legend*."

This time when our eyes met, she held my gaze. Realizing she'd tracked down the book from the poster in my room, I smirked. Had little Jane Doe been paying attention to me? "Yeah? What did you think?"

"It was good. Exciting. Sad too." She sighed, and I heard a tremble in it, betraying her nervousness. I almost felt bad for her, but there was a part of me that thought maybe I liked that she was this hyperaware of me. "I read *Stir of Echoes* after it. I enjoyed that one too."

"I didn't think you read books like that."

"I'll read anything that's good."

That made me smile. "Yeah," I agreed.

When we fell into a longer silence, I considered that maybe Jane had used up all her courage for one night. Usually, I'd stay silent. But there was something about her presence, a quiet stillness that I liked. It made me curious about her.

"Why didn't you call your foster parents to come get you? You know you shouldn't be walking this far on your own at night."

Jane bit her lip. "I'm sorry if I've put you out."

"I didn't say that. And it doesn't answer my question."

"I don't like to bother them."

Bother them? She was their foster kid. Her job was to bother them. "They're paid to look after you, right?" I knew right away it was the wrong thing to say. Guilt pricked me, seeing her face fall. "That's not what I—"

"It's fine. I just ... I don't want to rock the boat. There're only four more years until I'm eighteen, and I want to stay with them until then. I don't want to move again."

"How long have you been with them?"

"Almost four years."

I frowned. "Who were you with before that?"

She shrugged. "A few families."

"And the Greens are the nicest of them all?" My friend, Lip, back in Dorchester, was a foster kid. He'd spent most of his life with a good woman called Maggie. Her asshole husband was lazy, and Maggie was constantly preoccupied with the five other kids they fostered, so Lip got away with a lot of bad shit.

Jane hesitated, and I felt a strange lurch in my chest. "Yeah."

"What's the hesitation about?"

"They just ... they're fine. They're not around much, but they make sure I have everything I need, and they don't yell at me or ... anything else."

"Anything else? Has someone done 'anything else' to you?" Why was I suddenly so aggravated?

Jane looked up at me, and the small smile and knowing look in her eyes made me feel like a naive little kid. "Jamie, the system is kind of flawed. Too many kids in care, not enough social workers, and definitely not enough foster parents. I've had it both ways. Good and bad."

For a moment, I forgot I was talking to a fourteen-year-old and not a grown-up. The world weariness in her eyes made me feel shitty. Growing up how I did meant growing up fast. But, I realized, growing up alone like Jane had made her grow up fast too. It didn't seem fair. "I'm sorry."

She was quiet a while, and then she took in a deep breath, as if preparing herself for something. She then blurted out, "You seem different. Less angry."

Yeah, I think Jane Doe *had* been paying attention to me. I frowned. "What does that mean?"

"You used to be kind of ..."

"Kind of what?"

Jane's lips twitched, and she flicked me an amused look before staring ahead. "Moody."

I had a feeling that wasn't the word she was looking for. And I was *still* a moody bastard. "Yeah, well, so would you be if your dad took off, leaving you with the kind of mom I had, and bad mom or not, she died anyway." I frowned, wondering why I'd said that.

This time when she looked at me, Jane held my gaze in a way that unnerved me. There was a wisdom in her eyes that made me feel weirdly younger than she was. "Can I tell you something? Something I haven't told even Lorna."

I nodded, knowing whatever it was, it was important. I didn't know why she wanted to tell me, and I didn't know why I wanted to know whatever it was, but I did.

"I got adopted as a baby."

What?

Seeing my confusion, she nodded, her expression so sad, it made my pulse speed up. "Marissa and Calvin Higgins adopted me when I was nine months old. My name was Margot Higgins."

"I don't understand."

"They couldn't have kids. The only family they had was Calvin's mom. She didn't like Marissa. She didn't like me. She didn't like anyone that Calvin loved more than her. I didn't realize that then." She gave me a sad smirk. "It's all the things you piece together when you're older, you know. All the memories that make sense when you're not a kid anymore."

"Jane ... I don't ..." How could she be adopted and then end up back in foster care?

"They loved me," she whispered mournfully. "They were Mom and Dad. I was seven when it happened. Car crash. I was at school. They car-shared to work. After they died, that's when I found out they'd adopted me. That they weren't my real mom and dad."

I felt my stomach sink for her.

"I used to dance." She was lost in her thoughts now. "Ballet. But it's expensive, and I moved from foster parent to foster parent. Paying for ballet lessons wasn't even a remote possibility. For a while, it's all I could draw. Ballerinas. Sometimes I still do. Anytime I see a dancer, it reminds me that my life could have been different." She gave a sad laugh. "But it's not. It is what it is, and we make the most of what we have. Still, I like to dream about that life. Marissa, my mom, she'd promised when I was a little older, she'd take me to see my first real performance. I've still never been to the ballet."

"One day, you will." It was out of my mouth before I could stop it. A promise. A conviction. "Why is your name Jane Doe?"

"Dad's mom didn't want me, even though she was my next of kin. Willa thinks my parents had to have left everything, including me, to my adoptive grandmother. That she didn't abide by their wishes. I found out about the adoption when they died. My dad's mom didn't even want me to have my dad's name. Social Services didn't want a fight about it, and I was only seven. My name was legally reverted to Jane Doe and I went back into the system."

Jesus Fucking Christ. "I'm sorry."

She nodded, the crest of her cheeks red. "I told you so you'd know you're not alone, Jamie. I think we walk through the halls at high school thinking no one can understand the crap we've been through, but almost everyone has a secret. A pain they don't talk about."

My throat closed with an emotion that hit me like I'd run into a wall. My heart hammered too hard in my chest, and I felt a kernel of shame in my chest. I'd been a dick to Skye for a year. Sometimes my anger and resentment still made me act out. And I dismissed girls. Impatient with them if they started pretending like I hadn't laid it out at the beginning that I didn't want to date. I got good grades, but I could be mouthy with teachers. And there were times I itched for a fight.

All that came from the same place.

And here was little Jane Doe, grieving for a life she should have had, and treating everyone with patience and kindness and respect.

I was, in that moment, being schooled by a freshman.

Seeing my struggle, Jane gave me a sweet smile. A dimple I'd never noticed before appeared in her left cheek. It was cute. I felt an unexpected twist in my gut.

Fuck.

I looked away, mentally reminding myself that not only was she a freshman, she was my little sister's best friend.

"Let's pick up the pace," I said, my voice flat. I didn't know what to say to her. "I've got shit to do."

The words made her blush, and I cursed myself for being a prick.

She remained silent the rest of the way to the apartment complex.

More than a few times, I had to stop myself from asking her something else about herself. I was interested in what Jane had to say. I wanted to hear her opinion on books and music ... and stuff.

It bugged me that she didn't say goodbye as she hurried upstairs to the Greens' apartment. It worried me that I might have hurt her feelings after she'd told me her secret. I cursed myself all the way back to the house, wishing I'd said something different.

Maybe even hugged her.

Shit. That wouldn't do. That wouldn't do at all. Jane was off-limits. She was just a kid. Those big, soulful eyes or the mature way she talked shouldn't fool me—or the impression she'd left on me with her sad tale.

Maybe Lorna and Jane's friendship was over, and I wouldn't have to see her again, anyway.

That hope deflated when I stepped into the house and saw Lorna sitting on the couch, her phone pressed to her ear. "No, it was my fault. I'm so sorry, Jane. I was such a bitch. You don't have to go to the party. I just don't want you to be mad if I do."

As tired as I was of her little drama tonight, I softened toward my sister when I heard her apology. Maybe Skye was right, and Jane was a good influence on Lorna. I ruffled Lorna's hair as I passed her to get a drink from the kitchen, and she looked up at me with such hero worship in her eyes, I felt a stab of guilt.

I should probably try to be a better big brother.

My phone buzzed in my pocket. It was Bethany.

> Yeah, I'm free tomorrow. My parents are out
> and the pool house is empty. Xxxx

My Sunday and Monday were looking up. Despite being cock-blocked by having to babysit Lorna, the turn of events appeased me.

"What do you want to order for takeout?" I asked my little sister as she got off the phone.

Her eyes lit up. "I get to choose?"

"You do."

She bounced off the sofa. "Is this to make up for choosing Jane over me tonight?"

All good feeling left me.

See, that was the crap that made me mad at her. "I didn't choose Jane. I don't choose sides in your petty little friendship dramas. She's fourteen, and I wasn't going to let her walk home alone. End of story."

"But you left *me* alone in the house." Lorna crossed her arms over her chest and glared at me.

I looked at her and saw my mother. When I was a kid, Mom had me in knots with that crap—making me feel like no matter what I did, I didn't love her enough—until I got a little older and knew better. It was exhausting. "Fine," I snapped, pressing speed dial on my cell. "We're getting pizza."

"Jamie!"

I ignored her whining and ordered what the fuck I wanted to order, my mood officially obliterated.

But that night as I laid in bed, I heard Jane's voice in my head.

I think we walk through the halls at high school thinking no one can understand the crap we've been through ... but almost everyone has a secret. A pain they don't talk about.

It was a simple but loaded moment. Wise words that would stay with me. They'd make me look beyond myself. Those words would make me a better writer ... but more, they would make me a better person.

As I laid there in the silence, I let her words truly sink in. I stopped being so fucking angry at the world that night because I realized there were people out there who'd been through worse shit than me.

I stopped feeling so goddamn alone.

Because of her.

Chapter Three
Two Years Later

JANE

Sixteen years old

As hurt flared in terrible heat in my chest, I realized I wasn't mad that Christopher Cruz had made out with Lorna over me.

It hurt me that Lorna deliberately went after Chris because she knew I had a crush on him.

The rules she'd made up when we were thirteen had been broken so many times, I'd lost count.

I wasn't stupid. I knew our friendship was partly beautiful, partly toxic. Fifty percent toxic was enough that I should've wiped my hands clean of her. Truthfully, I didn't want to sever our friendship because there were moments when Lorna was sweet and supportive and fiercely protective of me. And I stuck around because I loved Skye like a big sister, and my feelings for her brother Jamie had grown to epic levels. Their three-bedroom house in Glendale had become like a second home to me. If I broke off my friendship with Lorna, I'd lose her brother and sister too.

Not that Jamie and I had much of a relationship.

I loved him from afar.

But Skye ... I just loved her.

I was the one nine months ago who forced Jamie to confront Skye when I noticed she was drinking too much. She seemed so sad. Jamie talked to her, and she admitted she was partying too hard. Part of the lifestyle. After their talk, she stopped the parties and drinking. Instead, she worked all the time.

Still, having just a little of Skye's sunshine in my life was better than nothing at all.

And I lived for my weekly glimpses of Jamie and our casual interactions.

He was eighteen now, more beautiful than ever, and to my relief, he hadn't left for some far-off college. Jamie won a track-and-field scholarship to the University of Southern California and was in his freshman year there. To Lorna's dismay, he was majoring in English, which was a travesty to her because, as she said, "He will be an impoverished writer for the rest of his life."

To my delight, Jamie was staying at home to save money, which meant I still got to see him.

I just dreaded the day he met and fell in love with a smart, sexy college girl.

Jamie would never see me as anything but his little sister's annoyingly shy best friend. Sometimes I still felt pangs of mortification when I remembered I'd told him I'd been adopted. Not even Lorna knew that. And Jamie had reacted with impatience after I'd offered my secret. The painful moment still made me question my feelings for him. As did his moods. Sometimes he was funny and easy to talk to; other times, he could be kind of a dick.

In fact, it was only about a month ago that Lorna had left me hanging out by their pool to take a call with some college guy she'd met at the mall. I was drying off on a lounger, enjoying the break from school when a shadow fell over me.

Opening my eyes, I found Jamie glaring down at me.

"What are you wearing?"

Confused, I glanced down at the string bikini. "Uh ..."

"Nothing. The answer is nothing. Get back in the house and put something on."

At his high-handedness, my annoyance surged. Frowning, I stood, and he stepped back quickly, as if afraid I was about to bite him. "I'm wearing a bikini," I replied. As angry as I ever got, I didn't like shouting. I didn't see the point in people screaming in each other's faces. Lorna did enough yelling for the both of us. "I borrowed it from your sister."

His eyes flickered downward to my breasts and then quickly away. A muscle ticked in his jaw as he refused to look at me. "Yeah, well, she's smaller. That bikini doesn't fit you, and it's obscene. Go change."

Was he calling me fat?

My cheeks burned, but I stood my ground. "You're being ridiculous."

Jamie's head whipped around. That brooding gaze slightly intimidated me, but I kept my chin up. "I'm what?" His tone was edgy. I knew it well. It was his soft, dangerous tone before he exploded.

I shivered a little. "You're being ridiculous," I repeated patiently. "Jamie, you're not my brother. You can't tell me what to wear or where to wear it. And to be honest, you shouldn't be telling any woman, sister or not, what she should or shouldn't wear. It pushes women's lib back a few decades, and I didn't think you were that kind of guy."

With a shrug of disappointment, I brushed past him and made my way into the house. I was proud of myself. Usually,

Jamie flustered me beyond reason. Apparently, the key was for him to irritate me enough for me to become my normal, articulate self around him.

He refused to speak to me at dinner that night, and I'd questioned my feelings for him. Shouldn't I think about dating someone who liked me in return? Who didn't give me emotional whiplash?

Thus began my crush hunt.

I'd decided on Christopher Cruz. He straddled the social circles at school nicely. He was a surfer. Chilled out, nice to everyone, and California cute with sun-bleached hair and a crooked, sexy smile.

After making my selection, I did what all best friends do —I told Lorna. During the subsequent four weeks, she'd plotted happily to get Chris to notice me. The party at his parents' Malibu beach house was supposed to be the culmination of all the hours I'd spent at school getting to know him better.

Yet there was my supposed best friend, making out with my supposed crush by his parents' pool.

The twisted thing was, I didn't think Lorna was doing it because she didn't want me to have a cute boyfriend. Lorna was doing it because she didn't want me to have anyone but her.

My best friend was always complaining that Jamie loved Skye more than he loved her. That their mom had loved Jamie and Skye more than she'd loved Lorna. That her dad hated her, but he adored Jamie and even put up with Skye. And that I loved Skye more than I loved my best friend.

In Lorna's messed-up heart, everyone always loved someone better than they'd ever love her.

I was hers.

No one else's.

That was her point.

Her point reeked. I resented her and her jealous possessiveness.

Turning away from the pool where she was thrusting her tongue into Chris's mouth, I pushed through the crowd of high schoolers and made my way to the front door.

Malibu was over an hour from Glendale, and Lorna was my ride. She'd gotten her license six weeks ago. So had I. I just couldn't afford a car.

Cursing her under my breath as I stepped outside, I pulled my phone out of the pocket of my shorts and glared at my phone screen. If I called Willa to come pick me up, she'd have a shit fit. There was no way I was supposed to be at a party in Malibu where underage drinking was going on.

There was only one person I could call, and Lorna would be so mad at me.

I decided I didn't care.

Skye picked up after five rings. "Hey, sweetie, can I call you —" She broke off into laughter and shushed someone. "Sorry, Jane, I'm kind of busy. Can I call you back?"

"Skye, I'm stuck in Malibu. Lorna is my ride but I want to leave and … she doesn't."

"Give me a second." There was a moment of silence from her and I could hear the thud of music in the background. After a few seconds, the music dulled. "Okay," she said, "I'm back. What the hell are you doing at a party in Malibu?"

"A guy from school threw it. His parents have a beach house. Anyway, I want to go home but Lorna is my ride and …"

"I'm going to kill her," Skye huffed. "Okay, text me the address. I'll be there as soon as possible." She hung up before I could respond.

Hands trembling, because I hated making Skye mad, I texted her the address. Five minutes later, she texted me back and my heart fell.

I can't drive. I've been drinking. Jamie's in Reseda at a friend's and is closer. He's on his way. Tell Lorna I want her ass home. NOW. Xx

It was Lorna who came to me. She found me at the end of the drive, waiting on Jamie. I stared balefully at her, refusing to engage in an argument about what she'd done.

She sighed at my expression, jutting out one hip. "I can't help it if he likes me more."

"I couldn't care less."

Lorna flinched and glanced away. She nibbled on her lower lip for a second before turning back to me. "I'm sorry, okay. I should have told you I liked him too."

"Yes, you should have. Because you know I would have stepped aside."

"Yeah, because you're so much better than me. We all know that." She shook her head and heaved a dramatic sigh. "Are you just going to stay out here all night?"

Dreading her reaction, I wanted to stall but knew I couldn't. "I called Skye for a ride. She's sending Jamie. He should be here any minute."

As predicted, Lorna exploded, cursing at me and calling me a buzzkill. That I shouldn't be calling her family for rides when I had foster parents. That I'd deliberately done it to get her in trouble. That I was selfish and manipulative. I stared straight ahead, trying not to let her words sting.

The idea of being stuck in a car with Jamie for over an hour made me feel slightly nauseated, but I was relieved when he pulled up to the house in his black Ford Mustang.

He got out of the car, storming toward us, bristling with six foot two inches of aggravation. "Are you kidding me with this shit?" He gestured to the beach house. "Malibu, Lorna? Really?"

She rolled her eyes. "It's just a party."

"In fucking Malibu. You're sixteen. Get in the car." His angry gaze swung to me. "Both of you."

"I have my car here, and I haven't been drinking. I'll take us home. You can go away." Lorna shooed him.

Stuck in a car with Lorna while she berated me for calling Skye, or stuck in the car for an hour while Jamie silently seethed?

Without saying a word, I strode past them both and rounded the hood of Jamie's Mustang. I yanked open the passenger-side door and got in.

Jamie's voice carried down the drive. "Get in your car—I better see you following us all the way home."

"Would you even care about this whole situation if precious Jane wasn't here?"

I stiffened. Why did she have to do that all the time?

"Lorna"—there was an unyielding quality to his tone—"if you don't want to push everyone in your life away like Mom did, you'll cut that crap out. Now get in your car and follow us home."

I tensed as Jamie marched back to the Mustang. The car lowered with his weight as he got in and slammed the door. His jaw locked as he watched Lorna stomp like a five-year-old down the street to her Mini Cooper. As soon as she was in it, he swung a U-turn and took off.

Every muscle in my body was taut with the tension radiating off him, so it was a surprise when he asked if I was okay. He shot me quick, worried looks between watching the road ahead.

"I'm fine."

"Why did you call Skye? Why did you want to leave?"

Ugh. My reason sounded so pathetic and immature now. "Just because."

Jamie sighed. "Jane, what happened?"

I shrugged. "It's just girl stuff, okay? It's fine. I'm sorry your evening got ruined."

"I was just hanging at one of the guy's uncle's house in Reseda. There wasn't a lot going on."

I nodded and let silence fall between us. He had the rock station on low, so I watched the scenery pass by and tried to forget who I was with and how much I wished he'd notice me more.

My phone buzzed in my pocket. Frowning, I pulled it out and saw I had a text from Chris. We'd exchanged numbers a week ago.

> Hey, did u leave? Sorry bout Lorna. Dnt know y I did that? Had 2 many beers.

I frowned at his excuse just as my phone buzzed again.

> Ure gorgeous. Liked u for long time. Not in2 Lorna. Want u. Okay?

No, not okay. I must have huffed out loud.

"What's going on? Who's texting?" Jamie asked.

"Just a stupid guy." I turned my phone over on my lap.

Jamie didn't reply right away, so I assumed he was uninterested in my stupid-guy story. I was glad because I didn't want to tell it.

"Stupid how?"

I was pretty sure my eyebrows hit my hairline. I looked at him. He glanced at me, saw my expression, and frowned.

"What?"

"You want to know my stupid-guy story?"

"Considering you are the way you are, and you look the way you do, yet I've never seen you with a guy ... yeah, I want to know."

I was the way I was? I looked the way I did? What did that

mean? "Uh ... I thought I liked a guy. I told Lorna. We plotted to get him to notice me—"

"Like you need to plot," he muttered.

Huh? Did he mean what I thought he meant? My heart raced a little faster. "Anyway, that was his parents' beach house and tonight was supposed to be the night ..."

Jamie turned to look at me so fast, it surprised me he didn't get whiplash. "The night you what?"

Realizing where his thoughts had gone, I smacked his arm. "Not that."

His hands tightened around the wheel. "Good," he bit out.

"Tonight was supposed to be the night that we kissed. Maybe agreed to go on a date. Instead ...your sister pounced first. And now he's texting me to say that he didn't mean to stick his tongue down Lorna's throat for fifteen minutes and that it's me he wants."

At Jamie's silence, I suddenly felt idiotic telling him. "It's whatever."

"It's not whatever." He shook his head. "You're her best friend. Why would she do that to you?"

"It's not as though I really liked him," I confessed, not wanting Jamie to come down on Lorna for anything else. Even when she was horrible to me, I still found myself protecting her. It was confusing. "I just *wanted* to like him. Does that make sense?"

Jamie frowned. "Are you ... are you not into guys?"

I laughed at his assumption. "Yes, I am. Just not anyone in my class."

He seemed to relax a little. "Well, that's fair enough. Still, Lorna thought you liked him. She shouldn't have done that."

"She's possessive of me." I tried to explain her reasoning. "She doesn't want anyone to take my attention away from her."

"And you think that's okay? Jane, that's not okay."

I knew that. I sighed. Heavily. I tried to change the subject. "Are you enjoying college?"

He smirked and flicked me a knowing look. That smirk set off a flutter of butterflies low in my belly. "Four more years of school. Should I be enjoying it?"

"Yes," I insisted. "Jamie, you're surrounded by other students passionate about literature and writing. You're among your people."

His lips twitched. "My people?"

"Your people."

He considered this, nodded, and then asked, "You read anything good lately?"

Ask a bookworm that question and expect a lengthy answer. "I found a new author to obsess over. Haruki Murakami. I read *A Wild Sheep Chase* first, and I've just finished *Norwegian Wood*. Now I'm starting *Kafka on the Shore*." From there, I waxed lyrical about the Japanese writer's prose and how I loved the surrealism of the worlds he created, of the fatalistic loneliness of the characters.

When I realized I was rambling, I abruptly shut up.

"What is it?" Jamie asked in confusion.

"I was talking too much."

"No, you weren't." He smiled at me. Again. "I'll need to check out his books. Recommendation to start?"

"*Norwegian Wood*."

"Then I'll read that first."

Something about the way he said it, his voice deep, his expression almost affectionate, made me squirm hotly in the passenger seat.

Jamie returned his attention to the road. His eyes flickered to the rearview mirror. "She's following us. Good."

I realized that I hadn't even thought to ask if Lorna was making her way home too.

"Hey?"

There was a question in his voice. "Yeah?"

"I know I'm two years late with this, but I'm sorry I was a dick the night you told me about being adopted."

My breathing stuttered and my cheeks grew hot. Why was he mentioning this now?

"I ..." He let out a little huff of laughter. "What you said really got to me. I didn't know how to react, and I was a dick. I'm sorry if I hurt your feelings."

"You did." I didn't know who was more surprised by my honesty, him or me.

Remorse softened his features. "Shit, Jane, I'm really, really sorry."

Something that had been aching inside me for a while finally soothed. "You're forgiven."

There was a moment of silence between us, and then, "You schooled me that night. You know that?"

Shocked, I shook my head. "In what way?"

"Reminded me that I wasn't the only one who'd been through something. And that having a shitty dad or being angry at my mom for dying before I could stop being angry at her for being a shitty mom wasn't an excuse to be a dick."

Wow.

"I don't know what to say."

"You've already said it. And I've never forgotten it."

Jamie looked nervous. I'd never seen him look nervous. He swallowed hard and glanced between the road and me, his fingers white-knuckling the steering wheel. "I ... uh ... I've never asked anyone other than my professors to read anything I've written before, but ... would you? I mean, would you ..." He rolled his eyes at himself. "Would you want to read something of mine?"

It took everything within me not to shout a big, fat YES at the top of my lungs. My pounding heart was now speeding at a hundred miles per hour, my palms clammy. *Be cool, Jane. Be cool.* "Sure." I was proud I sounded normal, in control. I smiled when he looked at me again. "I'd like that."

Jamie released a breath. Like what I thought mattered or something. "Okay. Great."

I tried to lose my smile and failed spectacularly. He caught me and grinned. A full, wide, gorgeous grin. For me.

Something passed between us.

Something new.

And exciting.

Holy fluttering butterflies.

I'd always been hyperaware of Jamie McKenna, but it felt like, in that moment, maybe he was just as aware of me.

"So, what about you?" he asked.

"What about me what?"

"College. You're a senior after the summer and then it's college. What are your plans?"

College made me anxious. I knew what my heart wanted, but my head, a.k.a. Lorna, told me something else.

"Well, Lorna thinks I should consider pre-law with her."

Jamie snorted. Hard.

I scowled. "What?"

He looked at me in disbelief. "You, a lawyer? No. *No.* I asked what *you* wanted to do. Not what Lorna wants you to do."

Well, that was obvious, surely. "Jamie, I want to go to art school. But what the hell will I do with an art degree?"

"Something that makes you happy." He might as well have added "duh" onto the end of his sentence. "Jane, you're talented. And way too creative to be stuck in a job that won't allow you to explore that side of you. Plus, college is for discovering shit about yourself. Go to art school. Try different classes. Do things you never thought you'd like or be good at —see where it leads."

My palms were clammy for a different reason now. "And what about money and security?"

"All good things. I didn't say they weren't. But there's a reason they say money can't buy happiness." He flicked me an assessing look. "Back in Dorchester, we had this neighbor. Alejandro Elba. He was a jazz player. Didn't have a lot of money but he had a shit ton of records, had played the sax alongside Miles Davis, Charles Mingus, and Herbie Hancock. Unlike them, Alejandro didn't find fame. And it didn't seem to matter to him. He went out on the streets of Boston and played that sax like a legend. Scooped up his takings for the day, bought a coffee, and sat in the neighborhood, chatting with his friends and anyone who wanted his time.

"He was the happiest guy I'd ever met. Way fucking happier than all of Skye's rich-and-famous friends put together. I will never do something because it'll make me a crap ton of money. My life will be about what *feels* right."

A smile pulled at my lips as I stared at Jamie McKenna's handsome profile. Those butterflies he caused in my belly, that sweet ache in my chest, his words amplified them all.

Feeling my stare, he asked, "What?"

"I'm just wondering when you got so wise?"

"I don't know." He shrugged. "It might have been around the time a cute freshman reminded me to look beyond myself."

My cheeks bloomed with heat. I couldn't believe Jamie was so affected by our moment that night while all this time, I'd felt weird about telling him my story.

And did he just call me cute?

It wasn't "sexy," but I'd take it.

"Jane."

"Yeah?"

"I have to apologize for something else. I was wrong. A few weeks back. At the pool."

Remembering the moment he'd chastised me about the bikini, I shifted uncomfortably. "Okay."

"I mean it. You were right. I shouldn't tell you what you can and cannot wear. It was high-handed and assholian."

Laughter bubbled on my lips. "Assholian?"

Jamie grinned. "Yes, it was extremely assholian."

"So, you're just inventing words now?"

"When appropriate, yeah."

I laughed and he flashed me a warm look, affection bright in his eyes. "I like it. It's a good word."

"Thank you." His smile fell a little. "But I mean it. I didn't intend to make you uncomfortable. My issue with the bikini is my issue, and I shouldn't have made it yours."

Confused, I furrowed my brow. "What issue is that exactly?"

His eyes swung to me and flickered down my body, lingering on my bare legs, before returning to the road ahead.

After a few seconds, I realized he had no intention of replying. He didn't need to. A thick, hot tension I'd never felt before had fallen between us. It pressed on my chest, and my skin felt too tight, too hot.

Lorna, who had lost her virginity to Xavier Highland last year, had told me that sometimes she just needed to be touched. I didn't understand what she meant—until now. I needed Jamie to touch me. To soothe this feeling. Somehow, I knew only his touch could.

It was a long car ride after that, and when we finally pulled up to my apartment complex, I didn't know what to say to break the loaded moment between us.

Realizing Jamie wasn't going to say anything either, I pushed open the door.

"I'll, uh—"

At the sound of his voice, I looked over my shoulder at him.

"Why don't you come over to the house after school on Monday? Lorna has track practice then, right?"

"Right." I barely got the word out. Lorna had joined the track-and-field team sophomore year. I didn't know if it was because she liked it or because she thought it would give her something in common with Jamie. I voted the latter.

"I'll see you then?" He stared at me with an intensity I'd never seen in his eyes before. It matched the vibe that had sizzled between us the entire car ride. Excitement fluttered its rapid little wings near my heart.

"See you then. And thanks for the ride. I appreciate it."

"I know you do."

I moved to leave again and he stopped me with another "hey."

I laughed under my breath and turned back to him. "Yeah?"

But he wasn't laughing. "Do you have my number?"

I shook my head.

"Give me your phone. Anytime you need a ride again, you call me."

"Jamie—"

"No arguments. I don't like the idea of you being stranded somewhere."

Fumbling for my phone, I quickly handed it over. He typed in his number and then called his cell, shifting in his seat to pull it out of his pocket. After a few seconds of fiddling around with it, he handed mine back to me. As I took it, our fingers brushed, and a shock of electricity rippled up my hand.

My eyes flew to his face to find him staring at me, wide-eyed.

Like he'd felt it too.

"I'll, uh ..." His gaze dropped. "See you Monday."

Trembling with my reaction to him, I nodded and hopped out of the car. He waited until I walked through the gate into the complex. One look over my shoulder told me he was still waiting.

Jamie waited until I got all the way to my door before I heard the sound of his Mustang purr.

I didn't sleep a wink that night.

Chapter Four

JAMIE

Eighteen years old (almost nineteen)

I WAS in a hurry to get home. It was the one day of the week we didn't have practice, and while the guys were all getting ready for some party at a frat house that night, I was heading back to Glendale.

They called me on it, but I didn't care.

There was someone waiting for me at home. Someone who excited me. Someone I couldn't stop thinking about. Over the last few months, I'd become closer to this person than I'd ever imagined I was capable of.

Jane.

She'd asked for the latest chapters of the novel I was writing to distract her from a crazy start to senior year. A friend of Lorna's had died in a drunk-driving accident. Greta. She was a girl Jane had practically grown up with. They hadn't been friends. In fact, it was kind of the opposite, but Lorna and Greta had hung out a lot. I knew the past few weeks had been tough on them both for different reasons, and that there was some tension between them. Lorna had a ton of friends to turn to, but Jane didn't. And I didn't want her to be alone.

I liked our secret get-togethers because I loved being around Jane, but I also liked being able to keep my finger on the pulse of what was going on with her.

We grabbed secret time together whenever we could. That afternoon she was going to tell me what she thought about my chapters. I always got a little nervous because it turned out shy little Jane wasn't timid about telling me exactly what she thought about my writing. Her critique was always insightful and fair, and it made her praise even more satisfying. I fucking glowed when she rhapsodized about the parts she loved.

It didn't surprise me to find Jane curled up on the couch with her laptop open on her lap. Skye gave her a key to the house not long after we'd moved there.

The tension that had coiled tightly around my muscles as I'd hurried home relaxed immediately.

"Hey," I said, dumping my backpack by the coffee table.

Jane looked up at me with those gorgeous eyes. "Hey."

"Lorna at practice?"

She nodded.

"Want a drink?"

"Sure."

I frowned at her less than loquacious responses but retrieved bottled water from the refrigerator without questioning it. Instead, I waited until I got to the sectional and sat as close as I could without it being too obvious how close I wanted to be to her.

The smell of watermelon and some other fruity, undefinable scent tickled my senses. Jane always smelled amazing.

"What's up?"

She heaved a sigh and turned her body toward me, her laptop slipping. She grabbed hold of it and then peered up at me from beneath her lashes. It was a shy, uncertain look. I thought we were past that.

"What is it?" My tone was more impatient than I meant.

A frown creased her brow. "Nothing." She flicked her finger over the mouse pad. "Let's talk about this book of yours."

Realizing I'd fucked up with my attitude, I covered her hand with mine. "Hey, you can tell me."

Her gorgeous olive skin turned a little pink on the crest of her cheekbones. I tried not to be smug about it, but I loved that I could make Jane react to me. It made up for the fact that ever since I'd driven her home that night from Malibu, I hadn't been able to stop thinking about her.

Before that night, I'd realized I was attracted to her. And I didn't want to be—she was my little sister's best friend, and there were eighteen months between us. That wasn't a lot, true. But we were at the awkward place in our ages where I was legal, and she wasn't.

I'd tried to ignore my attraction, but it was more than physical. That was the problem. I wanted her, not just because she was beautiful, but because I couldn't always work her out, and I liked that. She was quiet and thoughtful, and she had the ability to shut me up with her intelligent observations without even raising her voice. Mostly, though, she was smart, cute, authentically herself, and so fucking kind, it was unreal.

"Jane?" I took my hand off hers since I seemed to have struck her mute with the action.

Finally, she met my eyes. To my shock, I saw something like guilt in them. "I hate school right now. Everyone is ... People are still crying in huddles and constantly talking about Greta. Lorna and her friends are organizing a memorial for the end of the semester, and a drunk-driving campaign, and they keep trying to get everyone to talk about how they're feeling about Greta's death."

Understanding dawned, along with a deep sense of kinship. "You don't want to share that shit with people who aren't your friends."

"Yes." Her eyes filled with relief that I understood, and it took everything within me not to kiss her. "I'm horrified this happened to Greta. But she was not a nice person to me. And she got in a car drunk—we're lucky she didn't kill anyone else. I have very mixed feelings about the whole thing, and I don't want to talk about it. Sometimes what they're doing doesn't feel genuine. Like, it's for attention ... Does that make me sound like a bad person?"

"No." I frowned. "You and Lorna are different people. Let her draw out the grief with her friends the way she wants to." I sighed. "You just do you. Like hell I'd want to talk to people who aren't my real friends about something like that ... If you need to talk, you can talk to me."

Jane gave me a grateful smile, the sadness in her eyes dimming but never disappearing. As if she read my thoughts, she whispered, "I just did. And I feel like the shittiest person for feeling only sad instead of heartbroken. And for truly believing Greta's friends are using her death for attention. There. I said it. I'm a terrible person."

I couldn't help it. I needed to touch her. To comfort her. I reached out and slid my hand along her jaw until I buried it in her hair. I clasped her nape and bent my forehead to hers. Closing my eyes, I breathed her in. She was like oxygen in that moment.

"You're not a terrible person. You couldn't be if you tried. You're actually the best person I know."

I felt her hand curl around my elbow, gripping on to me. My hand tightened around her neck in reaction, the silky strands of her hair tickling my skin. What I wouldn't give to bury myself inside her. Sex had always been just a relief, a satisfaction. But with Jane ... I bet she could take out all her worries and sadness in my body. I'd soak them right up, so she'd never have to feel that way again. Steal moments of euphoria in a time she needed reminding it existed.

Fuck, I would take on all her sadness and frustrations if I could.

Realizing if I didn't let her go, I'd never let her go, I pulled back and pressed a kiss to her forehead. The way she looked at me as I released her made me feel ten feet tall.

"Do you want to talk about these chapters?" Her voice was lower, a little hoarse with emotion. Its sultry sound caused another flare of heat to shoot from my gut to my groin.

Fuck.

Seventeen, I reminded myself. *She's seventeen and tomorrow is my nineteenth birthday.*

Nine months. I could wait nine months for her to turn eighteen. Then there would be no stopping us. Because I wasn't imagining the two-way attraction, right?

"Okay." I gave her a wry grin. "Hit me with it."

She returned my grin and then looked at the laptop screen. "Pacing and plotting is excellent."

Was it ridiculous how hot I found it when she got all serious about my writing? "Good to know." I watched her nibble her lower lip and lost focus for a second. Jane had the most beautiful mouth I'd ever seen. Her lips were everything. Full, lush, so fucking kissable. My eyes traveled down her throat, across the expanse of smooth, olive skin revealed by the wide neckline of her T-shirt. Her full tits were a generous handful. She was way too sexy for my own good.

"Your hero is great. He's flawed but intriguing. He *can* be a dick, but he also shows moments of warmth. Between that and how smart he is, you've gotten that balance just right."

I dragged my dirty, horny gaze off her body and back to her beautiful face. When I wrote women in my books now, they always had a little of Jane in them. Which was why what she said next bothered me.

"Your heroine, however, needs work." She shot me an apologetic wince. "She's a little weak, Jamie."

I frowned. "Weak, how?"

"You spend more time describing her looks than you do the heroes. So right away, you're setting this up as somehow important."

Yes, but did she not notice the resemblance between my heroine and her? "O ... kay?"

"That would be fine if it were the only problem." She pointed to the screen. "You haven't given her motivation. Her actions are defined by the actions of the hero."

Really? I scowled at the screen.

"Is that what you want?" Jane studied me. "For her to do what the hero tells her to do, with no thoughts of her own?"

"Not at all. But they both want the same thing."

"That's fine. Their goals align. But you have to clarify that her actions are motivated by what *she* wants. Not that she wants to give the hero what he wants with no thought to her own needs. Do you get me?"

Her passion and investment in my writing suddenly lifted my mood like nothing could these days. I smiled at her, not caring if my feelings were reflected in my eyes. "You're going to make sure I write badass heroines, aren't you?"

"Yes." She laughed. "Jamie McKenna will not write bad heroines while I'm around."

"Then I guess you better stick around forever." The words were out of my mouth before I could stop them.

Her breath caught as our eyes met and held. A little part of me panicked that she might take more from my meaning, but then I realized ... maybe I wanted her to.

Because the thought of a future without Jane filled me with dread.

"Hey, guys."

I jolted at the sound of my big sister's voice, whipping my head around to see her standing at the bottom of the stairs.

"Sorry to interrupt. I was upstairs napping." Skye smiled, but it was inquisitive.

I hadn't even noticed her car outside.

"That's okay." Jane closed her laptop and pushed up off the couch. "I need to get back, anyway. I promised Willa I'd babysit the kids tonight."

Disappointment filled me. I didn't want her to go. I stood, towering over her curvy, five-foot-six figure. "You're coming to my party tomorrow, right?"

I hadn't wanted a birthday party. I wasn't a birthday-party kind of guy, but Skye had convinced me that inviting guys from the track team and their friends to a party would help me find my place at USC. It was harder for me to fit in when I wasn't staying on campus. Or at least that was Skye's worry.

"Jamie, you know I'm not a party person."

"But I also know Lorna will browbeat you into coming, so I'll see you there," I teased.

Jane laughed. "Yeah, I'll see you tomorrow." She waved at Skye.

"See you tomorrow, sweetie."

As soon as the door closed behind Jane, my big sister pounced. "So, I'm not imagining the fact that (a) Jane is allowed to read your writing, and (b) you were flirting with her —am I?"

I groaned and strode past her into the kitchen. "Skye, leave it."

"Uh, if it were anyone else but Jane, I would." She followed me in and leaned against the peninsula counter. Her gaze bored into me. "What's going on there?"

"Nothing that will happen while she's not eighteen," I promised.

"You like her," Skye surmised. "It's not just that she's drop-dead gorgeous. You're letting her read your work, so you must like her. Respect her opinion?"

"I do," I admitted.

She exhaled slowly. "Jamie ... Lorna won't have it. As far as she's concerned, that sweet kid has belonged to her from the day they met."

Anger churned in my gut, and I glared at Skye. "And you don't think that's a little fucked up?"

Concern flashed across my sister's face. "Lorna has insecurities you and I seem incapable of helping her with. She met Jane when she needed someone to be hers, only hers, and at the time Jane needed that just as much."

"That doesn't answer my question."

"Do I like the way Lorna manipulates Jane sometimes? No. But they're both grown-ups now. It's up to them to work out their relationship."

"Here's what I know: Jane *doesn't* belong to Lorna. And Lorna's feelings on the matter won't stop me."

Skye scrutinized me. "Are you ... are you in love with her?"

The thought made my heart race fast and my palms sweat. "Fucking hell, what kind of question is that?"

"The kind of question a person asks when their little brother is the biggest player ever and he casts his sights on a young woman I adore and feel protective of."

That anger turned to indignation. "You think I'd hurt her?"

"Jamie, if your feelings are genuine, I'm all for it. Even if I have to deal with Lorna freaking out about it. Because it would make me happy if you ended up with someone like Jane. But"—she glowered at me—"if you're thinking with your dick because the girl is a knockout, then don't go there. Please. She ..." Skye heaved a sigh. "I'm betraying the sisterhood when I tell you this, but, Jamie, that girl has had a crush on you since forever."

My heart lurched at the thought. Happiness warmed me all over. "Really?"

Skye narrowed her eyes. "Really. And if you aren't serious about her, you'll *crush* her."

This wasn't the kind of conversation I wanted to have with my sister. In fact, I didn't think it was right to tell her this shit before I even told Jane, but since Skye would probably worry over it for the next nine months, I gave her what she needed to hear.

"That girl deserves to be loved," I said, my voice hoarse with emotion and a little discomfort. "No one has ever loved her right, except for you. Not even Lorna. When a guy comes along, he needs to love her *hard*. To make up for all the times people forgot to love her." Or the times it was taken away from her, like with her adoptive parents. Just the thought of Jane feeling unloved made me want to punch a fist through the wall. "I plan to be the guy who loves her like that."

Tears brightened Skye's eyes. She reached up and brushed the backs of her fingers over my cheek. "Wow. Well ... it sounds like you already might be that guy. Don't you think?"

My heart pounded hard. Yeah. I did think.

She squeezed my shoulder and gave me a tight smile. "You wait until she's eighteen."

I nodded, already willing nine months to fly by at the speed of light.

We fell into silence as we made fajitas, both lost in our own thoughts. But it occurred to me as Skye stood grating cheese and I stirred the chicken, spices, and peppers in the pan, that Skye was here at an odd time of day for her. "What are you doing home?"

"We finished filming the season finale at 4.00 a.m. I needed some sleep, so I came home for a nap. I fly out to New York for the Benson film the morning after your birthday."

It was still so surreal to see Skye in magazines and in photographs online. *The Sorcerer* had provided her with a certain level of fame, and now that she was getting secondary roles in big movies, it might not be long before she got starring roles. Once that happened, I couldn't imagine our lives would ever be the same. Not that they were normal now. There was nothing normal about seeing bikini shots of your big sister as the home screen on a teammate's phone.

The guys were annoyingly excited about the fact that Skye and her friends would be at the party tomorrow night.

"Patricia told me there's a small role in *The Sorcerer* she thinks Jane should audition for."

My heart faltered. "No." I cut my sister a dark look. "They just want her because she's beautiful. Which is exploitation, FYI."

She sighed. "They just want to see if she can act. She has the face for camera. And although I'm not sure I want her in this life, it should be up to Jane."

Sometimes I wondered if my sister even enjoyed acting or if she only did it for the money. There were times I caught a flicker of darkness in her eyes that I didn't like. But anytime I tried to talk to her about it, she shut me down. "No," I repeated. There would be no bikini shots of Jane on my team-mates' phones.

"It's not up to you, Jamie. You're not her keeper, and I hope you won't act like that if you two start seeing each other."

I curled my lip in annoyance and tried not to say some-thing I'd regret. Then I remembered who we were talking about. "Jane hates acting. She'll never go for it."

"Then you have nothing to worry about."

But I would worry because Jane would do almost anything

to make Skye happy. "Just don't sell it as if it's something *you* want."

My big sister understood. "I won't. I promise."

Jane would say no.

I closed my eyes.

Fuck.

I'd never been a possessive guy ... until now.

And I wasn't sure I was comfortable with the depth of my feelings for Jane Doe.

However, I also knew I no longer had a choice in the matter.

CHAPTER FIVE

JANE
Seventeen years old

IT SEEMED wrong to feel butterflies of excitement in my belly instead of the ones of dread I'd felt for the last eleven days.

However, yesterday, Jamie had successfully distracted me from my discomfort at school these days. He'd comforted me, held me, and he'd stared at me like he wanted me.

I'd had enough boys look at me with that heat in their eyes to recognize it when I saw it.

I just never thought I'd see it from Jamie.

And he'd flirted with me, hadn't he?

Lorna's rule from long ago about not crushing on her brother niggled at me. I didn't want to cause problems between us, but no one made me feel alive like Jamie McKenna did, and I couldn't ignore that. When he specifically asked if I'd be at his party, it felt like a different kind of invitation.

Something was changing between us, and I hoped that this party would be the start of it.

Dealing with Lorna would be worth it, if it meant I got to be with Jamie.

Music thudded from behind their door as I followed guests I didn't recognize up the walk to their porch. Two big guys—hired security—stood at the door with a guest list. I relaxed a little, seeing them there. Sometimes I worried Skye didn't take her own security seriously enough. Perhaps because there were other cast members invited to Jamie's party, she'd decided to be cautious, for once.

The guy with the clipboard barely looked at me when I approached. "Name?"

Before I could open my mouth, Lorna suddenly appeared in the doorway. "There you are!" She reached out to grab my wrist and hauled me inside.

She slammed the door shut behind us. "What are you wearing?"

Taking in the strapless minidress and five-inch heels she wore, I reluctantly understood her accusatory question. I was wearing skinny jeans and a Red Hot Chili Peppers T-shirt. And ballet flats. Don't forget the ballet flats.

I threw my hands up. "This is me, Lorna."

"Yeah, hiding your hotness, like always." She turned my hands palm upward. "Paint. You're covered in paint."

I wasn't covered in paint. I had *speckles* of paint on my hands.

"More ways you cover your hotness."

My best friend confused the hell out of me. Anytime she thought someone was paying me more attention than her, she freaked out. But anytime she thought I was "hiding my potential," as she called it, she got in my face. There was no one more complicated than Lorna McKenna.

For example, after she kissed Chris Cruz, Chris attempted

to win me over at school. A tough senior, Dana Rogers, known for slapping other girls around when she decided she didn't like them, had a thing for Chris. When she got word that he had a thing for me, she jumped me in the girls' restroom and busted my lip open.

When Lorna found out, she rounded up her friends and jumped Dana off school grounds. She broke Dana's nose.

Skye was furious.

Jamie was impressed.

And my loyalty to Lorna re-cemented.

No matter how she hurt me, she had my back.

I didn't know how to walk away from that and didn't know if I could. Sometimes it felt like the only person in the world who truly needed me was Lorna McKenna.

"I had a feeling you might come dressed like this. You're borrowing a dress from me." She eyeballed my shoes. "The flats will just have to do, I guess." Lorna and Skye both wore a shoe size bigger than me.

Still holding one of my wrists, Lorna maneuvered us through the very crowded living area. I searched for Jamie. I saw Skye and gave her a wave, but no birthday boy.

"You came." I heard his deep voice seconds before I felt the heat of his hand on my lower back.

I tugged on Lorna, who stopped as I turned toward Jamie. The movement meant he dropped his hand from my back. A pang flared across my chest as the fluttering in my belly intensified. He wore his usual uniform of casual T-shirt and jeans, somehow always looking like a broody Calvin Klein model.

"Happy birthday." I grinned and held out the wrapped present in my hand.

Lorna snatched it before Jamie could. "It goes on the pile."

Jamie raised an eyebrow at her. He held out his hand for the gift. "Isn't that up to me?"

"Nope. Now, go back to your harem. Jane needs to change."

Harem? I frowned, suddenly realizing there was a group of college girls standing behind Jamie. One girl with champagne-blond hair glowered like she wanted a black hole to open behind me.

My heart sank.

"Change?" Jamie's voice brought my attention back to him.

His staring made me shiver.

"Into something more party appropriate."

"I keep trying to tell her this is me."

Jamie's gaze drifted down my body and back up again, and a flush of heat between my legs made me take a step back. He flicked an annoyed look at his sister. "There's nothing wrong with her."

"Says the guy who wouldn't know what tailoring was if it bit him in the ass."

"Jamie." The champagne blond suddenly pressed her chest against Jamie's arm. She flicked me a catty look before gazing at him in open invitation. "Why don't you show me that book we were talking about it?"

"Now?"

She shrugged and trailed a fingertip over his heart. "Now."

His eyes dropped to her mouth and my heart dropped out of my body.

I was such an idiot.

Lorna tugged on my wrist, and I followed her without knowing where I was going or what was happening. I was vaguely aware of her putting my present with a pile of other presents. It wasn't until we dashed upstairs that I realized I needed to take that gift back.

Jamie would know what it cost me.

A huge chunk of my savings.

That gift was splaying my heart to him and asking him to punch a hole through it.

"Ugh, those college girls," Lorna complained as she hauled me into her bedroom. She slammed the door shut and reached for the hem of my shirt.

I brushed her hands off in irritation. "I can dress myself."

"Fine." She raised her hands defensively. "Dress is on the bed."

Was the champagne blond Jamie's girlfriend? Had I made up the connection I'd felt growing between us these last few months? Feeling nauseated, my fingers trembled as I tore off my shirt and then unzipped my jeans.

"You know, I don't get this thing about my brother," Lorna huffed.

I tensed, my pulse racing a little faster. *Does she know how I feel?*

"All these girls, I mean. You know he's made out with three since this party started."

I swallowed hard.

I wanted to cry.

I wanted to shove my face in a pillow somewhere and cry until it didn't hurt so bad.

Was this love?

Because if it was, it sucked!

Biting my lip, forcing the burn in my eyes back, I reached for the dress Lorna had laid out for me on her bed.

"The blond. The one hanging all over him ... no self-respect. Who watches a guy make out with three girls and volunteers to be the fourth?"

Who indeed? I thought bitterly.

"Anyway, enough about my lothario of a brother. There's a guy here perfect for you. He's one of Jamie's teammates."

Pulling the hem of the dress down, I wandered over to

Lorna's full-length mirror. The dress had straps, at least. Lorna knew my boobs could not hold up a strapless.

But it was scarlet red. And it clung to my curves, showing *everything*.

"Uh, I don't think so." I gestured to my reflection.

"I do think so. The red is great against your skin tone. It makes your eyes pop. And look at your boobs. There are women at that party who have paid surgeons a lot of money to have boobs like the ones God gave you."

"Yes, and now everyone and his father can see what God gave me."

Without answering, she took hold of my wrist again and led me out of her room and across the hall. "Wash your hands."

"Yes, Mom." I teased but did as I was told. Catching sight of my cleavage in the mirror above the sink, I sighed. "Seriously, Lorna, you know I'm not used to dressing like this."

"I'm not arguing with you about it. The ballet flats calm down the look, okay. Heels would take this dress to slutty on you, but the flats leave it at sexy."

"Don't say slutty."

She rolled her eyes. "PC Brigade alert."

"We don't need women perpetuating rhetoric that men use to denigrate our sex."

"Can we, like, *not*?" Lorna took hold of my hand after I dried them and led me out of the bathroom.

"You know, for someone who wants to be a litigator, you don't like conversations deeper than a kiddie pool," I teased.

"Yeah." Lorna cut me a serious look. "Right now, I don't. I've spent the past few weeks having deep conversations and sleeping fitfully. Tonight, I want to be shallow. Is that okay with you?"

I squeezed her hand. "You know it is."

She pulled me into her side, wrapping her arm around my

shoulders as we walked downstairs. "I can't wait to introduce you to Wex. I'm interested in his buddy Ryan."

My instinct was to pull away. To tell her I didn't want to flirt with some strange college guy. But from our vantage point on the stairs, I saw Jamie pressed against the wall in the far corner of the living room. The champagne blond was kissing the hell out of him, and he didn't seem to do much to stop her.

I was an idiot.

Those damn tears burned my eyes again as I looked away. Unfortunately, they snagged on Skye, who was watching me. She stood with a few of her actor friends in a huddle in the kitchen. She glanced through the crowd toward Jamie and then back to me. Concern flickered across her expression.

"Come on." Lorna pulled me down the last few stairs and past the kitchen.

I refused to look at Skye again.

She saw too much.

Wex and Ryan were out by the pool, sitting with the rest of Jamie's team and some girls.

Despite no one being legal drinking age, Skye was cool with everyone of college age having a few beers, as long as she was there to supervise. Lorna and I were excluded from this rule, of course.

It didn't stop my friend from plopping down on a guy's lap and helping herself to his beer bottle. The guy had dark hair and eyes, and as he cupped Lorna's hip and grinned at her, I saw he had an attractively crooked smile.

The guy next to Lorna's playmate for the evening nudged him. "I don't know how Jamie will feel about his sister being in your lap, Ryan."

Ryan shrugged as Lorna whispered something in his ear that made his neck flush.

She pulled back, a wicked smile on her face, and

gestured to me with the beer bottle. "Everyone, this is Jane, my best friend and the most beautiful soul you will ever meet."

I flushed at her praise and threw her an annoyed look.

She knew I hated being the center of attention.

"Jane, this is Ryan, and this"—she pointed to the guy who'd warned Ryan—"is Wex. Wex, make room for Jane."

Wex was tall with a similar build to Jamie. He had blue eyes that were startling against his dark coloring. Wex was good-looking. I could see that.

But he didn't give me butterflies.

However, he was looking at me as if I had struck him dumb.

Ryan nudged him, laughter in his voice. "Are you going to speak again, idiot?"

"Uh, yeah." Wex stood abruptly, not taking his eyes off me. "Here, please, sit." He gestured to the lounger he was on. I didn't really want to share the lounger with him, but it felt like the entire team was watching our interaction.

The image of Jamie and the champagne blond filled my head.

Maybe Lorna was right.

Maybe I should just let go for tonight after the hellishness of the last few weeks.

And Wex was cute.

I gave him a small smile, aware that my cheeks were probably sporting two bright spots of embarrassment.

"Remember, she's seventeen," Ryan teased under his breath, loud enough for me and Wex to hear.

Lorna giggled. "Uh, what age do you think I am?"

"Nah, you've been here before." Ryan nuzzled her neck. "And you're the devil."

"You're not wrong," I said before I could stop myself.

"Hey!" Lorna laughed.

I felt Wex chuckle because his body was pressed against mine.

Glancing shyly at him, I pulled on the hem of Lorna's stupid dress and inadvertently drew his attention to my legs. He swallowed hard and looked away from them. Our eyes met.

"So, you're on Jamie's team?"

"Yeah." He held out his hand to me. "Wex. Pete Wexham. Everyone calls me Wex."

I shook his hand. "I'm Jane."

He held on far longer than appropriate and gave me a boyish smile when he released my hand. "Sorry."

I didn't know what to say.

I wasn't exactly great at making small talk with strangers.

It turned out Wex was. He peppered me with questions about school and my interests, and I relaxed into the conversation, returning question for question. He seemed like a nice enough guy.

I didn't know how much time passed, and I wasn't aware of anything else going on around me because I was trying to focus on Wex and not on the horrifying thought of Jamie having sex with the champagne blond in his room above us.

That's why when Wex suddenly leaned in to kiss me, I was completely taken aback.

I'd been kissed before, of course.

My first kiss was in the eighth grade when we played spin the bottle at a party Lorna forced me to go to.

The last few years, I'd even gone on a few dates that involved first-date kisses, but I'd never wanted it to go beyond a first date because I was hung up on Jamie.

Wex's tongue flicked at my lips and I opened them on instinct, all the while screaming at myself, "What are you doing?!"

He groaned into my mouth as I kissed him back, and then his hand was on my nape, clutching me closer.

It wasn't a bad kiss.

What it was, though, was a mouth against mine, one that tasted of beer, and a strong hand on my neck.

I didn't feel the kiss anywhere else.

I never did.

Was there something wrong with me?

I pulled back, pressing a hand to Wex's chest. "No," I said. "I can't."

"Shit. Sorry if I read you wrong." He looked genuinely worried he had.

"I have to go." I pushed up off the lounger and stepped around people who were sitting on the floor of the deck.

I was shaking.

Why was I shaking?

Because there's something wrong with you. Something missing.

Wex seemed nice. And he was hot.

Why didn't I want him to kiss me?

There were too many people inside the house. I needed somewhere to be alone. Remembering Jamie's gift, I spotted it on the pile on the table in the kitchen, grabbed it, and hurried upstairs. I was dismayed to find the main bathroom occupied. Knowing Skye wouldn't mind, I slipped into her bedroom and fumbled through the dark to her private bathroom.

With a sigh, I flipped the light switch and closed the door behind me. I threw Jamie's gift on the counter and leaned on Skye's cool porcelain sink. I stared at my reflection in the mirror. Sometimes I wished my happiness weren't dependent on how other people felt about me. Wouldn't life be easier if we weren't all so preoccupied with the need to be loved, the need to be needed?

And if I was so desperate to be loved and needed, why didn't I keep kissing Wex?

The door to the bathroom flew open, jerking me out of my musings. I jolted in fright.

The sight of Jamie storming through and slamming it shut made my breath catch.

There were those butterflies again.

And the heat ... the heat that was always missing when someone else kissed me flared to life just being in Jamie's presence.

At night, in bed, under the cover of darkness, when I slipped my hand beneath my underwear and touched myself, I did it imagining it was Jamie.

There is nothing wrong with my body, I reminded myself.

It was just my desire wired inextricably to my heart.

Even with him standing there pissed about something, I wanted him.

"Jamie?"

He dragged his gaze down my body, lingering on my cleavage, before traveling south, leisurely. Almost insultingly.

I stiffened. "What is it?"

Those ocean eyes came back to mine.

Was it Wex?

My breath caught at the thought. No. It couldn't be.

"Jamie?"

"So, you put on a sexy dress and suddenly my teammates are fair game?"

I noticed his fists were clenched at his sides.

Anger flushed through me, and I knew I was blushing with it. "I didn't think you'd notice or care, what with the champagne blond and the three girls before her."

Jamie's head jerked back like I'd hit him. "What the fuck are you talking about?"

"Lorna filled me in on the girls, and I saw the blond for myself."

"What girls?"

"The three girls you made out with before the party even got started."

He scowled and closed the distance between us, his chest against mine, forcing me against the sink. I leaned away, curling my fingers around the edge of the porcelain. I couldn't breathe properly with him this close.

"Lorna is talking shit as usual. There were no girls. As for the blond"—he bent his head toward me, eyes hot with anger —"she cornered me. I didn't initiate that."

I ignored the fact that Lorna lied about the girls. "Yeah, you looked like you were not enjoying that at all."

His eyes narrowed at my sarcasm. "Why do you care who kisses me?"

"Why do you care who kisses me?" I countered.

Jamie leaned his hands on the sink, caging me in. "My teammates are off-limits to you." His breath whispered against my lips as he pressed his whole body against mine.

He was hard.

I gasped and his eyes flashed.

"Everyone but me is off-limits to you, Jane. You got that?"

"I don't belong to you," I whispered. It sounded weak. I hated that it sounded weak. Why did he do this to me? How could one person affect me so much?

"Yes, you do." His voice was hoarse. "And I belong to you." He swallowed hard. "I was going to wait. I'm supposed to wait."

"For what?"

"For you to turn eighteen."

I knew that I should feel euphoric that Jamie wanted me, but his words hurt. He could wait? And what would he be doing while he waited? I mean, according to him, all other men were off-limits to me, but a player like Jamie didn't give up sex for nine months.

He must have seen the fury in my eyes because he tensed. I pushed against his chest, but he wouldn't budge. "Move."

"What just happened?" He pressed even deeper against me. "What is going on in that busy head of yours?"

"You were going to wait nine months? And I'm to believe you weren't going to have sex with other girls in that time?"

That telltale muscle in his jaw ticked. "I'll never lie to you, Jane."

Bastard!

I pushed against him harder, but he wouldn't be moved. "Move out of my way."

"You never yell," he suddenly whispered, dropping his head to the crook of my neck. I felt his lips on my skin and shivered, despite myself.

God, I hated him in that moment.

He pressed a soft, sweet kiss to my neck and then lifted his head to whisper in my ear, "I've tried to fuck other girls. To fuck you out of my head." He pulled back to stare into my eyes. The intensity of his searing emotion caused a ripple of need low and deep inside me. "I can't," he confessed. "I try to be with them and it's like a thirst that's never sated. I can't go through with it— with being with them."

"Why?" My voice sounded hoarse.

"Because they're not you. I don't want to be with anyone but you."

"You don't mean that." I shook my head, afraid to believe him.

He cupped my face in his hands and brought our lips to almost touching. "I will never lie to you," he promised. Then he crushed his mouth over mine and I was lost.

It wasn't a sweet kiss.

It was deep and searching, tongue licking against tongue,

lips pushing against lips, and hands pulling at each other. I tugged at his T-shirt, trying to haul him closer, while he couldn't seem to decide which part of me he wanted to touch the most. My hips, my waist, my breasts. When he squeezed my breasts in his palms, his thumbs catching over my nipples, I throbbed with desperate need between my legs. I moaned into his mouth.

"Fuck." Jamie broke the kiss, panting. His eyes were bright with desire, desire I could feel pulsing against my stomach through his jeans. "I have to touch you."

I smiled shakily. The moment felt so surreal. Years of longing finally realized. "I thought you were."

He gave me a quick shake of his head as he gathered the hem of my dress in his hands. "Let me touch you."

Understanding what he meant, I blushed and felt that throb intensify. My body swayed with need, and I grabbed hold of the sink for balance. Unable to speak, I nodded.

All those nights of fantasizing about this, and it was going to happen.

Jamie leaned his forehead against mine, his breath quickening even more as he pushed the dress up to my waist. "I've imagined this," he whispered, his voice thick with lust. "More times than I count. Lying in bed, in the shower, hand around my dick. You in my head."

I shook with increasing need.

"Have you fantasized about me?"

I nodded, blushing harder.

"Say it." He lifted his forehead from mine, his expression as demanding as his tone. "Tell me you've thought about me like I've thought about you."

I think I surprised myself more than I surprised Jamie when I whispered, "I lie in bed and I touch myself only ever thinking about you."

Jamie kissed me again, ferocious, consuming, until I clung

to his shoulders to hold myself up. I shivered against him as his fingers tickled my stomach, and then I tensed as he slipped his hand down my belly and pushed beneath my underwear.

"You okay?" he broke the kiss to ask, his fingers stilling.

As strange as it was to have someone touch me where only I ever had, this wasn't just "someone." This was Jamie. My instinct was to push against his touch. "Please."

He didn't kiss me again.

Instead, Jamie held my gaze, his jaw clenched with tension, as he pressed his thumb over my clit and pushed two longer fingers inside me. I cried out against the unexpected pressure, my fingers biting into his shoulders.

"Fuck, Jane," he panted.

My eyes fluttered closed with sensation as he circled my clit. "Jamie," I breathed out his name on a pleasured sigh.

"Open your eyes."

They flew open.

"Good." He grunted. "Eyes on me."

It was so much more intimate like that, holding his gaze as he slid his fingers in and out.

"So tight." He bared his teeth at me. "So fucking tight, Doe."

I smiled on a gasp at the return of his Boston accent. "Jamie." I dug my fingers in deeper as I pushed against his touch, riding his fingers.

"That's it, fuck me, Jane, fuck me," he murmured hoarsely against my lips. He groaned as I physically responded to his dirty talk. "So full of surprises. You're perfect. Made for me."

As the tension built, little cries choked in my throat as Jamie pushed me toward climax.

"Don't stifle it," Jamie demanded. "No one can hear you back here but me. And I want to hear how much you want this."

"Jamie." I pushed under his T-shirt, wanting to feel him,

caressing the ridges of his abs with one hand, as I held onto his waist with the other. Instinct made me raise my leg against his hip, opening myself further to him. The thrust of his fingers sped up. "Oh God," I panted, eyes still locked on his. "Jamie."

"One day I'll be inside you completely," he promised. "I'm going to be your first and your only, Jane."

That made me even hotter than the dirty talk. My cries grew louder, and Jamie brushed my lips with his. "More."

"Oh my God." I let go, riding his fingers with desperation, clawing at his abs with my nails.

One last rub on my clit.

"Jamie!" I cried out, shuddering and jerking against his hand, throbbing and contracting around his fingers.

All the strength went out of my body. I melted into him. Nothing but a satisfied heap of hot-skinned Jane.

He slipped his fingers out of me and gently tugged down the hem of the dress. Lips on mine, his erection digging into my stomach, he whispered, "Why? Why is making you come the sexiest thing I've ever seen and heard in my life?"

"I don't know." I shook my head, unable to do much of anything at that moment.

"I do." He took my chin beneath his fingers with one hand, forcing my head up, my eyes to his. The look in them made me want to melt all over again. "It's because it's you. No one does it for me like you do. You have no idea."

I laughed, because I absolutely did. And it was amazing to me that Jamie felt the same. "I do. I understand completely."

"Yeah?" He kissed my lips, soft, sweet, just a caress. Then he pulled back, his expression stern. "Then you'll know it's no laughing matter. You should be worried, Doe."

"Why?"

"Because I feel like I'm coming out of my skin. You're all I think about. You're all I want. When I want someone's opinion on something, you're the first person I think of. I don't want to be in class because it means I'm not hanging out with you, talking about important shit and not-so-important shit ... I want to be buried deep inside you."

He nodded, swallowing hard. "Not just ..." He slid his free hand under my dress and cupped me in a possessive gesture. "Not just buried in here." He lifted his hand from my chin and tapped my temple. "But in here." Then he moved it to cover my breast where my heart pounded beneath it. "And I want to be so deep in here, you'll never get me out. Because *you're* buried in *me*."

Joy suffused me in such a wave of bliss and relief, tears blurred my vision. "You're already there, Jamie. You have been for a long time."

A tear spilled over and Jamie cursed under his breath, catching it on his thumb as he clasped my face in his big hands. "I'm such a moron." His voice was harsh. Then he kissed me. He kissed me like I was oxygen. "Forgive me," he begged between kisses. "Forgive me for being so slow on the uptake."

I laughed against his mouth. "You got there in the end. That's all that matters."

We kissed until my lips felt sensitive and swollen, until Jamie was clutching at my thigh and grinding his erection into my stomach.

"We need to stop." He pulled back, panting. "Before we go too far."

"Maybe I want to go too far."

"No." He shook his head. "Not until you're eighteen."

"You can't mean that."

"I don't want to rush you. I want this to be right."

His jaw set stubbornly. With a groan of frustration, he released me and stepped back toward the door. "You should go out first." He gestured to his erection tenting his jeans. "I need a minute."

Although nervousness filled me, I didn't want to leave him just yet.

"I have your gift here." I held it out to him. "Maybe that'll give you a chance to ... cool off."

He flashed me a smile and took the gift in hand. "This was on the pile downstairs. I know, because I've been eyeballing it since Lorna took it from you."

That thrilled me and made me even more nervous about his reaction.

"Why is it up here now?"

"I, uh, when I saw you kissing the blond, I suddenly realized that if you opened this, you'd probably guess what you mean to me and then you'd feel sorry for me."

"One, she kissed me, and if you'd stuck around long enough, you would've seen me push her off and search the room frantically to see if you'd caught her doing it."

I laughed at his teasing, my worries eased. "Okay."

"And two"—he stepped into my personal space, eyes hooked on mine—"I would never be sorry or feel sorry about you having feelings for me. The opposite, in fact."

"I get that now," I teased right back.

With a nod, Jamie's eyes dropped to the gift. Then, with an exasperating slowness, he opened it. When he pulled out the somewhat tattered copy of *I Am Legend*, he raised an eyebrow.

"Open it."

When he did, he tensed at the sight of the author's signature. "Is this a signed first edition?"

"Yeah."

His eyes flew to mine and my breath hitched at the hunger I saw on his face.

"You like it?" I whispered.

"It's the best gift I've ever gotten." He placed the book

carefully down on the sink and then shot me a wry look. "And now I'm hard again."

My laughter cut off when he suddenly lowered to his knees. "What are you doing?"

"I want to say thank you."

I gasped as he pushed my dress back up to my waist and then curled his fingers around my underwear. "Shouldn't we get back to the party? People will notice."

"Fuck 'em." He pulled down my underwear, and I stepped out of them. Eyes on mine, he watched as I shivered at the feel of his hands caressing my inner thighs before pushing them apart. I widened my stance, dragging in shallow breaths.

Jamie's eyes dipped to the shadow between my thighs. He groaned, and then his mouth was on me, and I forgot about anything else but him.

There was a moment as I rode his mouth, abandoned myself to pleasure, that I wondered if this was the beginning of something we couldn't control.

And should it scare me?

Probably.

But Jamie McKenna just felt too damn good, and too damn right, for me to care about anything else.

Chapter Six

JAMIE

Nineteen years old

THE SWIPE of Jane's pencil against the sketch paper was driving me nuts. Who knew posing for a drawing would be so sexy?

Jane sat on my desk chair, her eyes moving over my body and flicking down to the pad in her hand as she followed the lines of my body with her pencil. There was a smoky heat in her gaze that made me hot all over.

"Isn't this objectification?" I teased.

"It's art," she replied, her lips twitching with amusement.

"I'm not sure I need to be wearing only boxers for you to sketch me."

Our eyes met, and the blood that was making my heart pound quickly made its way south. I wanted to tell her to get over on the bed, but we'd only been seeing each other for six weeks, and the no-sex thing was already testing my limits.

"You're beautiful," she whispered, and I could tell she

meant it. "The lines of your body are beautiful. I want to see them."

She wanted to see all of them.

It was me who insisted I keep my boxers on. We needed some boundaries; otherwise I'd lose myself in her. Which was exactly what my shy, not-so-shy-with-me, sexy girl wanted.

"It would be better if you lost the boxers," Jane said.

See?

I grinned at her and shook my head. "What if Lorna came home? It would be pretty hard to explain why I'm letting you draw me naked."

"It'll be pretty hard to explain why you're letting me draw you half-naked," she argued.

For the sake of peace, and so we got to know each other as boyfriend and girlfriend before World War III broke out, we'd kept our relationship a secret from everyone. The truth was, we didn't want to have to deal with Lorna just yet. However, I didn't know how much longer I could handle the secret. It had only been a month, and the small moments of time we stole when I didn't have practice and Lorna had practice after school was quickly becoming not enough.

"Hmm." Jane bit on the end of her pencil, her eyes moving between me and the sketch.

"What is it?"

"I can't get your left nipple right."

I chuckled. "Nipple problems, huh?"

She sent me a smile that caused a flutter in my stomach. A fucking flutter. These past few weeks, I'd discovered a new side to Jane. She was quiet, reserved, kind of shy, yes ... but not with sex. She was uninhibited with me. Jane just had to look at me, how she looked at me right then, and my dick got hard.

Not that we'd had sex. I was determined not to until she was eighteen. But we were doing other shit, and Jane was so beyond passionate and exciting, I was losing my mind.

Holding out for another eight months ... well, it might as well have been ten years.

I watched as she put the sketch pad on my desk and then got up to cross the room to me. My eyes dipped down her body and back up. She was wearing jean shorts and a T-shirt, and it made me as hot as sexy lingerie on her would have.

"Jane ..." Her name came out hoarse. "What are you doing?"

"I need a closer look." She placed a knee on the bed and crawled toward me on all fours.

Fuck.

Her citrusy scent tickled me as she pressed a hand to my chest and gave it a little push.

I obliged by rolling onto my back, already hard.

Then she straddled me, resting her ass right on my erection.

I hissed in a breath as her eyelids lowered and she gave a little moan.

"Jane." I gripped her hips, half wanting to push her off and half needing to grind her on me.

"Let's have a look," she murmured, bending her head toward my nipple. Her thumb rotated over it and I shifted beneath her, my skin flushing. Then she kissed it, tongue flicking against the nub.

"Fuck." My fingers bit into her hips and I pushed her down over me.

Jane's breathing stuttered as she undulated, rubbing against me.

"Fuck, fuck." I grabbed her hips and tried to lift her off, but she wouldn't budge. I glowered up at her. "You need to get off me."

Sighing, she sat up straight and then lifted her T-shirt up over her head and threw it across the room. Any words of discouragement died in my throat as she unclipped her bra and took it off. Her full breasts jiggled as she threw the bra away, her dusky nipples tightening into mouthwatering little buds.

Fuck, fuck, fuck.

"I'll get off you." She smoothed her hands up my abs and bent toward my mouth. "If that's what you really want."

"You're a temptress." I cupped her beautiful face in my hands. "You know that, right?"

I didn't give her time to answer. I lifted off my back, crushing her mouth to mine as my hands caressed her breasts, kneading them. My thumbs dragged over her nipples as she rocked against me.

I broke the kiss and pulled roughly on her hair to arch her back, and she whimpered with excitement.

I took her right nipple in my mouth and sucked it hard, groaning in satisfaction as she cried out and raked her nails down my back. Everything else ceased to matter. We were just lips and tongues and hands and fingers and skin.

Heat and sweat enveloped us.

The tension deep in our guts became more important than rational thinking.

Soon Jane was naked, her sexy, beautiful body spread out beneath me. My boxers gone, my dick hard and throbbing between her legs.

I couldn't think straight.

I couldn't think beyond the need to be inside her.

She was panting, her eyes smoke, her pussy wet against my tip, and I had her right thigh gripped tight against my hip, opening her to me. I nudged, gritting my teeth, already anticipating how tight she'd be but worried about hurting her, wanting it to be good for her.

"Jamie," she begged, lifting her hips toward me. "Please."

Her face was flushed, her eyes on me, and I felt like the

only man in the world. She always made me feel like the only man in the world.

I pushed into her. "Jane—"

My head jerked up at the sound of my bedroom door crashing against the wall. Heart pounding, my first instinct was to cover Jane's body with mine as my little sister barged into the room.

"Shit!" I grabbed at the duvet we'd cast aside and tried to cover us. "Get the fuck out!" I yelled.

"I knew it!" Lorna screamed, her face screwed up in outrage and hurt. "I fucking knew it!" Her eyes flew to Jane, who was trying to hide under my body. Feeling her shaking beneath me, her embarrassment and worry made me even more pissed.

I shielded her as much as I could and addressed my sister. "If you don't get out right now, I'll lose my shit like you've never seen me lose my shit, Lor."

Whatever she heard in my voice made her take a step back. "I'll be downstairs, waiting for you two assholes to explain yourselves!"

With that, she stomped out of the room.

I cursed again and pulled away from Jane, worried I was crushing her. "You okay?"

She tried to scramble out from underneath me, and the desperate way she attempted to get away caused my panic. I took hold of her biceps to stop her. She wouldn't look me in the eye. *Jesus Christ.*

"Hey." I forced her chin up, her eyes on me. "We aren't doing anything wrong."

Jane trembled. But she nodded and I calmed a little. "I'm just embarrassed. And not prepared to face her."

"This is you and me," I reminded her. "We're allowed to date. This is not something she gets to dictate."

At her slow nod, I kissed her. Long, deep, and with every

ounce of emotion I felt for Jane so she'd know that I'd put up with anyone's shit, including Lorna's, as long as I got to keep her.

After we'd dressed, I held Jane's hand tight in mine as we made the descent into hell.

As soon as we stepped off the last stair, Lorna launched off the couch, eyes on Jane as she charged toward us.

I pushed Jane behind me, and Lorna stumbled to a halt.

"What did you think I would do?" She blinked, paling, as if I'd hit her.

"I wasn't sure."

"I'd never hurt Jane."

Jane stepped out from behind me. "Lorna, we were going to tell you."

"I'd never hurt Jane," Lorna repeated, glaring at me, before turning to her best friend. "Unlike my brother."

Anger churned in my gut. "Lorna."

"No. This is ridiculous." She gestured between the two of us. "You two don't make sense at all, and Jane is not ruining our friendship over a fling with you, Jamie McKenna." She crossed her arms over her chest and stared defiantly at Jane. "It's him or me."

Jane's expression was as shocked as mine. "What?"

"I said, it's Jamie or me. If you date him, our friendship is officially over."

The color disappeared from Jane's face.

That was it. I lost it. "Are you serious?" I yelled. "You can't make her choose between us. You're fucking nuts, do you know that?"

"No." Lorna's eyes filled with tears. Crocodile tears. Manipulative brat. "What I know is that no one ever picked me. Until Jane. She's my best friend and I *need* her. If you two split up, what happens then, huh? What happens to me and Jane?"

"We won't split up."

"Oh please, Jamie, you're a man-whore. As soon as you get bored, you'll dump her."

"You don't know shit!"

Jane flinched at my side with the impact of my roar.

It didn't even touch Lorna. Not even an earthquake could intimidate her. "I know she's *my* best friend and I love her. You don't!" She turned toward Jane, her eyes beseeching. "I'm the only one in the world who loves you."

I remembered overhearing her say something similar to Jane years ago. I should've done something about it then. I pushed between Jane and Lorna, and my sister stumbled back. "Do you even hear yourself?" I asked, my voice calm but hoarse with the fury I was trying to check. "Do you hear the sick, manipulative bullshit you're trying to fill her head with? And how long, huh? How long have you been filling her head with this shit?" I spun away from her to take Jane by the hands, putting her palms on my chest.

She stared up at me, wide-eyed. "Jamie?"

"I don't want you to ever believe her bullshit, okay? She's only saying it to get you to do what she wants, the same way she has done your entire friendship."

A weariness entered Jane's eyes that I didn't like. "I know that."

I relaxed, slipping my arms around her shoulders as I turned to my sister. She wasn't getting into Jane's head with that toxic crap. That's all I cared about.

Lorna's face crumbled. "You're supposed to be my big brother. It's my feelings you're supposed to protect. And you never have. I don't want you to do this. Why won't you choose me?"

I squeezed my eyes closed, hearing the real pain in her voice. The problem was twofold. For reasons I didn't care to think on too long, our dad hadn't been kind to my little sister.

In fact, he only ever had time for me, but he was at least sweet enough to Skye. Lorna, he treated like shit. I knew this had affected my little sister.

And then Lorna was just like our mom. Unlike when I was a kid, pandering to my mom, I wouldn't sacrifice my happiness for someone who would never be happy, no matter the choices I made. "I love you, Lor. You're my kid sister and I will always love you. But this isn't about you."

"Jane's my best friend."

"Yeah. And you just told her no one would love her like you do. Do you not understand how fucked up that is? That's shit sociopaths say to people."

She glared at me. "That's not fair."

"Yeah? You say you love Jane, but you haven't asked her how she feels about me, if being with me makes her happy. Because you don't care. You don't care about anyone's happiness but your own. You hand out your love to her in exchange for her obedience."

Jane stiffened under my arm, and I gave her a reassuring squeeze.

"I don't hand out love in exchange for anything," I said, swallowing hard, my heart pounding. "I love Jane and ..." I turned, looking down at her as she stared up at me in shock. I think it was a good shock, though. "I love you. And it isn't dependent on you loving me back or doing what I want you to do. I just love you."

It wasn't how I wanted to tell her, but I needed her to know before she let Lorna mess with her head.

"Talk about manipulative," Lorna scoffed, completely ruining the moment. "How many girls have you said that to?"

"None."

"Liar. You're such a nasty, dirty fucking liar. You'll saying anything to get into a girl's pants."

Stupidly, I let her draw me into an immature yelling

match, but it didn't take me long to realize Jane was strangely silent. She just stood there, looking pale.

I petered off into silence as I stared down at her, feeling my heart sink.

Maybe I'd gotten it wrong.

Maybe I was the only one falling here.

Perhaps I couldn't compete with years of Lorna telling Jane that only she would ever truly love her. It would've been easy for my sister to mess with Jane's head like that. An orphan who had moved from foster home to foster home, and even when she ended up at a good one, her foster parents didn't have time for her. Willa and Nick always seemed relieved that my family had enveloped Jane into ours.

A kid who'd had no one since she was seven until Lorna gave her someone.

Fuck.

"Jane?" I whispered.

She glanced up at me and then back to Lorna. "Since we were thirteen, I've spent days loving you and resenting you in equal measure. Being grateful to you and resenting you for trying to make me feel like no one could ever love me but you. If it hadn't been for Skye and Jamie, our friendship might never have survived, Lorna."

Holy. Shit.

Lorna's eyes filled with genuine, hurt tears.

I felt that prickle of guilt and protectiveness that I'd always feel as a brother, but I knew Jane needed to say this. And Lorna needed to hear it.

"You think I didn't know." Jane's eyes filled with tears, and I wanted to reach out and hold her, but I refrained. This was about them, not me. "That you used the fact that no one loved or needed me, against me?"

Just like that, any brotherly protectiveness I'd been feeling was decimated as I heard the pain in Jane's voice.

Anger burned in my throat.

"I ... I didn't mean to do that," Lorna sobbed. "If that's the way it came across ... I didn't mean to do that. Not really."

"Then stop." Jane took a step toward her. "Please, Lorna. Despite everything, I *do* love you. But I'm in love with Jamie." She glanced up at me, and I saw it. I saw all that love for me, and for the first time in my life, I knew what happiness felt like. "I've been in love with you for a long time." She gave me a shy smile as my heart grew so big, I thought it might explode every-fucking-where.

Then she addressed Lor again. "If you love me the way you say you do, you'll want me to be happy. You won't make me choose between my best friend and the guy I'm in love with. And we'll move forward, treating each other with more respect than we have in the past."

Silence fell among us, the clock above the mantel ticking so loudly, I wanted to rip it off the wall.

Finally, Lorna wiped the tears off her face and shook her head. Her anger and disappointment were palpable. "I can't. If I do, I'm saying it's okay. And it's not. Because he will hurt you, and then you won't want to be around us anymore. So, I might as well cut myself off from you now. It's him or me, Jane. Choose me, and I promise I'll be a better friend. I promise."

My fucking sister.

"Lorna—"

Jane lifted a hand and I shut up. "I'm sorry. I don't want to choose, but if you make me ... I'll choose Jamie."

With a heartbreaking sob, my sister whirled around and rushed out of the house.

That hurt.

I wanted to run after her.

But the consequent sobs coming out of Jane hurt too. Gathering her up in my arms, I carried her upstairs, feeling her tears soak into my T-shirt. She cried like her heart was breaking, and guilt suffused me. For years, Lorna had been Jane's family. Was I being a selfish bastard?

See, this was what Lorna did. She turned it all around on everyone else.

Tucking Jane into my side of the bed, I held her until she cried herself to sleep, promising myself she'd never regret making that choice.

———

AT SOME POINT, I must have drifted off, because the next thing I knew, a loud crash jolted me awake.

Jane jerked awake too. "What was that?"

It was dark in the room.

We'd been asleep awhile.

Heart racing, I reached over for my phone and saw it was one in the morning.

"Wait here," I whispered. "It's probably just Lorna."

Except Lorna wasn't in her room, which was something I'd worry about once I investigated the crash. I was about to head downstairs when I saw a light coming from Skye's room.

"Skye?" I called out, striding down the hall. The door was wedged open a little, but I knocked anyway. "Skye, you in there?"

When there was no answer, I pushed inside.

My stomach lurched at what I found.

My big sister sprawled motionless on her bedroom floor.

"Skye!" I fell to my knees beside her and felt her skin; it was clammy. She was soaked in sweat. Her head twitched on her neck, her eyes fluttering behind her lids. What the fuck?

"Skye?" I checked her pulse. It was slow and faint. "Jane!" I yelled. "Call 911!"

Fear coursed through my body as I tried to determine

what the hell had happened to my sister. I could smell the alcohol on her. Alcohol poisoning? Rolling her into the recovery position, my gaze caught on something on her nose.

I bent over and swiped my thumb over her nostrils, glaring down at the white powder sitting on my skin.

"Skye." I groaned, tears choking my throat. "Jane!" My voice cracked as I tried to yell.

The door burst open as Jane rushed into the room, the phone pressed to her ear. Her eyes widened. "Oh ... it's my ... it's my boyfriend's sister ... I don't know." She looked at me, tears in her eyes. "What happened?"

I shook my head. "I think it's an overdose."

"We think it's an overdose. I don't ... Jamie, what did she take?"

I shook my head. "Maybe coke and alcohol. I don't know."

She repeated the words and then rushed out of the room to wait at the front door. An ambulance was on its way.

Everything was a blur as I waited helplessly, hoping Skye would open her eyes and tell me this was just a big joke. Instead, paramedics were suddenly there, pushing me aside and lifting my sister onto a stretcher.

Jane and I followed.

She drove my car.

I didn't say a word. I couldn't speak through my fear.

I was vaguely aware of Jane calling Lorna and leaving her a voicemail.

At the hospital, minutes felt like hours. My skin was on fire. Every noise irritated me. My toes curled inside my sneakers as my nerve endings screamed with agitation. Dread was a sickening weight in my gut.

The only thing that kept me from roaring my outrage at the world was Jane's small hand in mine. She kept me anchored inside my skin. The place where her palm touched mine was the only place that was cool and soothed.

Sometimes she'd whisper reassuring words in my ear, and I'd bend toward her because her breath on my skin was a comfort too. Nuzzling my face into her throat, I stifled frightened tears and wished I could somehow hide inside Jane.

"Skye McKenna's family?"

I lurched out of the uncomfortable waiting-room chair and dragged Jane toward where the doctor stood. I was barely aware of anyone else or the pain radiating off them as they awaited news of their loved ones.

All I cared about was Skye.

"Skye McKenna?" the doctor asked.

"I'm Jamie McKenna. I'm her brother."

"You called it in?"

I nodded. "Is my sister okay?"

The doctor sighed. "Mr. McKenna, your sister had a heart attack."

Jane's hand tightened in mine while I shook my head, not sure I'd heard right. "What?"

"We found high traces of cocaine in your sister's blood, along with high alcohol levels. Alcohol is often used to temper the effects of cocaine because it's a depressant. Were you aware your sister was using cocaine?"

I shook my head.

No.

But I should have been.

"I was worried about her drinking a while back but I ... thought ..." I thought she was okay.

I hadn't been paying attention.

"Will my sister be okay?"

"The drugs and alcohol caused your sister to go into cardiac arrest. She has a recovery period ahead, and I can give you recommendations for rehabilitation facilities. Her road won't be easy, but your sister can recover from this."

"She's okay," Jane whispered, kissing the back of my hand.

I disagreed. Skye wasn't okay.

Apparently, she hadn't been okay for a while.

And I never even noticed.

Guilt wracked through me.

CHAPTER SEVEN

JANE
Seventeen years old

As we walked hand in hand through Glendale, I turned to Jamie for the third time and asked him where we were going.

He wore a secretive smile. "You'll see."

It wasn't my birthday until June. It wasn't his birthday until September. There didn't seem to be anything to celebrate that required me wearing "my nicest dress." But that's what Jamie had asked me to wear, and when he picked me up, he did it wearing a shirt, suit pants, dress shoes, and a tailored, mid-length overcoat Skye had bought him. He'd never worn it until now.

This surprise date was killing me. I had butterflies in my belly.

Strolling through the tree-lined neighborhood a block from the McKennas' rented Spanish Revival house, I wondered if we had much farther to walk. I'd worn heels and wasn't used to walking in them. I threaded my arm through

Jamie's and snuggled closer. He smelled like lime and tangerine from his shower wash. "I'm nervous."

"Don't be." He pressed a sweet kiss to my temple. "You're going to love it."

"Why the surprise? Have I missed an anniversary or something?"

Jamie's smile tinged with sadness. "No, Doe. I just wanted to do something special for you. It's been a rough few months."

He could say that again.

The important factor in it all was that Skye was doing well. But after recovering from a heart attack at twenty-five years old, it didn't take much convincing from the three of us for her to go to rehab. Jamie attempted to talk to her, to see why she'd turned to drugs and alcohol. He worried it was the pressure of taking care of him and Lorna at too young an age. Skye was adamant that wasn't true. She said the drugs were just too readily available during a time when she felt stressed about finding stable work.

Ironically, she got dropped from her current show because she had to go into rehab. Now that she was out, the last few weeks had been difficult. Her agent was struggling to find her work. Jamie had given up his car, and Lorna had agreed to trade hers in for something cheaper.

While Skye reassured them she had savings, Jamie took over managing the household and budgeting their monthly expenses. He also got a job working on campus at a coffeehouse. His coach wasn't too happy about it, but if he promised not to let it interfere with his training, the guy didn't give him too much crap.

Following in Jamie's footsteps, I'd started taking on babysitting jobs. Between looking out for Skye, being with Jamie any minute we both had free, and schoolwork and babysitting, I had less time to think about the fact that school was not a great place to be.

Lorna had frozen me out. She remained a popular girl jock, and I went back to being kind of anonymous. I kept texting Lorna, trying to get her to talk to me. Or at least to Jamie, whom she also wasn't talking to. Jamie said I was just feeding Lorna's need for attention, but I didn't want my former best friend to feel like I'd taken her family from her. Still, she ignored me.

There were kids at school I was friendly with, and I still got asked out occasionally, but as a not entirely social person, things were quiet at school. Lonely, even. Most days that was fine. But there were the days when Lorna's so-called friends liked to make snide comments about me whenever I was in the vicinity.

I didn't tell Jamie. There was no point. He'd just get pissed at Lorna when she wasn't the one saying anything. Whenever Jamie and I were together, I didn't want to talk about his little sister.

"We're getting closer." Jamie tugged on my hand as we rounded the corner and turned left onto North Brand Boulevard. We were in the hub of it all. Restaurants, shops, nightclubs and all.

There was a lot going on here, so Jamie could be taking me anywhere. To dinner? Only fancy places required you to dress up, though, and I thought he was trying to watch what he spent.

Crossing the street, hand tight around mine, I laughed under my breath. "Why does it have to be such a mystery where we're going?"

"Why not?" He grinned down at me. "Do you really hate surprises that much?"

"Not when you're giving them." I knew everything I felt

for him was probably beaming out of my eyes. "But with you, I'm impatient."

His ocean eyes turned a lagoon blue. They always did when something turned him on. "I like that I bring out your impatient side."

"You enjoy corrupting me," I corrected him, teasing him.

Yet I wasn't sure it wasn't true.

"You're right," he agreed, sounding serious. "I like that with everyone else, you're patient, you're controlled, calm, you never raise your voice, you'd never hurt a soul ... But with me" —he bent his head to whisper in my ear—"you cry, you yell, and you claw my back with your nails."

I flushed hot, but not from embarrassment.

After the humiliating moment with Lorna when Jamie and I were almost about to have sex for the first time and she busted in on us, life had distracted us from our fast-moving relationship. Skye's mental and physical well-being became our priority. There was a lot going on, and it made Jamie reevaluate. He was back to wanting to wait until I was eighteen before we had sex.

I didn't get it. We were doing everything else. What were a few months?

Jamie McKenna had the ability to make me lose my ever-loving mind.

His expression was smug as he pressed a hard kiss to my mouth.

"Watch it," a woman said as we almost walked right into her.

I threw a "sorry" over my shoulder and Jamie chuckled, wrapping his arm around me as he guided me past more stores.

I knew we were getting closer to wherever it was we were going when Jamie's strides slowed.

Then he stopped outside the Alex Theatre.

"This is it?" I asked.

He looked a little uncertain as he nodded.

Glancing up at the marquee, I read the signage and understanding dawned.

LOS ANGELES BALLET PRESENTS *THE SLEEPING BEAUTY*.

The breath whooshed out of my body and emotion thickened my throat. My vision grew a little blurry.

"I've still never been to the ballet."

"One day you will."

"Are those happy tears or did I fuck up?"

Not caring where we were, I slid my arms around his neck, went up on my tiptoes, and crushed my lips against his. I poured every ounce of love and gratitude I could into that kiss, breathing my very life into it, my soul spilling into his.

We were panting by the time I let him up for air.

"I guess that's a yes." He squeezed my hips in his hands, searching my face. "You like?"

"I love," I whispered, brushing my mouth over his once more. "Jamie, no one has ever cared like you care. I love you so much."

He groaned and wrapped his arms around my waist, pressing his face into the crook of my neck as we hugged. After a minute, Jamie lifted his head, caressed my ear with his lips, and said, "There are no words for how much I love you, Jane Doe."

I'd always hated my name. For obvious reasons. Not anymore. Not the way Jamie said it.

Grinning, I stared up at the marquee again. "I can't believe you're taking me to the ballet." I side-eyed him. "You're going to be so bored."

He took my hand and led me inside. "Bored with you is still my version of bliss, Doe."

I grinned so hard my cheeks hurt.

After we'd handed over our tickets and were walking into the auditorium, Jamie started laughing.

"What?"

"You're so fucking adorable." He squeezed me into his side and kissed my temple again. "If I'd known it would make you this happy, I'd have done it sooner."

It wasn't until we were settling into our seats that I realized how great they were. We were in the middle of the first row of the Alexander Terrace that hung over the orchestra section. We had a clear view all the way to the stage.

"Jamie," I whispered in his ear, "these tickets ... the cost."

He pulled back at me and scowled. "You don't need to worry about that."

"But—"

"We're not talking about it."

His snippy tone irritated me. "No need to snap."

Jamie's answer was to kiss me. Hard, deep, his warm hand clasping my face as his tongue danced with mine. It was incredibly inappropriate in the theater and was one reason it made me so hot. I breathed a little hard as he finally let me up for air. His thumb pulled on my swollen lower lip. "Just let me do something nice for you."

I narrowed my eyes. "You could just say that without getting me all turned on."

He threw his head back, his chuckle deep and amused. "Someone put you on this planet just to stroke my ego."

I raised an eyebrow. "Just your ego?"

"Thankfully, no."

We shared a knowing, heated smile that was interrupted by a couple who were trying to get past us to their seats.

Twenty minutes later, the vibrations from the orchestra below tickled my feet. Goose bumps prickled my skin and I sat tense in my seat, fingers gripped to the arms of the theater chair as I strained to take in everything that happened on stage.

Female dancers in traditional costume with stiff tutus and brocaded, sparkling corsets danced across the stage and into the arms of male dancers who had bodies like Roman sculptures. The dancers' bodies were machines, honed and muscular, sleek and powerful, and they moved with such grace and elegance, emoting so much with a mere flourish of their arms.

Memories assailed me. Ballet classes. Standing at the barre, learning how to turn my feet out. How to plié. My mom, Marissa, who was now just a shadowy impression in my memories, gushing over me after my first recital.

The longing when I'd see advertisements for ballet or a little girl in a tutu going to class. The crushing envy I felt when I heard Keelie Meyers in seventh grade telling our whole class she was attending a ballet school in Paris during the summer.

All of it had symbolized a life I'd wanted.

A life that should have been mine.

A life I hadn't known how to let go of until Lorna McKenna hauled me into her world.

Yet, it wasn't until Jamie that I finally felt I'd found home. That I finally gave up longing for Margot Higgins and grew content with being Jane Doe. I could watch the stunning dancers tell a beautiful story, and it didn't hurt anymore.

I didn't realize I was crying until I felt Jamie's hand on my cheek. I turned to him in the theater's dark as he caught one on his thumb, his frown severe.

Grabbing his wrist, I pressed a kiss to his knuckles and smiled. "They're good tears," I whispered. I leaned in and pressed a quick kiss to his mouth. "Thank you."

Assured I was happy, he settled in his seat.

I did the same, drawn back to the stage, where I fell in love all over again with ballet. It swept me up in the music and the feeling and the utter beauty of how many ways humans were capable of telling stories that enraptured.

Jamie didn't say a word as we left the theater ninety minutes later. His hand clenched mine tight, and I realized he was waiting for me to say something. Traffic sounded, laughter, music, lights flared from headlights, from streetlights, from neon signs hanging on buildings as we walked through the evening world that was Brand Boulevard.

"Were you bored?" I asked.

"I thought I would be. But I wasn't. It was beautiful."

I loved that he could admit that. *It's his artist's soul*, I thought. "Maybe we can go again sometime?"

"If it'll make you happy, we'll go anytime you want."

Hugging into him, I inhaled a deep breath and let it go. "It made me forget everything for a little while."

"Yeah, me too."

The mood between us was somewhat intense as Jamie stopped at a taco place and got us a quick bite to eat. We ate as we walked back to his house, a silent agreement between us that we weren't ready for the night to be over. Every inch of me vibrated as we strolled through Glendale. Now and then, he'd squeeze my hand, as if reassuring himself I was there. Or perhaps reassuring me that he felt what I felt.

Something had cemented deep inside me as soon as I stood outside the Alex and realized what Jamie had done for me.

I knew I loved him.

But now I knew that he was so deeply, intrinsically a part of me, to lose him would be like someone tearing me in half. For someone who'd always been slightly detached, even from the people I cared about, this should have terrified me.

Instead, I was electrified. And desperately wanting.

I was done waiting to be with him.

The house was empty when Jamie let us in. He called out anyway, double-checking, but there was no response. It was a

Saturday night. Lorna would be out with the latest guy she was seeing, and Skye had left Jamie a note.

"She's with Sheridan." He waved the note she'd left on the kitchen counter. Sheridan was an actress Skye had met through rehab. She was a little older and had been sober for seven years. She and Skye had bonded.

"That's good." My voice was thick with need.

Jamie eyed me. "What do you want to do?"

Heart pounding, I gave him a loaded look as I walked past him and ascended the stairs.

He didn't say anything, but his footsteps soon sounded behind me.

Once inside his room, I turned to him and shrugged off my light jacket. It pooled at my feet as I kicked off my heels. Jamie stepped inside, his eyes dropping to my thighs where I clutched the hem of my dress. He pushed the door shut without taking his attention off me.

Shivering at the heat in those ocean eyes, I pulled the dress up and over my head and let it fall to the floor.

"Jane ...?"

I unclipped my bra, and the straps slipped down my arms, the cups catching on my taut nipples before finding my dress on the floor. "I adore you, Jamie McKenna. And I don't want to be with anyone but you. Ever."

His eyes were now vibrant with need as they devoured my body. His voice was hoarse. "You know I feel the same way."

"Then what are we waiting for?" I curled my fingers into the waistband of my cotton underwear and taking a deep breath, arms shaking—not with fear but with anticipation—I pushed them down until they dropped around my ankles.

Jamie sucked in a harsh breath, his chest rising and falling a little faster as I stepped out of them.

I shrugged a little, every inch of my naked body tingling, goose bumps prickling all over my skin. I was hot and shivery.

My heart slammed hard in my chest. My palms felt clammy. "Jamie, I want you. And life is too damn short. We both know that. Tomorrow something might take me away from you, and I don't want us to never have been together in every way we can be. I don't want to wait anymore."

He seemed a little lost, dazed, as he drank me in from head to toe. Not that he hadn't seen me naked. We'd fooled around naked before.

But it felt like this was the first time.

I could see his erection straining against the zipper of his suit pants, his hands flexed at his sides as if he was desperate to touch me. Cheeks flushed, breathing uneven, he looked up from gazing at my body. "I'm coming out of my skin. What are you doing to me?"

He didn't give me a chance to answer. He shrugged off his coat and crossed the distance between us, plucking at a few buttons on his shirt before hauling it up and over his head. Then his hands were clutching my face as he kissed me, deep and wet, his tongue licking hungrily at mine. The sensation of falling soon followed, the mattress depressing under our bodies, our lips losing contact as we bounced a little with the impact.

I gasped as Jamie held himself up over me so as not to crush me and nudged his throbbing hardness between my legs. The fabric of his pants caused delicious friction against me. My hands slid over the smooth, steel sleekness of muscle on his back, my fingers bruising his skin as my hips rose to meet his thrusts.

We'd done this before. Just last weekend after watching a movie on the couch, a movie we didn't realize had a hot sex scene in it until it was too late, he'd pinned me to the sofa. To both our delights, we discovered that night I liked it when he held me down. Sex was the only time I enjoyed him being in total control. Determined not to go too far, though, we kept our clothes on, his thrusts hard between my legs, sweat glistening on his temple, as the friction pushed us to orgasm. We came hard.

But I knew we were both still unsatisfied.

I didn't want that tonight. As good as it felt, I wanted more.

I fumbled for the buttons above the zipper on his pants.

When one of his hands covered mine, I feared he wanted to stop.

He broke our kiss and pushed up off the bed, straddling me. Jamie held my gaze as he unbuttoned his pants, unzipped them, and stepped from the bed to shuck them off completely. Along with his boxer briefs.

Jamie was impressive, to say the least.

There was ... girth.

The tingling between my legs intensified, and slickness accompanied this familiar tugging flip in my lower belly.

"Jamie," I gasped, reaching for him.

Instead of coming down over me, his features hardened. Gripping my hips in his strong hands, he yanked me toward him. His hands moved to the back of my thighs, fingers squeezing as he lifted my lower body off the bed and forced my legs wide.

His head descended between them and then his mouth was on me.

I was flooded with sensation as he licked and sucked at me. Pleasure coiled tightly, deep and low, the pressure building as I undulated against his tongue. The urge to throw back my head and descend into bliss was strong, but it was turning me on even more to watch him.

I came on a scream, my body falling against the bed, my hips jerking with climax as Jamie lapped up my orgasm. At one point I was vaguely aware of Jamie leaving my body, of the crinkling sound of foil, as I melted into the mattress, my body pulsing.

Then I was being lifted under the arms, maneuvered back up the bed, and I wrapped my legs around his hips as he fell over me, kissing me. I could taste myself on his tongue. He was hard and hot between my legs, a slight pressure against my wet.

Jamie groaned, breaking the kiss, eyes on me as he pushed up onto his hands to brace himself over me. "Hold on," he demanded hoarsely.

I gripped his waist, my panting increasing with the anticipation. "Jamie."

He pushed against me, feeling impossibly big, and my fingernails dug into his skin. "Fuck." His expression strained as he gently nudged in a little more.

It burned and I winced. Oh my God, he wasn't going to fit. How was that possible? "Jamie?"

As if he'd read my mind, he gave a huff of breathless laughter. "It'll happen. You're just so tight." He groaned and leaned his forehead against mine, his body trembling as he held himself suspended. "Give me a minute."

Feeling the damp sweat coat his body, I lifted my hips upward into him. "Just do it fast," I whispered.

"I don't want to hurt you."

"I think it'll be better." The burning pressure was uncomfortable.

Lifting his head, he stared into my eyes. "You sure?"

I nodded, my hands sliding down to rest on his waist. "Please."

Jamie took in a breath, expression fierce. He moved his hips back, retreating slightly, and then he thrust into me hard. His guttural growl filled the room as he seated himself deep inside me. "Jane, fuck me, fuck me," he murmured, eyes squeezed closed, face suffused with utter pleasure.

For me, it hurt. I hadn't expected it would hurt like that.

Tears burned in my eyes and when Jamie opened his and saw, his expression instantly changed from bliss to horror. "Jane," he panted, cupping my face with one hand while he held himself up with the other. "Do you want me to stop?"

In that moment, my body did. It wanted to eject him and retreat, but my mind reminded me I loved him and that I'd read that a girl's first time could be painful. But that it got better.

Knowing the joy I'd felt from the orgasm Jamie had just given me, I had to believe it got better. We just had to work through the awkward virginity part.

He began to pull out and I gripped him tight. "Don't."

Jamie hovered over me, unsure.

I gave him a reassuring smile, blinking back the tears. "Don't stop."

"I don't want to hurt you," he whispered. "I love you."

Adoration suffused me and I relaxed, and as I relaxed, the pain receded. The sensation of him was overwhelming and it burned still, but there was a pleasure pain in it. "I love you so much, Jamie. Keep going." I flexed my hips a little. "I want this."

Jamie kissed me. Deep. Full of feeling. And as we kissed, he moved. It stung with the first few glides, but then it changed.

That beautiful tension built.

I gasped into his mouth and we broke apart, holding each other's eyes as he moved in and out of me. "Jamie." I gripped his shoulders, shifting my hips to meet his thrusts. He was hitting a place inside of me that felt amazing.

"Jane." He pushed back up on his hands, his thrusts growing more confident again. "Fuck, Doe, you feel amazing." His voice was guttural. "You're fucking heaven around my dick."

I pulsed around him and groaned.

His eyes flashed. "So tight and hot. I love your pussy."

My breath hitched as his words caused a ripple of hot pleasure.

Jamie's eyes widened a little and he bent over me, his lips whispering against mine as he grunted with each push into my body. "You like dirty talk, my sweet Jane?"

I think I might.

"You know what I like?" he growled, flexing his hips faster, deeper. "I like that I'm the only one who's been inside your beautiful body. And I'm the only man you'll ever feel inside you for the rest of your life."

"Yes!" I gasped, my orgasm hovering on the horizon. "Jamie!"

"You gotta come, baby." His thumb pressed down on my clit. "You're squeezing my dick so good, I'm gonna blow. I need you to come."

He circled my clit as he slammed into me and the tension shattered.

The sensation of coming while he was inside me was so different to anything we'd done before. I pulsed and throbbed around his hardness, milking him. It felt so good, it already wasn't enough. I wanted more. God, it felt *amazing*.

Jamie clearly thought so too as he suddenly froze above me and then called out my name in a hoarse shout. His hips juddered hard against mine.

Jamie collapsed, our panting chests crashing together, as he continued to pulse inside me. He weighed heavily on me and I let out a breathless gasp. "Jamie."

He mumbled something and then pushed off, sliding out of me with a slight burn. He landed on his back but grabbed my hand to pull me over him. My head rested on his damp chest as his fingers played in my hair and his other hand cupped my breast. His thumb stroked my nipple as we laid there trying to catch our breaths. I could hear both our hearts pounding.

"Fuck," Jamie muttered. "I need to deal with the condom, but I don't want to move."

I chuckled lazily. "Don't move. I don't want you to move."

He took a breath. "Are you okay?"

Lifting my head, I grinned at him. "Do I not seem okay?"

Jamie searched my face and relaxed at what he found there. "You surprise me all the time."

"In what way?"

He squeezed my breast and I gasped as I felt renewed heat flush between my legs. "You like it when I talk to you."

I blushed.

His voice was thick. "Sweet, shy little Jane likes it when I hold her down, likes it when I talk dirty ... What else will you like?"

Getting turned on all over again, I shifted over him, my lips hovering above his. "I'm willing to try anything with you."

His grip on me tightened. "Anything?"

"As long as it's you."

"Fuck, I'm getting hard again." He pushed up, kissing me.

When we finally came up for air, he brushed his thumb over my lips, eyes holding mine. "Let's get cleaned up."

Thankfully, we were still alone in the house. Holding Jamie's hand, I followed him into the bathroom and watched as he took care of the condom. My attention got him hot.

He ignored his hard-on as he placed me on the edge of the bathtub and pushed open my legs. He lowered before me with a washcloth and I saw why. There was a little smear of blood on the inside of my thighs.

"Does it make me a sick bastard that this turns me on?"

"What?"

"Knowing no one else will ever get this from you. I'll always be your first. It's caveman bullshit, right?" He grinned, that wicked smile of his causing a flutter of butterflies in my belly. "Guys aren't supposed to say that shit anymore."

"If it's how you feel," I said, cupping his face in my hands, "it's how you feel."

"How do you feel about it?"

I considered this, loving that he'd asked. That he cared. I thought about how I liked him being in control. His physical strength over me invoked some kind of cavewoman bullshit in me too. I chuckled at the thought.

He smiled at the sound. "What?"

"I'm independent because I've had to be," I told him, serious. "I like making my own decisions."

Jamie frowned. "Okay?"

"Now that I have you, you will factor in my life decisions ... but they will be *my* decisions."

He nodded.

"However ..." I bent my head toward him, my lips brushing his. "I don't mind handing the reins over to you in the bedroom. If you like it. I mean ... I think I might really like that."

His breathing deepened. "We'll try. If you like it, great. If you don't, it won't matter to me. I'll give you anything you need, Jane." He coasted his hands up my thighs. "Doe, I ..."

"What?" I curled my hands in his hair, playing with it.

Jamie surprised me by pressing his forehead between my breasts, his breath hot on my skin.

"Jamie?"

His arms bound tight around and worry filled me.

"Jamie?"

He exhaled and then finally lifted his head. The fierceness of his expression made my breath catch. "I've never loved anyone like this. It feels too much."

My heart leapt in my chest. "I feel it too."

It was scary. Terrifying, even. Yet it was the most exhilarating ride of my life.

"Don't break my heart," he growled, his fingers digging

into my skin. "Don't break my fucking heart. You break my heart ... and ... fuck, I'm afraid what I'll become without you. Fuck, I shouldn't say that." He tried to pull away. "I'm sorry, that's too much pressure—"

"No." My eyes widened as I cut him off. Jamie was concerned *I'd* break *his* heart? "I feel the same way. Don't break my heart, and I won't break yours." I nodded, pulling him back to me. "Promise?"

"I promise." He kissed me hard. So hard it almost hurt. "I want you again."

"Okay."

"No, we can't." Jamie shook his head. "You'll be sore, swollen."

I pulsed between my legs. "I need you. I want you."

His nostrils flared. I found the words Jamie couldn't resist. Hauling me into his arms, he carried me back to his bed. His hands circled my wrists, holding me down, and I flushed with renewed desire. "And you'll always have me," he promised.

CHAPTER EIGHT

JANE
Eighteen years old

ART WAS SUBJECTIVE.

Everyone knew that.

However, if you wanted to make a living as an artist, you had to appeal to a great number of people. If you didn't, it didn't make you any less of an artist. It just made you a less commercially successful one.

Every art major at Pomona wanted to be successful in their art. I believed that. No matter if it was digital art, photography, fine art, sculpture, graphic design, or performance. We wanted to shine.

Already, only a few months into my first semester as a freshman at Pomona College, I was discovering new skills and ways of expressing myself that I never thought I'd enjoy. As yet, however, nothing quite eclipsed my love of fine art. Though my small class seemed to think life drawing was basic, I loved it.

As a small group, however, it was too easy to become distracted when you could overhear the professor talking to your neighbor about their work.

Cassie Newman had the easel next to mine.

I glanced from my work to hers.

Our model was a dance student. Lola disrobed with no visible insecurities about her near nakedness and positioned herself like a ballet dancer in repose. Although she wore a nude leotard, she might as well have been naked for all it didn't disguise.

Her hair was pulled up in a tight bun, her head bent forward as if she was looking at her foot. One leg and foot straight, the other knee bent, her foot *en pointe*.

Her hands sat on her slender hips, and she wore a thoughtful expression.

Neither Cassie nor I had created a mirror image of the dancer on the paper.

We'd interpreted what we saw in different ways.

My brush strokes were loose, creating movement, as if the young women were about to lift off the page into dance—movement that was incongruous to her expression. As though she felt trapped by the rigidity of tradition and wanted to let loose. I chose soft grays, peaches, and pale pinks with some harder grays. I'd imagined a mirror and barre behind her, and her reflection portrayed her back arched dramatically, arms flourishing, the leg that was bent pushing out, foot straight in the style of a contemporary dancer, not a ballerina.

Cassie's brushstrokes were even less defined than mine. Much less. Her painting was abstract—that was her style. I knew this wasn't what bothered Professor Pullman.

"I just ..." He tilted his head to the side and sighed. "I question your color choice. The reason behind it."

It was dark, gothic even, heavy and foreboding.

I liked it.

It had *mood*.

It was clear our professor did not agree.

Cassie scowled at her work, refusing to look at Professor Pullman. To be fair, he questioned her choices all the time. While he was encouraging to students who didn't share his particular style, Cassie was a different story. He didn't seem to appreciate her "darkness."

He didn't have to. He just needed to support her and guide her. Right?

I tried not to sigh heavily as he suggested she start over.

"Why?"

"Because I don't believe this." He tapped her paper. "I can't see your point of view on the paper. I can't understand it. And you can't explain it to me."

I stopped what I was doing, not wanting to look but finding it hard not to. Everyone else listened in too.

Cassie glowered. "Fine. You know what I see? I see years of goddamn ballet lessons I hated, years of instruction, and years of being told I couldn't goddamn eat what I wanted to eat. That's what I goddamn see."

I grimaced.

Wow. We had different memories of ballet, huh? I wondered if that's how I'd felt about ballet. I had tits and an ass, which seemed like it might have become a problem for me at some point.

"There's no need to curse." Professor Pullman sniffed in pompous outrage. "Continue, then."

I tried to hide my scowl and probably failed.

What was his problem with Cassie?

"Time's up!" He raised his voice and stepped toward the model. "Thank you, Lola."

She grabbed her robe, pulled it on, flashed him a quick smile, and disappeared into the supply closet to get changed.

Our classmates moved their easels to the back of the

room. I followed Cassie, who had a slouch to her shoulders I didn't like. I hovered as a few people said goodbye to me and walked out. Lola left with the professor and that left only me, Cassie, and a guy called Devin we were both friendly with. Devin was in the far corner taking his sweet time leaving the classroom.

I wanted to get home and couldn't wait around much longer to say what I wanted to say.

Screw it. I stepped up next to Cassie, who was staring forlornly at her painting.

She jerked her head around, blinking in surprise. "I didn't know you were still here."

I placed my hand on her shoulder and her brow puckered. "I love your painting."

She bit her lip. "You're just saying that."

"I'm not." I sighed. "He shouldn't give you such a hard time. As an artist, he should know that art is subjective. Just because he's doesn't get it doesn't mean there isn't a place for it."

Cassie shrugged. "I'm supposed to paint what I feel when I see something. That's what I'm doing. I see Lola and I hear Madame Renee berating me for putting on a pound. I remember my mother snatching a candy bar out of my hand and stuffing a carrot in its place. I see swollen and wounded feet, my toenails pushing painfully into my skin, forced by the pressure of being *en pointe*." She flicked me a sour look. "I danced for ten years, and I was good at it. But I hated every minute. Misery. Never feeling good enough. Always hungry. You have to love ballet to want to go through that. For me it was restraining, and I was dying to break free. Which I did. And it was an angry, resentful, huge, explosive argument between me and my mom. We've never been the same since. That's what I feel when I look at Lola. That's what's on the paper."

"Then you're doing what Professor Pullman asked. That's all anyone can do. He needs to back off."

"You're right."

I tensed at the sound of the professor's voice.

Cassie's eyes widened.

Wincing, I hesitantly turned to look at him.

Professor Pullman stood behind us and wore an unreadable expression. "As much as I don't appreciate the discussion behind my back," he said, raising one eyebrow at me, "your friend is right, Cassandra." He sighed. "I ... I misinterpreted your choices." He gestured to the painting. "Jane is right. As an artist, I should know better. I'm sorry if I've been hard on you. I just ... I wanted to make sure you were truly painting from your gut and not some leftover teenage emo ... whatever."

"Uh ... thanks. I think." Cassie grimaced.

"Jane, Devin, do you mind giving us a minute?" he asked.

I'd totally forgotten Devin was in the room. I shot Cassie a look, and she gave me a reassuring smirk. Gathering my stuff, I gave the professor a tight, embarrassed smile and hurried out of the room after Devin.

As soon as we were in the hall, Devin waited for me to catch up.

I'd spoken to Devin Albright our first week in art history. He'd asked to borrow a pen, and we'd shared some get-to-know-you stuff while we waited for class to start. Tall, lanky, and cute in that guy-in-an-indie-rock-band sort of way, Devin's passion was in digital media.

"You okay?" he asked.

"I'm fine. A little embarrassed for getting caught talking shit about my professor." I chuckled. "But I'm okay."

I couldn't wait to tell Jamie.

He'd laugh his ass off.

Devin smiled down at me from his great height. The guy

had to be at least six four. "It was kind what you did. Talking to Cassie. Sticking up for her. No one else seemed to give a shit that he's been on her for weeks, and she looked seconds from bursting into tears."

"Well, at least he apologized."

"Yeah, because of you and what you said. I still think he's a dick."

I shrugged. "I think he's just a tough critic. A dick wouldn't admit he was wrong."

"Do you always see the best in people?"

Had Devin been around me enough to surmise that? I shot him a look.

He laughed. "I notice you, Jane. You're sweet to everyone. And someone ... someone who looks like you doesn't need to be nice to anyone."

Irritated, I huffed, "That's a little cynical and shallow, isn't it?"

It bothered me that people automatically assumed something about a person based on their looks. Cassie didn't even want to be friends with me at first because she assumed I was one of those "gorgeous cheerleader types" she had nothing in common with. I gave her another shot, despite her judginess. We lived in a shallow world, and it affected us whether we wanted it to. Even Skye had once asked me to audition for *The Sorcerer*, and God knows I'd shown no talent for acting, so that offer was based on how good her agent thought I might look on camera, and nothing else.

I should cut Devin a break.

"I didn't mean it like that." He ran a hand through his dark hair and drew to a stop.

I hesitated but halted with him as he struggled with his words.

My heart beat a little fast, my suspicion growing.

Devin nervously licked his lips. "So, okay, I'm just going to say it, so I stop messing it up. Jane, will ... would you go on a date with me?"

I felt my cheeks grow hot. "I have a boyfriend, Devin," I reminded him. "You know that."

He nodded, his neck turning red. "I just ... I just thought ... I didn't know if you were serious, and we have a lot in common ..."

Did we?

I wracked my brain trying to think over the conversations we'd had. Devin and I spoke to each other in class. We'd eaten together at lunch with a few of our other classmates, including Cassie, but I couldn't remember us having any deep, meaningful conversations. "Well, I appreciate it, but I love my boyfriend. I'm sorry."

Devin flushed hard, rubbing his neck. "Right. Sure. Okay. Bye." He strode off, leaving me in the wake of the awful awkwardness.

Crap.

I hoped things wouldn't be too weird between us.

I talked about Jamie all the time. He'd even had lunch with me at school on a number of occasions. My friends all knew I had a boyfriend; so did some of my other classmates. I didn't expect to be asked out by someone who knew about Jamie.

Did that mean girls were still asking Jamie out at USC?

Of course, it did.

Classes were way bigger at USC. They wouldn't know he had a girlfriend.

Possessiveness bothered me as I walked out of school toward the bus stop.

I trusted Jamie.

It didn't mean I liked the idea of girls hovering around him. And they must. He was protective, sexy, witty, talented, brooding, and a track star.

But he's also all mine, I reminded myself with utmost certainty.

I smiled as I put in my earbuds and flicked through Spotify to my latest playlist. *Seven Nation Army* by the White Stripes thundered in my ears as I strolled to the bus stop. Pomona College was only a forty-minute bus ride from the house I now lived in with the McKennas.

Despite my distant but polite relationship with Willa and Nick, they'd offered to let me stay at their apartment while I was in college. They weren't legally obligated to as I was an adult, so it was kind of them to offer. However, Jamie had spoken to Skye, and Skye had offered me Lorna's room now that she was pre-law at Columbia in New York.

I'd jumped at the chance.

If Jamie was cool with me living with them, then I was all for it.

Skye had insisted I have my own room to create "boundaries," but I spent every night in Jamie's bed. Lorna's room became my art studio. There was a moment where I worried I was intruding too much in Jamie's space and suggested I sleep in my room instead. He got pissed and did what he always did to stop me discussing anything that annoyed him.

He kissed me and then screwed my insecurities right out of me.

I didn't mind his methods at all. They'd only become a problem if he avoided talking about something I really, *really* wanted to discuss.

As I found a seat on the bus, I bit my lip, staring out the window, feeling the ghost of Jamie's hands and mouth on me. The last eight months had been intoxicating. I couldn't think of a better word.

Our appetite for one another was insatiable.

Sex had only drawn us more tightly into our little bubble of two.

Yeah, we hung out with friends, mostly his track team-mates from USC (even Wex, who got over his crush on me pretty fast), but if we were together, we were rarely not touching. I knew his friends gave him shit about it, but Jamie didn't care.

I was his entire world.

And he was mine.

The bus let me off a block from the house, the October sun beating hard on my back as I sauntered happily home.

It was the first home I'd truly had since I was seven years old.

With Lorna gone, the horrible atmosphere she created whenever she was around went with her. My relief to have her on the other side of the country made me feel like a traitor, but I couldn't deny Jamie and I were more relaxed without her around.

I knew Skye missed her, and I'd feel bad about it if I thought Jamie and I had chased Lorna away. But Columbia had been Lorna's dream school since she was fourteen. Her not staying in close contact with her big sister was not anyone's fault but Lorna's.

She pushed everyone away.

I missed my best friend.

Not who she was now. But the little kid who enveloped me in her love without hesitation and offered me a home.

I missed that Lorna.

It was the only thing in my life now that was tainted by sadness. Still, it couldn't touch my overall satisfaction. I'd gotten into my college of choice, I was living with people I loved, and I was the kind of "in love" that other people only read about or saw in movies.

It seemed that Fate was trying to make up for our hard start in life when She gave me and Jamie to one another.

As for Skye, she had won a role on a popular TV hospital

drama. Approval ratings for her character were high, and she'd already signed a contract for the next season. This meant she'd insisted that Jamie lease a car. *He'd* insisted on nothing fancy and was driving a practical hybrid. Skye was driving around in a shiny white Mercedes convertible.

Two weeks ago, a woman turned up at the house asking for Skye's autograph. How she found Skye's address, we didn't know, but it freaked Jamie out. He wanted us to move. Skye was calm about it all. Her social media followers had increased exponentially since joining the show, and she'd appeared in the gossip rags again, snapped out and around Hollywood with her friends. Skye took it in stride. It pissed her off when they'd posted a photo of her and Jamie, insinuating she had a boy toy, but that was the only time I'd seen her harassed by her increasing fame.

At the sight of Jamie's and Skye's cars parked outside the house, I smiled. They were my family now, and I appreciated returning to a house where my family was waiting. I really hoped I never lost that appreciation. I had a feeling that kind of gratitude was the key to happiness.

They weren't inside the air-conditioned house, but I could hear raised voices coming from out back. The weather was especially hot this fall, and we were enjoying a rare break from the Santa Ana winds, so it didn't surprise me they were probably enjoying the pool. The kitchen window was open as I passed, their conversation halting me on my progress to join them.

"You're getting defensive," Skye groaned.

I frowned, pausing.

"You just said you didn't want Jane living here."

My heart stopped. *What?*

"I did not," she hissed. "I said, I wanted the sleeping-in-the-same-room thing to stop."

"Why? We're both adults."

"No, Jamie. You're twenty and she's eighteen. I said yes to Jane living here because I love her, and I want her to be somewhere she feels wanted. But Jane is also your girlfriend, and I'm slightly concerned about my little brother living with his girlfriend at such a young age. However, to assuage my fears, you said that Jane would stay in Lorna's room, and she hasn't been staying in Lorna's room. I'm not an idiot. I know she sleeps in your room. *Every* night."

Oh, God ... were we ... loud?

"What is the damn problem?"

I knew that tone—Jamie was about to explode.

I wondered if I should go out there, but I was too hurt to move.

All this time, I'd thought Skye was more than happy with our arrangement, and I'd been blissfully ignorant.

"Jamie, I'm not trying to upset you. I love you both and I just ... I'm concerned that you're too young to be this deep into it with each other. I was happy for you both when you first started dating, but I've never seen anything like you two. I mean ... you are consumed by one another. As a recovering addict, believe me when I say that you need other interests outside of Jane."

There was silence.

Was Skye suggesting that our relationship was as unhealthy as an addiction?

"She's not my fucking drug. I'm not hers. This isn't some destructive addiction—"

"Jamie, please don't curse at me."

"You just insinuated that I'm in a bad relationship. You compared us to your addiction." His tone reflected my hurt.

"God, that's not—"

"Just because you've never loved someone like I love Jane doesn't mean it's unhealthy. You just don't understand."

I flinched, feeling terrible for Skye. Sometimes Jamie could cut a person to the quick when he was angry.

"You're right." She sounded sad. "A guy has never loved me like that, or vice versa. I'm sorry. I didn't ... I *shouldn't* have compared your relationship to my addiction. I just ... I wish that you two had other interests."

"We have other interests," Jamie argued as I muttered the same under my breath.

My hands were covered in paint from my other interest.

Art and Jamie and books. Those were interests. What was so wrong about that?

"You know what I mean. I think Jane should sleep in Lorna's bed from now on and that you two should practice a little distance. I don't want you to lose yourself inside one another. It scares me."

Jamie's tone softened. "What scares you about it?"

"Love is one thing. We all need it. But ... we have to stand on our own. To survive on our own. Jamie, God forbid something happened to either of you ... I see how you are with one another, and I'm so worried about what will become of you if something happened to Jane. Or to Jane if something happened to you."

To my surprise, Jamie chuckled. "Skye, the actress in you is being melodramatic."

"Don't be condescending."

He laughed. "Sorry. I don't mean to be."

"I know you think I'm worrying about nothing, but I saw you today with that girl, and I thought ... maybe you and Jane shouldn't shut down all your options. Isn't there a part of you that went to USC to stay close to her? And I know she chose Pomona to stay close to you. But what if Jane hadn't done that? What if she'd followed Lorna to New York? Maybe you would have met someone else. Someone you're not so wrapped up in. Someone easier ... It's not like you don't notice other girls. Like the girl today, for instance."

What girl? I frowned.

"One, Lacey is my project partner. Nothing more—"

"It didn't seem that way for her."

What? I knew Lacey Gibbins was working with Jamie on a presentation for children's literature.

"Well, it's that way for me."

"I'm just saying, you two seemed to get along great. And what about Jane? She's only eighteen, Jamie. And she's not just a typical teen girl. She hasn't had a lot of love in her life, and maybe that's why she clings to her relationship with you so much. It might be healthier for her to be out there, having fun."

"Having fun?" His tone was back to biting. "You mean, screwing other guys."

"Don't be crass. I meant dating."

"She doesn't want to. She wants me. And I want her. End of story. Jesus Christ, Skye, she makes me happier than I've ever been. Why the hell would I give that up? Why would you want me to?"

My cheeks flushed hot at his words, my heart aching in recognition of everything he was feeling because I felt it too.

Water splashed, and his voice drew a little closer to the house as he said, "Jane looks up to you. She listens to you. You say any of this ridiculous shit to her and mess with her head ... I swear, Skye, I won't forgive you."

"Jamie, I'm sorry, I won't. This is ... I'm putting my crap on you, okay. I love you. I want you to be happy. I want Jane to be happy." Her voice broke. "I just worry about you. Please don't be mad at me."

At his silence, I glanced out the window and saw the siblings were hugging.

I took that moment to disappear upstairs and dump my bag.

Sitting on the bed in Lorna's room, I stared a little unseeing at the artwork that cluttered the room. I wondered if Skye was right. Were Jamie and I setting ourselves up for heartbreak?

So lost in my thoughts, it took Jamie sitting down beside me on the bed for me to notice his presence. I drew in a breath, startled.

Our eyes locked. His narrowed. "You heard, didn't you?"

I nodded.

Frustration tightened his features, but I knew it wasn't directed at me.

"I'm making things weird for you two."

"No." He kissed me. Hard, deep, trying to pull me under his spell so I'd forget about their argument.

"Jamie," I pulled away. "Are you and Skye okay?"

"We're fine," he assured me, tucking my hair behind my ear. "And you're not sleeping in here so don't get any ideas." His lips brushed over mine as he curled his hand gently around my neck. It was claiming, dominant, and it made me shiver. "You know you need me at night," he teased. "I need to be readily available to you."

I rolled my eyes. Smug bastard. Often, I woke in the middle of the night, wanting him. It was me who kissed him awake. It was me who straddled him in the dark of the night, desperate to have him.

"Fuck, you excite me," he whispered harshly, gripping my hips as I slid up and down on him.

I frowned, pushing out the memories before they distracted me. "We do have a lot of sex. Is that normal?"

Jamie burst out laughing, pulling me into his body, his laughter fluttering against my neck as he buried his head there.

"Jamie."

My annoyed tone only made him laugh harder. Finally, he lifted his head, but only to kiss my pinched lips open. "You're sleeping in my bed, and you'll reach for me anytime you want. Discussion over." He moved to stand, hand in mine, attempting to pull me up. I tugged on it, refusing to budge. "What?"

"What did Skye mean about Lacey?"

Jamie sighed and let go of me to run a hand through his hair. "Jane—"

"Well?"

He crossed his arms over his chest and shrugged. "She was here this afternoon. We were going over our presentation for tomorrow."

"She likes you?"

"She kissed me."

My heart lurched.

"Something I would have told you without Skye's help." Seeing my dubious expression, his brow puckered. "Jesus, Jane, you don't think I actually wanted her to kiss me."

I shook my head.

Still, I hated the idea of her lips anywhere near his.

His lips were mine.

My hands clenched into fists in my lap, and Jamie's gaze dropped to them. "Jane, I pushed her off. I told her it wasn't happening, and it would never happen. Skye walked in on the whole thing. Mortifying for Lacey. I felt bad for her."

I narrowed my eyes. "She knows you have a girlfriend." It wasn't a question. "*I* don't feel bad for her. She wasn't thinking of *my* feelings when she kissed you." I stood and threw him a displeased glare. "I'm hungry."

I heard his heavy sigh as he followed at my back. "Doe, girls will come onto me. Ask me out. Guys will do the same to you. Doesn't mean anything. Other than that, we're both extremely irresistible."

My lips twitched at his teasing as I thundered down the stairs. Skye was nowhere in sight. Feeling Jamie at my back as I opened the refrigerator, I said, "Well, since you were open with me, I should tell you I got asked out today." I grabbed some carrots and hummus and shut the door, turning to Jamie, struggling to hide my smile.

His face had darkened. "Who?"

I tried not to laugh at his changed tone. "What happened to 'it doesn't mean anything'?"

"Are you messing with me or did someone ask you out?"

"Devin." I shrugged. "He hoped you and I weren't serious. I put him straight." I dipped a carrot into the hummus and took a loud, noisy bite, relishing Jamie's obvious annoyance. It made me feel better about mine.

"The tall, gangly moron?"

"He's not a moron." I offered him a carrot. "I felt bad for him."

Jamie impatiently waved off the proffered carrot. "I don't feel bad for him. He knows you have a boyfriend." He echoed my words. Then Jamie's expression turned suspicious. "Are you telling the truth?"

"Yes," I promised. "He asked me out. I told him I was in love with my boyfriend. Note, however, that he didn't kiss me. *My* lips don't have someone else's lip print on them."

Suddenly, Jamie sprung at me, bending into my belly before he threw me over his shoulder. I squealed, dropping my carrot. "Jamie!" The world rushed by upside down as he took the stairs two at a time. My excited laughter filled the halls as he rushed toward his bedroom.

I was promptly thrown onto the queen-sized bed, my giggles swallowed in Jamie's hungry kisses until they turned to moans. Just like that, our world condensed to just the two of us.

There was a small part of me that heard Skye's voice in my

head as Jamie moved inside me. Perhaps our love *was* all-consuming. Perhaps it *would* devour us.

But as Jamie held my gaze in his and murmured how much he loved me over and over, her voice disappeared, along with my worries.

Who cared if it devoured us?

At least we'd die happy.

CHAPTER NINE

JAMIE
Twenty years old

AROUND 6.00 A.M. I awoke from a dream I couldn't shake. It had been like a movie in my head. I was stuck in this apocalyptic world where Jane was missing. I'd been trying to find her and instead kept getting caught up with these strange individuals who had their own problems.

I was spooning Jane, my face buried in her hair as she slept beside me, not making a sound. The only reason I knew she was alive was because of the gentle rise of her body as she breathed. Not wanting to wake her, I eased out of bed and crossed the room to my desk. I wrote on my laptop, pouring the images that had been in my head into what would become a short story. It might work for my sophomore fiction project.

As always when I wrote, time passed without my awareness of it.

Fingers aching a little, I stretched, cracking my upper back.

Glancing over my shoulder, I saw my bed was empty.

A little smile prodded my mouth.

Jane never disturbed me when I was writing. She treated those times like they were sacred, making me, and what I loved to do, feel more important than anyone had ever made me feel.

Still, I wished she'd stuck around. I would have been happy diving back into bed and fooling around. Not that I was sure she'd be up for that. Her room, which reverted to Lorna's room during the holidays, was right across the hall from mine, and Jane hadn't wanted to have sex since Lorna's arrival from the East Coast a few days ago.

Just in case Lor overheard or some shit.

I tried to convince Jane we could be quiet.

Or at least *I* could be quiet. I grinned to myself. For someone who was the quietest person I'd ever met, Jane wasn't very good at keeping her voice down when we made love. Chuckling to myself, I crossed the hall and got in the shower. She had no idea what that did to my ego.

Afterward, I made my way downstairs. The place was empty.

It wasn't until I switched on the coffee maker that I saw Jane and Lorna out by the pool. I walked over to the sliding glass door, which was already partially open. The murmur of their conversation met my ears as I leaned against the counter to chug back some caffeine. I couldn't really make out what they were saying, and I didn't want to.

It was just nice to see them talking.

While Lorna had been surprisingly nice to me since she got back from school, she'd been giving Skye and Jane the cold shoulder. Skye, I didn't get. And her attitude was driving my big sister into herself.

They'd given her character in the hospital TV show a huge storyline. Since it was about her character being raped by a colleague, a long, drawn-out, months-long storyline, Skye was emotionally drained. I worried about her. Yeah, I was proud of her because I'd caught some clips of the show and she was awesome in it, but the pressure she was under was unreal. I only watched clips, though. No way in hell could I watch my big sister in a simulated rape scene.

Fuck no.

Jane and I barely saw Skye these days, and when we did, she was completely withdrawn. I was concerned about her relapsing, but there wasn't a lot I could do when Skye kept telling me she was fine and there was no evidence of drug or alcohol abuse in the house.

Still, I didn't need Lorna giving Skye crap for apparently no reason.

Yet I didn't want to start anything with my little sis since she and I were in a good place.

I was sitting at the counter eating a bowl of cereal when my girl and Lorna strolled back into the house. Lorna smiled brightly when she saw me.

"Jane says you've been writing this morning."

My eyes flicked to Jane, who wore a pensive expression. "That I have."

"Well, fingers crossed it's a huge best seller so I don't end up looking after you in your old age," Lorna teased and pressed a quick kiss to my temple before she breezed past. "I'm heading out. I promised my old track mates I'd meet them for lunch on Rodeo Drive. I'll be back tonight in time for Santa!"

The door slammed shut behind her, and I raised an eyebrow at Jane. "Is it just me or does she seem in a good mood?"

Jane shrugged, grabbed a spoon out of the drawer, and leaned over the counter to spoon a bunch of Cheerios from the mountain I was depleting. She chewed, pretty eyes on me, crunching the Cheerios loudly.

I grinned at her.

She swallowed. "What?"

"You're cute."

She wrinkled her nose, but the dimple in her left cheek creased. I wanted to kiss it. I had the urge to kiss it every time she smiled. "Where's Skye?"

"I don't know." I jerked my chin to the patio door. "What were you and Lor talking about?"

Jane leaned her chin in her palm, knocking my spoon out of the way with hers as she reached for more cereal.

"You could get your own," I teased.

"Why?" She grinned and took another bite. Her words were muffled as she ate, but I think she said, "Yours are delicious."

"Are you avoiding my question?"

"No. You keep distracting me from the question." She rounded the counter and hopped onto the stool next to mine.

Reaching for her, I ate with one hand while I rested my other hand on her leg, my fingers caressing the silky skin of her inner thigh. "What's going on?"

"Nothing. It was ... it was awkward and weird." Melancholy darkened her face. I didn't like it. "For years, Lorna was my best friend, my confidante ... and now it's almost like those years didn't happen. Or they were part of some other life."

I pushed away the bowl and grabbed her by the back of the knees until she was up and on my lap. She gave a bark of laughter and took hold of my shoulders before shimmying comfortably into place. Her legs dangled over the side of the stool as she ran her fingers through my hair.

Unable to help myself, I kissed her. Soft, sweet, not trying to take it anywhere. Just a comforting kiss. I stared into her eyes when I pulled back. "She's talking to you, though. Isn't that a step forward?"

"I guess." Jane's brow furrowed. "And she told me she wants to be friends again, that time away has given her perspective, and she can see how close you and I are. She can see that you love me, and she's over it." She smiled and I couldn't help but kiss her again.

"I sense a *but*," I murmured against her lips.

"Well, don't you think it's odd how mad she is at Skye? I asked her about it, and she said she didn't really want to talk about it, only that it hurt her that Skye took our side in the whole thing."

"Fuck," I muttered. That didn't sound like someone who was "over it." "Skye didn't take sides. And she doesn't need that shit right now. I'll talk to Lorna."

"I can see that idea brings you much joy."

"I was kind of enjoying her being nice to me, but I'll sacrifice it if I have to."

"You're such a good brother." Jane kissed me. "And such a good boyfriend." Her voice was huskier, her kiss deeper.

I groaned, nipping at her mouth. "If I'm such a good boyfriend, don't I deserve an early Christmas present?"

"Didn't I give that to you four days ago?"

I laughed at the way she quirked her eyebrow. Four days ago, I'd taken her to the ballet again as *her* Christmas present. *The Nutcracker*. Turned out, I wasn't a fan. Bored, I'd nodded off. Next thing I knew, Jane was waking me and telling me to follow her out of the theater, but to wait two minutes before I did.

"I'll be in the ladies' restroom on this level."

Instead of sitting through the rest of *The Nutcracker*, I'd fucked my girlfriend in the empty restroom. I'd bent her over the sink, while she'd held my gaze in the mirror above it, and I'd thrust in and out of her, mindless with want. Jane was so into it, she came harder than I'd ever felt her come. I had to cover her mouth so no one would hear us.

I felt myself getting hard just remembering it.

"That was my Christmas present to you."

She guffawed. "Oh, baby." She shook her head, pouting

condescendingly. "When a guy's girlfriend gives it to him in a public place, it's *always* her gift to him. In fact, let's broaden that. When a guy's girlfriend lets him do anything sexual to her, it's *always* her gift to him."

Shaking with laughter at the cocky little brat, I squeezed her hips and ground her over my throbbing dick, loving the little hitch in her breathing. "Yeah? So, all those times I've made you come so hard you lose your mind, they weren't gifts from me to you?"

"Well …" She considered this as she undulated in my lap. My grip on her tightened and I hissed through my teeth as my pleasure sharpened. "I think maybe I need you to do it again, so I can decide."

I jumped off the stool, and she wrapped her legs around my waist, biting her lip between her teeth. When I didn't start walking her upstairs, I saw her eyebrows furrow with confusion. I rested her on the edge of the dining table and pulled savagely at her pajama shorts.

My jeans and boxers were around my ankles by the time she gasped, "Jamie, here?"

Her shock was edged with excitement. I crushed my mouth down over hers and thrust into her tight, sleek, warm heat. Our lips parted as we groaned together.

"Anyone could walk in," I grunted, fucking into her and feeling her pussy ripple around me at the words.

Her fingers bit into my waist as she tried to lift her hips off the table to meet mine, but I gripped them, holding her still so I could slam into her at the angle I knew would blow her mind.

"Anyone passes on the street and looks in, they'll see me fucking you, baby," I panted. "They'll see how much you love taking my dick."

Just with those words, she shuddered against me as she climaxed.

It only took a couple more drives inside her and I followed her into heaven.

Grabbing her by the nape, I kissed her deep and wet, already needing her again. Gathering her in my arms, I carried her upstairs to my room and laid her down on our bed. As we kissed and petted and caressed, I felt her wet on my fingers and lost myself in her all over again.

I made love to her, our eyes locked, gliding gently in and out of her beautiful body, lost in our private world. "Jane, I'm coming, baby," I huffed against her lips, and slipped my hand between us to help her reach climax before me.

Not too much later, she came, gasping my name against my mouth. I kissed her deep and hungry as I throbbed inside her.

"Jesus Christ!" Someone hammered against my bedroom door seconds after I melted into Jane. "Is that all you two ever do?"

My girl tensed at Skye's interruption. Maybe because of the irritation in my big sister's tone, or the humiliation of her overhearing us, or the fact that my sister sounded like she was slurring.

"Fuck."

We heard something fall in the hall seconds before Skye's bedroom door slammed. Jane stared at me wide-eyed.

"You okay?" Anger coursed through me.

"Jamie ... was she ... did she sound ..."

"Drunk?" I gently eased out of Jane and launched off the bed. "Yeah, she did. Wait here."

"Maybe you should give her some time." Jane sat up as I pulled on my underwear and jeans.

"Time?" I cut my girlfriend an incredulous look. "It's Christmas Eve. Lorna's home. And Skye decides now is the time to fall off the wagon?"

"Jamie—"

"No, if she's drunk, I'm driving her straight to rehab. Wait here."

I shook with adrenaline as I marched out of my room. One second, everything in my world was good. School was great, Lorna and I were cool, and while I'd been a little worried about Skye, it wasn't to the point it could eclipse the bliss of making love to my girl after several days of going without.

Until now.

"Fuck my life," I muttered.

I knocked on Skye's bedroom door. Getting no response, I charged right in.

Shit, her room was a mess. Her clothes were strewn everywhere and there was a musty smell as though she hadn't aired it out in days. Hearing a noise from the bathroom, I rounded the bed and came to an abrupt halt at the open bathroom door.

Skye was bent over the sink, snorting white powder.

She blinked rapidly as she stood up straight and leaned into the mirror to wipe that shit off her nostrils.

Fury and worry and despair held me in place.

What the hell could I do?

How was I going to keep her clean if she was determined not to be?

Don't give up. It's not time to give up.

She is not Mom.

Skye turned toward the door and stopped when she saw me.

Her eyes filled with tears. "I'm sorry."

Emotion choked me. "Skye ..." My voice was hoarse.

Moving toward me, she stumbled. Was she drunk too? Remembering the last time she'd had so much to drink and so much fucking coke she'd given herself a heart attack, I moved to steady her. I needed to stay calm. "Skye, how much have you had to drink?"

"I dunno." She shrugged, holding on to me as I led her to the bed. "A lot, maybe."

"And how much coke?"

She waved her finger at me. "I just got it. Treenie gave it to me before she dropped me off."

I didn't know who Treenie was, but it was the last time she was getting near my sister. "Okay, up, let's go."

"Where are we going? Are you mad?"

"I'm disappointed."

"Ugh, that's worse."

"Come on." I put my arm under her and helped her out of her room.

Jane was waiting in the hall, dressed, eyes round with worry. "What's going on?"

"Doe, run out to the car. You're going to drive."

I didn't need to say anything else. My girl knew where we were going.

Skye kept asking as we drove, but I distracted her. By the time I had her in the ER, it was too late for her to do anything about it.

Thankfully, nothing happened. The docs kept a watch on her overnight, while Jane, Lorna, and I spent Christmas at her bedside in the hospital.

When they discharged Skye the next day, I let her convince me she could get clean again on her own. That she didn't need rehab, she just needed to go back to her AA meetings and get back in touch with Sheridan.

Skye was so convincing. So contrite. So determined.

I gave in.

Not long later, I'd question that decision over and over again.

Chapter Ten

JANE
Eighteen years old

I COULDN'T STOP SHAKING.

It felt like my bones were rattling with the force of it.

Nausea covered my skin in a cold sweat, but I'd already thrown up the contents of my stomach as well as bile. There was nothing left to eject.

Staring at the phone in my hands, I wondered how I was supposed to do this.

It didn't feel real.

I'd felt anguish before.

I'd felt grief, way too young to know how to deal with it.

This was different.

This wasn't just my pain. It was ... his.

I couldn't breathe.

"Would you like us to make the call, Ms. Doe?"

Swiping at the tears that rolled in continuous tracks down my face was pointless. They kept coming; I kept brushing them away. The police officer who'd spoken was gazing down at me, his expression kind, capable.

Instead of his dark eyes, I saw Jamie's ocean ones.

Yesterday morning, I'd dropped him off at the university where he was meeting his teammates. They were heading to the airport together to catch their flight to San Francisco. Usually, I went to as many of Jamie's track meets as possible to support him, but I couldn't afford a flight to San Francisco. And I had a paper to finish for art history.

Jamie had kissed me goodbye and then before he'd gotten out of the car, he'd turned to me and said, "If you get Skye to talk to you, my love for you will turn to adoration."

"You already adore me," I replied.

"True." He grinned, but his smile fell quickly. "Just keep an eye out while I'm gone this weekend. She's so goddamn secretive lately."

"Jamie, she's been going to her meetings and talking with Sheridan every day."

"I know. I just ... my gut keeps telling me something isn't right."

Considering this, I nodded. "Always trust your gut. I'll keep an eye out."

He kissed me again, told me he loved me, and hopped out of his car.

Back at the house, I found Skye at the dining table, sipping coffee and reading a magazine. She wasn't home a lot lately, and free weekends for her were rare.

Sitting down beside her with my coffee, I stared at her magazine, trying to think of something to say. Jamie was right. Skye was secretive and distant. After the last trip to the ER, Lorna had taken off for school early. She said she had no patience for her sister's "bullshit weakness" and wouldn't be back until "it was over."

"And you said I'm the one who's like Mom," Lorna had said to Jamie.

I didn't need to ask what she'd meant. Jamie had told me a lot of stories about his mom over the past eighteen months we'd been dating. Among being mentally and emotionally manipulative with her kids, she'd also been an alcoholic.

Frankly, I was glad Lorna was gone. Skye didn't need her sister's toxic attitude. She needed understanding and support from the people who loved her.

Yet, I was afraid it was Lorna's rejection that was the root cause of Skye's current solemnity.

"Talk to me."

Skye glanced up from the magazine. She sighed and pushed the magazine toward me, flipping the pages. She'd left it open on a particular page.

One that featured an unflattering shot of Skye coming out of her AA meeting. The words "BACK IN REHAB ALREADY?" were printed across the top of the image.

I swallowed hard, hurting for her. "Skye, I'm sorry. Does your producer know?"

She gave a brittle nod. "I promised them I'm on top of it. I'm not fired."

"Good," I murmured. What was I supposed to say? "No one pays attention to this crap."

Her lips twitched, but the amusement didn't reach her eyes. "You don't. Many people do." Tears burned in her eyes. "I don't want Lorna's friends at school seeing it."

Ah.

I got up from my seat and rounded Skye, sliding my arms around her and resting my chin on the top of her head. She gripped tight to my arms. "Lorna loves you."

"Does she?" Skye whispered. "It doesn't feel like it. It feels like I lost her ... and I felt that way before Christmas."

"She's just finding her feet at Columbia and wrapped up

in her own little world right now." I came around to her side, lowering to my haunches to smile reassuringly up at her. "Lorna loves you best of all, Skye. She's just not very good at showing it sometimes."

Skye nodded, sniffling. "I just miss her. Sometimes I wonder if I miss her, or if I miss the kid she used to be. When we'd dance around the apartment and she'd look at me like I was Wonder Woman." She glanced away in apparent embarrassment. "Kids grow up, I guess. They start to see reality and it's a bitter disappointment, huh?"

"No, you know it's not like that with Lorna," I chided. "You are not a disappointment. Skye, you gave me a home. A family. You gave Lorna and Jamie the home they deserved and opportunities they never would've had without you. They know that. You are the best big sister anyone could ask for. And the best big sister I never even dreamed I'd one day have."

Her eyes widened with hope.

"You're just human. And we make mistakes. But no matter how many times you need it, I will be here to hold your hand. That's what you do for the people you love."

More tears slipped down Skye's cheeks as she reached out to clasp my face in her hands. "What did I ever do to deserve you, kid?"

"We deserve each other."

"Do you mean it? You'll be there, no matter what?"

"Absolutely." A thought occurred to me and I stood, crossing the room to my phone. "I think we need a little pick-me-up." I scrolled through Spotify and found the track I wanted.

"The Whole of the Moon" by the Waterboys played.

Skye gave me a sad smile but didn't get to her feet.

"Come on." I danced into the middle of the room. "It'll make you feel better!"

With a huff of laughter, Skye got to her feet. I grabbed her hand and forced her into a twirl. It took a verse and chorus, but soon we danced energetically around the room, shouting the lyrics at each other.

When the song ended, we collapsed on the couch laughing, and I felt some uneasiness shift off my chest. Rolling my head to the side, I smiled at Skye.

Her return smile was filled with love, but still a lot of melancholy.

"I think I'm going to see if I can get time off work," she said, her voice soft in the now-quiet room. "I need a real break. I've always wanted to go back to Monterey after we shot there during season four of *The Sorcerer*. Maybe I could rent a place for a few weeks. I was even"—she shot me an embarrassed grin —"thinking I could try screenwriting."

Excited that Skye was talking about things that would give her focus and direction, I nodded eagerly. "That sounds amazing."

"Yeah?"

"Of course. You can do anything you put your mind to."

She patted my knee. "Thanks, kid."

"What are your plans today?"

"You got time to grab some lunch?"

"Absolutely."

We spent the rest of the afternoon in town, eating out and window shopping. I texted Jamie that everything was good and wished him luck at his meet. I sent him a snap of me and Skye trying on ridiculous hats. He replied with three words: "I love you."

Skye saw and rolled her eyes. "Sometimes, I can't even believe Jamie is the same person when he's around you. You know," she said, sighing a little shakily, "I used to worry that you guys were a little too intense. But now I envy you." She squeezed my hand. "What you two have is miraculous. Never let go of it."

"I have no intention of letting go," I promised.

By the time we returned home, it was evening, and Skye looked exhausted. I knew she was having a harder time than she let on, so when she excused herself for an early night, I understood. I curled up on the sofa with my laptop and worked on my paper.

Sunlight bursting through the windows woke me the next morning. I realized I'd fallen asleep on the couch. After I showered, I decided to see if Skye was awake and whether she wanted breakfast. I wasn't the best cook, but I was getting better, and I wanted this weekend to be a good one for my pseudo-big sister.

I could bring her a little breakfast in bed if it would cheer her up.

There was no reply when I knocked on her door, so I pushed it open and called out her name.

Seeing her lying above the duvet in the dim light of the room, my pulse raced.

"Skye?"

No response.

"Skye." I was a little louder.

Not even a twitch.

I searched for the light switch and heard it click a millisecond before light flooded the room.

Skye was sprawled across the top of the bed, her arm dangling over the side.

There was something unnervingly still about her.

Fear climbed up my legs, making my knees shake. "Skye?"

Somehow, I forced myself to come unstuck from the door, and I almost stumbled into the bed as I neared it. My attention caught on the pill bottle by her bedside table before returning to her.

Her chest wasn't moving.

"Skye?" I grabbed her, the fear now terror as I felt how cold she was. How stiff. I sobbed. "Skye!" I cried, shaking her.

But she wouldn't wake up.

She wouldn't wake up!

"SKYE!"

"MS. DOE," the police officer's voice brought me back into the hospital corridor. "Would you like us to make the call for you?"

I shook my head. It hurt to move it. "No."

I fumbled with the phone in my hand and swiped the edge of the screen for my speed-dial numbers.

What did I tell him?

"I don't know what to tell him," I muttered under my breath.

It wasn't deliberate.

I knew that. I knew that, even though we wouldn't get the coroner's report for days.

She'd been making plans for her future. It wasn't deliberate.

Jamie picked up on the fourth ring. "Hey, Doe, I'm just about to race, can I call you back?"

"Jamie." His name came out on a sob.

He was silent a moment, then his voice was frantic as he asked me what was wrong.

"You need to come home," I cried. "Jamie, you need to come home."

"You're scaring the shit out of me. What's going on?"

I took in a shuddering breath that caused something to rattle audibly from inside me. "Skye ... I'm so sorry. Baby, Skye is gone. She ... she died, Jamie. She's dead."

CHAPTER ELEVEN

JANE
Eighteen years old

GAZING OUT THE WINDOW, I watched as Lorna hugged Jamie goodbye.

I'd stayed inside the house because my ex-best friend had made it clear my presence was not appreciated.

The last ten days had been a blur. I wish I could say that grief had numbed me to any other emotion, but I couldn't. Anger played center stage. Anger at Skye. At Lorna.

And mostly at myself.

I didn't want to be angry at Skye.

She hadn't meant to go away.

Waiting five days for the coroner's report was the most excruciating wait of our lives. Jamie was a mess. Despite the way he clung to me through the night, there was this mile-high wall around him I couldn't scale. I understood that no matter how we all might be in agony together, grieving was a solitary journey. No one else could do it for you. Though someone might mourn at your side, that didn't mean they were mourning the same way you were.

I knew Jamie.

I knew he was a writhing ball of devastation, loss, anger, and guilt. Moreover, for those five days, there was the terror. That maybe it hadn't been an accident. That someone we loved was in extreme pain, and we didn't look deep enough below the surface to clue in.

During those days, I clung to one of my last conversations with Skye, and Jamie made me repeat it word for word over and over again, finding solace in it. His sister had been making plans for the future, that much was certain.

It had been an accident.

Raiding her bathroom, we found pills that substantiated that belief.

And the coroner's report corroborated my gut feeling.

Skye had gotten her hands on a friend's prescription medication. We hadn't known it, but she was taking two different antianxiety meds. That day she'd not only taken those meds, she'd taken painkillers, and something to help her sleep. She died of acute intoxication. An accidental overdose.

There were days as I pondered a future of never seeing her again that I wondered if I could survive the physical sorrow crushing my chest. Then I'd look at Jamie, his face drawn, dark circles under his eyes, those beautiful eyes dim— the light gone out—and my suffering would increase by a million as I took on his. I wished I could bear the weight of this loss for the both of us. Knowing I never could devastated me.

The powerlessness was almost as agonizing as the grief.

Through it, I had my own guilt. I'd convinced Jamie that Skye was okay. However, if she was taking antianxiety meds, then she wasn't okay. He'd known something was wrong, and I convinced him not to push her.

We were also plagued by the paparazzi that camped outside our house for days and hounded us to and from the funeral.

Today was the first day they hadn't shown up.

I couldn't bear to look at the internet to see what they were saying about Skye. Through the messages of love and grief, there would be gossip about her addiction and speculation over her death. There was no point reading all of that. It would be like picking at a fresh wound.

Watching Lorna lower herself into the cab, I felt relieved to see her go.

From the moment she'd flown in, she'd treated me with a cold fury. Three nights after her arrival, she got drunk and told me I was to blame for the distance between her and Skye before she died. That she wished she'd never brought me into her life.

It was hard to shut those words out.

If it hadn't been for Jamie, I might never have bothered trying to.

But he needed me.

Although Lorna clung to him at the funeral and made it clear she didn't want me in their space, Jamie needed me. He wouldn't sit in the front pew until Lorna moved to his other side to let me in.

The day Skye died, Jamie got a flight home and I met him at the morgue. He wanted to go in alone. When he came out, he collapsed at my feet, and I held him while he sobbed deep, wrenching cries that I could still hear in my head when I closed my eyes.

That was the last time he cried.

Until the funeral.

Lorna organized everything. The place was packed with friends, celebrities, and industry people. I was barely aware of them or those who approached Lorna and Jamie to offer condolences. Despite the ill feeling she had toward me, I was proud of Lorna as she stood up in front of the congregation and delivered a beautiful memorial to a sister who had changed her life to look after her and Jamie. It was a relief to hear Lorna speak of Skye's drive to give her and her brother a future they never would've had without her.

I hoped Skye was somewhere listening, finally realizing how much she'd meant to us all. And to the little sister she thought didn't look up to her anymore. Lorna's voice broke a few times, but she got through that speech in a way I wasn't sure I could have.

As Skye was taken away for cremation, a video overhead played clips of her through the years. Photos and home-video shots. The Waterboys' "The Whole of the Moon" played over the footage.

I wanted to be strong for Jamie. To hold back my tears, but I couldn't. His grip on my hand tightened and I felt his shoulder shake against mine. I looked at him and saw the tears rolling silently down his face as he stared up at the memorial.

I broke.

Because he was broken.

And I knew it was a wound that would never fully heal.

I couldn't help him.

So, I just held on tighter and laid my head on his shoulder. He gripped at my arm, keeping me as close as he could as I attempted to absorb some of his grief.

I wanted to offer the same to Lorna. I tried to.

But as I held out my arms to her afterward, she cut me a dark look and brushed past.

Two days later, we took Skye's ashes to Santa Monica and poured them into the ocean. Lorna threw a fit when Jamie told her I'd be attending the private moment. As though I hadn't been a part of their family for years. Jamie had no patience for Lorna's antics normally, so to say he was on a knife's edge was an understatement.

I'd never heard him roar at anyone the way he roared at Lorna that day.

She burst into tears, apologized to him, and didn't say another word about me coming.

The three of us said a silent goodbye to Skye.

Lorna never spoke to me again.

So, yes, I was relieved to see her go. My fragile heart could not take the tension between us.

Jamie returned to the house and enveloped me in his arms. He buried his head in my neck, his embrace tight and reassuring—even though I knew it was me he sought the reassurance from.

I kissed his shoulder and caressed his back, trying to soothe him.

After a while, he lifted his head. Beneath the unbearable sadness was a resigned weariness.

The previous night, we'd discussed giving up the house. We couldn't afford the rent on our own, so we'd need to find a smaller apartment. That meant packing.

Lorna packed up the things she'd left behind when she left for college and still wanted to keep. She said we could donate everything else.

That wasn't our concern. The concern was that it meant going through Skye's things and deciding what to keep and what to donate.

Lorna didn't want to do it, and I didn't want Jamie to have to do it, so I'd volunteered.

And since I was not looking forward to it, I wanted to get it over with.

"The guys dropped off the boxes." Jamie pointed to the dining room where I'd already spotted the pile of packing boxes. His teammates had been a huge support to him through this whole nightmare, and I would never forget them for it. "I'll get started down here."

The house came furnished, so we didn't have to worry about moving furniture, just knickknacks and clothing.

"Remember, we need to donate a lot. We won't be able to take it all with us. I'll go upstairs and get started."

Sorrow rippled over his expression before he got control of it. Nodding, he pressed a hard kiss to my lips, murmured a hoarse "thank you," and moved to the kitchen to get started in there.

Carrying a few boxes upstairs with me, I hesitated outside Skye's bedroom door.

We hadn't gone in since we raided her bathroom for clues to her death.

Taking a deep, shuddering breath, I threw back my shoulders and soldiered into the room. Dropping the boxes, I flicked the light switch.

The room smelled like her. Like the Gucci perfume she wore.

Tears clouded my eyes and I took a deep breath, letting out a shaky exhale. Memories of finding her on her bed played over in my head. All the time.

I'd never be rid of them.

I knew it.

And I'd have to find a way to live with their permanent residence in my head.

Fighting down the nausea, I started in the bathroom. Most of everything in there could be thrown out. From there I moved on to her shoes and clothes. I tried to numb myself. To not associate any of the items with memories as I created donation boxes filled with her beautiful things.

Along the top of her closet were trinket boxes, hatboxes, and jewelry boxes. I pulled them all out and started going through them. I was there a few hours, putting aside items I thought Lorna might want to keep.

Pulling over the stool from Skye's dresser, I stepped up

onto it to make sure I hadn't missed anything in the closet and found a large shoebox buried at the back. It was much too heavy to have shoes inside.

Dragging it down, its weight caused it to spill from my hands, and journals fell out, slamming to the carpet one after the other.

As I stared at them in surprise, I heard Jamie call upstairs to ask if I was okay.

I called back my affirmative and lowered to my knees, reaching for the leather-bound journals. There were eight of them. They were thick. And as I flicked open the pages, I saw they were all filled with Skye's handwriting.

She'd kept diaries.

I had no idea.

I glanced at the door, wondering what I should do.

I shouldn't read them. I should take them to Jamie and ask him what he wanted to do with them.

Instead, I tremored with adrenaline. Inside these diaries were possible answers. Why was Skye on antianxiety meds? What drove her to alcohol and drugs? Was it a genetic predisposition toward addiction, or was there another reason?

That roiling sensation moved through my gut—the one you get when you know you're doing something you shouldn't be doing—as I fumbled through the diaries, trying to find the most recent entry.

Her last entry was days before her death.

What I discovered had me tearing through the diaries, traveling back through her words to four and a half years ago.

The entry was dated November, my freshman year of high school.

Her writing was messier in this entry. Instead of the beautiful, cursive handwriting in most of her entries, here it was spiky and frantic. It was a detailed entry of how she'd gone to a meeting with the powerful Hollywood producer Foster Steadman. How he'd tried to coerce her into sex in exchange for advancing her career. How she'd said no.

And how he'd taken what he wanted anyway and raped her on the floor of his office.

Tears poured out of me and I tried to stifle sobs as I read on through the diaries, reading her pain and violation and shame through the months. How small and disgusted she'd felt by her own silence. The fear of losing her career if she spoke up. Losing the money she needed to take care of Lorna and Jamie. How she was repulsed anytime she looked in the mirror and that alcohol and cocaine made her forget for a little while.

Her entries changed after rehab. Her self-loathing eased. She'd confided to Sheridan what had happened, and Sheridan had convinced her to go to therapy, which we never knew about. The therapy helped.

Until the hospital TV drama. The rape storyline. It dragged Skye right back to that place Foster Steadman had taken her four years before.

Shaking hard, I cast aside the last journal and stumbled into the bathroom to throw up. As I cast up my sorrow and bile, rage, guilt, and grief fought to overwhelm me.

We never knew.

None of us knew.

And as far as I was concerned, Foster Steadman was the real reason my beautiful Skye was gone.

I leaned back against the bathroom wall, trembling so hard, my back moved against the tile. Shock. I think I was in shock.

That's how Jamie found me.

As he lowered beside me, I stared at him, at his concerned eyes and furrowed brow, and terror flooded me.

If I gave Jamie those diaries ... would I lose him too?

Chapter Twelve
Months Later

JAMIE

Twenty-one years old

THERE WEREN'T a lot of things I was afraid of in life. After Skye died, I was sure the only thing I feared was losing Jane and Lorna.

Somehow, I'd convinced myself that I wasn't afraid of prison. Yeah, I was afraid of losing out on five to seven years of a life with Jane. I was worried about my future, my career, once I got out.

It wasn't until I found myself inside a cell in medium security at the state prison that the fear set in. I'd been there a week and some sick, twisted bastards that haunted the halls were eyeing me like I wasn't human, but just a walking, talking orifice for them to stick something into.

"You're too pretty for here, son," a biker warned me in the cafeteria the first day. "Find yourself some protection, or you ain't gonna last."

It was like something out of a bad prison movie, except it was real. It was happening. To me.

And I was fucking scared all the time and pretending like I wasn't.

Walking into the visitation room, seeing Jane sitting behind the Plexiglas of a visitor booth, I felt my feet touch the ground for the first time in a week. Lying in my cell at night, I missed her as much as I missed not being afraid.

I despised that she was seeing me like this.

She gave me a sad smile and that cute dimple in her cheek eased the ache in my chest as I sat down opposite her and reached for the phone.

"Hey, baby," she said as she pressed her palm flat to the thick barrier.

I placed my palm over hers, wishing I could feel her skin. "Doe."

She let out a shuddering breath. "How are you?"

"I'm okay," I lied.

Jane knew. "Jamie."

There was no way I would tell her anything that might keep her awake at night. "How's it going with you? You and Cassie find a place?"

After my arrest, we couldn't post bail, so I'd waited in remand. My case went to court quicker than expected, probably because Steadman wanted me there as fast as possible. My lawyer wanted me to plead guilty; I told my lawyer to go fuck himself. So I went to trial, was convicted, and ended up with a longer sentence for standing up for myself.

Jane had given up the small apartment we'd only just moved into and shacked up with her friend Cassie from art school in her one-bedroom apartment. After my sentencing, they got a place together.

"Yeah. We found an apartment in Pomona. Near school."

"Tell me about it."

"Jamie, I don't want to talk about the apartment. I want to talk about you."

Frustration blew through me. "About what? There's nothing to talk about."

"I need to know you're okay."

"Do you love me?"

Jane blinked at the seemingly random question. "You know I do. You're my everything."

I let out a slow exhalation. "Then I'm okay. He thought he took everything from me ... but he didn't take you, and you're all that fucking matters. So, I'm okay."

She squeezed her eyes closed.

"It'll get easier, Doe," I promised her.

I hoped it was a promise I could keep.

With the rage that stirred inside me, I wasn't sure I could. I wasn't sure I could live with myself if I let this go once I got out. My sentence was seven years, but my lawyer told me they'd let me out in five if I behaved myself and kept my head down.

"They've got classes here. Computing, stuff like that. There's even a workshop. I'll keep busy," I promised.

"Can you write?"

"There's a computer lounge. I can write there."

"Good." She nodded, seeming somewhat appeased.

"Now tell me about you. I want to know what you're up to."

I let Jane's voice soothe me as she talked about her sophomore classes at Pomona. The projects she was working on. Dramas unfolding with her friends. That stuff seemed juvenile to us both now, I knew, but it was a distraction.

A distraction from the knowledge that we wouldn't be able to touch each other for at least five years. Sometimes that thought took my breath away.

What would Skye think of me here?

That I'd been a naive, stupid, impulsive asshole, that's
what.

A moronic kid who had no idea what he was doing when
he broke into Foster Steadman's office and confronted him
about Skye and what Jane had found in her journals. I wanted
to kill him. I wanted to rip his fucking dick off so he could
never hurt another woman again.

I knew I would do just that when I grabbed the letter
opener off his desk. His security arrived before I could touch
him and threw me out.

It was enough to calm my ass down. As was the tongue-
lashing from Jane. We would do it right, she said. We'd take
the journals to the police and they'd investigate Steadman.

We went out that night. Trying to distract ourselves. Skye
had left a far more substantial amount of money than I'd been
expecting, to be split three ways among Jane, Lorna, and me.
My little sister threatened to contest Jane's share, but I shut
her down, promising I'd never speak to her again if she didn't
abide by Skye's wishes.

The money allowed Jane and me to rent a decent apartment in Glendale and go out for the occasional nice meal if we
felt like it.

That night we'd come back to our apartment.

It was ransacked.

And I knew why immediately.

Panicked, I'd hurried into the bedroom where I kept
Skye's journals in the closet, and they were gone.

That wasn't even the worst of it. The next morning, there
were cops at the door, and I was in handcuffs being arrested
for armed robbery.

Armed. Fucking. Robbery.

"You tried to fuck with the wrong guy," one of the cops
whispered in my ear as he lowered me into the police car. Dirty
bastard cop. On Steadman's payroll.

The next few months were even more of a nightmare than I thought they could be after losing Skye. Steadman had paid a cashier near the studio offices to lie. And it must have been some amount of cash he bribed her with because she took a bullet. The footage from inside the store didn't show my face —it just showed some guy with a similar build to mine, wearing a hoodie that hid his face from the security cameras, coming into the store and robbing the cashier at gunpoint. The attacker clipped the cashier in the shoulder with a bullet.

That woman took a bullet to bury me.

She miraculously identified me. Said I came into the store a lot. She remembered my name from when I used my card there.

The fuck of it was, I'd gone into the store the day I attacked Steadman to grab bottled water. With no cash on me, I'd used my card.

Steadman's security must have followed me. Put all this together.

Cops were paid off. He paid for the cashier's lawyer. No one would listen when I tried to tell them about Skye, and my defense attorney said there was nothing he could do without any evidence.

There was no record of me showing up at Steadman's office that day.

I spent all the money Skye left me on my defense fees. Worse, Jane had to give me a chunk of her share too to cover my legal costs. It didn't matter. I got seven years for a crime I didn't commit. To shut me up. To shut up anyone who knew about Skye.

Look what I can do, Steadman was saying. *You're a fucking bug and I'm a lion. I can squash you just by taking a stroll.*

But I would get him.

I had patience. And I was smarter now.

As long as I could protect Jane while I did it, Foster

Steadman was going to wish he'd kept his sick hands off my sister. I didn't care how long it took.

I would bury the bastard.

CHAPTER THIRTEEN
ONE YEAR LATER

JANE
Nineteen years old

FOR OVER A YEAR, every Thursday, I'd gotten up early and driven Jamie's car three and a half hours north to the state prison to make visiting hours at 11:00 a.m. I had not missed a week.

Nothing short of fire and brimstone could make me miss a week.

Not even the changes in Jamie. The coldness. The distance.

He hadn't told me he loved me in weeks.

Yet still I said it. It was the last thing I said before I left him after every visit. Just for a moment, something would spark in his grim gaze and he'd lift his chin in acknowledgment.

I had to believe he still loved me.

Prison was chipping away at who he was.

Three weeks after he was put away, I got a call from the prison telling me Jamie was in the hospital. I had to leave a message for Lorna because she wouldn't answer my calls, and she, thankfully, listened to my message and got the next flight to LA. We found ourselves paying vigil at his bedside for the next few days as he recovered from a stab wound to the gut.

It was only after he was back in prison that he told me he'd deliberately stepped between the attacker and a guy called Irwin Alderidge.

I'd googled Alderidge after our conversation.

He was this billionaire real estate mogul. He had properties all over the world, but his home was in Los Angeles. He'd been tried and sentenced to seven years for paying millions in bribes to two elected officials to be his eyes and ears in California's government. The government officials were also convicted. It was a high sentence for the crime, but the jury had decided to make an example out of Alderidge.

Despite the large fine Alderidge received, the guy was still dripping in money. According to Jamie, that money kept him safe while he was behind bars. He paid the toughest sons of bitches in that place to watch his back.

But Jamie had been keeping his ear to the ground, and some psycho little shit who tried to blackmail cash out of Alderidge decided he was going to shiv him. Jamie watched. Waited. And took the shiv instead.

For the first time in my life, I wanted to scream at him. He'd almost died! And that's when it all came out. That there were guys who wanted to *hurt* him. As much as it killed his pride, he needed protection. It was the shiv, or his life wouldn't be worth living, he'd said.

Thankfully, Jamie recovered, and his risk paid off.

Turned out Irwin Alderidge wasn't someone who let a debt go unpaid. I also got the impression from what my boyfriend had told me that Alderidge genuinely liked Jamie. They shared varied interests, were educated, and were avid readers. They spent a lot of their time keeping each other sane.

Jamie didn't speak about it, but I knew he'd witnessed things in that prison that haunted him.

It wasn't just isolation and injustice eating away at him.

It was the whole damn place.

That Thursday I waited impatiently in a booth in the visitation room, desperate to see him. He stepped into the room behind a guard and the constant ache in my chest bloomed, spreading through my whole body.

To say I missed him was an understatement.

I'd lost all the McKennas, and even though Cassie was a good friend, my family was gone. Sometimes it felt like I was just going through the motions. Wasting time until Jamie was out of prison.

He looked tired when he sat across from me.

I smiled and his eyes dropped to my dimple, his harsh countenance softening a little.

"Decided not to shave today?" I teased into the phone.

He scratched at his stubbled jaw with those long, big-knuckled fingers. I missed his hands. "It makes me look older, no?"

I grinned. "It's very sexy."

His eyes glimmered a little. "*You're* very sexy."

My cheeks flushed.

I missed sex with Jamie.

It wasn't the thing I missed most. I missed his laugh the most. I missed lying next to him at night while he slept. I missed waking up to find him writing, tiptoeing out of the room so as not to disturb him. I missed the way he used to look at me, like I was the one who made the world turn. Like I was the sun and the waves and the moon.

I missed hearing him whisper, "I love you, Doe."

I missed the feel of his arms around me. The way a Jamie hug made me feel safe and loved and needed.

But I missed sex with Jamie too.

I missed the hunger in his eyes. The way he'd bare his teeth as he fucked me. The way he murmured my name across my lips as he made love to me.

I *missed* Jamie.

"How are you?" I asked as I always asked.

"Good," he replied like he always replied. "What's been happening?"

I regaled him with the dull minutiae of my life. At least it was dull to me, but Jamie seemed to enjoy listening to me talk. I told him about how my friend Tom had just found out Cassie was seeing a guy fifteen years her senior, and Tom was jealous as hell. He'd asked Cassie out a bunch of times over the last year and she'd said no every time, and now he knew it was because of this older firefighter named Cal.

I was the only one who knew she'd been seeing Cal since our freshman year. Considering she was eighteen and he was thirty-three when they'd first started dating, they'd kept the relationship on the down low. But a few of her friends found out the longer their relationship went on, and now it was no longer a secret.

Tom was not happy.

"I think she's afraid he's going to tell someone. Cal might lose his job."

Jamie's brow puckered. "She's nineteen."

"Yeah, but people can be judgmental about these age gaps. He's worried he comes off as some cradle-robbing creep." In truth, Cassie had lied to Cal about her age when they'd first met. By the time he realized she was only eighteen, he was already in love with her.

Jamie nodded slowly, but he frowned. "You haven't mentioned Devin in a while."

My stomach dropped. Despite Devin asking me out freshman year, Jamie had been cool that he was still part of the group I hung out with at school. He'd never been insecure or possessive that way. He didn't have to be. I loved him, and he knew that.

So Devin and I were friends.

Good friends, as far as I was aware.

That's why when he followed me into a bathroom at a party six weeks ago, I never saw it coming. He was wasted. He told me he loved me and that I needed to be with someone who wasn't going to drag me down like Jamie. I told him to get out. That he didn't know what he was talking about.

And he decided to kiss me to prove me wrong.

Cassie had talked me into taking self-defense classes just after Jamie was sentenced. Thank God she did.

At first Devin was too strong, too big at six four, and I was so busy struggling to breathe through the kiss and the panic that it took a minute for me to realize he'd shoved his hand up my skirt. Fury kicked in.

I grabbed his wrist and twisted it as hard as I could; then I disabled him with a swift kick to the nuts.

Cassie wanted to kill him, and she just might have if I hadn't talked her out of it.

Instead, I went to the police and had Devin charged with assault.

He got a slap on the wrist since it was my word against his. He lied to the cops about it all being a big misunderstanding, but then he tried to apologize to me. There was no coming back from either that moment in the bathroom or making me out to be a liar afterward.

I'd cut him out of my life and most of our friends had done the same.

Becoming a social pariah was a kind of punishment, I guess.

What I hadn't done was tell Jamie any of this.

Over a year ago, I made the choice to tell him about Skye's

diaries. A choice I would never have made if I'd been able to see the future.

I knew Jamie would confront Steadman, and yet, I still told him.

I was part of the reason Jamie was behind bars.

Cassie tried to rationalize with me, and of course, I knew that this was Foster Steadman's fault, but I couldn't let go of my guilt.

Jamie scowled. "Well? Why haven't you mentioned Devin?" His cheeks reddened before I could reply. "Has something happened between you two? Have you fucked him?"

I blinked rapidly, and shock made the phone slip in my hand.

Had Jamie, *my* Jamie, really just asked me that? "Are you kidding me?" I couldn't even raise my voice above a whisper.

A manner of insolence took over his body, reminding me so much of fifteen-year-old Jamie. He leaned forward on his elbows, his eyes dark with jealousy. "You like sex, Jane. What am I supposed to think you're doing out there without me? Especially when you never mention Devin anymore? And I know when you're not telling me something. You got real weird there when I said his name."

"So, I'm screwing him?" Tears of fury brightened my eyes. "Because I like sex?"

Uncertainty flickered over his expression, and he swallowed hard. "Well?"

I glared at him in wounded indignation. "I like sex with *you*. There's a difference. That you would even suggest otherwise makes me want to knee you in the gonads."

His breathing was shallower, and he shifted in agitation. "What aren't you telling me, then?"

But I couldn't let it go. "Do you think I'd cheat on you?"

"Is it cheating if I'm stuck in here for five to seven?"

"Yes," I snapped. "I am yours. You are mine. That has

never changed. What the hell do you think I'm doing out there?" I gestured behind me. "My life is in limbo, Jamie. It's not even living. It's just wasting time until you're out."

His own eyes were bright, and he shook his head at me. "I'm not asking you to do that. I don't want that. I want you out there, being happy."

"Well, I'm not. I'm not happy." It was the truth, whether or not he wanted to hear it.

"Skye was right." He sank back in his chair, looking so goddamn weary. "She warned me that the way we feel about each other would fuck us up in the end."

"Only if you lose faith in me." I leaned forward, my hand pressed to the glass. I was terrified. Terrified of losing him. "I will wait however long it takes for you. Do you understand me?"

Jamie swallowed hard, a shimmer glazing his eyes. He blinked rapidly as he looked away, swallowing again and again, as if swallowing back his emotions, until he had himself under control.

"I love you, Jamie."

He glared at the ground but nodded tightly. Without looking at me, he pressed his hand to the glass where mine was and then put down the phone. He waited a moment, head bowed. His hand strained against the glass, he pressed it so hard.

Standing up, he caressed the Plex as if caressing my palm and then walked away without looking at me.

Hot tears rolled down my cheeks.

CHAPTER FOURTEEN
TWO DAYS LATER

JANE

"YOU DO REALIZE you've barely said a word in two days, ever since you got back from your visit with Jamie."

I looked up from sitting crossed-legged. The words in my art history paper blurred on my laptop screen, I'd been staring at them so long. The interruption from my roommate, Cassie, would have been welcome under normal circumstances.

However, I'd barely said a word in two days because I didn't know what to say. It felt like Jamie was slipping through my fingers, and I was terrified of losing him. If I didn't talk about it, the possibility seemed less ... possible.

"I haven't?" I evaded.

Cassie leaned against my doorjamb. She wore a wry, unhappy smirk. "Come out with me and Cal tonight. His friend, Rig, is having a party."

"I don't feel like it."

"Hmm." She pushed up off the jamb. "Do you want to tell me what happened with Jamie?"

"Nothing happened."

Something flickered over Cassie's expression. Something like disappointment. "You know ... in all the time we've been friends, I've told you almost everything there is to know about me. You were the only one I told about Cal in the beginning ... And yet, you never *talk* to me."

I stiffened with discomfort. "That's not true." It wasn't. Cassie knew I'd been left at a police station as a baby. She didn't know about my adoptive parents because no one but Jamie knew that. But she knew about foster care. She knew about Skye. Lorna.

I'd told her about Jamie and what he meant to me.

That was more than most people in my life knew.

"It is true, Jane." Cassie sighed. "I saw how hard it was for you when Jamie went to prison. You're strong, and you got on with it. But the last few months ... it's like you're not even here anymore. You're stuck inside your head, and I'm thinking that's not a great place to be right now. So ... talk to me. You can trust me."

The urge to confide in my friend was there. To tell her about how Jamie was acting. To get her advice. To have her, *hopefully*, reassure me that Jamie was just dealing with things that I couldn't possibly understand but that it didn't mean he didn't love me anymore.

However, trusting people wasn't exactly my forte these days.

I stared at her, mute with frustration. I wanted to trust her. But I was scared to.

And more than that, I was terrified if I said the words out loud, if I told her about Jamie's behavior, that by making it real I'd only be ushering on the demise of my relationship with the man I loved.

As irrational as I knew that was, the fear choked the words in my throat.

With a sigh of dejection, and not a little anger, Cassie bit out, "Fine," and strode from sight. I heard our apartment door close behind her seconds later, and tears pricked my eyes.

I should have told her.

I should have reached out to my friend and maybe changed the course of our friendship over the years.

Because I'd know, within only a matter of hours, that *not* voicing my fears over losing Jamie wouldn't stop it from happening anyway.

I STARED at the crumpled paper through blurred vision. It felt like someone had shoved a knife in my chest. I couldn't breathe.

It was Jamie's handwriting.

I'd know his handwriting anywhere.

The paper had wrinkles like it had been balled up. And then folded carefully into a square.

It was short, succinct. No need to sign it.

I looked up at Lorna. Her expression was flat.

Like she didn't care that she'd just delivered the kind of news that had torn my world to shreds. "He doesn't mean it," I whispered.

Jamie couldn't mean it.

No. I felt my head shaking *no, no, no.*

Lorna stood, staring dispassionately down at me. She'd flown in from the East Coast to visit Jamie and some old high school friends. She said he'd asked her to deliver this letter to me. Which she'd done, only hours after Cassie left the apartment. "He blames you too. Don't you get that? If you'd just kept your mouth shut about those damn diaries, he'd be in his last year at school. He'd have a future." Her voice broke. "You leave him alone, Jane. He's all I have left, and I won't let you hold him back anymore."

I was barely even aware of her leaving.

I just kept reading the letter ... over and over.

Remembering our visits over the past few months.

How he'd stopped saying he loved me.

It hurt like grief.

It was an agonizing pain greater than any physical pain I'd ever felt. I didn't know how to breathe through it. I wanted a black shroud of numbness to fall over me and take away the pain.

Jamie didn't want me anymore.

CHAPTER FIFTEEN
FOUR YEARS LATER

JAMIE
Twenty-six years old

IN A PERFECT WORLD, she'd be as haggard and as ugly as her weak soul.

Instead, Jane was even more beautiful than I remembered. Even more beautiful than the shots of her I'd seen online.

My freedom was within reach. I was up for parole, and things looked good for me. From within the confines of prison, I'd found a literary agent who wanted to find a publisher for the book I'd written.

Yeah, things were looking up for Jamie McKenna.

I just wished seeing her wasn't still a knife in the gut.

No, correction: I'd had a knife in the gut.

Seeing Jane was much worse.

When they told me she'd requested a visit, I was shocked as shit. Four years ago, the love of my goddamn life ghosted me. The visits stopped with no explanation.

I guess she didn't need to explain.

It was obvious. She couldn't take that I'd changed. I knew I hadn't made the visits easy for her, but I'd stupidly assumed Jane would stick by me through anything. What a naive asshole. The time apart was too much for her. What future did I have with a criminal record? She was only nineteen back then. What kind of life was it for her to wait around for her boyfriend to get out of prison?

The rational part of me understood. The Jamie who loved her back then had even wanted that for her.

However, Jane hadn't even taken time to face me. To come to the prison and tell me to my face that it was over between us.

Instead, she just never showed up again.

Maybe I could have forgiven that, if she hadn't reinvented herself as Margot Higgins and started spreading her legs for the son of the evil fucker who took my life for five years and ruined my sister.

What was Jane doing here? I thought as I strolled across the room toward the booth where she was waiting. Had she heard I was up for parole, that I was probably getting out soon? Did that make me worthy of her time again?

Fuck her.

I sat down, staring at her. She had the phone pressed to her ear, waiting.

Those stunning, hazel-green eyes stared into mine, and the longing I felt was so devastating, fury erupted from me. I grabbed the phone off the hook, held it to my ear, and didn't give her a chance to speak. "What's it like to fuck the son of the man who raped Skye and framed me for a crime I didn't commit?"

Her shocked gasp sent blood pumping to my dick, and I resented her for that too. Those plump lips parted, eyes filled with pain. Or was that guilt?

"I hate you," I told her. I was cold as ice. "You disgust me."

You abandoned me and then took up with Asher Steadman. What the hell else did you expect?

The boy who used to love her wanted to believe there was a reason she'd hooked her star to Asher Steadman. Because the Jane I knew would never have done that.

In saying that, the Jane I knew would never have abandoned me either.

"When I get out, I'm heading back to Massachusetts," I said. "I expect I'll never have to look at your fucking face ever again." It was a warning.

Slamming the phone on the hook, I pushed back my chair and walked away from her.

She needed to stay out of my life. I had plans to put in motion, and I didn't need her screwing them up.

Not until I was ready.

Then I'd be back for her.

And Jane Doe would wish she'd never laid eyes on me.

PART TWO
THE PRESENT

CHAPTER SIXTEEN

JANE

IT WAS the last place I wanted to be.

I was surrounded by famous and not-so-famous faces, features blurring as guests moved around me, some nodding hello, others stopping to chat. I smiled, asked questions I couldn't remember the answers to seconds later, and willed the minute hand on the giant, frameless clock above Patel's fireplace to move faster.

Patel Smith was the Academy Award-winning producer on the movie I was working on. It was the second time I'd worked for Patel. The first time was five years ago, and I was a mere art department assistant at the time. Now I was his art director.

Despite the uber-contemporary (and expensive) home in Laurel Canyon—a house he bought two years ago after a landslide scared off its previous owner—Patel insisted he wasn't "Hollywood." It was obvious by his home and car that he liked the money, the sun, and the lifestyle, but according to him, he was still the working-class guy who grew up in Liverpool, England.

While his wife, Shireen, lived a designer life, Patel didn't seem interested in conversation unless it was about books, film, music, or Liverpool Football Club. Since I had no interest in soccer, I fell upon books and music as my go-to topics for conversation with Patel. But mostly we talked about set design.

Patel's house had a panoramic view of Los Angeles and an infinity pool that merged with the sky reflected in it. As Shireen told everyone who entered the house, they were lucky not to have lost everything in the cyclonic fires that had ripped through the Hollywood Hills a year ago.

I personally thought the house was a risk.

Beautiful, but unreliable.

Who wanted to invest themselves emotionally in something that might get wiped out by a landslide or climate change?

The party was a crush. Patel wasn't a guy who just invited actors and "important" crew members to his parties. Everyone working for him got an invitation. It was a large cast and crew on this movie, and I didn't know everyone by name.

The cast and crew appeared and disappeared through the rotation of guests while I longed for Asher's steadying presence.

Strike that. If I was wishing for stuff, I wished to replace the spritzed partygoers with the bitter scent of linseed oil, pungent turpentine, and the piney aroma of a new canvas frame. Instead of the mansion, I wanted to be in my bedroom/art studio in my apartment in Silver Lake.

I'd spent seven years building a career I never meant to pursue. Not that I was unhappy, but working in Hollywood was far more frenetic than the future I had envisioned.

I chose this life. And for what? I was no closer to my goal, even with Asher's help.

These parties reminded me of all the things I could gladly do without. I was an introvert by nature and being forced to schmooze was akin to someone scoring their nails down a chalkboard.

Still, I might never have wanted this life—to be dealing with people day in and out, collaborating with production designers, delegating, keeping to deadline, working crazy hours —but I didn't mind it. The movie Patel was directing and producing was a musical, which meant elaborate, expensive sets and a huge amount of work I could disappear into.

Filming would start on Monday, so Patel's party was kind of a kickoff event that I'd felt obligated to attend. For now, I estimated I had to put in another hour at this party before I could leave without being rude. While the cast might not have to work tomorrow, I'd be up at the crack of dawn and on the lot to make sure the set Patel wanted to work with first was ready.

I squeezed through the crowds gathered in the open-plan sitting room and strode into the kitchen. The music playing throughout the house, mixed with the cacophony of voices, meant I couldn't even hear my booted heels click against the ceramic-tile floor. Like the living room, the kitchen also had a bank of bifold glass doors along one wall that looked out onto the infinity pool and the city beyond. The doors were pushed all the way open as guests wandered in and out of the house.

Seeing a waiter pick up a tray of hors d'oeuvres, I moved toward him and took a few. As I reached for another, the waiter eyeballed me. It was clear he was trying to place me. I scrambled to grab several of the little pastries before he had his "ah-ha" moment, but I was too late.

"You're Margot Higgins, right?"

I nodded. My name used to be Jane Doe. For reasons, I had it legally changed while I was still in college.

"You're Asher Steadman's girlfriend." He grinned, apparently pleased with himself.

Only someone who wanted to be in the business would pay close enough attention to know that. Yes, I'd been photographed with Asher a few times, but it wasn't like paparazzi hounded us. We weren't actors or singers or models … so we weren't all that exciting. The only reason the public cared even a little was because Asher was Hollywood royalty.

I gave the waiter a tight smile and popped a pastry in my mouth. Unlike many of the actors around me, I didn't have a love-hate relationship with carbs. There was only love between us. I loved them. They loved my ass.

The waiter dragged his gaze down my body and back up again. "You are way hotter in real life."

I swiped a couple more puff pastries and whirled away from him with a two-fingered salute. It was that or throw food at him, and that was just a waste of good catering.

After art college, I'd done something I thought I'd never do and asked my ex-foster dad, Nick, to help me get a job in a studio. He found me a position working as an art department runner. After a year of keeping everyone on set caffeinated, I got promoted to an assistant, which meant I got to use my art skills. Making my voice heard in the sea of chatter that was film wasn't easy for me, but I was determined to be noticed. I had to be noticed so I could find the "in" I needed in Hollywood.

I'd worked on a few big movies, including one of Patel's previous films, but lowly assistants weren't on people's radars. However, art director Marsha Kowalski was my boss on an *Indiana Jones*-style flick, and she noticed me. I worked my ass off. I offered my talents as a scenic artist, I painted, I constructed, I kept people more organized on that movie than

Marsha herself. Marsha hired me on her next movie as *her* assistant, which was several steps up the ladder in one promotion.

That movie was a Foster Steadman film.

My "in."

From there I met Asher and my career moved at warp speed.

Now I was an art director. At only twenty-six years old. When Patel asked for me specifically for this musical, I couldn't believe it. He *asked* for me. People were asking for me now.

Which brought me to the party at Patel's swanky house in the hills.

Remembering Patel's mention of a home library, I moved away from the crowd, avoiding eye contact so I didn't get drawn into conversation. Instead, I skirted the edges of the sitting room and disappeared into the hallway. I found the room in question toward the back of the first floor.

The door was open, but there was no one else inside. It was much darker than the other rooms in the home because there was only one window and a blind had been drawn over it. A comfy sectional, a few armchairs, side tables, and a coffee table were situated stylishly throughout the large room. White-painted bookcases wrapped around every inch of wall space. I envied Patel this room.

I felt relieved to be alone, surrounded by books, the music a dull thud in the background. My lungs opened and I breathed freely as I stepped into the room. It smelled like furniture polish, which was a welcome change to the colognes and perfumes out at the party fighting for supremacy over one another.

I relaxed as I stopped at the first row and began to catalogue Patel's collection in my head.

After a while of perusing the shelves, my attention snagged on a copy of *Brent 29*.

I pulled out the worn paperback and flicked through the pages. Patel had underlined sentences in ink. The horror! I shook my head at the defacement but smirked. He'd underlined all the lines I'd highlighted in my e-reader edition.

The book was a runaway bestseller last year by a mysterious author called Griffin Stone. He didn't share his photo, no one really knew who he was, but it didn't seem to matter because the guy had sold over two million copies of his book. It was about a man, Charlie Brent, who was wrongfully imprisoned for the death of his son. His young wife, Una, worked relentlessly to have him exonerated and succeeded, but it took her and the lawyer almost seven years. By then, Charlie had been badly affected by everything that happened to him and others while he was in prison, and he convinced Una to go on a devastating journey to find the man who'd killed their son. Through everything that happened to them, the couple's bond and faith in each other was unshakeable.

The book didn't have a happy ending.

I cried when I finished it. Not just because Charlie sacrificed himself for justice (or was it vengeance? It was up to the reader to decide) and left Una on her own, but because the story was chillingly relatable. Moreover, the writing style reminded me of Jamie McKenna's.

The boy I'd loved.

My phone buzzed in the ass pocket of my jeans, making me jolt, my heart racing a little. Pulling it out, shaking off my memories, I opened a text from Asher.

Hang in there. I'm on my way.

He knew me so well.

I texted back.

I'm hiding in the library

My phone buzzed again.

You're adorable.

Chuckling, I shook my head and put my phone back in my pocket. Asher didn't mind the parties and the glamor. He grew up in the Hollywood environment and was far better suited to faking his way through it.

Putting *Brent 29* back on the shelf, I ran my fingers along the walnut cases as I studied Patel's collection. He'd shelved the books by genre, then alphabetically. When I found a bookcase of mixed genres and authors, I frowned. Why was this case unorganized? Reaching up for a book by Stephen King, I flipped it open and grew still at the sight of the scrawl across the title page.

It was signed.

My attention caught on a pristine hardback copy of *Brent 29,* just a few books along from where the Stephen King book sat.

Putting the Stephen King title back, I reached for Griffin Stone's instead. Sure enough, the pristine copy was signed. I traced my finger over the autograph, liking the way his G and S stood out in big, attractive loops in comparison to the brutal stiffness of the rest of the letters. I wondered how Patel got a signed copy.

And not for the first time, I wondered what Stone was like.

I felt strangely connected to his book.

I enjoyed his ability to make me care for a deeply flawed character like Charlie and a determined, loyal woman like Una, even though she followed love into chaos.

A shuffling noise behind me drew my attention over my shoulder and—

My heart stopped.

A man stood in the doorway.

There was something incredibly familiar about him.

As his face began to make sense, a cold sweat prickled my body as though I'd stepped into a shower of ice water.

"Jamie?" I breathed.

He glared at me with Jamie McKenna's face. Older, harder, scruff covering his angular jaw. His hair was a little darker, too, but I'd know that moody brow and those soulful eyes anywhere. The book slipped from my fingers, making a soft thump against the hardwood. I took a step toward him. "Jamie?"

He moved swiftly from the doorway, disappearing down the hall.

No!

Heart pounding so hard all I could hear was the blood rushing in my ears, I hurried after him, hitting my leg on a goddamn coffee table in my rush to keep up. Bursting out of the library, I turned right down the hall, but he was gone.

"No, no, no," I whispered, frantic, tears burning in my eyes.

I searched the house from top to bottom, all thoughts of Patel's privacy overshadowed by the blast from the past I'd just seen.

Yet ... there was no Jamie.

Stepping into the huge entrance hall where the floating stairs led down to the first floor, I gazed into the crowded sitting room and tried to make sense of what had just happened.

Had I imagined that Jamie McKenna, love of my life, had somehow appeared at a party in the Hollywood Hills? Wasn't he supposed to be on the East Coast?

Trying to breathe through the panic tightening my chest, my cheeks tingled as everything around me began to feel very far away.

I was having an anxiety attack.

Stumbling toward the staircase, I slumped onto the second step as I let the sensation move through me. It took a while for the chest pressure to alleviate, for the faraway feeling to fade, and for the noise of the party to return. Exhausted, I pressed my hands to my forehead and waited. I knew if I got up, it would be on trembling limbs. Nausea always accompanied my anxiety attacks, so I needed a minute to compose myself or I would eject the hors d'oeuvres I'd just eaten.

Releasing a shaky breath, I chastised myself. After the last time I'd visited Jamie in prison, the doc wanted to put me on antianxiety medication, but there was no way. I did not have good memories associated with those meds. Instead, I fought my way through the anxiety and depression and thankfully made it to the other side.

I hadn't felt anxious in a long while, and I hadn't had an anxiety attack in an even longer while.

Fuck.

That goddamn book. It reminded me of Jamie. It was making me see things that weren't there. Shit.

"Okay, I did not expect to find you like this." Asher's soft voice brought my head up.

He was there. Lowered to his haunches in front of me, concern creasing his brow.

Relieved to see him, I reached out a shaky hand and he drew it against his chest. I felt his slow, steady heartbeat and relaxed a little. God, I loved him.

"Anxiety attack," I admitted.

"Honey." He gave me a commiserating look and pulled me to my feet. Anxiety was something we unfortunately shared.

He got it. I cuddled into his strong chest as he wrapped his arms around me. "You want to go?"

"I'm sorry," I mumbled. "I'm just so tired now."

"Do you want to tell Patel you're leaving?"

"No. Let's just go." I knew it was rude, but I was probably pale and shaken, and truthfully, I didn't think he'd notice his art director's absence.

"What brought it on?" Asher asked as we walked out of the house. There was a cool evening breeze, welcome against my clammy skin. Parked cars lined the drive and two valet guys sat drinking coffee near the end of the driveway at a pop-up table. Since Asher's car was parked near the gates, he hadn't surrendered a key fob. Not that he could or would.

Asher drove a Rimac Concept Two. The hypercar was fully electric, combining Asher's eco-heart with his love for horsepower. I waited as the $2 million car scanned his face with its facial recognition software. The doors opened upward, like the Batmobile.

I'd never get used to Asher's wealth, no matter how hard he tried to insinuate me into almost every aspect of his life.

Sliding into the tan, leather passenger seat, I didn't speak until the doors closed. "I think I'm just exhausted," I lied. "We've been working flat out."

I didn't want to tell Asher about hallucinating Jamie. I didn't want him to suggest, for the thousandth time, that I see a therapist.

My best friend studied me, and I squirmed beneath his dark gaze. I hated lying to him. Those chocolate-brown eyes were so kind and warm, it felt evil to deceive him.

"You're doing a great job, Jane. No one is questioning how you got promoted. It's not about me—it's about how good you are at this job."

I gave him a grateful smile. He was the only one in my life who still called me Jane. To everyone else, I was Margot. I thought I could shed the name Jane easily. However, when our connection deepened, I realized how much I missed just being Jane and had asked Asher to call me by that name. He and Cassie, my friend from college, were the only people who did. It might have been confusing for some people, but not for me. There was still a part of me that wanted to hold on to a piece of the girl I used to be.

As the car reversed out of the driveway, barely making a sound, I forced my tired eyes to stay open.

"Anything on Foster?" I asked.

I hadn't asked in a while. But hallucinating Jamie tugged at my guilty conscience.

"I can't get Lisa to talk." His fingers tightened around the steering wheel. "He's paid her off. Like he has the last few. And they're too scared he'll ruin their careers. I have to be careful too. If Foster discovers I'm investigating him, it's all over."

My chest ached with sadness while bitter helplessness burned my throat. "Maybe it's time I went in."

"No," Asher snapped. "We will not have this conversation again."

At my dejected silence, he sighed. "Jane, a honey trap is too dangerous. And who's to say whatever you discover would stand up in court? Worst-case scenario—and the most likely scenario—he takes what he wants from you and you'll be just another one of his victims."

I flinched at the thought. "It's been seven years," I whispered. "And I've done nothing."

"We're trying." He reached over to rub a soothing hand down my arm. "And we've got time. This isn't a movie where the bad guy gets his within the two-hour run time. Foster is smart, but one day he'll slip up, and we'll be there when he does." He suddenly grinned at me. "Here's something that might cheer you up: he's got a black eye and he's cradling his left side like he has cracked ribs."

I frowned. "Huh?"

"Someone beat him up."

"Why?" Not that I cared. I would've liked to have seen it.

"No clue. But he's not talking, so whoever it was managed to get one over on him. You should see him. He's using makeup to try to hide it."

His laughter made me chuckle. I rolled my head toward him, my hair rustling in my ear with the movement. "I love you, Ash."

His face softened. "Love you too."

CHAPTER SEVENTEEN

JAMIE

THE BLACK PORSCHE Taycan glided down the hills toward Glendale with smooth quietness, and the view of LA from Laurel Canyon barely registered. It was a valley of lights in the distance, of life and humanity. Where once I'd seen the beauty in it, all I saw now were the shadows in between the lights. The dark places where dark deeds were done.

Seeing *her* for the first time in two years didn't help my mood.

Jane.

I gripped the steering wheel tighter and seethed.

She left the party with Asher Steadman.

And for the first time in two years, I felt my control slip.

The one thing Irwin Alderidge taught me was to keep my emotions locked down tight. When you were a cold, emotionless bastard, no one could guess what you were thinking. What you were planning.

I thought I'd heeded his lessons well ... but whenever Jane

entered the equation, my fucking heart raced and a cold sweat dampened my skin. Watching her leave with the son of the bastard who destroyed my life was one of the hardest things I'd ever done. And I'd done a lot of difficult shit in my life.

I locked down. Stopped myself from racing out of Patel Smith's house to confront Jane.

It wasn't part of the plan.

I'd spooked her. Just like I'd hoped. It was the beginning.

When I first discovered Jane was working in Hollywood, I felt betrayed. Sure, the job was art related, but our plans involved a quiet, creative life away from the glitz and lights of Hollywood. Money had never been our priority. Fame was to be avoided at all costs. Yet, there she was: Steadman's woman. Captured in gossip rags in her bikini on a resort vacation with him. I hated those photos when I first saw them online. Jane sprawled across the pages for any fucker to fantasize over.

It was out of my hands, and now I couldn't care less. I stopped caring the moment I found out she was sleeping with the enemy.

Traitor.

"Anything on Foster?" Jane's voice filled the Porsche.

The question made my breath catch.

Getting into Patel Smith's party had been way too easy. These people needed to up their security. What was even easier was planting a listening device in Asher Steadman's $2 million car. It shouldn't have been. But Asher's friend, Kent Bishop, had an expensive drug problem and was willing to do anything for cash. He'd put the bug in his friend's car when they drove out to Malibu for a surf that morning.

Asher hadn't said anything of importance so far.

Hearing Jane's voice, though, made my heart pound.

"I can't get Lisa to talk," Asher replied. "He's paid her off. Like he has the last few. And they're too scared he'll ruin their careers. I have to be careful too. If Foster discovers I'm investigating him, it's all over."

What the fuck? My hands tightened around the steering wheel. Did this conversation mean what I thought it meant? Were Jane and Asher investigating Foster too?

"Maybe it's time I went in," Jane said.

"No," Asher snapped. "We will not have this conversation again."

What was she talking about?

"Jane, a honey trap is too dangerous. And who is to say whatever you discover would stand up in court? Worst-case scenario—and the most likely scenario—he takes what he wants from you and you'll be just another one of his victims."

Fucking hell. She was talking about luring Foster Steadman into ... what? Trying to attack her? Was she insane?

And why do you care?

Well, thirty seconds ago, I didn't. However, if Jane and Asher were trying to find evidence against Asher's father, it was because of what he did to Skye. Because of what he did to me. It had to be.

But that didn't make any sense.

Shit.

"It's been seven years," she whispered. "And I've done nothing."

My eyes widened. It *was* about Skye. Maybe even about me. "Jane?" I murmured, feeling a little sick. "What the hell is going on?"

"We're trying." Asher spoke again. "And we've got time. This isn't a movie where the bad guy gets his within the two-hour run time. Foster is smart, but one day he'll slip up, and we'll be there when he does ... Here's something that might cheer you up: he's got a black eye and he's cradling his left side like he has cracked ribs."

My brows pinched together.

"Huh?" Jane asked, mirroring my confusion.

"Someone beat him up."

Who? I wasn't aware of that.

"Why?"

"No clue. But he's not talking, so whoever it was managed to get one over on him. You should see him. He's using makeup to try to hide it."

I heard them chuckle together over Foster's misfortune, and again, I questioned everything.

All my plans suddenly hovered in the air, suspended.

"I love you, Ash," Jane whispered.

Just like that, my plans were back in place.

"Love you too."

Jealousy, a thick, writhing, painful feeling that turned my blood so hot I couldn't think straight, cut through me. I thought I was past the jealousy.

Yet somehow, knowing Jane hadn't forgotten about Skye made everything that little bit more complicated again. She hadn't moved on from Skye but she'd moved on from me. And I hated her for the latter.

Maybe I could've gotten over it if she hadn't moved on with my enemy's fucking son.

Screw whatever plans Jane had in motion. I was still coming for them all.

Silence filled the Porsche as my ex and her boyfriend's conversation drew to a halt. Lost in seething thoughts, it surprised me to realize I was almost at the small house I was renting in Glendale.

For now.

Sheila had agreed to my price, which meant I was moving to Silver Lake.

Shaking my head, I cursed how clammy and slick my palms felt against the wheel. I had to get my shit together. Sweaty palms were not the palms of a guy in control.

Look how far you've come, I tried to calm myself.

Never would I have imagined my book would become a runaway best seller, that I'd have the financial freedom to come to California and plan my vengeance.

Two years I'd been out.

Two years it had taken me to get to this point, and Jane Doe or Margot Higgins or whatever bullshit name she went by wouldn't stop me now.

Swinging the car into my drive, I noted the red Lotus parked on the street in front of the house.

Dakota.

Hoping that meant news, I parked my rental and eyed the Lotus as I got out. The driver's side door opened, and a long, gorgeous leg set off by a red stiletto appeared first. The rest of Dakota Jones followed it.

The tall, exceptionally built madam, wearing a tight dress, short on bottom but conservative on top, sashayed up the walk to the small porch. For once, I couldn't see *her*. I kept seeing Jane standing in that library.

Separated from everyone else.

Finding refuge in books.

Holding *my* book in her hand.

Still so fucking beautiful, just one look cut me off at the knees.

"You okay?" Dakota asked, yanking me back to the present.

I grunted and turned toward the front door, letting us inside.

"Drink?" I offered.

"Water if you have it."

The house was an open concept, and I could see Dakota settling into a leather armchair as I strode into the kitchen to get her bottled water from the fridge. I took one for myself, enjoying the chilled sweat on its surface. My skin burned; it had since seeing *her*.

Immersing myself in an ocean of cold water didn't sound so bad.

I handed Dakota her bottle and took the seat across from her. We watched one another in silence as we each took a swig.

Her intelligent blue eyes studied me. "You're on edge."

Jane's eyes, rounded with shock, filled my vision.

Those plump lips parted on a gasp.

Then I heard her whisper, "I love you, Ash."

Fury flooded me.

Trying to stem the tide of emotion, I waved at Dakota. "You got news?"

Dakota had been hired by Irwin Alderidge, a powerful man I saved and befriended in prison. He knew Dakota because she ran the most elite brothel in Los Angeles. And she owed Irwin. I didn't know why. It was none of my business. All I knew was that it must've been some debt for her to jeopardize her brothel's reputation for me.

If I were a better man, I wouldn't have put her in that position, but all I cared about was that her debt meant a chance to give Skye the justice she deserved. Dakota agreed to infiltrate Foster Steadman's wife's social circle. It took her three months. None of the morons realized Dakota wasn't the wife of a rich CEO. She *was* the rich CEO. If someone wanted to make money selling sex, there was no better or safer place to look than Dakota's. She took care of her people. No one fucked with a Dakota employee.

Getting close to Rita Steadman meant getting close to Foster. Dakota gained his trust enough to tell him about her brothel. He'd heard of it, of course. She'd opened the golden gates to him. VIP access. The bastard bit the bait and for the last six months, we'd been recording and filming him at the brothel. He liked the girls to play out a forced-seduction scenario. That was putting it politely.

"We're done," Dakota said. Her tone was ice. Firm. "He hurt one of my girls, which means he's banned. No exceptions. I also had Lucifer fuck him up enough to send a message. I don't care who he is."

That explained the conversation between Asher and Jane in the car about Steadman's black eye.

As disappointed and concerned as I was, I wished I'd been there to see that. Lucifer was one of Dakota's security guys—six foot seven and built like a Mack Truck.

"You have enough to ruin him, Griffin."

Not flinching at the name everyone but Irwin and Lorna used now, I shrugged. Like this didn't matter to me, when it mattered the most. "It isn't enough." What we had on Steadman could ruin his marriage and his social reputation, but how long would that last? He'd be back to making movies and money within weeks when some other scandal came along.

No, I needed evidence that would put him in prison.

"How bad was it?"

"He ... was trying to do something she didn't want to do. Lucifer heard her screaming down the hall."

Jesus Christ.

"We have it on tape. But, of course, my girl's face will be blurred out when we give it to you."

Which meant it might be useless in court. If no one wanted to step up and press charges, all it might do was ruin his rep. For a while. I wasn't going to manipulate anyone into testifying against the bastard, not after what he'd already put them through.

"She okay?"

Dakota's face softened. "She'll be fine."

What now? Where did I go from there? Rubbing the

strain between my brows, I let out a slow exhalation. Frustration didn't even cover how I felt.

"I could stay," Dakota offered in that soft, sexy voice. "Let you work out that pent-up anger you're not hiding very well tonight."

I considered it. Looking at her, watching as she got up and walked toward me. Feeling the heat curl in my gut as she lowered to her haunches in that tight dress and smoothed a hand up my hard thigh.

But instead of blue eyes, I saw hazel-green ones.

Instead of sweetheart lips, I saw a full, lush mouth.

Blond hair was replaced with hair the color of dark chocolate.

My fingers itched to reach out and touch ... but in my mind, I wouldn't be touching Dakota. "Not tonight."

The madam saw too much. She pressed a hand to my chest. "I know there's someone else in there. I've always known. That's not what we are. It's just sex, Griffin. Let me make you feel better."

Part of me wanted to say yes. To immerse myself in the fantasy. "No." I grabbed her wrist and gently removed it from my thigh. "When we've fucked, I've always been fucking you. I wouldn't be tonight. I may be a bastard, but I'm not asshole enough to fuck a woman while pretending she's someone else."

Dakota processed this, her lips pressed together. Finally, she nodded and stood. I stared at her, wondering if I should be a selfish dick. Take her offer. Burn off this writhing energy that was making my blood too hot.

She was older than me. Who knew by how much? Could be ten or twenty years. Her face was ageless, either due to good genes or an amazing plastic surgeon. It didn't matter. Her experience drew me to her. Good sex with no strings attached.

Yet, when she reached out, caressed my cheek in soft affection and said, "I worry about you, Griffin Stone," I knew I'd made the right decision. She was a good woman. Few people might think that, doing what she did, but I saw her heart. And I thought it was a good one. Much better than mine.

"Send me what you have."

She nodded and stepped back. "I'll send over the last tape once we've manipulated it. Along with the others."

Always taking care of her people.

"Are you going to drop them?" she asked. "I just want to know what I'm facing here."

"I won't fuck you over. I'm sending them to Rita Steadman and if that last tape doesn't make her want to leave the prick, I'll blackmail her. I'll tell her those tapes will go public. But I won't do it."

At least ... I didn't think I would.

I didn't want to screw over Dakota, but I wasn't sure what I was capable of anymore.

Dakota seemed assured, though, and left me to it.

When the front door closed behind her, I slumped against the armchair. I should think of my next move with Steadman. If I couldn't get anything out of him through Dakota's, then I needed another way in. I'd start with his personal life.

Wife, gone. And hopefully she'd take half of everything he had in the divorce.

What next, though?

Jane's voice whispered in my mind. "I love you, Ash."

I couldn't get *her* out of my head.

I needed her out of my head so I could concentrate.

Instead, I heard her whisper again. *"I love you so much, Jamie. Keep going. I want this."*

I groaned and closed my eyes. If I let myself, I could drown in the memories.

Chapter Eighteen

JANE

It was so hot, the asphalt within the studio lot had a haze over it. The air outside was dry and thick, causing sweat to bead across my skin. Despite the heat, I hurried across the lot with a fresh cup of hot coffee in my hand. Coffee was a necessity of life, after all.

Behind me was a massive hangar on a studio lot within the grounds of one of the six majors: Chimera Studios. Inside that hangar were several soundstages, with multiple sets I'd helped design for Patel's musical.

Butterflies flapped around like crazy in my belly as I hurried toward my car. I'd been at the lot since 5:00 a.m., making sure the sets were ready for the first day of filming the next day. Patel arrived not too long after, which surprised me considering he was probably hungover. It was just a pop-in visit to see how things were going.

Now that he was gone, I had an hour for lunch, and I was taking it before someone stopped me—

"Margot!" a voice called across the lot.

Damn.

I turned toward the hangar. Luke, Patel's PA, stood in the doorway waving me over. Grumbling under my breath, I hurried back across the lot and stepped inside. Sliding my sunglasses up into my hair, I smirked at the way Luke bounced on his feet as if readying to take off on his next mission. I swear to God, he made me feel old; the kid had so much energy.

"Sandy wants you."

Sandy was the production designer, Vale was the construction coordinator and Joe was the the head of the art department. Sandy and I worked closely together and delegated work to Vale and Joe.

Pushing aside my irritation, I nodded. "Where is he?"

"Second soundstage."

The first stage we passed was one of several sets for a prison interior. The fake prison felt pretty real as I walked past the visitors' room. It would. I'd helped design it based on my time spent in the visitation room at the state prison. It hadn't been easy working on that set. In fact, I'd fought back a lot of painful memories.

"Margot!" Sandy called from the second stage. It was bigger and hosted several prison cells. The production designer stood next to my assistant, Lea. "We've got this old poster of Kate Upton in Berrio's cell, but Leo says it should be in Pax's."

"It's Pax's!" I called back. "It was in Pax's this morning. What is it doing in Berrio's?" What the hell?

"Someone's been messing around with the set! They've moved things. I don't have time for this shit. Can you come over here and sort this out?"

"It's my lunch break. Lea knows what she's doing." I was all about giving my trust to the assistants in the art department, since that's where I'd started.

Sandy, not so much. "I want it done right."

Seeing Lea's wince, I narrowed my eyes on Sandy. "And Lea will do it right."

She brightened and gave me a grateful smile.

"But—"

"Not 'but,' Sandy. I have an amazing assistant who can fix this very minor issue. Now, if you don't mind, I've been here since five and I need sustenance. Lea, take care of this?"

"You got it, boss. I'll talk to the set dec. She should have the polaroids we took for continuity."

I winked at her, ignored Sandy's scowl, and turned on my heel to leave.

I wasn't the type to yell. I didn't boss people around; I delegated and asked politely. The only time I was less than polite was when someone gave me shit, but even then, I never yelled. I was always calm. In a room filled with lots of people, I was reserved. A little shy, even. Somehow, people always mistook these personality traits for timidity, perhaps even spinelessness.

I enjoyed proving them wrong.

The relief of getting in my car was great. I wasn't lying when I said I needed sustenance. But I also just needed a breather. Sleep failed me last night after I'd hallucinated Jamie.

Not hallucinated.

There was definitely a guy standing in that doorway last night. It just hadn't been Jamie.

Jamie was long gone from my life, and after what happened to him here, I doubt he'd ever return to LA.

Driving out of Studio City, I headed east through Toluca Lake, following the freeway toward Glendale. I lived in Silver Lake now, but memories were pulling me home.

When would Glendale stop being home?

When would someplace else finally *feel* like home?

Would it ever?

I shrugged off my melancholy and concentrated on finding a parking spot several blocks from the Brand.

Brand Boulevard was so familiar to me, but I hadn't visited in at least two years. My favorite panini place was still there, so I stopped in to grab a bite to eat, to fill the empty, nauseating hole in my gut. While I people watched, I was too aware of the time. It was fifteen-minute drive to the lot and I only had half an hour left on my break. I considered where to go before heading back.

It hit me as soon as I stepped out onto the sidewalk.

Years ago, Jamie and I would come here and hang out at Brand Bookshop. It closed about a year after he went to prison, not long after Lorna passed along his letter. The one that shattered me.

However, Asher had mentioned there was a big-chain bookstore in Americana, the mall. So that's where I headed. I took the long way around, following the path along the edge of the large musical, dancing fountain. I winced at the sight of the large, gold-plated sculpture of a mostly-naked man. It was a recasting of the famous D-Day sculpture, "The Spirit of American Youth Rising from the Waves," by Donald Harcourt. There were water jets circling the sculpture and now and then they'd come to life around it.

One of my favorite photos was of me and Jamie standing in front of that sculpture, the jets of water rising behind us. Skye had taken it not long after we'd started dating. Jamie had his arm around me. While I beamed at the camera, still giddy with disbelief that Jamie was mine, he stared down at me with a look of adoration.

I'd teased him about it, but I secretly loved his expression.

The photo was still tucked away inside a shoebox in my closet.

Picking up my pace, I strode around the fountain and headed toward the bookstore. The store was air-conditioned, and that was always welcome on a day like today. I breezed past the coffee shop on the first level and took in the space. It was huge, three levels, with escalators. I searched for signs for the mystery section and made my way toward it. However, as I casually strolled, scanning all the aisle signs, a table in the center of the first floor caught my eye.

A sign on the table read SIGNED COPIES.

And sitting on a section of it were two upright books facing outward.

Brent 29.

Signed.

And there were only two copies left.

I hurried over to the table and snatched up the crisp hardback edition. The booklover in me felt a heady rush of happiness welcome on a day I felt melancholy.

"You know, we only put these out this morning and they're already nearly gone," the cashier said as she rang up the signed edition. "We thought putting them out on a Sunday might give people a chance to get one, but word of mouth seems to have spread."

"It's because he won't do a tour," her colleague butted in. "No one knows what the guy looks like. A hermit or something. Signed copies will fly out the door when they come in."

"Who says he's a guy?" the other girl argued, handing over my copy and receipt.

I thanked her and left them bickering over the sexual identity of Griffin Stone.

Personally, I believed he was a guy. Maybe because his writing reminded me so much of Jamie's.

Once outside the store, I pressed back against the shop window and cracked open the hardback. There on the title page was the same autograph I'd seen in Patel's copy. Except my copy had a handwritten quote from the author too.

My favorite quote from the book.

I smiled to myself, delighted.

Suddenly, a shadow cast over the page, and I realized someone had come to a stop beside me.

Invading my personal space.

Frowning, I glanced up.

Then my stomach dropped, as though I'd just plunged down the Big Dipper on a roller coaster. Staring down at me, ocean eyes flat beneath his moody brow, was Jamie McKenna.

I *had* seen him last night.

My pulse rushed in my ears, and my whole body shook. "Jamie?"

His expressionless gaze flicked down to the book I now clutched to my chest, as if it were a life float. "It surprises me—"

I gasped at the sound of his deep, rumbling, familiar voice, with the East Coast accent he'd never fully rid himself of.

"—that a woman like you would enjoy a novel that traverses the dark forest of abiding love."

His words barely penetrated. I couldn't stop staring at him.

I wanted to reach out and touch him.

It had been so long since I'd done that.

In that moment, I forgot our last meeting. I forgot how he'd made me bleed inside. I reached for him. "Jamie—"

He flinched, the blank expression gone in a blaze of fury. He glowered in disbelief, and my hand dropped limply at my side.

In that moment, he reminded me of a wounded animal.

How could that be?

He wasn't the one whose heart had been broken.

"What are you doing here?" My voice was barely above a whisper.

Yet he heard me. His lips pinched together, and my eyes dropped to them. Longing coursed through me in an agonizing wave, and I hated myself for it. Dragging my gaze back up to his eyes, I saw something calculating in them.

"What are you doing here?" I was louder now. Attempting to sound in control.

Jamie smirked, as though he knew better.

He probably did.

The bastard.

"It's not safe for you to be here, Jamie." I might despise him for hurting me, but I still ... Jesus Christ, I still needed to protect him.

His eyes flashed dangerously as he bent his head toward mine. My breath caught and held as his scent flooded me. Jamie smelled different, I realized. When we were younger, he always smelled citrusy. Now, there was a hint of that, but something darker, earthier ... almost like lime drenched in leather and tobacco. "Is that a threat?" he purred.

My lashes fluttered and I took a wary step back.

Was this happening? Was he really here?

"It wasn't a threat."

"No?" His cheek brushed mine, and I shivered involuntarily as he pressed his lips to my ear. "Well, this is."

I tried to pull away, but he gripped my biceps tight, holding me in place so he could whisper, "'A love that consumes, consumes everything unto utter desolation.'"

It was my favorite quote from *Brent 29*.

"When I'm done with you, there won't be anything left." He pulled back and gave me a benign smile that was an unsettling contrast to his threat. "I'll be seeing you."

Then he was gone.

And I felt like I might be sick.

"A love that consumes, consumes everything unto utter desolation."

Oh my God.

Pushing away from the store window, I looked left and

right to see if I could find him. Jamie had disappeared in the crowds. But my suspicion grew, and I needed to know if I was right.

My lunch break was almost over, but I didn't care. Instead, I took the Glendale freeway to my rental in Silver Lake. Sliding into my allocated parking spot, I clutched my signed book to my chest and charged toward the main door, hitting the entry code. My feet pounded upstairs to the second floor, where I fumbled with my key as I hurried into my one-bedroom apartment. Marching into my bedroom/art studio, I thrust open the closet door at the rear of the room and dug through my art supplies until I found the shoebox I stored my keepsakes in.

Dropping the hardback, I hauled out the box and threw it open. Digging to the very bottom, I found the letter I'd kept, even though I should've thrown it away years ago.

Masochist that I was, I couldn't let it go.

Fingers shaking, I grabbed the paper and unfolded it flat as I opened *Brent 29* and held the letter against the inscription and autograph on the book.

"A love that consumes, consumes everything unto utter desolation." Griffin Stone.

Jamie had appeared outside the store before I could pay much attention to the handwriting.

Now I could see it.

"Oh my God." I sank back on my heels.

The handwriting matched.

Jamie was the mystery author. Griffin Stone.

Of course, he was. Perhaps, deep down inside, I'd even hoped he was.

"When I'm done with you, there won't be anything left."

He still blamed me. Still hated me. Still saw a faithless girl instead of the girl he'd loved.

He wanted to hurt me.

Tears of outrage spilled down my cheeks, sobs escaping me

to release the pain. Skye had been right all along. She worried that our love was too much and that when it ended, it would destroy us.

I laughed bitterly. It *had* almost destroyed me.

And now he wanted to take away what I'd salvaged from the ruins.

Rage burned through my grief.

If he planned to punish me for my supposed crimes, let him try. I would not take his shit lying down.

If he was no longer Jamie McKenna, I was no longer Jane Doe.

I was Margot Higgins, and he was Griffin Stone.

Enemies.

Here lies Jamie and Jane, I thought. *Once upon a time, they adored each other to distraction.*

RIP, sweet lovers.

Chapter Nineteen

JANE

As I DOTTED a little white against the tip of a petal, I heard a soft curse from my left. It reminded me I'd been too close to my painting for a while now. It was time to look at it from a new point of view.

Putting the paintbrush down, I cracked my neck and arched my back, groaning at how stiff they both were. "What are you cursing at?" I said through a yawn as I slipped off the stool.

I flicked a look at Asher before striding away from the painting.

He stretched out on my bed, glowering at the phone in his hand. When he glanced up from it, his dark eyes glittered with irritation. "My parents' divorce has found its way onto the gossip rags."

I winced. Guilt pricked me. As much as it delighted me that Rita Steadman had decided to divorce Foster Steadman, I felt bad for Asher. Not that he wasn't happy to see his mom break away from his father, but he was concerned about Rita.

They'd only just told him last night. How the hell was it online already?

"Mom doesn't need this shit." He shook his head in frustration. "Those bastards don't care, as long as people hit their clickbait or buy their fucking magazines."

"She'll be okay. I promise. She'll be better than okay. And hey, at least she's no longer in the dark about Foster. To some extent."

"I'm not sure I'm happy about that."

I knew it was hard for Asher. He'd spent most of his teenage and young adult years protecting his mother from the truth about her husband. Someone had decided enough was enough, however. And I had a feeling I knew who that person was—hence my guilt.

Someone had anonymously sent Rita footage and images of Foster screwing young, pretty things at a swanky LA brothel. She wanted a divorce, and Foster wasn't going to contest it because he didn't want anyone to find out about the brothel visits.

"I have to find out who sent those tapes before my father does."

I glanced guiltily away.

Jamie.

He was back for revenge. That's what my gut told me.

"I can't have this person out there doing whatever they like. They could destroy my mom."

It wasn't even on the tip of my tongue to tell Asher my suspicions, which made me the worst best friend in the world. Why was I still protecting Jamie McKenna? Or was I protecting myself? If I'd told Asher sooner about Jamie, he could've prepared for something like this.

Jamie had reemerged in my life a week ago, and I still

hadn't told Asher about it. Despite Jamie's threat, I didn't want Foster Steadman to discover what Jamie was up to.

"Things will be okay," I promised as I squinted at my painting.

"Yeah, I guess I should just concentrate on being happy that he'll be out of her life soon." He paused. "You happy with it?"

Looking at him in confusion, I found him staring at the painting. Realizing what he meant, I nodded. Yeah, I was satisfied with the second layer. "Time to put the resin on. Which means I need to put the varnish on first. I know how you love the smell."

"Is that your subtle way of telling me to leave?" He sat up on the bed.

"Like I would." I pretended to be affronted by the idea.

Instead of playing along, Asher narrowed his eyes. "You know I know there's something going on with you, right?"

Asher, I should say, *Jamie's back and he hates me. He hates me because he blames me for everything that happened. And he hates me because of you.*

Despite what Jamie thought, and what the world thought, Asher was just my best friend. We became friends over three years ago. By accident. I'd gotten an invitation to a party at Foster Steadman's home. I had no strategy, but I'd naively hoped some great master plan would come to me when I got within touching distance of the bastard.

Instead, upon seeing Foster, I was sick to my stomach. Skye's voice, her words, filled my head, and tears had swum in my eyes. Until that moment, I had never considered myself to be a violent person, but I'd wanted to claw Foster Steadman's face off.

I'd followed him as he left the main area of the party and watched him and his son disappear into a private room. Eavesdropping, I'd overheard Foster verbally ripping Asher to shreds. No parent should ever say what he said to his son that night. While they argued, I found my way to Steadman's office and ransacked it.

It was Asher who caught me. He was furious to find me there.

Frightened he would call the police, I'd taken a risk, thinking about what I'd heard between him and his dad. I'd told him the truth. I'd told him everything.

To both of our surprise, we formed a connection.

And it turned out he already knew about his father. He'd witnessed the cover-ups.

Asher wanted to bring his father to justice, even if it meant damaging his family's reputation. He was a good man. Together, we'd tried to bring Foster down, but we couldn't find any solid evidence to do so. We'd descended into minor sabotage, which left us both feeling hollow, just half-hearted attempts because Asher couldn't be pushed, and I, despite what I wanted, didn't want to push my friend.

We ruined a relationship between Foster and his favorite mistress by sending her photographs of Foster visiting the same well-known, high-end brothel depicted in the photos Rita received. We also leaked a script that he'd wanted to buy to his competitor, who then outbid him. And Asher played a game of telephone to recommend a crappy investment that lost Foster a million dollars.

I knew Asher was finally ready to drop the ax on his father, but all the seedier stuff amounted to rumors at this point. As Asher had explained to me many times, none of the girls were willing to talk. Foster had paid them off, and they were afraid of jeopardizing their careers. That's what they said. But I knew they were also afraid no one would believe them. I knew because that's how *she* felt.

Tears burned in my eyes.

"I'm worried about you," Asher said. "I know there's something else going on."

I should just tell Asher about Jamie. To let go of all the pain his faithlessness had caused. It was eating at me. A festering wound. A scream I couldn't let go. Because if I did, if I told Asher, he would tell me to tell Jamie the truth. He'd give up his secret for me.

Asher would tell me it was unhealthy to hold a grudge against Jamie. To deliberately withhold the truth. To be at war with him when I didn't have to be. To keep causing him pain in return for the hurt he'd inflicted when he broke up with me.

I didn't want that from Asher.

I was already constantly arguing with my conscience.

But the hurt Jamie had caused was too great.

"I'm worried about you, that's all." I avoided his question with a truth.

"I'll be fine. If this person wasn't out there knowing shit about my family he or she shouldn't know, I'd be dancing a jig right now that my mother is leaving my father." He sighed and stood up. "I'm going to let you get on with the varnishing."

"I'll walk you out."

We strolled through the apartment, making plans to meet up after work tomorrow. I hated the worry darkening my friend's expression.

He turned to me before I opened the door. "I don't care anymore about what *he* thinks. What the world thinks. Now that Mom is out from under his influence, I think—no, I know—things will be okay between me and her. And that's all that matters."

Surprised by the random turn of conversation, I raised a questioning eyebrow.

"What I'm trying to say is, we don't have to make people

think we're dating anymore. It's unnecessary. And maybe you could start *actually* dating."

The thought of no longer hiding behind Asher as an excuse was scary. I didn't want to admit that to him, though. Not knowing what to say, I was dazed as Asher opened my front door. Realizing he was just trying to be a good friend, even as all this craziness was happening to him, affection filled me. I pulled him back for a hug.

Asher's arms tightened around me.

"What would I do without you, huh?"

"You'll never have to know," I promised him.

As we pulled back, he brushed his thumb over my cheek.

"Show me the dimple," he demanded.

I grinned as his thumb caressed the hollow in my cheek, but the sound of a woman's giggle drew my attention from Asher.

We both turned toward the sound coming from the apartment across the hall.

Oh my God.

Pressed against the doorjamb of the open apartment door was a tall blond. A very familiar, gorgeous guy crushed his body against hers as he kissed her.

There was a moment where I forgot the last seven years had happened.

And all I saw was the man I loved kissing another woman.

No ... devouring her.

Jealousy, outrage, and pain were my foremost emotions. They made my skin hot, my chest ache, and my throat painfully thick.

But then Jamie released the woman. Despite the passionate kiss, his expression was blank, unaffected. "Thanks, gorgeous. We're done here. Leave."

With crashing reality, I remembered this wasn't Jamie

from my past. This was Griffin Stone. My Jamie would never talk to a woman like that.

And what the hell was he doing in the apartment across from mine?

The blond was breathing fast and shallow. She scowled, confused. "Your mood swings are giving me a migraine."

"Then go see a doctor."

"Asshole." She huffed and pushed off the jamb. She faltered when she saw Asher and me, a red stain flushing her cheeks, before she disappeared downstairs. The sound of her heels clattering against the concrete steps echoed up to us. I gazed incredulously at Jamie.

He stared back.

"Uh. Hey," Asher said, breaking the strained tension. He strode toward Jamie, pulling me along with him. Holding out his hand, he said, "Are you new to the building?"

To my shock, Jamie shook his hand. "I am. I'm Griffin. Are you my neighbors?"

"Ja—Margot is." Asher faltered on my name and gave me an apologetic smile. "I'm her friend, Asher."

"Asher, good to meet you." Jamie held out his hand to me. "Margot."

There was a smug understanding in his eyes as he looked at me. He knew I hadn't told Asher about him. Realizing Asher would figure out something was going on if I didn't shake Jamie's hand, I hesitated before letting him touch me.

A shiver skated down my spine as his warm, strong fingers enveloped mine.

Memories washed over me as we held each other's gazes.

Kisses and hugs and soft laughter in the dark.

Jamie's grip tightened ever so slightly before he dropped my hand like a hot potato. "Nice to meet you."

"Yeah, you too," I muttered. I turned to Asher. "I'll see you later." I caressed his arm in affection and then tried to walk calmly back to my apartment. Thankfully, I could hear Asher and Jamie saying goodbye before I closed myself back in my apartment.

What the hell was he doing here?

Was this part of a sick plan to torment me?

Limbs trembling, I moved distractedly back into my bedroom and heard my phone beep. Grabbing it off my dresser, I saw it was a text from Asher.

> Holy hot chemistry. He forgot that blond as soon as he saw you. xx

The blond. I practically hissed.

That fucker. How many women had he had since he got out of prison?

I couldn't bear to let anyone that close to me again, and he'd gone back to his old ways. Except worse. My Jamie, even before we dated, didn't treat women like they were disposable.

I texted Asher back.

> He forgot that blond while he was still kissing her. Yuck. No thanks. xx

I stared dully at my painting. My creative mood had left the building, under the weight of the many questions going around and around in my head. Adrenaline made it hard for me to sit still. Cursing Jamie under my breath, I grabbed my laundry basket and headed toward the front door. Peering through the peephole, I double-checked his door was shut before I left my apartment. Glowering at his door as I passed, I hurried downstairs. How the hell had he maneuvered himself into my building? And why?

What was he planning?

And did he really think I was just going to sit around and wait to see what he'd come up with?

To my gratitude, the laundry room was empty as I crashed around inside it. I hauled out my stash of detergent and softener from my allocated locker and started separating my whites. That rat bastard. My heart raced, sweat gathered under my arms, and it agitated me. An encounter with Jamie was the equivalent of fifteen shots of caffeine.

And I hated that he knew I was lying to Asher. Something he could easily hold over my head.

"You are a very angry laundry doer."

Jamie's deep, rich voice startled me. Trying to control my breathing, I glared over at him standing in the doorway. Arms and ankles crossed as he leaned casually against the jamb. He wore a T-shirt and jeans. Nothing had changed there.

He was still the sexiest man I'd ever seen.

God, I hate him.

"What the hell are you doing in this building?" I turned my back on him, marching over to the stacked washers and dryers.

"I had no idea you lived here," he lied, his voice growing closer as he crossed the room toward me.

Attempting not to react physically, to not hunch my shoulders in tension, I stared unseeing at the machines. What was I in the middle of doing again?

"What a surprise to find out you're my neighbor."

I snorted in disbelief and turned around, shocked to find him already in my personal space. "Liar." I dragged my gaze insolently down his body and back up. "Move away. And I mean that in more ways than one."

"Oh, does my presence bother you?" His wicked smile caused somersaults in my belly.

"What are you doing here?" I ignored his proximity. Okay, I *tried* to ignore his proximity.

In answer, he stepped into me and I stumbled against the machines at my back. Jamie pressed the palms of his hands on the dryer, caging me in. My breath caught and held as his scent flooded me. That dark, earthy scent was enticing, and my body betrayed my emotions.

Feeling panic rise, I pushed at his chest, but he wouldn't budge. "Jamie?"

Those ocean eyes wandered over my face, cold, calculating. "He doesn't know who I am. You haven't told him."

I lowered my hands. Touching him was even more discombobulating. "No."

He bent his head toward mine until our noses almost touched. I sucked in a breath. "I wonder why you're keeping it from him?"

Determined not to let him see how much he affected me, I glared up at him. He'd only have to touch me, hold my hand, to realize I was trembling. His face was so familiar. His lips were lips I'd thought I'd kiss for the rest of my life. Why did the pain of it never dull? Why did it still feel like a shard of glass through my chest? "Did you leak those tapes of Foster Steadman to Asher's mom?"

Something menacing flashed in his eyes before he banked it. "And if I did?"

"Are you being smart, Jamie?"

"Are you asking out of concern for me or for your billionaire boy toy?"

"Jamie."

"Never mind. I don't care." The bastard dipped his nose to my throat, and I tensed against the stacked machines. He inhaled, his nose brushing my skin, and my fingers bit into the washer behind me. "You smell different," he whispered, lifting his head to my ear. "Expensive perfume. You've come up in the world."

I felt his breath caress my skin seconds before his teeth touched my earlobe. Gasping, I instinctively pushed my palms against his stomach as he bit down hard, causing a flush of heat between my legs.

With a dark chuckle, Jamie released my ear after one last nibble and whispered, "Is he the jealous type, Jane? Would it bother him to see you with me, knowing I'm the first man who ever slid his dick into you?"

My body reacted to his words in opposition to my mind. While my skin flushed and heat pooled low in my belly, I despised him for throwing me away and then losing all faith in me. For talking to me like this. And that war between my physical desire and my emotions made me hate him even more. I wanted to tear him up.

"Does he know how you like it?" His voice was thick now, hoarse, and he leaned the length of his strong body into mine, pushing me into the machines at my back. I could feel him. Throbbing. Hard. My breath skittered and my fingers curled into the cotton fabric of his T-shirt. "Does he know sweet, shy, Jane Doe loves a good, hard fucking as much as gentle lovemaking? That when the mood takes you, you like to be tied up, held down ..." Jamie trailed his lips across my flushed cheek and brushed them against my mouth. "And fucked until you scream?"

Memories assailed me. Memories of our youthful adventures in sex. How together, we were open to anything. How exciting it had been to explore that side of ourselves with someone who made us feel safe and loved.

"Does he know you like to be fucked in public places?"

I shivered, remembering the hottest sex we ever had in a restroom at the theater.

"Does he hold you all night long, just the way you like?" Jamie trailed his fingertips along my collarbone, gentle, caressing. Almost loving. "Does he keep his dick buried inside you while you sleep like I did? How many nights did you want that from me? How you needed me to stay inside you, connected."

Tears burned in my throat.

I'd been desperate for him. Wanted him to never leave me. To hold me always.

No one had held me in such a long time. Not like that.

Not since him.

I glared at his throat, half of me wanting to lick it and the other to rip it out with my teeth.

"Nothing to say?" He pressed a soft kiss to the side of my neck, one hand sliding down the curve of my waist to rest on my hip. He squeezed it. "Huh?"

Did it hurt him to be near me like it hurt me to be near him?

Was this causing him pain, or did he only find pleasure in trying to humiliate me, trying to make me feel guilty about Asher?

The dark ugliness he woke in me spread upward, searching for release. I turned my head toward his ear and whispered, "He likes it when I cry out his name." I pressed a kiss to his jaw and curled my hand around the wrist of his hand resting on my hip. My nails dug into his skin as I undulated against his hard body. "Asher," I groaned and felt Jamie stiffen. "Oh, Asher, yes, harder ... Oh, Asher, I love you."

Jamie slammed his hand hard against the dryer beside my head, and I flinched. He glared balefully down at me, hatred pouring out of him.

Yeah, pal, the feeling is mutual.

He bared his teeth before he opened his mouth to speak and then snapped it shut. Pushing off the dryer and out of my space, the tension in my body deflated a little as Jamie retreated. Then he chuckled. A harsh, unhappy sound. His expression was mock impressed, his voice hoarse as he said, "Baby Doe knows how to play the game. Good." Malice glittered in his eyes. "Wouldn't want you to make this easy for me."

Turning on his heel, he strode out of the laundry room and called over his shoulder, "See you soon, neighbor."

It was a threat.

Shuddering, indignation built inside me.

When Jamie broke up with me in that letter, I thought I'd never get over it. If it hadn't been for my friend Cassie's no-nonsense approach to seeing me through my heartache—i.e. refusing to let me lie in a dark room alone for months like I wanted to—I might never have moved on.

But I'd gotten on with my life because there was no other option.

It occurred to me, despite how shaken I was by his presence, I wasn't panicking. I wasn't anxious. No. I felt like fighting.

I'd been dealt so many blows in my twenty-six years on this planet, I'd developed an undetectable armor. People didn't realize it even existed until they tried to push me too far.

Did Jamie really think I would just sit back and let him come at me?

No way.

Jamie was back in LA to make Steadman pay. And clearly, I was also a target.

However, I wouldn't sit on defense and wait for him to come get me.

It was time to go on the offense.

And I knew just where to start.

Chapter Twenty

JAMIE

Opening our apartment doors at the same time had just been nice timing.

Candice showed up at the apartment on behalf of Dakota. I'd met Dakota's cousin at a party a few weeks ago, and she'd made it clear she'd like to "get to know me better." Her appearance at my new apartment with the last of the Steadman tapes pissed me off.

I didn't trust Candice. I didn't want her in my business.

It was clear, however, from what she had to say, that she didn't have a clue what was on those tapes. I wondered why Dakota hadn't brought me the tapes herself, but it didn't matter.

The tapes I'd already sent to Rita Steadman, along with my blackmail note, had done the job. The Steadmans' divorce was all over the internet. Before I ushered Candice out of the apartment I was subletting at a ridiculous price to be close to dear Jane, the madam's cousin had thrown herself at me.

I'd not so politely declined.

Then, just as I opened the door for her to leave, I saw Asher and Jane in her doorway, looking so cozy and in love, I could've knocked Asher into Timbuktu and it still wouldn't have been far enough out of my sight.

On impulse, I'd kissed Candice.

And I'd impressively held my shit together when I shook that son of a bitch's hand.

Yet even so, despite all my maneuvering, Jane had gotten one up on me in that laundry room.

"Oh, Asher, yes, harder ... Oh, Asher, I love you."

I took the stairs two at a time, hurrying back to my apartment, heart hammering in my chest. The taste of her skin still lingered on my tongue, her scent thick in my nose.

Note to self: corner Jane and her goddamn claws come out.

Yet my body throbbed with need.

You could cut someone out of your heart, but apparently, the dick wanted what the dick wanted. Curling my lip in outrage, feeling hot blood fill my cock as the image of fucking Jane in that laundry room filled my head, I made a decision.

I'd have her again.

I'd screw her until I'd had my fill. Fuck her out of my system.

It was just another way to insinuate myself into her life. Because once I knew her again, knew what mattered most to her, I would rip it away.

Taking a calming breath, I sat down on the couch, put in earphones, and turned on the recordings from the device I'd had planted in Asher Steadman's car.

I still hadn't found anything incriminating and neither had my PI. This morning, Asher had driven to Jane's, listening to the radio the whole time. Settling back on the couch, I listened to Steadman in his car now. Just the hum of the road filled the headphones. Not even a radio this time. *Well, this is boring.*

A minute or so later, however, I heard the ringing of a phone, and then a man's voice I didn't recognize filled the car.

"Asher, is there a problem?"

"Do you have time for a quick phone session?" Asher asked.

"Well, uh, yes, I can do that. I have an appointment in fifteen minutes, though. What can I help you with today?"

"Did you see the news, Dr. Jensen?"

"I can't say that I have."

"My parents are getting divorced. They told me last night. My mother found out about the brothel."

I frowned and got up, moving over to my laptop to open the digital folder of information I had on Asher.

"I see. You're worried about her?"

Clicking through the files, I found the report from the PI that stated Asher visited a building on Wilshire Boulevard in Beverly Hills every second Wednesday. Dr. Jensen was his therapist.

"I think the divorce is good. I'm glad she knows some truth now. But someone sent her tapes of my father at that brothel. Someone's been watching him."

"And how does that make you feel?"

"Concerned about my mother's safety. What she would go through if those tapes went public."

Now I was really confused. Wasn't Asher in cahoots with Jane? I thought they were trying to bring down Steadman together.

"I can assume you haven't been able to share those exact worries with Jane."

I tensed. Dr. Jensen knew about Jane.

"No. But I still have her support."

"At our last session, you said that you would tell Jane the truth. Does this mean you're not ready to do that?"

What truth?

"I can't. Not yet. She wouldn't understand. I have to wait … until certain things come to fruition. I need her in my life and without being able to explain fully just yet, I might lose her."

"Remember, Asher, the longer you wait, the greater chance of you pushing Jane away when the truth comes out."

"I'm protecting her."

"Deliberately sabotaging her attempts to find evidence that may incriminate your father is protecting her?" The doc's tone was neutral. No judgment.

Me? I was judging.

A grin crawled across my face.

"Whether you agree or disagree with Jane's methods, you're pretending to support her in her plans. You might not realize it, Asher, but this lie is causing you a great amount of stress. Considering this latest development, we need to find ways to reduce your stress."

I'd stopped listening.

"Deliberately sabotaging her attempts to find evidence that may incriminate your father is protecting her?"

"Whether you agree or disagree with Jane's methods, you're pretending to support her in her plans."

If Asher Steadman meant as much to Jane as I suspected he did, I'd just found something important to rip away from her.

Chapter Twenty-One

JANE

It was almost too easy.

Well, it would have been if I hadn't been worried Jamie would find out and blame Ivy.

Ivy Martin was our building manager and had been for thirty years.

Her office was across the hall from her apartment on the ground floor, and I had to wait for Jamie to leave his apartment until I could make my move. Standing by the peephole of my apartment door for hours was not a fun way to spend my Sunday afternoon, but I was determined to find some information that would put me ahead of Jamie's plans.

He left around three o'clock, about four hours since he'd tormented me in the laundry room, and I waited until I saw him drive his Porsche out of his parking spot before going downstairs.

Sometimes Ivy wasn't in her office on Sundays, but I was pleasantly surprised to see the door open and the building manager standing over her desk reading through some papers. Probably notes left by my neighbors on things they wanted fixed. It was an old building—the place kept Ivy busy.

I rapped my knuckles on the open door and Ivy glanced over at me.

In her midsixties, Ivy looked like a spry woman in her late forties. She told me it was the California sun, yoga, and drinking plenty of water that kept her looking young. It wasn't often you came across a female building manager, but Ivy used to work with her dad in construction, so she learned skills across a variety of trades from the age of five. That woman could fix anything.

Turning her twinkling dark eyes on me, she lifted her chin in greeting.

"Margot, problem?"

I moved into the room and gave her a pained smile. "Ivy, I'm so sorry, but I locked myself out of my apartment when I went to the laundry room. Can you let me back in with your spare?"

"Of course, no problem." She dropped the papers in her hand and moved to the locked cabinet where she kept the spare keys. I moved around her, so she was the one nearest to the door, and leaned into peer at the photos above her desk. "Is that you?" I pointed to a washed-out photo of a beautiful woman in an old-fashioned bikini, standing in front of a lake with her arms wrapped around a handsome guy in swim shorts. "And Mal?"

Mal was Ivy's husband. He'd passed away two months after I moved into the building.

Ivy gave me a soft smile as she unlocked the cabinet, throwing the doors wide.

Thank you, Ivy.

"That's my Mal. Our fifth anniversary at Lake Tahoe."

"Good-looking couple," I said.

"Thank you, doll. I was a very lucky woman. My Mal was even more gorgeous on the inside."

My heart squeezed, feeling a prickle of envy and a sting of grief for her. I knew what it was like to lose the one you loved. Guilt accompanied those feelings.

Unfortunately, guilt didn't stop me. As she unhooked my key off its hook, I jumped, pretending to be startled as I gaped at the open doorway. "Was that a dog?"

"What?" Ivy turned.

I snatched the keys next to the empty hook where mine had hung and hid my hand behind my back, the metal biting into my fingers. Sweat dampened my palms. "A dog. I just saw a dog run past."

"Are you sure?" Ivy looked back at me.

"Absolutely."

She sighed heavily. There was a strict no-pet policy for this building. "I'll let you into your apartment and then look for it." Her eyes trained on the hall outside as she locked the key cabinet.

I'd gotten away with it.

I couldn't believe it.

"Now you're sure?" she asked me again as we left her office.

"I'm positive."

"I bet it's that girl on four," Ivy muttered under her breath. "First she smuggles in a cat. Now a goddamn dog."

Trying not to laugh while feeling bad at the same time made me slightly hysterical. I had to stifle my snorts of guilty amusement as Ivy let me into my apartment. I thanked her, went inside, and hid behind my door, waiting for her to leave.

As soon as the coast was clear, I shot across the hall to Jamie's apartment.

My heart was pounding so fast, I could barely hear anything else over the rushing blood in my ears.

Hands shaking, I let myself into his unit and closed the door behind me with a soft snick.

His place was just like mine. Open living and kitchen area, with a large bedroom and bathroom off a narrow hallway at the rear. I'd half expected to find a wall of the living room covered in papers and pictures and timeline arrows. You know, like a stalker wall.

Unfortunately, it wasn't that straightforward.

In fact, the apartment was depressingly bare and piled with opened boxes. Rummaging through them, I found a lot of books. Either Jamie hadn't found time to unpack, or he had no intention of doing so considering this was a temporary situation. To torment me.

Growling under my breath, I ripped open another box and stilled at what I found inside. Lifting out a pristine hardback, I turned it over in my hand, feeling a rush of longing.

He had copies of *Brent 29*.

Despite all the shit that had happened to him, he'd made his dream come true. He was a published author. Not just any author either, but a huge best seller. There was a small kernel of Jane from the past who was proud of him. The percentage of authors who achieved what he'd achieved was probably less than 1 percent.

Sighing, I put the copy back.

"Not why you're here," I muttered as I stood and moved toward the desk at the back of the room. The drawers held receipts. That was it.

I glared at his laptop.

Everything I wanted to know was probably on there.

Then my eyes moved to the pile of paper sitting beside the laptop, and my breath caught at the text printed across the middle of the top piece.

DOE

A novel by Griffin Stone

I lifted the top few pages to discover it was a printout of a new manuscript. From the red pen and notes scrawled on the pages, it was obviously copy edits for the book. Considering the title, the urge to read the pages was overwhelming.

However, I'd never read something Jamie didn't want me to.

Even if the title was my surname.

Ignoring the belly butterflies, I placed the pages back in order and slipped into Jamie's computer chair to flip open the laptop. The password box appeared. A memory came flooding back from when we lived together. Jamie's passwords for everything were so complicated that he kept them all written in a little black notebook.

Pulling open the drawers, I rummaged through them, searching.

Nothing.

I moved into the kitchen and raided those drawers.

No luck.

The only place left was the bedroom, and I'd really been hoping to avoid it. I nearly walked into a dark red boxing bag that hung from the ceiling.

Jamie boxed?

The image of him doing just that made me shiver with longing. Another reason to hate him. Jamie's smell hit me as I moved around the bag. That new, darker scent of his. Curiosity drew me into the bathroom, and I opened the cabinet above the sink. The bottle of cologne sat on the top shelf; I brought it to my nose.

Yup.

That was Jamie's new scent. Except, not quite. His own personal scent signature changed the cologne slightly, so it was even sexier on him. Jamie never used to wear cologne. Just body wash.

Putting the bottle back, I returned to the bedroom. There

was a bed, bedside cabinets, and a dresser. Remembering Jamie always slept on the right, I targeted that bedside cabinet first.

Sliding the drawer open, my heart leapt in triumph.

Bingo. I pulled out the small black notebook and was about to open it when my attention was caught by what had been underneath it.

An ache scored across my chest as I picked up the small stack of photos.

Skye and Jamie.

Jamie, Skye, and Lorna.

Five photos of them at different stages of their lives.

It was the final photo that made me slump down on the bed in confusion.

It was a photo of me on my own, one of a bunch Skye had taken with her phone and printed later. I was sitting down, my elbow on a bench table, my chin resting in my palm, and I was laughing at the person behind the camera—Skye. My eyes were bright, my dimple creased my left cheek, and I looked happy.

I caressed the image with my fingertips, tears burning in my eyes.

I couldn't remember the last time I was that happy.

Remembering the day it was taken, I choked down building emotion. I was seventeen, and Skye and Lorna and I had spent a girls' day at Disneyland. I'd had a secret that day.

Jamie.

We were seeing each other in secret, and despite our secrecy, I was in heaven. In love. Excited for the future.

Why did Jamie have this picture? Why did he keep it?

After he had Lorna deliver his letter to me, she'd packed up his stuff and put it in storage. I'd have thought she would have destroyed all evidence of my existence, but this photo must have escaped her.

And Jamie had kept it.

If someone didn't love you anymore, if someone did, in fact, hate you, why would they hold on to a photograph like this? Why would they keep it close?

Deciding I didn't have time to ponder the complex nature of Jamie's feelings toward me, I shoved the photos back in the drawer and tried to force them out of my mind. Back at his desk, I flipped through his little black book, ignoring a few phone numbers written beside women's names, until I found his password list.

There was one password that didn't have any information next to it, and I guessed this was his main one.

I guessed correctly.

Shaking with anticipation and the knowledge that what I was doing was not only very wrong but illegal, I made my way through the folders on his desktop. The curious bookworm in me wanted to read his works in progress, novels and short stories, but if I could refrain from reading *Doe*, I could refrain from reading those too.

I groaned at that realization, eyeing the manuscript I wanted to steal but knew I wouldn't.

Finally, I came across a folder titled *The Count of Monte Cristo*. Frowning, I clicked on it and my breath caught.

Laughing under my breath, I shook my head. "Jamie, you sneaky bastard."

It was his revenge folder.

He'd named it after a famous revenge novel about a guy who was framed for a crime he didn't commit.

There were five folders with people's names on them.

Foster Steadman.

Frank Kramer.

Elena Marshall.

Ethan Wright.

Jane Doe.

Foster: The producer who raped Skye and framed Jamie for armed robbery.

Frank Kramer: Foster's right-hand man, and the guy Jamie had deduced was the one behind the setup.

Elena Marshall: the cashier who lied and identified Jamie as the robber.

Ethan Wright: the crooked cop working for Foster.

I clicked on my folder first. Jamie had collected a copy of my legal name-change document, a detailed and correct résumé, my closest friends (pitifully short list of one: Asher), my work colleagues, the films I'd worked on, and my Hollywood connections. He had a list of all the galleries in California who bought and sold my artwork.

There were photographs of me. They looked like surveillance shots.

And that's when I found Jamie's notes file. This document was written almost like a diary. Every time Jamie found a new piece of information, he wrote it down next to the date and time. I scowled as I read his emotionless descriptions of my relationship with Asher. He questioned why Asher didn't spend the night with me, and vice versa, and pondered the depths of our connection. He surmised, however, that we spent enough time together to be important to one another.

I cursed him under my breath when I read his notes on bribing my neighbor Sheila to sublet her apartment to him. He'd told her it was because he'd grown up in the building and wanted to "come home." In reality, it was so he could get a "better handle on Jane's personal life and what was important to her."

There was a document on Asher, and I realized why when I saw a single file titled "Jane: Most Important." Written on it were two things: *Asher* and *art career*.

Feeling more than a little sick, I went through the other folders, making my way backwards, starting with Ethan

Wright. Each person had the same last file with that "Most Important" list.

It wasn't until I got to Frank Kramer's folder that I realized exactly what Jamie was doing. On Kramer's Most Important list was one name: Juanita Kramer. His wife. Unbeknownst to me, and obviously Asher because he'd never mentioned it, Frank Kramer had been abusing his wife.

For years, it seemed.

Jamie had police reports and photographs of Juanita after Frank had put her in the hospital. The charges never stuck, however, which Jamie attributed to Foster Steadman's influence. Unlike the other lists, Juanita's name was crossed off. Reading Jamie's notes, I knew why. It would seem Jamie had discovered the most important thing in Frank's life was his wife, Juanita. In fact, Jamie seemed certain that Frank was dangerously obsessed with her. She'd filed several reports against him over the years. Jealous attacks, locking her in a room for five days, and a plethora of other domestic abuse reports. No one had helped her.

The injustice of it made my blood boil.

According to Jamie's entries and via talks with her family, they'd tried to help Juanita run away, but Frank always found her. Jamie was determined to help Juanita get away. Reading between the lines, he'd used his own connections from prison to help her disappear. He admitted in writing what he might not have admitted to me. Yes, it served him that he wanted to take away the thing Frank coveted most, but Jamie was also glad he could assist in Juanita's escape.

His latest notes detailed that Frank was searching for her, but he wasn't even close to finding her.

Closing his file, I felt a complicated mix of emotions. As much as I was pissed at Jamie—unforgiving, hurt, and furious, and worried just how far prison and injustice had pushed him —I was also proud of him for helping Juanita Kramer. It gave me hope that he hadn't completely lost touch with the Jamie I'd loved.

Reading these files, I realized what Jamie's goal was. In order not to incriminate himself, he'd researched his targets to discover what was most important in their lives. And he'd decided to take it away.

"Because that's what they did to you," I muttered.

I still didn't understand my part in all this, other than that Jamie thought I was sleeping with Asher.

As for Ethan Wright, Jamie suspected the cop was taking bribes. However, he didn't have evidence. Wright had no personal ties either, so Jamie deduced his career—and the power trip he got from it—was the most important thing in his life. Take away his career, and he had nothing.

Elena Marshall, the cashier, had no deep, dark secrets. Jamie had searched her financial records, her personal life, and there was nothing on her. Yet, her daughter had a criminal record a mile long. Jamie had the daughter written on Elena's list, but there was a question mark next to her name.

I narrowed my eyes on the screen.

Don't you dare, Jamie McKenna.

I would not let him drag an innocent person into this mess.

Finally, I clicked on Foster Steadman's file.

There were photographs and videos in that file I wished I could unsee. I was right: Jamie had sent this stuff to Rita Steadman. Her name was crossed off Foster's Most Important list.

The last two on the list weren't: *Asher Steadman. Career.*

I didn't know how Jamie intended to take those things away from Foster Steadman, but there was no way I'd let him hurt a hair on Asher's head.

The lock turning in the door made my heart jolt.

Shit.

Before I could think how to react, Jamie strode into the room and came to an abrupt halt when he saw me sitting at his desk. Giving nothing away, he pushed against the door and it slammed so loudly, I flinched.

Then he turned the lock.

Sweat collected beneath my arms as I stood. My knees shook.

This is Jamie, I reminded myself. He won't really hurt me.

Will he?

His eyes flicked to the laptop as he moved toward me, throwing his keys in a bowl on a side table. He dumped the brown paper bag of groceries on the couch. Heart thundering, I found I couldn't move as he strode casually across the living room and stopped by my side. His gaze shifted to me as he reached out and closed the laptop.

"You have a key to this apartment," he murmured, his tone calm.

That tone was a dangerous lie.

I knew it.

I nodded, not wanting to get Ivy in trouble. "I used to water Sheila's plants."

"Did Sheila have plants?" Jamie mused, cocking his head to the side. "I don't remember that."

"She had plants." I lifted my chin stubbornly. Staring up into those familiar ocean eyes, one of the foremost emotions I'd felt as I pored through Jamie's research hit me like a punch to the gut.

Fear.

Not for myself.

But for Jamie.

If Foster Steadman realized that Jamie was taking down the people involved in his wrongful incarceration, he'd come after him, and this time I worried he'd shut Jamie up for good. If Jamie's plans were to hurt innocents, I was way past concerned for him. No matter what he wanted to believe, I knew him. I knew his heart.

It might be all tangled and fucked up right now, but beneath the scarring was his goodness. He would never come back from hurting people who didn't deserve it.

"I saw everything," I admitted.

The muscle in his jaw ticked, letting me know he was pissed, despite his bland expression. "Am I supposed to be shaking in my boots now? Or congratulating you for surprising me? Because I am surprised." He reached out to chuck my chin and I jerked it away, glowering. He smirked. "My little Jane Doe and her hidden spunk."

"I know it's hard for you to not be condescending, but at least give it a try."

Jamie leaned back against the desk, crossing his arms over his chest. "I suppose you came in here with a master plan, not just to ruin my day by making me look at your face again. It's amazing how something once so beautiful can be so ugly to me now."

I lowered my gaze, not wanting the hurt that splintered through me to be reflected in my eyes. Straightening my spine, I looked back up at him. "Funny, I'm pretty sure I felt your hard-on digging into me down in the laundry room. Guess *it* still finds me attractive. On that note, never do that to me again." I walked away, crossing the room to stand by the sectional. I needed space from him.

Jamie flicked his eyes up and down my body and shrugged. "Get to the point, Jane. I'm bored."

No one made me want to rail and scream like Jamie McKenna. Swallowing the urge, I took a breath. "I know you're planning to take down everyone involved in putting you away. That you've already dealt with Kramer. That you're looking for an 'in' with the cashier, the cop, and Steadman." I gestured to myself. "I'm your 'in.'"

This time Jamie couldn't keep the shock off his face. "What?"

"I'm your 'in.'" I took a step toward him. There was no way I would let him take vengeance against these people without having their back, and his. If I was in control of this thing, I could control the line. I'd make sure Jamie didn't cross it. "In your notes, you state you can't get close to the cashier or the cop. He's paranoid, and she'd remember you. Well, no one will remember me. I can get close to them."

"You think I'll let you work with me when you're on my hit list?" He chuckled darkly. "Do you think helping me will save you, Jane?"

No. I think it'll save you. "This isn't a discussion. I want justice for what happened to you, Jamie. You and I might not like each other very much, but once upon a time, you and Skye were my family. If we can't give her justice for what happened to her, we can take Foster down a different way, and take down the others for what they did to the Jamie I *used* to love."

Jamie narrowed his eyes as he bit his lip. Hard. Like he wanted to say something that would cut me to the quick. Instead, he released his lower lip and replied, "No. I'd rather spend another five years in prison than make you the Bonnie to my Clyde."

"I wasn't asking."

He snorted. "You think you can force me to allow this?"

"I think I'm close, personal friends with Asher Steadman, and one phone call to his father would make him aware of your activities here." The words were like ash on my tongue. I might not forgive Jamie for breaking my heart and choosing to believe the worst of me, but I would never betray him. However, he didn't need to know that.

"You really are a heartless bitch now, huh?"

It was hard not to flinch, but I managed it. "Don't act like you're above blackmail, Jamie."

He sneered at me. "Fine. And Steadman?"

"He'll never know, as long as you keep me involved. As for how to take him down ... We'll figure it out."

"You've been plotting with Asher for years, and you still haven't figured it out."

How did he know that? I verbalized the question.

"You think everything's on this laptop? No." He pushed off the desk and crossed the room to tower over me.

I wanted to retreat.

I forced myself not to.

"You'll use Asher."

"Never."

His lips twitched. "I have a feeling one day, I'll change your mind. For now, we go after the cashier and the cop."

Relief eased through me. "Good. Where do you want to start?"

"Why don't we start with you giving me back that key?" He held out his palm.

Not seeing any reason to argue, I slipped it out of my back pocket and dropped it into his hand without touching him. If I wasn't mistaken, his eyes danced with laughter, like he knew I was afraid to make physical contact.

He closed his hand around the key. "Now, get out."

I glared at him. "The plan?"

"Well, I need to think about it now that I have a new player in the mix, don't I," he said in a tone that suggested I was a moron. He turned his back to me and walked toward the laptop. I flipped him off. It was childish, but it made me feel better. "I'll be in touch ..." His voice trailed off, and I realized why when I saw what he was looking at.

The manuscript on his desk. *Doe.*

He looked back at me, his expression guarded.

"I didn't read it," I assured him.

After a moment of speculation, as if trying to gauge if I

was telling the truth (the bastard), he turned his back on me again. "You can leave."

But I wasn't quite ready to. "Why?"

"Why what?" he snapped.

"Why is your new book titled *Doe*?"

Jamie laughed, his shoulders shaking a little with the movement. "Do you think it's about you, Jane?"

"It's a little coincidental ..." My cheeks flushed with embarrassment.

I hated that he could make me feel so small and stupid.

He turned toward me, leaning on the desk as his hand rested on top of the papers. "I guess I wanted to feel what it was like to ruin you before I actually do it."

Pain lashed across my chest, so acute, it was like six years hadn't passed. Like I was reading his letter all over again and wondering how *my* Jamie could do this to me.

He studied me, a deep melancholy slowly washing through his eyes. The darkness in them made my heart beat faster. "I want to ruin all of you. A lifetime of misery ought to do the trick."

Holding back the tears, I gave him a tight nod. "Well, they say misery loves company."

"Look at you. I think you're finally beginning to understand."

Marching away and slamming out of his apartment, I railed at him in my head. What did he think? That he was alone in his wounds? That the rest of us weren't in pain too?

All those years ago, I'd taught him to look beyond himself.

It would seem Jamie McKenna had forgotten that lesson.

I glanced back at his closed door as I leaned against mine. "It's up to me to remind you."

Chapter Twenty-Two

JAMIE

"What was the name again?" the security guard asked.

I leaned out of the car window and peered up at him through my dark sunglasses. "Jamie Stone."

"Here to see?"

Jesus Christ, how many times did I need to repeat myself? "Margot Higgins." I bit back my attitude, knowing it would get me nowhere. I'd save that for Jane.

A few minutes later, they opened the gate to the Chimera Studios grounds and I drove in, wearing a satisfied smirk. I knew Jane would let me in. She seemed determined to stick close. Blackmailing me. I was almost proud.

I should've known she wouldn't just sit back and let my plans unfold around her. Jane was made of tougher stuff than that. Would she hand my ass over to Steadman? I'm not sure I believed that. So why indulge her?

She might prove useful; it kept her where I could keep an eye on her; and it meant I could figure out what really made her tick. What would really screw up Jane? Personally, I hoped *I* could, that underneath her attitude, there was still a part of her that was attracted to me. That I could do to her what she had done to me:

Make her love me.

Only to abandon her.

I'd have to play it by ear. She definitely appeared moon-struck over that asshole Asher Steadman. My fingers tightened around the steering wheel. God, she pissed me off.

It was the most alive I'd felt in a long time, and I had to admit I was looking forward to our future interactions.

As I pulled up to the hangar the security guard had directed me to, I saw a door open and there she was, hovering in the doorway. My blood pumped as if I'd just downed a quart of caffeine.

By the time I made it to her, she'd disappeared inside the building and was holding the door open from the shadows. It closed behind me and there she was.

Jane in cut-off jean shorts, a red-and-black plaid shirt tied at the waist, and red and black sneakers. Long hair in a messy half-bun-ponytail thing that spilled all over the place. Barely any makeup.

I wanted to wrap her shapely tan legs around my waist and fuck her into next week.

"You're a mess." She was a mess. It didn't mean she was any less beautiful.

She made a face. "Is that what you came here to tell me? I'm working."

"Show me around." I moved past her, heading out of the short entryway and into the massive space. There were several soundstages inside.

A hand gripped me by the arm, and I glanced over my shoulder as Jane pressed a finger to her lips. I realized they were filming. A very famous actor was in the middle of delivering a line to another very famous actor. My eyebrows rose. I'd never been on a film set before. It was kind of interesting.

The soundstage they were on was made to look like a New York penthouse apartment. It was amazing how realistic it was, and it occurred to me that it was partly Jane's doing. She was the art director.

Another tug on my arm wrenched me from watching the scene play out. Jane gestured silently for me to follow her, and I shot a look at the actors before going after her. We disappeared out of the hangar into the back of the building.

"Was that Reesa Orland and Jack Sheen?" I asked Jane's back as she marched down the white hallway.

"Yeah." She stopped at a door, pushed it open, and gestured for me to go through first.

I smirked and waved my hand for her to precede me.

Jane quirked a brow. "You're being a gentleman now?"

"No. Walking in first gives you my back. Wouldn't want you to stick another knife in it."

She huffed, anger flickering in those pretty eyes.

I followed her into the room and shut the door behind us.

Taking in the space, I reckoned there was an office buried under all the props. "So, this is what you do, huh?"

"Small talk? Really?"

"No, not really." I held out my hand. "Give me your phone."

"Why?"

"So that when I have plans we need to enact, I don't have to chase you down."

With a beleaguered sigh, Jane pulled her phone out of her back pocket. "Number."

"Give it to me."

"I'm not an idiot, Jamie. You're not getting my phone. Just give me your number."

"Were you always this paranoid?"

"Not until my ex-boyfriend bribed my neighbor to sublet her apartment to him so he could plot his asinine and completely uncalled-for revenge against me." She smiled sweetly. "On that note, has anyone suggested therapy?"

"Ah, sweet Jane, I really am enjoying getting to know this side of you." I threw her a dirty look before I rhymed off my number. Almost immediately my cell rang in my jeans pocket.

"Now you have my number."

I quickly saved her number to my contact list.

"Is that it?" Jane asked, leaning against a cluttered desk. "Or was there something else you needed?"

Seeing photographs on the desk, I realized this was Jane's office. I ran my eyes over her legs as I brushed past her. "That's a loaded question."

"Stop, I'm blushing," she replied dryly. "What are you doing?"

I'd picked up one of the two framed photos—a photograph of Jane and her friend Cassie from art college. It looked like it was taken while Jane was still in school. I tried, and failed, not to notice how sad her smile was in the photo. "What happened to Cassie?" I asked, even though I couldn't take my eyes off my ex in the photo. Were we still together when this photo was taken? Was it before or after she ghosted me?

"You're telling me you don't know?"

I grinned as I put the frame down. I liked that I had her all worked up and worried about what I knew and didn't know about her life. "I actually don't. Last time you talked about her, she was shacking up with some older guy."

"She married that older guy. They moved to Florida. They have a kid now." I heard the slight hint of melancholy in Jane's voice.

"You miss her," I surmised.

Jane stiffened and shrugged.

"When did she leave?"

"Right after college."

Leaving Jane alone with no real friend until Asher. What had happened to their little art crew? "And Devin?" I looked away, perusing a shelf of props so she wouldn't see the curl to my lips. I'd hated that gangly prick and the way he was always ogling Jane.

There was a slight hesitation, and it brought back our conversation years ago. Something had happened with that guy. As much as I didn't believe it at the time, I knew better now. Jane had cheated on me.

I could feel my heart hammering harder in my chest.

"We stopped being friends a long time ago," she said, her tone weirdly emotionless. "Just a little before you made it clear you didn't trust me or want me in your life anymore, he attacked me at a house party."

I whipped around, blowing past the outright lie of "you made it clear you didn't trust me or want me in your life anymore" to the latter. "He what?"

Indignation and something like dark satisfaction mingled in her eyes as she glared at me. "No, Jamie, I didn't cheat on you with Devin. He assaulted me in a bathroom when he was drunk. Thankfully, Cassie and I had taken self-defense classes. I got away from him." She retold the story like it'd had no emotional impact on her, but I was coming out of my fucking skin. "I didn't want to tell you because I didn't want you to feel bad about not being there for me." She huffed at herself. "I'm surprised you didn't know about it. I reported it to the police."

As I tried to shove out the images my imagination was putting together, of that lanky, emo little fuck forcing himself on Jane, I shook my head. "I didn't know." I took a step toward her. "By assaulted ... you mean?"

"Not rape. He kissed me and wouldn't stop. I had to physically make him stop."

My stomach roiled at the thought. "What happened?"

"I just told you."

"No, what happened to him?" I snapped impatiently.

"Slap on the wrist."

That fucking fucker!

"But he became a pariah at school with our friends." She shrugged. "He transferred. I never saw him again."

Silence fell between us as I turned away, suddenly playing the memory of her last visit before she broke it off. Is that why she never came back? Because I accused her of cheating when that piece of shit had attacked her? Something crushed down on my chest.

Okay, she had every right to be pissed at me for that.

But she should have talked to me.

If she'd come to me and told me that's why she was ending things, I would have apologized. I would have promised I'd do better.

Listen to yourself, groveling to her in your fucking imagination.

Jane ended things without having the decency to do it to my face. End of story.

Still, I made a mental note to find out what had happened to Devin. Wouldn't want his life to be too comfortable these days after sexually assaulting my girlfriend.

Ex-girlfriend.

"So, I don't imagine you came here to talk about my old college friends and enemies." Jane broke the silence. "Why are you here?"

Pulling my shit together, I turned to face her again. "Ethan Wright."

"The cop?"

"The cop." The shit stain who had whispered in my ear

the night of my arrest, making it clear he was working for Foster Steadman. That only became clearer when I started investigating him. "I'm pretty sure he's taking bribes from all sorts. But I need more evidence I can hand over to the right people. Because he's a shiesty fuck, he's also paranoid. He'll recognize me, and he'd suspect a woman as beautiful as you coming on to him."

Jane raised an eyebrow.

"His partner is Lincoln Gaines." I pulled out my phone and brought up the photograph to show her. Jane gazed down at the good-looking cop. "As far as I can tell, he's clean." I eyed her carefully. "He's also single."

Jane's eyes met mine.

We were standing so close, I could see the specks of gold in them. Gold that flared with understanding. "You want me to get to know Lincoln Gaines?"

I nodded.

She scowled. "How well do you want me to get to know him?"

Before I'd walked into this office, I had no qualms about asking Jane to throw herself at this guy. I wasn't talking sex. Just flirting and some kissing if she had to. On the back of her Devin confession, however, I couldn't help but feel like a prick. "You don't have to do it," I said, my voice too gentle.

Jane harrumphed. "You going soft on me already?"

Brat.

"Fine. You have to do it."

"I'm not having sex with a stranger for this, Jamie. That's too far."

That thought was more than a little nauseating. "Who said you needed to have sex with him? Flirt with him, go on a few dates, and maneuver things so you're spending time with his *friends*."

"With Ethan."

"Exactly. You can be where he is. Watch what he's doing. Maybe even get a hold of his phone."

She considered this. And my heart raced like hell. *Say no*, a little voice whispered at the back of my mind.

"Okay, I'll do it. How do we start this?"

I shoved my phone back in my pocket. "Wright and Gaines frequent a nightclub in downtown LA on their night off. That's tomorrow night. You'll make sure Gaines doesn't leave the club without your number."

"And where will you be?"

At the club, making sure no one touched her without her permission. "I'll be there too, making sure you don't fuck up."

If looks could kill, I'd be dead.

However, the longer we stared at each other, the more the urge grew to kiss the attitude right out of her. "You like this, then?" I blurted out, gesturing around the room. "Miss Art Director."

Jane sighed heavily. "It's not what I intended to do with my life. I like things quieter than this. But I can't say I hate it."

"Why this?"

Her expression was incredulous. "Why do you think, Jamie?"

I frowned, not getting it.

"I needed an 'in.' This is Foster Steadman's world, and I didn't know how else to infiltrate it. So, I asked Nick to get me a job—he got me a job as a runner for the art department. Things escalated from there."

Sweat dampened my palms as I remembered her conversation with Asher in his car. It was true. All this time she had been trying to find a way to bring that bastard down. I didn't know how to feel about it.

"I loved her." Tears glimmered in Jane's eyes now. "I wanted him to pay."

Trying to fight back the emotion she incited, I chuckled. "My bloodthirsty little Doe."

She cut me a hard look. "I stopped being *your* anything a long time ago." She marched over to the door and threw it open. "Text me the time and place for tomorrow. I have to get back to work." She stalked off, leaving me alone in her office.

I stopped being your *anything a long time ago.*

She could be callous when she wanted to be.

Ignoring the ache in my chest, I moved back to her desk and picked up the second photo frame. It was a photo of Jane, Skye ... and me.

My fingers tightened around the frame, a sense of satisfaction moving through me.

Maybe deep down, Jane Doe still had feelings for me.

Chapter Twenty-Three

JANE

Between the chartreuse dress and gold tones in my eyeshadow, my eyes appeared to be light green rather than hazel green. The body-con dress had a simple silhouette—thin straps and a sweetheart neckline, and it hit mid-thigh. It hugged my every curve, and admittedly the vibrancy of the color worked nicely against my tan skin. Asher had convinced me to buy the daring dress when we were on Rodeo one day. It was the most expensive item in my wardrobe, and I'd never worn it because I always thought it was too sexy for any of the events I attended with him.

Tonight felt like the right night to wear the dress, and I'd paired it with my sexiest gold strappy heels.

"I could come over and look after you if you're feeling sick," Asher offered as I gave myself a final once-over. He was on speakerphone, my phone on my bed.

Lying to Asher was my least favorite thing in the world. I

winced as I grabbed a gold clutch out of my closet. "You know, I think I just want to go to bed early. But thank you."

"No problem, babe. If you'd take me up on my offer and move into this too-big-for-me home by the beach, I wouldn't have to worry about you being on your own when you're sick."

I smiled sadly as I slumped on the bed. "I thought you didn't need to hide behind me anymore?" Or was it the other way around?

"I don't. But I like you close."

I laughed. "I thought you wanted me to date?"

"I do. I do. I just don't like the idea of you being sick by yourself."

If I moved into Asher's Malibu home, people would definitely assume we were together. However, the commute into LA—I couldn't do that every day. "The commute would kill me."

"Well, I could buy a place in the hills."

"And be closer to dear old Dad?" He wasn't buying a house just so I didn't have to commute to the studio.

"Right."

"Asher, I like my apartment. I'm fine. I'm going to get an early night and hopefully feel better in the morning." I could feel my cheeks burning with my lie. "I'm off to bed. Love you."

"Love you too."

Guilt joined the kaleidoscope of butterflies in my belly as we hung up. I'd been avoiding my best friend because I didn't want to lie to his face. Having Jamie in my life was tumultuous, and I knew I couldn't hide the effect his presence had on me from Asher.

Still, I couldn't avoid my friend forever. It wasn't fair to him. Especially when he was going through so much upset with his parents' divorce.

Determined to be a better friend in the morning, I reluctantly pushed aside thoughts of Asher and tried to focus on the night ahead.

As if on cue, the doorbell rang. My heels clicked against the hardwood floor as I walked down the hall and into the main living room toward the door. Palms a little clammy, I took in calming breaths to slow my racing heart. The attempt failed miserably.

Pulling open the door, I found Jamie slouched in the doorway, as if he was bored already. There was no change in his usual uniform of T-shirt, jeans, and boots. Why? Because he didn't need to dress up for a club. He was sexy, and he knew it.

Bastard.

"Ready to go?" I asked, stepping outside and forcing him out of the doorway. I reluctantly gave him my back as I locked my apartment.

When I turned around, the boredom was suddenly absent from his expression. His eyes were on my shoes. Slowly, they traveled upward. By the time he made it to my face, my skin was hot and I was agitated.

Jamie stared resentfully at me.

Flustered, I brushed past him. "You said dress for a nightclub."

His cold silence followed me downstairs.

———

I'D NEVER BEEN SO glad in my life to escape a car.

When Jamie dropped me off a street over from the club, I practically threw myself out of the Porsche. At first, he wouldn't even talk to me as we drove into the city. Then he started talking to me like I was an idiot.

"Don't make it obvious you're watching Wright."

Well, of course not.

"Don't come on strong with Gaines either. Wright might see and get paranoid."

Commence eye rolling.

"This isn't going to be over in one night. This could take weeks."

No, really? I thought I'd just snap my fingers or wave my magic wand and find evidence against Wright in the first ten minutes.

There was no point responding to any of his "advice," especially when he said it in that patronizing tone. Jamie was always a little impatient with people he deemed morons. I'd just never been one of them before.

The line to get into the club was long. Unfortunately, that cliché shallow attitude depicted in movies and television really existed and "pretty people" got to jump the line. Problem was, there were a lot of "pretty people" in LA. However, Asher had taught me a thing or two over the years. It wasn't just about how you looked, but how you carried yourself. As an introvert, having attitude wasn't easy for me. However, if I was to be successful at convincing Lincoln Gaines that I wanted to date him, then I needed to find the actor within.

I sashayed past the line of waiting clubbers, wearing a small smirk as I neared the doormen. Their eyes moved to me, drifting down my body. When they met my gaze, I smiled, showing my dimple.

"Don't stop at the door, as if you know you need permission to enter," Asher's voice filled my head. *"Smile, say hello to the doormen, but keep on walking in as if you know you're hot enough to be there and not letting you in is not an option."*

"Hey, guys." I kept strolling toward the door as if it were my God-given right.

"Hey, gorgeous," one of them replied, grinning as I strutted by.

And right into the club without them stopping me.

Worked like a charm.

As soon as I was inside, my smile dropped.

The world and its shallow preoccupation with looks made me truly sad sometimes. But such was life, and I couldn't do anything to change it. What I *could* do was get tonight over with.

I'd never been to this club, but it was packed. Purple and blue lights gave the place an atmosphere without it being too dark. Massive crystal chandeliers hung from the ceiling, one over a dance floor packed with people. As I moved along the bar, I saw another chandelier suspended above a seating area. Leather, button-back booths edged the walls with tables centered in front of them. And in the middle of the seating area, the same style booths made rectangles—two U-shaped booths facing each other with two small tables, and a gap on either side so you and your friends could enter the cozy space.

The booths were all occupied.

Scanning faces as inconspicuously as possible, catching features as overhead lights and wall sconces illuminated them, I couldn't find Gaines or Wright.

But I knew the moment Jamie entered the club.

The skin at my nape prickled despite the heat, and I turned my head ever so slightly to watch him. He zoned in on me too, our gazes connecting and causing a warm shiver to tickle down my spine. He drew his eyes from me before striding through the crowded dance floor and disappearing among the bodies.

But I knew he'd be watching. For some stupid reason, I was less nervous knowing Jamie was there, keeping an eye on the situation.

Turning away, I searched the club, my eyes passing over the bar and veering back again, when I caught sight of a familiar profile.

Lincoln Gaines.

He stood at the bar chatting with the bartender.

Taking a deep breath, I sauntered over and squeezed into a space between the cop on my left and a woman on my right.

"A soda water and lime!" I yelled to be heard over the music.

A frown puckered the brow of the bartender who had been speaking to Gaines as she worked. She looked at me and I tipped my head to give her a sweet smile. Her frown melted and she grinned flirtatiously. "Sure thing, girl! Just let me finish up with this!"

"Hey."

I glanced to my left and found Lincoln Gaines staring down at me in interest. He had glittering dark eyes and gorgeous brown skin with warm, bronze undertones.

I cocked my head and gave him a flirty smile. "Hey."

He grinned, a sexy flash of perfect white teeth. "You waiting on someone?"

"I was here with a friend. She bailed."

"Lincoln." He held out his hand.

My palm was tiny in his, and I felt a flutter of attraction. "Jane."

Jamie and I had decided I'd use my birth name, since Margot Higgins was in the tabloids for dating Asher Steadman.

The cop's hand tightened around mine as his warm eyes focused on my face. "Nice to meet you, Jane."

"You too."

"Soda water and lime," the bartender interrupted us.

"Let me get this." Lincoln handed her some cash.

"Thanks."

"You're welcome. Not drinking tonight?"

"Not much of a drinker," I answered honestly.

"Me neither."

Curious, I leaned closer to him. "So, why are you in a nightclub?"

"Why are you?"

"I promised my friend I'd hang out with her."

"And she bailed on you, anyway."

"Yeah. But my night is looking up."

He chuckled, a deep, rich sound. "That's why I'm in a nightclub."

I raised a questioning eyebrow.

"On the off chance that a beautiful woman will flirt with me."

"Very smooth," I teased.

He flashed those pearly whites again. "So, why did your friend bail?"

It was disconcerting how easy it was to lie and play a role. The underlying fear of conning a cop—a good one, from what Jamie had gathered—buzzed low within me. However, it was strangely exciting to take charge of a situation that had controlled me and Jamie for seven years.

Moreover, I wasn't a perfect person. I was an angry person. Angry at several people. One of them was Jamie, and there was a spiteful voice inside me that liked to think it might bother him to see me flirt with this sexy cop. It was petty. It wasn't who I was. And that pissed me off too.

Lincoln relayed what I already knew: he was a police officer. I told him I was a freelance artist. Sticking to some truth seemed smart so I wouldn't trip myself up over details I'd concocted. Not too long later, fresh drinks in hand, Lincoln directed us over to the seating area. The chandelier above flickered over the occupants of one of the booths, and something ugly lurched in my gut at the sight of Ethan Wright.

As tall as Lincoln, Ethan sprawled on a leather booth, his arms along the back, two women sitting on either side of him.

One was talking with the guy on her other side, while the other had her lips almost on Ethan's ear as she spoke to him.

Wright wasn't traditionally attractive. But he worked out and was muscular. Even if I didn't already hate the piece of scum, he wouldn't do anything for me.

Lincoln gestured to the empty booth opposite his partner. Ethan's eyes came to me as I slid in. He ogled, not caring how obvious he was. Attempting not to shudder, I relaxed against the booth and turned to Lincoln as he squeezed in beside me.

Jamie thought Ethan would be paranoid that someone "as beautiful" as me would be interested in him. It hadn't escaped me that his words were incongruous to some insults he'd dealt since coming back into my life. What also didn't escape me was that Wright was arrogant. He would have no difficulty believing I was interested in him.

Flirting with Lincoln was easy.

Having to flirt with the dirtbag who helped put Jamie in prison would have been impossible. I was glad Jamie had chosen Gaines as the less obvious investigative option.

"This is my partner, Ethan!" Lincoln called over the music.

Ethan smirked. "Nice piece!" He gave Lincoln a look of approval before turning his attention to the girl at his side.

Nice piece?

A shock of surprise moved through me as I felt Lincoln's warm breath on my ear. "Sorry, he can be kind of a dick."

My eyebrows rose as I pulled back to look at him.

He shrugged and bent his head to my ear again. "The guy's my partner. He's got my back." His tone was of the "what can you do?" variety.

I could think of several things he could do. For a start, call his friend out for being repulsive.

On the one hand, Lincoln's reaction suggested he wasn't a man who talked about women that way. On the other hand, he wasn't a guy who stood up against his friend for talking about women that way. It was a mark against him in my book.

I had a feeling Lincoln wouldn't be so forgiving when he found out Wright was a dirty bastard, using his position of power to screw people over.

However, I smiled like I understood, and we tried to engage in conversation in the loud club. Now and then, I'd shoot looks across the table at Ethan, keeping a surreptitious eye on him.

Not once did I see Jamie.

But I could feel him.

He was watching us. I knew that. He would watch the fact that Ethan kept checking his phone, that he tensed and looked at it about an hour after I'd sat down in the booth with Lincoln. When he nudged the girl and guy next to him and asked them to let him out, Lincoln turned to him. "You off?"

"Yeah!" Ethan flashed a cocky smile. "Favorite pussy just texted!"

Ugh. Could he be any more disgusting?

Lincoln shook his head, apparently not impressed. *Well, say something to him about it*, I wanted to snap at him. He didn't. He just waved in a "whatever, man" gesture and turned back to me. My phone vibrated in my purse.

"I need to use the restroom. I'll be right back."

He nodded and got up to let me out, but touched my lower back as I shifted past him. "I'll be waiting."

Guilt pricked me as I made my way to the restroom. Despite his inability to call out Ethan on his gross rhetoric, Lincoln appeared to be a nice guy. He hadn't moved to kiss or touch me inappropriately. In fact, so far, it seemed he was treating this like a first date. I could be wrong, but my instincts told me Gaines was a nice guy.

I did not like screwing around with nice people.

In the privacy of the restroom hallway, I pulled out my cell.

> Following Wright. Will come back if he's leaving city. Don't make a move without me.

I huffed at Jamie's text and returned to Lincoln.

Instead of sliding into the booth, he asked if I wanted to dance.

We headed to the dance floor.

At first, we danced close but separately. Other than Asher, I'd never danced with a guy. Jamie and I hadn't been the clubbing types. But Lincoln could move, and he made it easy. Soon, however, he was gently pulling me against him, his big hands on my hips. Keeping up the flirt, I put my arms around his neck, which drew us closer, and the dancing turned a little more sensual. Concentrating on the movement of our hips, it was easier for me to keep up the ruse, if I didn't look into Lincoln's eyes. I hated the lie. And it was difficult to stop myself from tensing up.

Especially when I felt a prickle over my skin.

While the feel of Lincoln's hard body against mine did nothing but incite guilt, sensing Jamie's eyes on us made my breath hitch.

I didn't understand how I knew he was there, watching. I just did.

My heart raced, sweat dampened my skin, and my body relaxed as the thought of him watching me melted my insides.

It was Jamie I was dancing with in my imagination, his hips rolling gently against mine, his hands gripping tight to my hips, and his hot breath on my cheek as he bent his head toward me.

But he tensed suddenly.

"Hey, your phone is vibrating." Lincoln's deep rumble caused goose bumps behind my ear.

It jolted me out of my fantasy, and I flushed.

Realizing my clutch, still gripped in my hand, was resting against Lincoln's shoulder blade and thus he'd felt my phone's vibration, I released him.

He reluctantly let go of my hips, caressing my waist as his hands slowly dropped away.

Pulling out my cell and shielding the screen from Lincoln, I stiffened at Jamie's text.

We're done here. Meet me at the car.

I slid my cell back into my purse and gave Lincoln a regretful sigh. "It was my alarm," I called over the music. "I set it to remind me when I needed to leave. I have an early appointment tomorrow."

He nodded but stepped into my personal space, forcing my head back to meet his eyes. "Can I get your number? I'd like to take you out for dinner."

Smiling through my guilt, I nodded. "Of course."

He pulled his phone out of his back pocket and I gave him my real number. "I'll call you," he promised. "Let me walk you out."

"Oh, that's okay. My car's just down the street."

"Then I'm walking you to your car. It's not safe to walk out there alone." Lincoln wasn't taking no for an answer.

As he walked ahead to make space for me through the crowd, I quickly texted Jamie the situation.

By the time we got to the Porsche, Jamie was nowhere to be seen, but I knew he was around because he'd left the car open for me.

I opened the driver's side door. "Keyless entry," I explained.

Lincoln raised an eyebrow as he took in the car. "You must sell a lot of paintings."

I gave him a modest shrug.

He smiled down at me. "I had a great time tonight, Jane."

"Me too." And I did. In another life, I'd go out on a real date with Lincoln Gaines. "Call me?"

"Absolutely." Lincoln pressed a soft, sweet kiss to my cheek. Remorse was a swift kick to the gut as he retreated onto the sidewalk. "I'm not leaving until I see you drive off."

I couldn't do this.

He was too nice.

And let's not forget he's a cop.

With a little wave of my fingers, I got into the car and took off seconds later. I didn't go far though. I turned the corner out of sight and stopped. Getting out, I rounded the hood and let myself into the passenger side.

Minutes later, the driver's side opened, and Jamie slid in, slamming the door shut behind him.

Just like that, it was as if all the air in the car had been sucked out.

My skin buzzed, and there was a hot tension in my belly, a slick heat between my legs.

For a moment, he just sat there, not saying a word.

But this energy blazed from him. I wanted to ask about Wright. What he'd seen. Instead, I told him, "Lincoln's a nice guy. We shouldn't do this to him."

"You can back out any time." Jamie's tone was cold. Flat.

I shivered and pulled on my seat belt. "No." As much as I hated involving Lincoln Gaines in this, I hated the idea of leaving Jamie to his own devices even more.

Thick, horrible silence filled the space between us as Jamie drove back to the apartment. I hurried out of the car and felt him moving quickly to keep up with me. My skin burned as I rushed up the steps in front of him, feeling his eyes all over me.

I was trembling.

"Good night," I said as I pulled my keys out of my clutch, not looking at him.

His apartment door slammed behind me before I'd even put my keys in the lock. I glanced over my shoulder at the apartment. Tears burned my eyes.

Even after all he'd done to me, I still cared.

If it had been him flirting and dancing with another woman in front of me all night, I would have hated every minute.

When I'd been dancing with Lincoln, it only got good when I'd imagined Jamie in his place.

Did Jamie even care?

I hated him.

I hated that there would always be a part of me that wanted him. That when I needed to be a strong, independent woman who demanded respect and kindness, I let myself down because of him.

He was an unforgivable weakness.

"Bastard," I muttered under my breath, forcing back tears. He didn't deserve them.

I let myself into my apartment. I'd left a few table lamps blazing because I hated returning to darkness. Sitting down on the sofa and unbuckling my strappy heels, I tried not to think about what I'd done tonight. My feet ached as I got up and wandered into my bedroom to put my shoes away.

Just as I was setting them on a shelf in my closet, I thought I heard a knock on the door.

Pulse racing, I ambled into the hall and halted, ears pricked.

The knock was louder this time. More demanding.

My stomach flipped as I hurried through the living area to the front door.

Peeking through the peephole, I saw Jamie standing outside, glowering ferociously at my door.

What now?

I unlocked the chain and the dead bolt, yanking the door open. Before I could even ask what the hell he wanted, he reached out for me as he stepped inside.

And crushed my mouth beneath his.

CHAPTER TWENTY-FOUR

JAMIE

I'D BARELY STORMED into my apartment when I felt the walls closing in on me.

There were days in prison when a feeling of claustrophobia was so powerful, it was like I was losing my mind. Trapped. Airless. Stress crushing my lungs. Even two years later, I hated being stuck in traffic. Not being able to maneuver my car away to freedom, being stuck inside it ... I'd feel this pressure on my chest and become light-headed.

The same thing happened when I flew out to Boston to see Lorna after my release. It was so bad that when I decided to return to LA six months ago, I rented a car and drove back to California. Deciding to make the most of it, I took my sweet time. I arrived in LA fourteen days after I'd left Boston.

Now I'd do anything to avoid that feeling—like something was happening beyond my control.

Like I was coming out of my skin.

Like I needed air.

Seething, I turned around and stared at my door.

It was her fault.

No matter what she'd done to me, I couldn't stop caring. I hated putting her in this position. I hated her flirting with Gaines. Breathing the same air as Ethan Wright.

Yet, it wasn't until I returned from following Wright that my fury consumed everything. I no longer cared about Wright or Steadman, or anything else but the fact that Jane was rolling her hips against Gaines. That his hands were on her body.

She didn't look at him. Her eyes were closed as they moved against each other, but I knew her expression. Jane was enjoying herself a little too much.

Seeing the sweaty dew on her skin made my mouth dry.

Or was that my jealousy?

I couldn't watch any longer, so I'd sent her a text to end it.

The urge to pull over the entire way home and remind her that no one could satisfy her like I could was great. But I'd held it in check.

Until she was gone.

Until she was on the other side of the apartment door, a million miles away despite the short distance. And I couldn't stand it.

I wanted Jane to feel what I felt.

I wanted to consume her like she consumed me.

Needing a release worse than the nights I'd laid in my cell missing her, I stopped thinking straight. All my blood traveled south, cutting off the supply to my brain. One second I was in my apartment; the next I was knocking impatiently on her door.

It swung open.

There she was. In that fucking dress.

So beautiful and unreachable ... and so ... *Jane*.

I buried my hand in her hair and jerked her toward me as I stepped into the apartment, relief and euphoria like oxygen as

I kissed her. Her lips were soft and familiar beneath mine and I groaned, needing a deeper taste.

Hooking my foot around her door, I slammed it shut and then hauled Jane up into my arms. With a whimper that vibrated down my throat, Jane wrapped her legs around my waist and clung to me as we devoured each other's mouths on the way to the bedroom.

There was no thought of foreplay in my head. I needed inside her. End of story.

Following her down to the bed, I broke the kiss, but only to shove her dress up to her waist and pull her nude silk underwear down her legs. She panted beneath my body, staring up at me, dazed, face flushed.

She wasn't stopping this.

Relief made me frantic.

I wanted to sink into her bare, but at the back of my mind, I remembered Dakota, and the handful of women in Boston I'd screwed when I got out of prison. Cursing under my breath, I dug my wallet out of my jeans and found a condom. *The first chance I get*, I thought, looking down at Jane, legs spread for me, tits heaving against that flimsy dress, *I'm getting a clean bill of health so I can have her without anything between us.*

Fuck, no one made me harder. No one did it for me like she did.

That made me almost as pissed as it did hard.

My jeans shucked down just low enough to free me, condom on, I pinned Jane's wrists at either side of her head, ·enjoying her familiar gasps of excitement.

Without taking a moment, my only focus on being inside her, I pushed against her wet heat and thrust.

Hard.

I was so euphoric, her tight, hot clasp around my dick the

best thing I'd ever felt in my life, that her gasp of pain didn't immediately register with me.

Opening my eyes, I stared down at her face, her expression finally cutting through my pleasure. She pulsed and throbbed around me, as tight as I remembered her when we were teenagers.

And her face was pinched with discomfort, like it was the first time too.

There were even tears in her eyes.

"What the fuck?" I huffed out, desperate to move but too concerned to continue.

She was tight.

Too tight, I supposed, for a woman who'd been having regular sex.

Jane gazed up at me, and there was something unbearably sad behind the heat in her eyes. Emotion burned in my throat as I looked into her eyes. "Jane?"

"Don't stop," she whispered. She undulated, so I slid deeper inside.

Shivery heat sparked down my spine and swirled in my groin, making me groan.

I didn't know if Jane had been with anyone since me, but I knew she hadn't been with anyone in a long while. Which meant she wasn't sleeping with Asher Steadman.

There were a lot of questions that came with that realization, but the guy in me didn't care about asking them right then. The man that used to adore this woman to distraction felt relief and possessiveness flood him in a rush of primal need.

I drove into her again, baring my teeth against the kind of pleasure that made my eyes want to roll back in my head. Jane gasped, lifting her hips into my mine as I moved in and out of her.

My grip tightened on her wrists as my drives increased in

speed and strength. The whole bed shook as I growled her name over and over.

"You need this too," I panted hard. "You need this like I need this."

"Yes," Jane panted, her eyes closing.

"Open your eyes," I demanded.

She did.

"This is me," I breathed against her lips, before kissing her hungrily. I broke away to fuck her harder. "You can't hide from it, Jane. Don't hide from it."

"Jamie!" she screamed as she came, clenching around my driving cock in heartrending throbs.

That's all it took.

"Fuck!" I tensed between her legs seconds before I came, my dick pulsing and pulsing inside her. Bliss shuddered through me as I held myself over her, pouring myself into the condom when I wanted to pour it all into her.

Jesus, it was never ending.

My muscles turned to liquid as I slumped over her, pressing my face into her throat as I ground my dick into her, trying to prolong every second.

Jane.

Peace settled over me. Contentment I hadn't felt in who knew how long settled in as I laid on top of her soft body and breathed her in. Shit, I could have fallen asleep like that.

"Jamie," she whispered, pressing a hand to my side. "Jamie, I can't breathe."

Reluctantly, I lifted my head, pushing slowly onto my hands to raise my weight off her, and stared down at her flushed face.

She wouldn't look at me.

"Jane."

"I need to clean up," she muttered, still not meeting my eyes.

"Jane, look at me."

She raised those beautiful hazel-green eyes to mine. My heart thundered as hard as it had as I moved inside her just seconds before.

"You're not sleeping with Asher." It wasn't a question.

Angry tears shimmered in her eyes. "There's been no one since you."

With that shocking announcement, I felt the room spin.

Chapter Twenty-Five

JANE

"Get off me," I demanded, feeling vulnerable.

To my surprise, Jamie did as I asked. He rolled off and onto his back, his hands covering his face.

Trembling, I pushed down the dress that he'd practically ruined when I'd allowed him to screw me like the masochist I was.

I moved to get off the bed and his hand suddenly shot out, wrapping around my bicep.

"Stay. Talk," he demanded.

Why the hell did *he* sound angry? I was the one who should be angry. I was the one who had pined like an idiot over him, unable to move on, only to hand myself over to him, even when he'd treated me like I was the enemy.

As soon as he'd started kissing me, however, I'd felt like I was home.

No matter what my rational brain told me, I wanted him inside me more desperately than I'd wanted anything. At that moment, as the orgasm shattered through me, it had felt worth it.

But as soon as the pleasure faded, I was left with the reality.

"I have a better idea. Pull up your pants and get out." I wrenched out of his grasp, sliding off the bed and tugging my dress back into position. I throbbed between my legs, reminding me what I'd just done.

Marching out of the bedroom, not sure how I'd face that room again, I called over my shoulder, "That wasn't a request, Jamie."

Slamming into the bathroom, I leaned against the sink, afraid to look at my reflection in the mirror above it. I didn't want to face myself. Beyond the bathroom door, I could hear movement, and then Jamie's footsteps down the hall. My heart thudded as I waited for him to leave and then it skipped a beat as the bathroom door flew open.

The door banged back against the opposite wall as he stood in the hall, staring at me in disbelief. Although his jeans were pulled back up, he hadn't bothered to zip them. He looked disheveled, freshly screwed and unbearably sexy.

"Do you have a hearing problem?" I asked, quietly seething.

A muscle ticked in his jaw. "Tell me the truth."

"I hate strawberries."

"Stop fucking around, Jane. You just said there's been no one but me. What the hell is going on with you and Asher?"

"None of your business." I turned to face him, crossing my arms over my chest. "Please leave."

He didn't leave. Instead, for the first time since he'd stormed back into my life, his expression gentled with concern. My breath caught. In that moment, he reminded me so much of *my* Jamie. "Jane, talk to me. Tell me what the hell I'm missing here."

I didn't want to.

What was the point?

We'd had a moment of weakness. So what? It was better to pretend it never happened because nothing changed the fact that he'd broken up with me and then proceeded to make me the target of all his anger.

It was time to push him back across the hall, and asking nicely wasn't working. "You've had other women, right? The blond in the hall that day ..."

Something like discomfort flickered across his face.

"Well?" I demanded. "Are you going to tell me that you saved yourself for me, Jamie? Or have there been other women since you got out of prison?"

There went that muscle again, ticking away. He heaved a sigh. "There have been other women," he admitted.

Even though I'd known that, it still hurt, and I didn't do a very good job of hiding it.

"Jane ..." He took a placating step toward me.

"Don't." I retreated out of his reach. "Why is it always the way? Huh?" A tear slipped down my cheek before I could stop it, and I hated myself for the weakness. Jamie's eyes followed the tear as if he were entranced. "Why is the woman always the one who's faithful with her body, but the guy never is?"

Anger flashed over his face. "We weren't together. That was your doing. And I didn't cheat."

My doing?

Ugh, typical man, twisting history to suit himself and his agenda! I scoffed. "Yeah, right. But you moved on. And I couldn't. So, I guess that means you win."

He shook his head, taking another step toward me, and I held my hand up against him. He stopped, frustration mottling his cheeks. "I don't get it. I don't get this." He gestured between us.

I didn't get it either.

What I did know was that I was seconds from falling apart, and he was the last person I wanted to witness it.

"I asked you to leave. If you don't, I'm going to start screaming bloody murder."

Seeing the resolve on my face, Jamie cut me a dark look. "This discussion isn't over."

Fury still boiled inside me as he walked out of the bathroom, heading toward the front of the apartment. It's what propelled me out into the hall to call after him just as he reached the door.

He glanced over his shoulder. "Yeah?"

"Was it good?"

Confusion, wariness, and desire mingled in his expression. Then longing and weariness and something I couldn't quite decipher replaced it all. "It's fucking paradise with you," he said, his voice gruff. "Even though I wish it wasn't. I wish it were that with anyone but you."

My lips trembled as I tried to smile like I didn't care. Like his words didn't kill me. "Yeah, well, it's never happening again so you needn't flagellate yourself."

Jamie gave a bark of dark laughter as he pulled open the apartment door. "Don't make promises you can't keep."

I flinched when the door slammed behind him.

As I returned to the bedroom, tears slipping down my cheeks, I knew I should jump in the shower and wash the smell of him off me.

Instead, I curled on the bed, on top of the duvet, and closed my eyes, remembering the overwhelming feel of him pushing inside me. The pleasure burn that soon turned to rapture. Jamie's ocean eyes blazing with lust.

I grieved for the love in his eyes when he looked at me.

But it was with a dark smile of satisfaction that I finally drifted to sleep.

If tonight had proven anything, it was that I was still under his skin, just as much as he was under mine.

And I kind of liked being there.

Twisted little Jane Doe.

Guess Jamie's heart wasn't the only one all tangled up.

FILMING WAS ONLY HALFWAY DONE with Patel Smith's musical, and he'd decided to make a big change to one of the sets. Which meant I'd barely had an hour's sleep after Jamie left when I got the call from Sandy that I was needed in the studio. By some miracle we'd managed to pull the changes together in time for filming later that day.

I was just breathing a sigh of relief as Patel gave the changes his approval when my phone vibrated in my back pocket. Since Patel was deep in conversation with Sandy, I stepped away from the set, thinking it was probably Asher texting me. He'd already called that morning to see how I was feeling.

The urge to tell him everything was growing stronger. I needed to be there for my friend, and I couldn't because of the lies between us.

To protect Jamie, I'd kept my mouth shut and stewed in my crappy friend guilt.

The text wasn't from Asher.

> Jane, it's Lincoln. I had a great time
> meeting you last night. Would you still like
> to go to dinner with me?

Work had done little to get my mind off the nightclub or the events with Jamie after it.

The events.

I laughed at myself.

The screwing.

The screwing with Jamie.

Skin flushing, I pushed away those unhelpful images and texted Lincoln back that I would love to. We arranged to meet for dinner at an Italian place I liked downtown the following Thursday, his one of two nights off. At this rate, it would take months to infiltrate his friendship with Ethan Wright and use it to get what we needed.

On that thought, I realized I hadn't even asked Jamie what happened when he followed Wright after he'd left the club.

My hands shook as I shot Jamie a text to update him about Gaines.

He didn't respond.

Irritated, I tried to throw myself back into work, but my mind kept drifting to my ex and the bitter exchanges between us. We seemed at once incapable of letting go but also of forgiving each other.

An hour later Jamie still hadn't texted back, which bothered me more than I'd like. This was his grand plan, after all. He couldn't leave me hanging.

It was a surprise, then, when I got a call from security to say "Jamie Stone" was here to see me again. I told them to let him in, my heart pounding, my belly fluttering. It was a cruel fate that would make Jamie McKenna the only man who inspired such exhilaration.

"Is it your lunch break yet?" Jamie asked without preamble as I walked out of the soundstage to meet him by his car.

I wanted to pull my elbow back and then let my fist fly at his face. It didn't shock me that Jamie incited that violent passion in me.

He was seriously going to come here and just pretend like we didn't have sex?

"Earth to Jane," he said. "Come in, Jane."

He was!

"Are you kidding me?"

"We have somewhere to be." He opened the passenger side door. "Are you getting in? Or are you backing out of helping me *Count of Monte Cristo* the shit out of LA?"

I would not laugh or smile or be even remotely amused.

Fine.

If he wanted to play it that way, I could do that.

In fact, it was better. Pretending like it didn't happen was for the best. "Give me five minutes."

I returned a few minutes later with my purse after telling Lea I was taking my lunch break off the lot. Having gone from someone who lived and breathed every minute on the set to someone constantly distracted and taking lunch breaks, Jamie might just inadvertently ruin my career. Yay for him. Something to cross off that list of his.

Bastard.

Well, you didn't have to get in the car, Jane, I reminded myself.

True. Hello, self-sabotage.

As I got in, I tried to ignore how much the Porsche smelled like Jamie. When my gaze moved to his hands as he shifted into drive, I quickly wrenched my eyes away. All I saw were those gorgeous hands on me. I could still feel them wrapped tight around my wrists, pinning me to the bed while his hips thrust against mine.

Flushing hot, I stared out the passenger window. "Where are we going?"

"You'll see."

He drove across the river, past Universal City, heading south. His mysteriousness was making my irritation increase by the second. Moreover, I was hungry. I'd been promised a lunch break. As if reading my mind, Jamie drove the car off Barham Boulevard and pulled up to drive-thru at a sub place.

"What do you want?" He flicked his finger at the small restaurant.

"Where are we going?"

"Right now, we're grabbing some food." He pulled up to the outside menu. "What do you want?" Annoyingly, he read it to me. Every item, in detail, as if he were being paid to do it.

"I'll have the veggie sub," I cut him off, if only to make it end.

Jamie shot me a confused look. "You a vegetarian now?"

"No."

Not responding to my curtness, Jamie ordered our food and paid for it, handing over the bags to me as he drove back onto the main road and turned left, heading farther south.

Ten minutes from the studio lot, he parked along the sidewalk across from the hospital.

"Now will you tell me what we're doing here?"

He pointed down the street. "That yellow building is owned by a group of therapists who work at the hospital too. They host different therapy groups, including one called Coping with Cancer." The building was small compared to the others on this street; only two stories and painted a vibrant, sunny yellow.

Confused, I turned to him. "And we're here why?"

"You'll see. Keep your eyes on the door." He took his sub and drink from me and began eating. Casually. Like we were on a stakeout and this was an everyday occurrence for him.

Even though I was pissed at the subterfuge and drama, I was also hungry, so I ate as we waited. Ten minutes later, food gone, and tension still unbearably thick between us, I was about to complain when the door to the center swung open.

A few people stepped out onto the sidewalk, and I searched their faces for someone familiar.

Finally, a woman with short, silver-gray hair appeared and stopped to talk with a younger man. I recognized her from

Jamie's surveillance shots. I recognized her from court. My heart sped up.

I turned to Jamie. "Elena Marshall."

He was already looking at me, expression unreadable. "I checked everyone's financial records, and there were a lot of medical bills on Elena's. Considering how much money Foster Steadman must have paid her, that woman is up to her eyeballs in debt. Turns out she had breast cancer a few years ago. Now she volunteers and runs this support group for people suffering with cancer or who have lost a loved one to cancer."

Uneasiness churned in my gut as I watched Elena Marshall. She crossed the street, seeming in good health now, as she got into a small car. I was conflicted.

This woman had helped frame Jamie for a crime he didn't commit.

I hated her.

But I wondered if perhaps Karma hadn't already dealt with Elena Marshall. Cancer was no joke, and neither were the medical bills that came with it.

As if he could read my mind, Jamie spoke, his voice soft but hard at the same time. "Cancer happens to all kinds of people, Jane. It doesn't discriminate. Good, bad, and all in between. It doesn't exonerate her from what she did to me. She took five years of my life."

"Jamie ..." I thought I could do this, mete out a little justice, but maybe I wasn't built for it, after all.

"Do you know I can't go to the movies anymore? Something about the darkness and being trapped in a row of seats fucks me up."

Surprised he was telling me that, I turned to him.

His eyes were hard, filled with bitterness. "I don't like elevators. I can't stand being stuck in traffic. Flights are a nightmare. I need the windows open in my bedroom at night, and, even then, after years of being unable to sleep in that cell, it still takes me forever to fall asleep. I get a couple hours a night at most."

Prison had made Jamie claustrophobic and an insomniac.

Anguish filled me. "What else happened to you in there, Jamie?"

His ocean eyes turned stormy. "Not *that*. But there was nothing I could do when it happened to other guys. Guys younger than me, with no one to protect them. Irwin kept me safe, but the price of that was keeping my nose clean and out of everyone else's business. I didn't ..." Jamie wrenched his gaze away, probably because the haunted look on his face was bringing tears to my eyes. "Steadman made me realize there were evil bastards out there ... but there were a few prisoners who made me realize there are people in the world who take it to the next level. They take what they want, and they don't care who they hurt, as long as their needs are satisfied. Spending five years avoiding scum of the earth and feeling guilty for not doing anything to protect guys more vulnerable than me, it screws with your head ..."

My heart was breaking. "Why didn't you tell me this back then?"

His expression flattened. He scoffed. "Because I thought I was protecting you."

"Jamie—"

"Elena Marshall is one reason I lost five years of my life. That I now have a criminal record. If I didn't have my writing, I'd be struggling below minimum wage, doing shitty jobs under shitty employers willing to look the other way regarding my record so they could justify their shittiness." His tone was cold again, controlled. "I need you to attend the support group and connect with Elena. You'll find out personal details of her life, and we'll use that information to hit her where it hurts."

Hearing just a generalized summary of what Jamie had

gone through, what he'd seen, I knew the details were probably much worse. My anger for him chipped away at my uncertainty. But using a cancer support group made my stomach lurch. "Jamie, you cannot think that it's okay to use people going through what they're going through to get to Elena. I know you can't."

"Of course, I don't," he spat. "But I'm willing to do what it takes to get this done. I'm willing to bear the burden of my actions. Are you? Are you in or are you out, Jane?"

"Spending five years avoiding scum of the earth and feeling guilty for not doing anything to protect guys more vulnerable than me, it screws with your head ..."

Suddenly, I was nineteen again and looking at Jamie through Plexiglas.

"I need to know you're okay."

"Do you love me?"

"You know I do. You're my everything."

"Then I'm okay. He thought he took everything from me ... but he didn't take you, and you're all that fucking matters. So I'm okay. It'll get easier, Doe."

He *had* lied. To protect me.

I nodded, despite the nausea in my gut. "I'm in."

The tension drained out of Jamie, and he turned the ignition. Strained silence settled between us as he drove back toward the studio. Jake, the security guard, waved us through. Jamie parked near the soundstage door.

I unclipped my seat belt.

"If you tell me why you and Asher Steadman have been pretending to be in a relationship, maybe I can try to trust you again."

Disbelief stopped my departure. It really felt like Jamie had rewritten our history. He acted like *I* was the one who had broken up with him. "It's not my secret to tell. And I'm not the one in this relationship that broke us. *I* don't need to win back *your* trust. It's the other way around, Jamie."

His eyebrows hit his hairline and he let out a bark of incredulous laughter. "I broke your trust? You want me to trust you when you're protecting Asher Steadman over me?"

I shook my head at the childish dig. "It's not like that. I *can't* tell you. Not because I don't want to, but because it's not my right to tell you."

Jamie considered this. "Are you his beard? Is he gay?"

"No," I answered honestly.

"Then what is it?"

"Jamie—"

"You think you can trust this guy more than you can trust me?"

Was he serious? "You haven't given me any reason to trust you. You have me on your *Monte Cristo* hit list. Asher has been like family to me these past three years."

He sneered. "Asher Steadman is screwing with you, Jane. He told you he was helping you, right? That he would find something on his father that would help bring him down?"

"How did you know that?" How had he known I was going after Steadman in the first place?

"Am I right?"

I didn't respond.

Jamie leaned toward me, his voice lowered to a deep growl. "You put all your trust in that bastard, but he's never been helping you. He's been deliberately sabotaging your attempts."

Nausea rose inside me at the accusation, and I could feel the color draining from my face. *No. No way.* Jamie was just saying that to mess with my head. Asher was my friend. He was the one person in my life I could count on.

"I don't believe you."

"Fine. If you're so sure, why don't you ask him."

Needing to get away from him, I threw open the passenger door and practically jumped out, slamming it shut as hard as I could. I didn't waste another glance on Jamie as I hurried into the hangar.

I loved Asher.

He would never hurt me like Jamie had hurt me.

———

JAMIE

WATCHING Jane disappear into the studio, my fingers tightened around the steering wheel.

That morning, I'd woken up thinking about her. She was the first thing that popped into my head. I could even smell her on me.

Probably because I hadn't showered, not wanting to wash her away just yet.

Jane was messing everything up.

My focus was shot to pieces.

It was like we were kids again, and all I could think about was her. From the moment I realized I wanted her, that's how it had been between us. She was a constant thought in the back of my head, my every decision orbiting around her. And when she was in the room, I was aware of her every move.

I wanted to hate her.

Needed to.

Yet, I couldn't stop remembering that moment of peace as I melted inside her.

Everything had been quiet and pain-free—perfect—for the first time in seven years.

Skye warned me that needing someone the way I needed Jane would only cause sorrow in the end.

She was right.

Because I wanted that feeling of peace back. I wanted another taste.

And I was afraid I might do anything for it.

Something stupid. Something that would ruin everything.

Something like forgiving her.

Chapter Twenty-Six

JANE

Headlights flared, passing me on the 101 as I drove to Asher's Malibu beach house. Work had kept me at the studio late, so the highway wasn't clogged with traffic, but it was still busy.

I wondered where the strangers who passed me were going, and if they were just as afraid of their destination as I was. I hoped not. My palms were sweaty around the steering wheel and I couldn't get my heart to slow. I didn't want to believe Jamie was right. It was easier to think he was just trying to wound me again than to imagine that Asher had been playing me the whole time.

If one more person I loved screwed me over, I didn't know how I'd handle it.

Would I break?

My grip tightened on the wheel.

Or would I go numb?

Neither possibility sounded appealing.

Pulling up to the gates, I hit the clicker Asher had given me. The gates swung slowly open; I drove in as a tall figure stepped out of the open front door. The house was built in the 1950s and was of typical mid-century architecture. It sat on a cliff overlooking the ocean and had a private path that led down onto the beach.

Getting out of my car, my knees shook a little as I walked toward my best friend. His brow furrowed, most likely because I hadn't texted him to let him know I was on my way.

"Hey, baby." His tone was cautious, as though he could read my reason for being there in my body language.

"Have you been sabotaging my efforts to find incriminating evidence on Foster?"

Asher's eyes widened slightly.

Then I saw something in them that made me want to throw up.

Fear.

Guilt.

I squeezed my eyes closed, tears thick in my throat.

No, please, no.

"Jane, come in so I can explain." I felt him take my arm and then I was stumbling into the house.

The open-plan living space, the sunken living room that led into the kitchen, and the long bank of bifold doors that opened to a deck overlooking the ocean, suddenly didn't feel like the safe place it had felt for me these past few years.

I'd loved spending time at Asher's. He'd even given me my own room.

Wrenching my elbow out of his grip, I spun on him. "Tell me everything."

"Will you sit down?" Asher gestured to the sofa. "Please."

Blood rushing in my ears, I walked down into the seating area and perched on the end of the couch. Asher took the armchair next to me and leaned his elbows on his knees. His expression was so earnest.

Yet wasn't he about to tell me he'd screwed me over?

He exhaled slowly. "Jane, there are a few reasons I pretended to be investigating my father for *you*."

There it was.

My hands clenched into fists on my knees.

"One, I was afraid if he got suspicious, he'd start figuring out who you were. Two, I was afraid of hurting my mother in all this. The third reason ... I can't explain the third reason, but I will eventually."

"You will eventually? What does that mean?"

"I can't tell you." He sat forward, his expression desperate. "But you have to believe me when I say that I didn't lie to hurt you. I'm trying to protect you."

"No." I stood, needing physical distance. "You were protecting your family." Jamie was right. Jesus Christ. A sob caught in my throat. I couldn't trust anyone.

"Jane, how did you find out?"

I whirled on Asher and he flinched at my expression. "It doesn't matter."

"It does matter. Were you investigating me?"

"No." I'd let him think what he wanted. There was no way I could trust him to know that Jamie was in LA trying to get revenge against Foster. The thought of Asher telling Foster about Jamie made me feel sick. Thank God I'd decided not to confide in him. The consequences didn't even bear thinking about.

"Jane—"

I held up a hand against whatever else he would say. What other pitiful excuses he'd give for making a fool out of me. I stared into his dark eyes. Dark eyes that used to make me feel safe. "There have been only two men that I have ever loved.

Jamie. You. *Two.* And both of you broke my heart." I moved toward the door.

"Jane!" Asher grabbed my arm and I jerked out of his hold, stumbling back.

"Don't touch me," I hissed.

"One day I'll explain," he promised, determination hardening his features.

I wanted to believe him, but I was too afraid to.

The drive back to Silver Lake was a blur. I couldn't remember getting from Asher's beach house to my building. Emotions had me reeling. Noting Jamie's Porsche in his parking spot, I walked upstairs to our floor and knocked on his door.

Footsteps sounded behind it.

Then he was there. Leaning against the door frame, expressionless as he took in my tear-stained face.

"You were right," I told him dully.

Jamie just stared pitifully at me.

I curled my upper lip. "Don't worry, I didn't tell him how I found out. Although I'd be interested to know how *you* found out."

He smirked and gave a slight shake of his head.

That smirk ... that stupid little smirk in the face of my pain hurt worse than anything so far since he'd come back into my life. I stumbled back. "You don't even care. You don't even care that this hurts me."

Something flickered in Jamie's eyes as he straightened up from the door frame. "Do you love him?"

Would it wound him if I had? "I thought I did."

Jamie clenched his jaw, his gaze dropping to the floor, probably to hide whatever it was he felt.

I scoffed. "You asked me if I love him. You didn't ask me if I was *in* love with him." *There's a big difference, Jamie.*

His eyes met mine. "Are you in love with him?"

Did he deserve to even know the answer?

Shouldn't I torture him a little?

I slumped, so goddamn weary, I couldn't stand it. "No. And I never have been."

There's only one man I have ever been in love with.

When he continued to stare at me, not giving anything away, hoarding his thoughts and feelings to himself, I fought the urge to shove him. To slap him. To scream at him.

But that wasn't me.

I wouldn't let him turn me into that person.

With a snort of derision, I turned on my heel, walked toward my apartment, and stuck my key in the door. "Text me what I need to know about Elena." Before he could respond, I stepped inside and slammed the door behind me.

Agitation boiled my blood as I stalked through my apartment, restless and uneasy. I had an urge to curl up in a ball and sob for days.

But that wasn't me anymore.

Yes, I'd lost everything that mattered to me six years ago. However, I'd survived it.

"You survived it," I reminded myself, fists clenched at my side.

I would survive losing Asher.

I would survive once Jamie got what he'd come to LA for and left me again.

I wouldn't go numb to protect myself.

And no one ... *no one* would break me.

———

ASHER TRIED TO CALL. Jamie too. He even knocked on my apartment door a few times.

I ignored all of it and attempted to concentrate on the day-to-day routine of working on set and on a painting underway at home for an art gallery in San Francisco. However, I didn't ignore Jamie's text with the information on Elena Marshall. After several days away from Jamie, and having worked through the weekend and most of the week on Patel's movie, I took Thursday off. Around lunchtime, I got in my car and drove to the hospital in Hollywood.

After I parked, I strolled to the yellow building. My steps slowed as I neared it. Once inside, a receptionist directed me to the room I was looking for, but when I stopped outside the double doors and stared in through the inset windowpanes, I found I couldn't go any farther.

As much as I wanted to help Jamie find some peace, the idea of infiltrating a cancer support group made me sick to my stomach. I couldn't go in and pretend to be there because a loved one was suffering. It was a betrayal to the others who had come to that group to find people who understood what they were going through.

My gaze zeroed in on Elena. She'd been in her late thirties when she testified against Jamie. A perfectly ordinary woman, she'd worked night shift at the twenty-four-hour mini-mart for six years before Steadman paid her to lie. Jamie and I never knew if she'd known she'd get shot that night, but we surmised it had always been part of the plan because it meant a longer sentence for Jamie.

Right then, she leaned across from her chair to hold the hand of a young woman who was crying as she spoke. It was an act of kindness. Of comfort. Elena's eyes were sad but warm as she gave the girl's hand a squeeze.

I remembered at the time when she testified against Jamie in court that she didn't *seem* like the kind of person who would persecute an innocent man. I didn't care then, though. At nineteen, there were no shades of gray in the case against Jamie. As far as I was concerned, everyone involved in framing him was wicked and cruel.

The rage I'd felt toward her the day she stood on the stand and identified Jamie as the man who had shot her had cooled a lot since then. Now I longed for answers. I wanted to make sense of this woman's choices. I wanted to know if what she'd already been through would satisfy Jamie.

Would it satisfy me?

However, I couldn't go in there.

Every time I went to push inside, I faltered and paced outside the doors, trying to drum up the courage to walk in. It never came. Frustrated, I slumped down on a chair outside the room and buried my head in my hands. There had to be another way to get close to Elena without disrespecting a room filled with strangers.

Skye would not agree with this, and considering half the reason I was still on Jamie's side in all this was because of Skye, I couldn't go through with it. She was the voice in the back of my head. If it had all been about Skye and not Jamie, I wouldn't be doing any of it because Skye wouldn't want it. She'd want Jamie and I to move on and live our lives.

I knew that with absolute certainty.

But Jamie couldn't do that, so here I was. Helping him.

Or failing at helping him.

The feel of a hand on my shoulder brought my head up. Startled, I stared into the warm brown eyes of Elena Marshall. Taken aback, I realized that the support group had dispersed, a few shooting me curious looks as they departed.

"Are you okay?" Elena sat on the chair beside me. "I saw you hovering outside the entire time."

Stunned to be this close to her, I couldn't speak.

Emotion, anger being the foremost, clogged my throat, and I realized I hadn't let go of my fury toward her as much as I'd like to think.

"Are you sick or does someone you love have cancer?" she asked tentatively, as though she was afraid to spook me.

Look at her. That seemingly genuine concern in her eyes. Was it real? How could it be? How could a kind person do what she had done to Jamie? Did they talk about pain management in her support group? I could talk about that for days, how Jamie was in so much pain, there didn't seem to be anything I could do to take it away. "Someone I love," I whispered.

Elena nodded. "It's difficult, isn't it?"

"Very."

She held out her hand. "I'm Elena. I run the Coping with Cancer support group."

I stared at her held-out hand. I couldn't shake it.

Her smile wilted a little as she lowered it. "Why didn't you join us today?"

"It didn't … it didn't feel right," I answered honestly.

She nodded like she understood. "It can be difficult to open up to a room of strangers, but it's amazing how much relief can be found from talking with people who understand what you're going through. Or people who have cancer and can offer you advice on how to be there for your loved one."

"What is it for you?" I asked. "Did you have cancer or was it someone you loved?"

"I *have* cancer." Her smile trembled a little. "I fought breast cancer several years ago, but I just found out that it's back."

Fuck.

I bowed my head, looking at my feet. "I'm sorry."

"I've fought it before. I'll fight it again." Elena sighed heavily. "Why did you come today?"

Why did you do what you did?

That's what *I* really wanted to ask. Instead, I looked at her and let all my confusion and anger blaze out of my eyes. "Something took our power away. Both of us. His and mine." Not something. Someone. *You did. Foster did. Wright.*

Kramer. You all took his power away. "And it hasn't come back. I'm powerless to help him, and I think he blames me." *I know he blames me.* "I think he feels abandoned ..."

She nodded in understanding. "I can't tell you whether that's how your ..."

"Boyfriend," I offered.

"How your boyfriend feels. But is it possible you're projecting? That helplessness is making you feel you're not doing enough for him?" She edged closer. "All you can do is be there to offer comfort and hold his hand through this, to make sure he knows you're not going anywhere."

I glanced away, wondering if it would be enough. And was I a moron for even considering seeing Jamie through this, hoping I'd get the man I used to love back?

It was too confusing.

One minute I didn't want anything to do with Jamie, and the next I was desperate to find a way to bring him peace again.

"The others in the group can offer you great insight." Elena stood, and I followed suit. "Why don't you come back next week? We'll be here. Same time."

I nodded, muttering my thanks under my breath as I turned to walk out.

"Hey, I didn't get your name!" I heard her call after me.

I didn't answer. I just kept walking.

And it wasn't until I got into my car, I realized I hadn't asked Elena a thing about her life like I was supposed to.

My phone beeped just as I was about to pull away. It was a text from Lincoln.

Can't wait to see you tonight.

Just like that, I felt overwhelmed by resentment.

Jamie was sending me out on a fake date with a cop. I'd lied to get close to Elena Marshall.

I felt like I was losing myself.

And was I willing to do that for Jamie, when he didn't seem to care that my actions over the next few weeks could mark me forever?

"What do *you* want, Jane?" I bit out under my breath, my fists squeezing the steering wheel.

I wanted justice.

I wanted to know that the people who had hurt my family weren't getting to live life like they hadn't inflicted irreparable damage on others.

I wanted peace for Jamie, and for myself.

But I didn't want to lose myself to get it, and now I didn't know how to turn back.

I was frustrated. But it was easier to resent Jamie. That resentment simmered as I drove back to Silver Lake.

CHAPTER TWENTY-SEVEN

JAMIE

WITH EXPOSED DUCTS AND PIPES, oversized Edison bulbs as light fixtures, and wood and steel furniture, the Italian restaurant had a casual warehouse vibe. Sitting at the bar centered in a room crowded with tables, I had an eyeline to Jane and Lincoln Gaines.

I hadn't seen Jane in days. Although she answered my texts, she wouldn't answer my calls and I was itching to see her. My agent wanted me to sign off on the proof copy of my second manuscript, which provided me with little distraction since Jane was the inspiration for the twisted love story I'd written. Jane was like a hangnail. I could put her to the back of my mind, but the sting remained.

That's why I'd been watching for her return from the visit to Elena's support group. I stood in my doorway, waiting as her footsteps echoed up the stairwell. As soon as she turned the corner and came into view, my skin crackled to life.

Despite looking a little drawn, Jane was beautiful, as

always, as she caught sight of me and continued upstairs without faltering. She drew to a halt. "I didn't go in."

Somehow that didn't surprise me. And it didn't bother me. Jane was nothing if not respectful of other people's pain. "Okay."

"I did speak to her."

The idea of Jane anywhere near the dangerous bitch agitated me. But I was the bastard who'd asked her to do it. When she relayed she'd learned nothing from her, I told her it didn't matter. She'd made contact. It was a start.

Now I was the bastard encouraging her to go on a date with Gaines. If Jane was uncomfortable with it, she'd be gratified to know I was a goddamn mess. The two of them made a striking couple, dressed casually for the relaxed restaurant. They exchanged smiles as they chatted, each one of Jane's a dagger in my fucking gut.

When Gaines reached over and touched her hand for the fifth time, I almost aimed my table knife in his direction.

The plan was for Jane to not overengage in our agenda this evening. Get to know Gaines. Go in stealthy. Ask only a few questions about his job and his partner, Ethan Wright. This would be a slow game, and one I hadn't thought through.

There was no way Jane could keep Gaines at bay when it came to sex. At first, sure. But after a few weeks?

Sex? Touching and kissing was bad enough.

On what planet did I ever think I could stand by and let Jane do this? And not just because it was eating me alive with jealousy to see her on a date with another man, but because I was swinging her ass out there. She could get hurt. Never mind physically hurt. Jane hated lying to people. This subterfuge must be twisting her up inside.

"Lincoln's a nice guy. We shouldn't do this to him."

"You can back out anytime."

"No."

I thought I could do this. I thought I could use her.

I couldn't.

I sat there stewing over dinner for two hours as I watched Jane and Gaines through the passing bodies of people who came and went at the bar. *Fuck this.* Pulling my phone out of my pocket, I was about to send Jane a text to tell her to end it when I noted Gaines asking for the check.

Shit.

I hurried to do the same and had just paid as Jane and Gaines got up from the table. He put his hand on her lower back to lead her out, and my eyes zeroed in on the spot. I wanted to rip his hand off.

Seething, I followed them out of the restaurant at a distance and sent Jane a text to tell her to find an excuse to finish up the date. There had to be another way to get to Wright. One that didn't involve Jane lying to a cop for weeks.

To keep up the ruse, Jane had taken my Porsche and I was driving her car. Whatever she said to him had him leading her to where she'd parked the sports car a block around the corner from the restaurant. I couldn't get parked near her. Fucking downtown. It was a miracle she'd found a parking spot this close to the restaurant.

Keeping my distance, I watched as Gaines suddenly slipped his hand around Jane's waist and bent to kiss her.

Not just a peck either.

No, he went for it.

And she kissed him back.

My heart stumbled as I watched her press her palms to Gaines's chest. Wait, was she kissing him back or pushing him away? Panicked, I made to stride toward them when they suddenly broke apart and she gave the dickhead a shy smile. He brushed his thumb over her cheek, pressed a kiss to her nose, and stepped back.

Adrenaline shot through me, and I barely had time to turn

around and walk away before the cop spotted me. I disappeared around the corner and peeked back to see if Jane was in the Porsche.

What the hell was that? Why the fuck did she kiss him back?

What else was she supposed to do? I argued with myself as I marched to Jane's car.

By the time I got back to Silver Lake, my Porsche was in my parking space. I drove Jane's into hers and dashed inside the building. I didn't know what I expected when I hammered my fist on her apartment door.

I wanted to kiss her. To make the taste of Lincoln Gaines a distant fucking memory, and I didn't care what that said about me.

She called out that the door was open. I strode inside her apartment, slamming the door behind me, and came to an abrupt halt.

Jane stood in the middle of her living room, and she looked tortured.

Actually tortured.

Acid burned in my gut.

"I'm sorry," I blurted out before she could speak. "I shouldn't have asked you to do this."

"Because it made you jealous?"

"Yes, I was jealous." I surprised the hell out of myself by admitting it. "But that's not why I shouldn't have asked you. I'm putting you in a position I would kill someone else for putting you in."

"You hate me. Why do you care what any of this is doing to me? Isn't it part of your grand plan, Jamie? I mean, I'm just Asher Steadman's whore to you. I fucked around behind your back when you were in prison, right? That's what you told yourself. I'm a traitorous bitch you threw away because you stopped having faith in—"

I couldn't listen to this. "Jane—"

She stepped toward me, face mottled with fury and pain. "Who cares who I have to lie to, or what personal morals I have to compromise, or who I have to *fuck* so you can get your revenge, right? I should see it as a positive, shouldn't I? Fucking Gaines will expand my experience, let me catch up with yours."

I grabbed her biceps, forcing her to look at me. "Stop it."

"Oh, does that bother you, Jamie? Thinking of me and Lincoln. Or do you get off on it? Does the sting of jealousy feel good? The knowledge that you've pushed me right down to where you think I belong? I'm just scum, right? I don't need you to care about me anymore. I don't need you or Asher or Lorna to want me, to love me. I don't need to hide behind a name my adoptive parents gave me because I grieve for the life that should have been mine. I should stop living in a fantasy world.

"I'm just Jane Doe. I'm nothing. I'm unlovable. I'm an emotional punching bag. Use me for what gets you off and then just spit on what's left." She laughed hysterically.

Fear climbed through me. "Jane, stop it."

"I hate you." Her laughter turned to sobs.

"No, you don't." I pulled her toward me.

Then she shocked the shit out of me by wrenching away and screaming, "I HATE YOU!" with such anguish, she almost took me out at the knees.

Tears burned in my eyes as she stood, chest heaving with shallow breaths, and stared at me in disgust. "Jane—"

"Get out! I hate you, get out!" she yelled over and over.

Fuck! I hauled her into my arms, wrapping Jane in a constricting embrace as I pressed my lips to her ear and begged her to stop. This wasn't her. This wasn't my Jane.

I was terrified I'd broken her.

And I realized as I covered Jane's tear-stained face in kisses and felt her fingernails dig into my back as she held onto me that I would never hurt her.

I couldn't.

Not like I'd planned.

I couldn't even witness her in pain without it breaking me apart.

Because no matter the fact that she abandoned me when I needed her, I still loved her.

I would always love Jane.

It was the kind of love that would never fade.

I forgave her.

If the choice was between not forgiving her and being without her, then I forgave her.

I'd forgive Jane anything.

JANE

Shaking and trembling in Jamie's embrace, I felt in shock. I had no idea I would lose it like that.

Yet I knew it had been building all day. For days, actually. Seeing Elena had reminded me of how much pain I'd been in for Jamie when he went to prison. The pain I'd been in that visiting him behind bars. It was the first time I'd realized that loving someone meant hurting for them more than you would for yourself. I still felt that for him.

And he'd sent me on a date with another guy.

Not just any guy.

A cop.

One partnered with a dangerous cop.

I knew I'd volunteered to do it, but as I sat across from Lincoln Gaines, that fuse of resentment that sparked earlier in the day burned down to the wire. How could Jamie be all right with putting me in that position? In what reality was it okay that he not only let me do this, he handed me the keys to his Porsche for the date and reminded me "to treat tonight like an actual date and not push on anything regarding Wright."

I resented Jamie. I resented my feelings for him and his lack of feelings for me.

I was indignant that I be treated like the bad guy when he was the one who broke up with me.

Even if he had misunderstood the Asher situation, he knew the truth now, and yet he was still using me.

We'd had sex, and he pretended like it never happened.

Then there was me. A woman who'd changed her legal name to the one her adoptive parents gave her, clinging to something I should've let go a long time ago. I had, once. When Jamie and I fell in love, I'd finally let go of dreaming for a life as Margot Higgins.

But then he pushed me away.

And I was right back at square one.

Only for him to return—and now, wasn't I just clinging to him the same way I'd clung to a girl who didn't exist?

For days, I'd been telling myself I was okay. That I'd survive Jamie coming back into my life. That I'd survive Asher's lies.

I'd survive.

But you can keep telling yourself you're okay and not be okay. I was a goddamn swan on the water, calm on the surface, and kicking like hell beneath it.

Those feelings exploded out of me when I least expected them to.

"I'm sorry." Jamie's voice was hoarse with emotion. "I'm sorry, Doe."

I tensed at the old endearment.

Feeling me stiffen, Jamie's embrace only tightened. "I'm sorry. I'm so fucking sorry."

"You don't mean it," I whispered.

"You scared me." He kissed a tear track on my cheek and followed its trail to the corner of my mouth. Holding my face in his hands, he switched to the other cheek, his stubble prickling me with the movement. Then he kissed every bit of skin a tear had touched. I was afraid to move. Afraid to break the spell of his gentleness.

And I was exhausted from my meltdown.

I didn't understand what was happening.

When his lips brushed over mine, my breath hitched as they tingled, and I jerked my head back to stare into his eyes.

What I saw there made my heart stop.

Jamie, *my* Jamie, gazed down at me. Like he used to. Like he loved me. It chipped at my weakness. "Don't," I demanded hoarsely. "Don't look at me like that when you don't mean it."

"I do mean it." He leaned in to brush his mouth over mine again, and he groaned before burying his head in the crook of my neck. The rasp of his unshaven cheeks against my skin made me shiver. His hands moved around my back and he crushed me to him. "I need you to forgive me."

Astonished, I couldn't move. I couldn't lift my arms to return his embrace. What was happening?

Jamie sighed against me and then lifted his head. But he didn't let me go. His hands rested possessively on my hips. "I love you. I never stopped loving you."

My heart stopped.

"You don't treat someone you love the way you've treated me."

Remorse darkened his face. "I know. I wish I knew how to take it back."

"You pushed me away when you were in prison. You know that, don't you? It started back then. I'd tell you I loved you, and you stopped saying it back. I counted how many times." Fresh tears filled my eyes as I stared up him, thinking of all the years we lost and not because he was in prison. "Twelve times.

Twelve weeks I visited and said I love you, and you never said it back. It started then. You hated me then, didn't you? You blamed me for telling you about the diaries."

Disbelief slackened Jamie's expression, and his grip on me turned bruising. "Jane, no. No. I didn't then and I don't now."

"Then why?"

"I didn't ..." He exhaled shakily. "I didn't plan to push you away. But I guess I did, and once you were gone, I needed to hate you."

A score of anguish cut through my chest and I tried to pull away, but he wouldn't let me.

"No, Jane." He bent his head to me, gazing fiercely into my eyes. "I didn't believe I deserved happiness. I don't believe it. Not after what happened to Skye under my fucking nose. Not after I lost you. Not after the things I stood by and let happen in that place. Coming after you, hating you, I knew it would mean we'd be ruined forever. That I could never get you back."

Horrible understanding made me relax against him. *Oh, Jamie.* "It was self-destruction."

He flinched and looked down at where we touched. "I don't deserve you ..." His eyes returned to mine, tears shining in them. "But from the moment I saw you again, I wanted the past seven years to have been a nightmare that I *could* wake up from." He stumbled back, scrubbing his hand over his face. "Tell me to leave, Jane. Tell me to get the fuck out of your life because I can't let go of what they did to me. I can't move on, and you deserve the chance to move on."

I couldn't.

Whether it was right or wrong, I still wanted justice too.

But more than that, I wanted him.

I loved him.

Why couldn't I stop loving him?

"Jamie." I took a step toward him. "I can't tell you to leave. I want you to stay, but if you do, we're a team. You respect me, and I respect you. The first time you insult me or try to make me feel less than I am, I will walk away for good."

"A second chance?" His chest rose and fell in shallow breaths.

I nodded, my heart beating hard. "If we don't at least try, then those bastards really did win, didn't they?"

Suddenly, I was in Jamie's arms and he was kissing me like I was oxygen. The familiar taste of him, the hungry emotion in his kiss, flicked a switch in me. Everything else, all the worries, all the forgiveness that would be a daily endeavor to overcome, were gone. It was just me and Jamie. As if the last seven years had never happened.

His growl of need vibrated down my throat, tugging deep in my belly. We stumbled against the wall as Jamie gripped the back of my neck with one hand and slid the other down my stomach. His fingers hooked inside the waistband of my jeans, yanking me into his body.

I kissed him harder and clung to him, my fingers digging into his back as I lifted my leg, my thigh pressed to his hip as I undulated against the hard heat of him. He bent his knees and then rolled his hips up into mine so his erection nudged between my legs. My lips parted on a whimper of lust and seven years of need.

Yes, we'd had sex already.

But this was different.

Before, it was an angry submission to passion.

Now ... now we could be Jamie and Jane again.

Jamie's hand tightened around my neck, and he groaned. I felt my breasts swell, my nipples hardening into tight, needy points. Desire built low in my womb as I moved against him. God, it was like when we were teenagers.

His kisses grew more demanding, long, dizzying kisses,

each one seeming to make up for years of missing my lips. We were panting and pulling at each other's mouths like we couldn't get deep enough.

I slid my hands up his back and over his shoulders, my fingers sinking into his hair as I silently begged for more, for harder, for deeper, for everything.

From him.

Jamie.

Was this really happening?

Needing him to touch me, I took his hand off the waistband of my jeans and pressed it to my breast. His kiss turned almost savage as he crushed me deeper against the wall and squeezed. I gasped into his kiss as his thumb swiped across my nipple. I needed to be naked. I needed to feel him everywhere.

Jamie broke the kiss, but only to haul me into his arms. I held on and wrapped my legs around his waist as he walked us toward my bedroom. "I love you, Doe." His expression was harsh with emotion.

I brushed my thumb over his mouth, melting into him. My heart raced. The moment felt so surreal. "I love you, Jamie. I never stopped."

His eyes flashed with satisfaction as he kissed me on our descent to the bed. I expected it to be fast, hurried and explosive. Instead, he slowly undressed me until I was naked and shivering with need on the bed. I watched as Jamie stood over me, hungry eyes taking in every detail of my body as he removed his clothes. He was even more beautiful than I remembered. Lean but strong, defined abs and V-cut obliques that made my mouth water. An ache flared across my chest at the sight of the small white scar on the right side of his upper belly.

I caressed it, remembering the fear that accompanied the memory.

I met his gaze and saw the love in his moody ocean eyes, and everything within me tightened with anticipation.

His eyes darkened and my hips rose slightly off the bed.

He knew.

Jamie knew how much being loved by him turned me on.

He put a knee on the bed, his erection thick, throbbing, and proud as he straddled me. I whispered his name. He was quiet. When we were younger, Jamie would tell me everything he wanted to do to me, or how what he was doing to me made him feel. But this moment was too big for words.

I understood.

His fingertips trailed over the tops of my thighs as he hovered above me and bent to brush his lips over mine. I clung to his waist, loving the feel of his sleek, hard, warm strength, and I captured his mouth again before he could retreat.

I poured everything I felt into that kiss. *I love you, I love you, I love you.* Jamie clasped my face in his hand as he sunk into it, our tongues dancing together in the deepest kiss of my life. I felt tears burn in my throat but fought to keep them at bay as his lips reluctantly left mine to kiss a trail down my throat.

I loved the scratch of his stubble on my skin.

It was still new, reminding me this wasn't seven years ago, and what was happening between us was more poignant for it.

Jamie pressed soft kisses down my chest and took his time kissing and caressing my breasts. He spent so much time laving and licking and sucking my nipples that I writhed beneath him, on the verge of coming. My skin was on fire, my heart thundering in my chest, the tension coiled deep in my belly.

"Jamie," I gasped as he suckled my nipple until it was unbearably sensitive. "I'm going to come."

He lifted his head, his eyes blazing. "Not yet."

His lips left my breasts only to kiss a path down my stomach. He licked at my belly button and I shifted my hips impatiently. I wanted him to reach the destination already.

The sound of his soft laughter, his breath hot on my skin, caused a pang of sweet happiness. I grinned at the sound, my fingers shifting through his thick, silky hair as he glanced up my body to share a smile.

"I love you," I whispered.

Jamie's eyes brightened. "I love you more."

"So competitive," I teased.

He chuckled and then kissed me just above my sex, his eyes on me.

My breath caught as his lips skirted where I wanted them to go. He raised my left thigh off the bed and started at my knee. His kisses were wet, savoring, hungry, as his mouth made its way up my inner thigh. His stubble scratched and tickled, adding a whole new layer of sensation to the experience. When he licked the crease between my thigh and sex, my hips lifted off the bed with a startled gasp.

"You're so beautiful," he said reverently, his breath puffing against me.

"Please." I slid my fingers in his hair, staring down at him in torment. "Please."

His mouth came down on me.

I whimpered, throwing my head back, hands fisting the sheets at my sides as I let my legs fall open to him. He flicked my clit in a tease, circling it, tormenting me. Then something took him over. Jamie's hands gripped tight to my thighs as his mouth devoured.

I could feel my climax teetering on the edge, the muscles in my thighs trembling and tightening.

Then his fingers entered the playing field.

I gasped, moaning in growing need as he pushed me further toward orgasm.

It didn't take long. I stiffened and exploded, crying out his name as my inner muscles clamped around his fingers.

But he didn't stop.

Jamie kept sucking, licking me, groaning and growling like a starving man, until I was coming again. "Jamie!" I screamed his name in disbelief as another orgasm shuddered through me.

Then he was over me, his mouth on mine, his tongue licking at my tongue, until I could taste us both.

He broke the kiss, his expression pained. "Condom," he panted.

"I'm on the pill." I was frantic. I didn't want to wait. I could feel him hard and throbbing against my wet, and I wanted him.

Jamie looked in agony as he shook his head. "I haven't been checked in six months."

It was a cold, hard splash of reality.

Jamie had slept with another woman, perhaps several, in the last six months.

It cooled my skin.

"No, no." Jamie rested more of his weight into me as he stared into my eyes. "Don't think about it. Don't pull away. No one has ever meant anything to me but you ... and as much as I want to come inside you, I love you too much. I'm not going bare until I've been checked."

I nodded, my emotions swinging from left to right. This was *my* Jamie in my arms. The Jamie who protected me from everything, even himself. Still, "I don't have any condoms."

He lowered his forehead to my chest and took a deep, shaky breath. "Give me a second." Then he jumped off the bed and hurried out of the bedroom.

I raised myself onto my elbows as I listened to my front door open. Then I heard the distant sound of his apartment door opening and slamming a few seconds later.

Then my door banged shut.

Jamie marched into the bedroom, and I swear I had a mini orgasm at the sight of him rolling a condom onto his hard length.

"God, you're unfairly hot," I groaned, flopping back against the bed, my legs parting naturally for him.

"You're one to talk." He threw himself on me, and I laughed.

My laughter petered out into gasps, however, as he claimed my body with more kisses.

"Wrap your legs around me," he demanded gruffly against my lips.

I did as he asked, feeling him nudge between my legs. "Jamie." I sighed needfully.

Then he was there, pushing gently inside.

Our eyes locked as his thickness filled me, our soft pants falling against each other's lips as he moved deeper and deeper.

Under my skin.

Forever.

"No one but you," he promised, emotion making his eyes bright. "I missed you every day, Doe."

"Me too," I confessed. Nothing was right in this world if I wasn't connected with Jamie McKenna. Caressing his back, I moved my fingertips around to his abs and down, my touch making his hips falter. His breathing hitched as my fingers moved across his sensitive skin and through the crinkle of hair to where we were joined. I wanted to feel our connection.

"Oh, fuck." He bowed his head in pleasure as I felt him move in and out of me.

Reaching between us, he took my hand and pressed my fingers to my clit. He guided my fingers, bracing himself with one hand as he glided, slow and deep. He looked up from watching us touch me, and held my eyes as he made love to me. He pulled back, sliding out, but only so he could brace himself on his knees. Grabbing my hips in his big hands, he tilted them and drove back in at an angle, hitting me in a place that sent me to the stars.

"Jamie!" I cried out as he continued to move slow and easy, but each glide forcing a deeper penetration against the coiling tension inside. I trembled against him as he took pleasure in taking his time. Jamie was savoring this. Savoring us.

What made it sexier was my need to move against him and my inability to do so because he was holding my hips captive. With one more thick push in and slow drag out, I broke.

My hips stiffened for a beat and then I quivered, my inner muscles rippling in deep, tugging throbs around him.

"Jane." His grip loosened and he fell over me, bracing his hands at either side of my head as I came around him. He thrust into the sensation, fast, hard drives, guttural sounds of pleasure falling from his lips seconds before he tensed.

Then his hips stilled.

"Jane," he growled. I felt the pulsing waves of his release as he jerked and shuddered ... and shuddered some more.

"Fuck." Jamie breathed, falling against me. "Fuck, fuck, fuck." He rolled onto his back so he wouldn't crush me, his chest rising and falling in shallow pants. "What the fuck was that?"

My heart raced as I tried to calm.

Our skin was dewy, slick with sweat, as I turned my head to look at him.

I found him staring at me in awe.

I smiled.

"That happened, right?" His deep voice coiled around my heart. "That was the best sex of our lives, right? Of anyone's life."

Grinning, I felt giddy and scared and euphoric and worried all at once.

Jamie rolled onto his side and pulled me onto mine so he

could tangle our legs together, so he could feel my breasts against his chest. "I love you." He kissed me, intense, a little frantic. "You're here. We're here. And you'll never leave me again. Promise you'll never leave me again."

Just like that, anger bloomed in my gut.

Quick. Fiery. And dispelling the mood like a bomb.

I wrenched away from him. "Jamie McKenna, if we're going to make this work, you have to stop. Stop acting like *I* left *you*. *You* broke up with *me*. Remember? I still have the goddamn letter."

Jamie's brows furrowed. "What fucking letter?"

CHAPTER TWENTY-EIGHT

JANE

"WHAT FUCKING LETTER, JANE?" Jamie repeated, sitting up.

My pulse raced as an ominous feeling settled over me at the sight of his genuine confusion. I pushed up to sit beside him. "The letter Lorna gave me. The letter you wrote."

"When?" he demanded.

"A few days after I visited you. Six years ago." I made to move out of bed, and Jamie grabbed my wrist. "I'm getting the letter."

He released me, but his breathing was shallow, agitated.

So was mine.

I yanked his T-shirt up off the floor and pulled it on before I hurried to my closet. Hauling over my artist's stool so I could reach the top shelf, I pushed shoeboxes aside to find the one with my keepsakes. Taking it down and over to the bed, I threw off the lid, desperate to find the letter. The box was filled with old photos of me and the McKennas, even a few with Willa, Nick, Tarin, and Flo, though I rarely ever saw them now.

Shoving aside trinkets and ticket stubs, I found the letter buried at the bottom. My hands shook as I unfolded it. Looking at Jamie, I saw him studying the paper with a wrinkle between his brow.

I held it out to him.

He took it.

I still remembered every word.

I blame you. I know it all wasn't your fault but some of it was. I will always love you but I also think things might have been better if you'd never been a part of our lives. That way I couldn't miss what I'd had with you and hate you for how it all turned out. You being around just complicates things. I don't need you in my life anymore. There's just too much bad shit between us. I don't want to see you anymore, and I don't want you to visit. Don't try to call either. Just ... don't.

Jamie scanned it, his fingers biting so hard into the paper, it crumpled. His chest heaved, like he couldn't get enough air. He threw himself off the bed, running a shaky hand through his hair as he looked over at me. "Where and when did you get this?"

For me, that moment was like yesterday. "You'd been in prison for about a year. Things were getting more strained between us with every visit. My last visit—not the one running up to your parole, but the one six years ago—you were caustic about Devin. Do you remember?"

"I remember it, Jane. I remember every second because it was the last time I saw you until you came to visit me two years ago."

"That's why." I pointed to the letter. "Lorna came to see me just a few days after that visit. She was in LA to see you and catch up with some friends."

He nodded. "I remember."

"She gave me that letter and said you asked her to pass it along. That you didn't want to see me again. She told me I was to blame for everything and that I was to stay away." Tears streamed down my cheeks as his reaction awoke dark suspicion. "It's your handwriting, Jamie."

"From when I was fifteen!" he roared and spun, planting his fist through my floor-standing mirror.

I yelled his name as it shattered, pieces falling at his feet.

"Oh my God, Jamie." I rushed forward, trying to avoid the shards littering my floor.

There was blood on his knuckles. Taking hold of his wrist, I led him away from the glass, my heart thundering as I guided him into the bathroom. He was seething and silent, and my mind reeled as I tried to focus on cleaning up his knuckles with my first aid kit.

"I don't think you need stitches," I whispered, fighting back tears.

When I met his gaze, I saw he was holding back tears too. "How could she do that to us?"

Then it was like he couldn't bear his own weight. He slumped into me, falling to his knees as he wrapped his arms around my waist. His hands fisted in his T-shirt I'd thrown on, and he burrowed into me, desperate, as if he couldn't get close enough. I could feel him shaking.

I tried to be strong, but I couldn't hold back tears as the realization of Lorna's duplicity cut us both to the quick.

I didn't understand the full plot yet, but I got the general gist of it.

And it was heartbreakingly tragic.

Soon I was on the bathroom floor with him, our backs pressed to the tub, my head resting on his shoulder as we gripped tight to each other's hands. I don't know how long we sat there before Jamie finally spoke.

"I wrote that letter to my dad when I was fifteen, and I

never sent it. He'd started coming around again after Mom died. There was a part of me that wanted him around because he was good with me. But he was an absolute bastard to Lorna. Treated her like shit. Hurt her so much that it hurt me too.

"It made me suspect that Lor wasn't his. We all had Mom's eyes, but Skye and I looked so much like our dad, and Lor didn't. When I was younger, I never even thought that Lorna knew what I suspected, but when I got out of prison, I went to live in Boston for a while to be close to her. She works for a law firm there now. And she told me then that when she was ten, she overheard an argument between our parents. She wasn't Dad's. Mom had cheated. Lorna reached out to him when she was in college, asked him to do a DNA test so she could know once and for all.

"She definitely wasn't his daughter."

"Oh my God."

"Suddenly, all her insecurities made sense, and I'd wished that I'd known what she knew because I would've been more understanding. I would have been a better brother. I told her that. And when I left Boston to come here, Lorna and I were in a better place than we'd ever been."

I lifted my head to meet his gaze. The betrayal in his was soul destroying. "I wrote that letter to Dad when I was fifteen and she kept it." He shook his head. "I threw it away, but she must have found it and kept it. She had, uh, short stories of mine, scraps of things I'd thrown away ... I know she kept those too." Jamie let out a shuddering breath. "She must have come from New York planning this because she had the letter with her. I had stupidly told her that seeing you every week was getting harder because I was afraid I was stopping you from living your life.

"But none of that mattered. She was going to do this to us,

no matter what. She remembered she had that letter, and she planned this."

As much as it killed that Lorna had done this to me, I was more devastated that she'd done this to Jamie.

"She knew." I could hear the rage building him. "She knew what you meant to me. And she took you from me when I needed you most."

I grabbed hold of him tight, trying to calm him. "Jamie, I knew her. And I should have come to you. Instead, I let all those awkward visits with you mess with my head, with what I knew was true. Yes, she did this to us, but I let her."

"No," he bit out, shaking his head. "You don't put that shit on yourself. I am done with self-recrimination. This"—he jumped to his feet and I hurried to follow him into the bedroom where he snatched up the letter sitting among the glass shards, tearing the page in two—"this is done for us now. It's in the past. We know the truth." Anguish darkened his features before he fought to let it go. "Neither of us meant to abandon the other. We love each other."

"We love each other," I echoed the promise.

"But I am done with my sister, and she needs to know that we know the truth." He yanked on his jeans.

"Jamie ..."

"No, Jane. She's my sister so I won't go after her for this, even though she's almost as bad as the fuckers on my hit list. But I am *done* with her. There's no coming back from deliberately tearing us apart."

"Don't call her yet." I took hold of his hand. "Stay here with me. Stay the whole night with me. Screw everyone else. We can face all that in the morning."

He hesitated, making my breath hitch.

To my relief, however, he exhaled slowly and nodded.

Jamie joined me back in bed.

I'd clean up the broken mirror tomorrow.

"I just gave us seven years more bad luck," he groaned as I cuddled into him.

I chuckled, and it was a relief to do so. "I don't think it's possible for us to have any more bad luck."

"Don't jinx us, Doe."

I pressed a kiss to his chest. Despite sad revelations, I squirmed a little with happiness to hear the endearment again.

Jamie rubbed his hand down my arm as we tried to settle into each other, to leave all the ugly, messy emotions at the door until tomorrow. "You need to text Gaines and tell him you can't see him anymore."

"What about Wright?"

He took a deep breath. "I'll follow him. Plant a bug in his apartment. It was my last-resort plan."

The thought of anything happening to him now that I had him back made me tense with anxiety. "Jamie—"

"It'll be okay."

I wanted to believe that, and as I stewed on it, I realized what he'd just said. "A bug?" I pushed up off him and he stared at me warily. "Did you plant a bug at Asher's? Is that how you knew he was sabotaging my attempts?"

He nodded reluctantly. "In his car."

"How?"

"I bribed one of his so-called friends to do it."

"Jamie, you need to remove that bug."

His eyes narrowed. "Why do you care?"

"Asher hurt me, and I can't be around him right now, but he has been like family to me these last few years. Those feelings don't just go away. Removing the bug would be what's decent and right."

Jamie's lips twitched. "I'm not decent and right, Jane."

My heart lurched. I bent my head to his and pressed a soft, sweet kiss to his mouth. "Yes, you are. I just need to remind you."

HOURS LATER, after we'd made love again, as my eyelids grew heavy with sleep, I remembered that Jamie didn't sleep well, and that he needed the window open to even try. Feeling the smooth rise and fall of his chest beneath mine, I lifted my head to tell him I'd open the window but then halted.

Seeing his eyes closed, I whispered, "Jamie?"

No response.

"Baby?"

Not even a twitch.

Jamie was asleep.

A small, grateful smile tickled my lips as I carefully lowered my head back to his chest and closed my eyes.

CHAPTER TWENTY-NINE

JAMIE

AT SOME POINT IN TIME, I'd convinced myself to treat the loss of Jane like a death. I hadn't lied when I told her that I'd *needed* to hate her. To a certain extent, I'd always feel like I didn't deserve her, but I couldn't hate her anymore just to keep her at a distance.

The relief of knowing she'd never stop loving me was too great.

It was how I imagined it would feel to think someone you loved had passed away, only to discover they were still alive.

At first, I didn't feel that relief. Instead, the grief I'd felt over losing her, the grief that had made me bitter more than anything else, turned to hurt and betrayal. Realizing my sister was to blame for events that had rocked my life was more than I could handle at that moment.

However, when the shock passed and the relief of having Jane back seeped in, it allowed me time to calm down. To be grateful to have her lying in bed beside me.

All of that stopped me from facing my fears, jumping on a plane, and confronting Lorna. I wanted to cut her out of my life for good.

I wasn't a perfect man. I wasn't very good at forgiving. *Understatement.*

I couldn't forgive Lorna for taking Jane away, but I still needed to know why.

Slipping out of Jane's bed that morning, my chest aching with a sweetness it hadn't felt in a long time, I watched my girl sleep as I dressed. I didn't understand what pulled us together. I didn't know what made Jane Doe the only woman who satisfied my heart, body, and soul. I didn't need to know.

I just had to do what I could to not lose her again.

If that meant cutting Lorna out of my life for fear of her fucking with us, then I'd do it.

Leaving a note for Jane on her pillow, I let myself out of her apartment and took a shower in mine. Once dressed, I sat down on my sofa with my phone in hand. My heart beat a mile a minute.

I dialed Lorna's number.

And it went straight to voicemail.

Goddamn it!

I hung up, my knee bouncing with agitation.

"Screw it." I called her again and when it went to voicemail, I stayed on the line. "Lorna, it's me. I ... I know about the letter you gave to Jane. I know what you did. If you love me at all, you'll tell me why. Because"—I swallowed hard against my hurt and rage—"I don't get how my sister could do that to me. I—" I hung up because I knew I was about to lose my temper. And I wanted answers. She'd never give them to me if I raged at her.

Pissed that I'd have to wait to talk to her, I called my PI and arranged to meet him at his office in thirty minutes. Burt Wethers was an ex-cop and friend of Irwin Alderidge. Irwin had put me in touch with Burt when I came out to LA to do what needed to be done. He was the guy who taught me about surveillance equipment, and he's who I bought it from.

I glanced at Jane's door as I stepped out of mine, resisting the urge to walk on in and climb back into bed with her. As much as I loved her, there was still shit to do, and I couldn't let myself get lost in her. Not yet.

Thirty minutes later I strode into Wethers's dismal little downtown office. His AC must have been broken because the place was stifling. Sweat beaded across my skin as Wethers crossed the room to greet me.

He was short, balding, and probably hitting his fifties, but Wethers was also compact and strong, his biceps flexing with the handshake.

"What can I do for you?"

"I need more equipment. For Wright."

Since Irwin trusted Wethers, I gave the guy some of my trust too. He knew about my plans, and that's why he'd only do so much for me. As an ex-cop, he knew when the line was being crossed. It didn't mean he wasn't on my side. He'd left the force because he saw too much injustice. And he hated dirty fucking cops.

Wethers sighed heavily. "Well, funny you should call this morning because I was about to call you. And it's about Wright."

"What's going on?"

"I've been keeping my ear to the ground about the people who did this to you, and Wright's name popped up ... with my contact at Internal Affairs."

I slumped back in the plastic seat he'd offered me, my pulse speeding up. "What does that mean exactly?"

"They're onto him, Jamie. Wright's been taking bribes from all kinds of criminals in Los Angeles, as well as blackmailing prostitutes to give him part of their take to keep the cops off their backs."

That son of a bitch. I curled my lip in disgust.

Wethers wore a similar look. "He got a new partner two years ago. This guy clocked him. Internal Affairs have been on him ever since."

There was no part of me that wanted to like Lincoln Gaines after seeing him kiss Jane, but I couldn't help it. Jane had been right. Gaines was a good guy.

"You need to back off Wright. You go poking around while they're investigating him, you'll just draw unwanted attention."

"You're sure about this?"

"Absolutely. That guy is going down, and soon."

The uncertainty didn't sit right with me, but rationally, I knew Wethers made sense. I couldn't be caught doing illegal shit like planting a bug in a cop's apartment. It was out of my hands now. A waiting game to see what IA did.

Feeling a mixed bag of emotions, I thanked Wethers and left his office. If IA took down Wright, then I had my justice. I just had to hope they didn't fuck it up.

There was only one person I wanted to see, to tell, so I drove back to the apartment. My phone rang while I was driving, and a New York number popped up. My agent.

"Are you ignoring my emails?" Susan asked without preamble when I picked up.

"No." I wasn't. I'd just been preoccupied. "Just got some stuff going on."

"Well, I need an answer, Jamie."

Knowing Susan referred to her phone call of three weeks ago and the subsequent emails, I sighed. A popular streaming service wanted to buy the rights to *Brent 29*. They had a vision of turning it into a miniseries. Considering my complicated feelings about the TV and movie industry, I'd been dragging my heels.

Now, though, I had someone else I could talk to about it.

"I'll call you back tomorrow with an answer. I promise."

"One more day, Jamie."

We hung up just as I swung into my space at the apartment complex. I was unclipping my seat belt when the damn phone rang. This time it was my sister's number. Heart racing, I got out of the car and hit the answer button.

"Jamie ..." The line crackled as she breathed heavily.

I hurried into the building, stomach roiling as I waited for her to say more. "Well?"

Taking the steps two at a time, I heard my sister crying. Instinct was to protect, but I held fast to my anger as I let myself into Jane's apartment. She was sitting at her kitchen counter eating toast, and I lifted a finger to stop her from speaking. Then I hit the speaker button on my phone.

"Lorna, I'm not going to listen to you cry. It's not gonna work."

Jane's eyes widened and she dropped her toast to slide off the stool. She'd showered too, her hair still damp, but piled on top of her head in a messy bun. Wearing jean shorts and a tank top, she was so beautiful, it was a sting in my chest.

Despite my tangled emotions, something in me eased as she sat on the sofa and took my free hand, pulling me down beside her.

Finally, Lorna's sniffling stopped. "I'm just ... I'm afraid she's lied to you about me."

Jane's eyes narrowed in outrage, and I squeezed her hand in reassurance.

"No lies, Lorna. You gave her a letter I wrote to Dad when I was fifteen, and you pretended I wrote it to her. Why the fuck—" I cut off at Jane's returning squeeze. Looking at her, she shook her head. *Stay calm*, she mouthed. I took a deep breath. She was right. Losing it on Lorna would only make her hang up. "Why would you do that? You knew I needed her."

Lorna was silent so long, I thought she'd hung up. Then, "You couldn't see it, but I could. She ruined everything. She read Skye's diaries and gave them to you, knowing how you would react. She should have burned them."

Anger boiled inside me. "You really believe that? What about Skye?"

"What could we do for her now? She's gone." Lorna's voice broke. "We couldn't reveal what had been done because it wasn't our story to tell, and she couldn't give us permission to do that. It would've been better to have just left it alone. But, no, Jane had to tell you, knowing what it would do to you."

"So you fucked us over?"

"I didn't do it to fuck you over. I really believe you're better off without her. I ... I did it for that, and, yes, I did it to hurt Jane."

Jane stiffened beside me. She stared at the floor, her cheeks flushed with emotion. Lorna had once been her best friend, her family.

"Why?"

"Because ... Because I pushed Skye away because of her." Lorna cried, and this time it sounded genuine. "I was so mad at Skye for not seeing my side of things when you and Jane started dating. It was like Jane came along and gave her the kid sister she'd always wanted. And Jane ... I loved Jane, and she chose you over me, Jamie. Do you know how much that hurt?"

Jane winced and tried to tug her hand from mine, but I wouldn't let her.

"Lorna, you know you only felt that way because of Dad. Skye loved you. Jane loved you. You didn't have to make it a choice. You forced that."

"I didn't force Skye to play favorites, to choose sides. And she did. And I was so mad at her, Jamie, and I pushed her away and then ... she died while I was mad at her. I hate myself for that! But what could I do? So I took it out on Jane. I hurt Jane because I couldn't take it out on myself."

Jane pulled away and strode across the room. With her back to me, I could see her trying to get control of her breathing, to calm down.

I understood. I was struggling myself. "What about me? I'd just had my life stolen, and Jane was the only thing keeping me going. How the hell could you do that to *me*?"

"I thought I was doing you a favor."

She thought she was doing me a favor.

Six years of mourning Jane. Hating her. Loving her and hating myself for loving her.

Never mind the things I'd done and said to her in the last few weeks.

Things I'd spend the rest of our lives making up for.

All because my little sister was selfish to her fucking core.

"We're done, Lorna."

Jane whirled around, watching me carefully.

I nodded at her in reassurance, my jaw clenched so tight so I wouldn't say awful shit to my sister I couldn't take back.

"What do you mean?"

"I can't forgive you," I admitted. "I've had to live six years of my life without the person who makes my life worthwhile. I can't get those years back and neither can she. We can't forget how that's changed us. You did that to us. I'll never be able to look at you the same way again. I'll never be able to trust you enough to have you back in my life."

"Jamie," Lorna sobbed. "Please don't say that."

I swallowed down the emotion, hating that it still hurt to hurt her. "Goodbye, Lorna." I hung up and threw the phone on the table, trying to hold myself together.

"It's always something," I said, my voice hoarse. "The good shines in." I gazed up Jane. "It shines in so fucking bright, I can't believe my luck ... and then a cloud passes over and puts me back in the shade."

Jane crossed the room and I pulled her between my legs, resting my forehead against her stomach, binding my arms tightly around her. Her fingers smoothed through my hair and down my neck, her nails lightly scratching my nape, causing goose bumps to prickle across my skin.

I held on tighter, breathing her in.

"One day," she whispered, "we're going to have that future we always talked about. A little place in the quiet ... somewhere so beautiful that even the shade can't dull the shine."

CHAPTER THIRTY

JANE

THE YELLOW BUILDING gleamed in the morning sunshine. I imagined the owners painted it that color so people would feel happier about entering it to talk about all the shit that made them unhappy.

I still felt sick as I stared at it. My palms were clammy too.

Not just because I hated confrontation, but because I intended to ruin Jamie's plans.

It was a risk, considering I'd only just gotten him back, but I'd had a lot of time to think these last few days and, ultimately, I believed that what Jamie needed more than anything was peace. He needed to move on.

Although I'd called in sick to work the day of the Lorna phone call, I couldn't keep doing that. In the following days, I'd gone to work, like always, but when I came home at night, it was to Jamie McKenna. It felt like a little miracle. Sometimes he'd be at his computer, writing ... or plotting, maybe. To my relief, Jamie had told me that Ethan Wright was under investigation with Internal Affairs and we'd hopefully hear soon that charges had been filed against him.

Wright and Kramer were crossed off the list.

But that didn't stop the moments when I felt Jamie was somewhere far away, even when he was right there beside me. I knew he still planned to take down Foster Steadman, and I knew he still wanted me to find out what I could about Elena Marshall's personal life. I wasn't ignoring his need for closure. I still wanted that for him. However, I was afraid that we'd sacrifice what was important to get it.

So instead, I distracted him.

With sex. Hours and hours of sex that should have satisfied a craving but only exacerbated our thirst. We had years to make up for, after all.

I also distracted him with conversation.

I wanted to know what I'd missed these past six years and tell him about what he'd missed.

During those conversations, he asked me for advice regarding adaptation rights to *Brent 29*. It was my opinion that Jamie should do what made him feel comfortable, but I also explained how I thought the book read like a movie and was ripe for adaptation. I could see how it could be turned into a miniseries, too, and despite my proximity to movies and TV, I still thought it would be cool to see Jamie's story come to life.

He told his agent, Susan, that he'd sign the deal.

The only thing we'd argued about in the last week was Jamie's refusal to remove the bug from Asher's car. When I brought it up, he got moody and snapped at me.

So I stormed out of his apartment and wouldn't let him into mine.

"Open the door, Jane," he said in that dangerously calm tone of his.

"Not until you discuss this like a grown-up."

"I can hardly do that with a door between us. You want to talk about childish?"

Realizing he was right, I huffed in annoyance and threw the door open. Jamie crowded me back into the apartment, closing the door. His chest pushed into mine, forcing me against the wall where he caged me in.

My skin tingled with exhilaration even though I was pissed at him.

"It shouldn't matter to you what I do to Asher," Jamie said, his breath whispering over my lips. "He betrayed you."

"And I told you that I can't just switch off my feelings and stop caring about him."

His face clouded over. "I don't want you to care about him."

"I'm allowed to care about other people, Jamie."

"Not other men!"

"Don't yell at me!" I yelled back.

His eyes flashed. "Stop driving me crazy!"

"I don't have sexual feelings for Asher. He's like a brother. Remove that goddamn bug from his car, or so help me God, Jamie, I will find it and destroy what I'm guessing is a pretty expensive piece of equipment."

Jamie's answer was to slam his mouth down over mine to shut me up. I let him, caught up in the excitement and thrill of just being with him again. We were frantic and needy, him yanking my underwear down my legs, me plucking at the buttons on his jeans.

Only minutes after the argument I was in his arms, legs wrapped around his waist, and he was inside me, screwing me against my living room wall. My gasps and his grunts filled our ears as he took me hard and fast and without mercy.

The orgasm blew the roof off my head. When the shuddering shivers of climax finally settled, our breaths slowing, I curled my fingers in the hair at the nape of his neck. His face was pressed to my throat where he'd buried it as he came.

"Nice try." I still sounded breathless. "But you're removing that bug from Asher's car."

Jamie groaned as he lifted his head. He stared at me, sated heat and affection on his face. He kissed me and then whispered, "If it means that much to you, I'll get rid of the bug."

I was pulled from those heated memories by the sight of Elena departing the yellow building. My skin flushed. Not just with my body's constant readiness for Jamie McKenna but because I was about to do something that might cause another argument between us.

Or worse.

I hurried out of my car and across the street to where Elena was getting into hers. "Elena!" I called, stopping her.

She turned toward me, eyes narrowing in concentration and then widening a little in recognition. "Hi."

I stopped in front of her, my heart rate increasing with nervousness. "Hey."

"You didn't join us." She closed her car door and leaned into it, giving me a patient smile.

"No, but I wondered if you had time for a quick chat. I'm Jane."

Elena's eyebrows rose a little. "Well, Jane, okay. I was grabbing a book out of the car because I have an appointment soon ..." She gestured to the hospital along the street.

"Another time?"

"No, we can have a quick chat."

I gestured to her car.

"Okay." She opened the driver's side and slid in and I rounded the hood to the passenger side. My heart thundered.

The AC blew in the small car as I got in, but it was still stifling. Sweat gathered under my arms and behind my knees. I didn't think it was because of the heat.

My unlikely companion sat patiently waiting for me to speak.

I turned to look into her warm brown eyes. "What's the worst thing that's ever happened to you? Is it cancer?"

She blew out air between her lips, considering my question. "Does it have to be one thing?"

"Ouch," I whispered. "Life been that bad, huh?"

Her smile was wry but pained. "The worst thing that ever happened to me was losing my daughter. She's still alive, but she has a drug problem, and no matter how I tried to help her, I somehow just kept pushing her away. What about you, Jane? Your boyfriend, his cancer?"

I flinched at the lie I'd told and stared out the windshield at the haze on the road. "I've had a few. But I guess the worst ones are the ones I still dream about. One sounds stupid because it happens to everyone ... but it was the first time a guy broke my heart." I smiled sadly, remembering the dark days after I thought Jamie had pushed me away. "The second ... well, I still have nightmares about it." I turned to Elena. "Do you know how memories fade over time ... like the image loses its sharpness even if the emotion attached to it doesn't?"

"I know what you mean, yeah."

"This particular memory hasn't. I still see Skye lying on that bed, clear as day. I still feel the fear that started in my feet as soon as I walked into her bedroom, because I knew she was gone before I even checked her pulse."

"Oh, Jane." Elena grabbed my hand and squeezed. "I am so sorry."

"Overdose," I explained. "Accidental."

Sympathy brightened her eyes. "I found my kid like that. I was luckier in the end. She survived. I am so sorry, sweetheart. Was Skye your sister?"

"A friend. But like a big sister, really. She was my boyfriend's big sister. He never got over it."

"I imagine not."

"What's the worst thing you've ever done?" I tugged my hand from hers.

Whatever she saw in my expression made her flinch. "What do you mean?"

"I unwittingly abandoned my boyfriend when he needed me. That's one of mine. I also found and shared with him his big sister's diaries, where she unloaded all her secrets. Including the fact that this big-shot producer had raped her. His name is Foster Steadman. He has a man who works for him called Frank Kramer."

Elena faltered, the color leaching from her face. "Why are you telling me this?"

"What's the worst thing you've ever done, Elena?"

"Maybe we should continue this another time." She gestured nervously to the door. "I really need to get to my appointment."

I grabbed her by the wrist, my grip tight and unrelenting. "Jamie went to him. Confronted him. He had no idea what Steadman and Kramer were capable of. Like, for instance, paying off a cashier to take a bullet and identify an innocent man for a crime he didn't commit."

She tugged at my hand, her eyes bright. "No ... I ..."

"What's the worst thing you've ever done, Elena?" I bit out, my fingernails digging into her skin.

She cried out, her face crumpling as she sobbed.

I released her, my chest heaving with emotion. "Why? Why did you do that to Jamie?"

Covering her face with her hands, she shook her head as her shoulders shuddered.

I waited.

I waited with more patience than I knew I had in me.

After what felt like a lifetime, Elena lifted her head, her face splotched, her eyes red and haunted. "I ... I'm sorry," she cried, more tears spilling down her wan cheeks. "I wanted to believe that he was a bad kid. That he'd probably deserved it. I'm so sorry!"

"Why?" I yelled.

She flinched, swiping at her tears, her breathing so ragged, I felt a twinge of concern. "My daughter was in trouble. A lot of trouble with some very bad men. A crime family. She owed them a ton of money and when Kramer came to me, I couldn't believe it. It seemed like fate. I was desperate. But I wasn't supposed to get shot. That was never part of the deal, but Kramer threatened me afterward. He said he'd hurt my daughter if I didn't take it all the way."

Elena tried to reach for me, but I reeled back from her. She raised her hands, as if approaching a wild animal. "I was just trying to protect my daughter."

I understood that.

I did.

But I needed her to understand the consequences of what she'd done. "Jamie was innocent. Steadman violated his sister, and he just wanted justice. You helped steal an innocent man's life. You took away the man I love. He'll never be the same because of what you helped do to him. You ruined him." Tears spilled down my cheeks. "I needed you to know that."

I didn't think Elena Marshall was a bad person. In fact, I had a feeling she was once a good person who had done a very bad thing.

A weight lifted off my chest as I left her sobbing in her car.

She *had* helped destroy Jamie.

They all had.

And I had to guide him onto the path back from ruin.

JAMIE WOULDN'T LOOK at me.

He glared at my bookshelves.

"Jamie, say something."

He let out a disgusted huff. "What would you like me to say?"

"That you understand why I did this."

Jamie finally looked at me, those ocean eyes filled with storm. "Well, I don't."

I'd told Jamie about my encounter with Elena. He didn't take it so well. "Where is the satisfaction in ruining a woman who has nothing left to lose?"

"You don't know she has nothing left," Jamie snapped, standing. He placed his hands on his hips and glowered down at me. "You didn't even try."

"She's estranged from the one person she cares about. She took the money from Steadman and Kramer to protect her daughter. She got shot when that wasn't part of the deal. Then he threatened her. She has cancer. Debt up to her eyeballs. And when I told her who she helped put away and why you were put away, that woman broke, Jamie. I watched her break. Someone with a soul wouldn't care the way she cares about the truth." I stood, imploring him. "She won't forgive herself for this, and you and I know a little something about that. Don't you think that's enough?"

"No, I don't."

"Jamie." I tried to reach for him, but he pulled away. Shoving down the hurt, I shrugged helplessly. "Look what Lorna's revenge did to us. Do we really want to be the people who cause that kind of pain?"

"This isn't revenge. It's justice."

"No, Jamie. It's revenge. Justice would be Foster going to jail for raping Skye and framing you. We might never get the latter, but we'll definitely never get the former. No one will pay for hurting Skye because she's not here to see that they do. You have to make peace with that, Jamie. We both do. Because hurting these people in other ways will never be the kind of justice we need."

I watched him warily as he whirled away from me, marching across the room to stare out the window. He ran his hands through his hair, his knuckles white with tension.

I waited.

Finally, he turned to me, gaze searching. "You really believe Elena feels remorse?"

I nodded, hope rising. "I do."

My hope crashed and burned when he cursed under his breath and marched across the room, past me to the door. He strode out of my apartment without another word.

Fuck.

In turmoil, I did what I always did—I turned to my art. Setting up fresh vellum on my easel, I sat on the stool and let that part of me take over. To my shock, what came out was a dancer. A leaping dancer. In my mind, she'd been dancing with a sheet of sheer silk, using the movement of the fabric to create beautiful shapes. I'd captured her midair, the silk wrapped around her, tangled in its beauty.

Hours later, I sat back from the painting, exhausted, drained.

The dancer was me.

She was a reminder of the little girl who had longed for the life she'd been promised before her adoptive parents died. How that longing had made her reach for the McKennas. How she'd gotten tangled in their beauty.

I couldn't keep making decisions based on what I thought they needed or wanted.

It had to come from me.

No matter how much I loved Jamie, or how much I missed Skye.

Yes, I still wanted Foster Steadman to pay for what he'd

done, but I couldn't be a part of hurting people to get that justice. I couldn't be part of a revenge plot.

And I was scared.

Terrified.

Because if Jamie couldn't do the right thing, I knew there was a huge possibility I'd have to let him go again.

Chapter Thirty-One

JAMIE

Standing outside Jane's apartment, I wanted to be mad.

After my initial reaction to what she'd told me about her encounter with Elena Marshall, after I'd stormed out on her, I couldn't get Jane's voice out of my head. And I wanted to be pissed that I wasn't pissed at her.

She was changing the game.

She was reminding me daily of who I used to be.

"She's estranged from the one person she cares about. She took the money from Steadman and Kramer to protect her daughter. She got shot when that wasn't part of the deal. Then he threatened her. She has cancer. Debt up to her eyeballs. And when I told her who she helped put away and why you were put away, that woman broke, Jamie ... hurting these people in other ways will never be the kind of justice we need."

"Goddamn you, Jane," I muttered wearily, letting myself into the apartment with the key she'd given me just that morning. I kicked off my shoes at the door and locked up before wandering through the dark sitting room and into the hall.

I'd tried to sleep in my own bed, thinking the distance would be good. That maybe it would put things back in perspective, make me focus again.

That's when I realized I'd slept every night this past week. All night. With Jane.

No windows open.

It scared the utter shit out of me to realize Jane Doe could offer me that kind of peace. I wanted it, but I needed to find it without her too. There had to be a happy medium where my ability to move on with my life wasn't contingent upon Jane's presence.

I decided I could give her what she asked because I could see deep down that she was right. But I couldn't give it all up for her. Jane knew who I was when she let me back into her life.

The object of my thoughts and affection was curled up on the bed, facing the opposite wall. Moonlight spilled in through the window where she hadn't drawn the curtains. The sheets pooled around her waist so I could see the spill of her dark hair across the pillows, her shoulders bare in her tank top.

My fingers itched to touch her.

Taking off my jeans, I saw her stiffen and realized she was awake.

After I pulled off my T-shirt and dropped it on the chair at her dressing table, I climbed into bed beside her. I rolled into her, sliding my arm over her waist, pressing deep into her back until we were as close as we could get.

She'd tensed up as soon as I touched her, and my heart beat a little harder.

I shifted her silky hair and pressed a kiss to her warm skin. "I'll leave Elena Marshall alone," I promised into the dark.

Jane melted, pulling away ever so slightly but only to turn in my arms. We relaxed into each other as relief moved through me. She hugged me so tight, burrowing into me.

I kissed the top of her head, wanting to reassure her but be honest at the same time. "I can't let Foster Steadman get away with everything, Jane. I can't walk away until he's behind bars. I don't care what he does time for. I just want him there."

For a moment, I held my breath, waiting for her to respond.

Then slowly, she nodded against my chest and tightened her embrace.

Relief saturated me and my eyelids grew heavy with exhaustion.

I might not want to need her as much as I did. It might be dangerous. It might be stupid and self-destructive. But it was what it was.

My soul was connected to hers.

I doubted I could ever find true peace without Jane by my side.

I DIDN'T WAKE up the next morning the way I preferred, usually with the drowsy awareness that I was lying tangled up in Jane and my body was already hard for her.

Starting the day coming with her was a pretty fucking great way to start the day.

So, it was less than ideal to wake to the sound of raised voices filtering into the bedroom. As I became more conscious of it, I realized Jane was arguing with a guy.

My heart leapt and I pushed off the duvet, rolling out of bed to scramble into my jeans. Not even waiting to throw on a shirt, I marched out into the sitting room.

Jane and Asher Steadman turned from facing off to look at me.

What the fuck?

My fists clenched at my sides as I took a step toward them. "What the hell is going on?"

Asher didn't seem as shocked to see me as I'd expect. He frowned at Jane. "Why didn't you tell me we weren't alone?"

"You're not asking the questions here."

That's my girl. I strode to stand by her side, giving her my support. "What's he doing here?"

"He came to apologize since I won't answer his calls."

"Can we not talk like I'm not here?" Asher glanced between us. "So, you and Jamie are back together?"

Shit. He knew me.

Jane gaped at him in shock, while I prepared myself for the extremely bad news that Foster Steadman knew I was hanging around.

"How do you know who he is?" Jane asked, stepping protectively closer to me.

Asher noted it. "Jane, my father doesn't know." He looked at me, all wide-eyed and innocent. I didn't believe his good-guy bullshit for a second. "He doesn't know you're here, and he won't know. But you have to back off."

Oh no, he didn't.

Jane grabbed hold of me as I made to step toward the spoiled bastard.

"Back off?" she huffed, putting herself between us.

I rested my hands on her shoulders as she continued, "Like you wanted me to when you sabotaged my attempts to take down your dad?"

Asher nervously licked his lips. "How can you think that I would ever deliberately hurt you? You have to believe in me, Jane, and know that when the time is right, all of this will make sense."

"You lied to me."

"I did." He took an imploring step toward her. "But I love you."

A low growl buried its way out of me before I could stop. "Take another step toward her and I'll snap your fucking neck."

Jane tensed under my hands as Asher eyed me.

Then something I didn't quite understand crossed his face. He glanced at Jane, then back at me, and then back to Jane. "You think I don't care about you ... I do. I'd do anything for you." He shifted his attention to me. "Jane and I were never together. I know you said some pretty horrible things to her when she came to see you two years ago because you thought we were sleeping together. We weren't. We never will." He took a deep breath. "I'm asexual. I love Jane very much, but I don't have sexual feelings for her because I don't have those feelings at all."

Stunned, I slumped. "Why let the tabloids pretend you were dating, then?"

He looked at Jane and sadness tightened his expression. "Because when I tried to explain it to my mom, she told me I was just a late bloomer. And when I told my dad, he told me I was looking for attention, that I needed to act 'normal.' When I tried to push it with them both, Foster beat the shit out of me and called it 'kicking the heterosexuality into me.'" Asher scoffed. "People aren't just pricks to homosexuals, Jamie. It's anyone who sits outside the boundaries of 'heterosexual normality.'

"After that, I had to deal with a lot of shit from Foster. A lot of emotional abuse. I also figured out what he'd been doing to women long before Jane came along. I knew, and I know my father needs to be stopped, but when the tabloids put Jane and me together as a couple, Foster stepped off me. It was a relief. It was also a relief to have other friends stop questioning me about sex and dating. Whether they realized it or not, they made me feel like there was something wrong with me. I suffered from a lot of anxiety."

His eyes dropped to Jane again, affection bright in them. "Until Jane. She didn't mind going along with the lie that we were together."

My immediate concern was Jane and how I would ever make it up to her for having such little faith in her.

It would take me a lifetime, which wasn't exactly a punishment.

"Why are you telling me all this?"

"For Jane. So you can know for certain that she never forgot about you." He looked at her again. "You know how hard that was for me to trust him with that, so you have to know what I did wasn't to hurt you."

"Okay," she replied, her voice soft. "Thank you, Asher. I do appreciate it, and you know, as hurt as I am, I love you. Please don't betray that. You can't tell Foster about Jamie."

"I promise I would never do that." Asher's gaze shifted between us. "But you have to promise to do as I say. You have to promise to back off and let me deal with this."

No. Fucking. Way. "I can't do that."

Jane tensed beneath my hands again.

Asher sighed heavily. "Jane, talk some sense into your boyfriend."

Then he was gone and the vibe coming off Jane was not good.

Jesus, hadn't we sorted this out last night?

She stepped away to turn and face me. "You heard him."

"And I thought we agreed last night that I'd leave Elena out of this. I'll give you something else. I'll let Internal Affairs deal with Wright, and even if they don't come through, I'm gonna let the bastard go. I won't go after him. But I can't walk away from Foster Steadman, and you know it."

"Jamie, if he finds out you're here and you're gunning for him ..." Fear darkened her eyes. "I'm terrified that this time, he'll shut you up for good."

"He won't get away with murder, Jane."

She narrowed her eyes in disbelief. "Jamie, do you think Skye is the only woman he's sexually assaulted? From what Asher and I could deduce, he's been violating women for nearly three decades. How many victims do you think we're talking about here? And he's getting away with it. Somehow, he and Kramer would find a way of getting away with shutting you up for good. It doesn't have to be murder. They could just frame you for it."

I chuckled, and it was the wrong thing to do. I knew that when she smacked me in the face with a cushion off her sofa.

"Jane ..." I tried to placate her. "I'm not going to get caught."

"I'm not asking you to give up. I'm just asking you to step back for now. Do it for me. Please. It's the right thing to do. Until things calm down."

"What things? Your *bestie* barges in this morning, doesn't explain his reasons for making a fool out of you, and suddenly you want me to step back? You knew why I was in LA. You knew exactly who I was when you let me back in. I'm doing this and I will not be manipulated out of it. Fuck!" I was beyond furious at her for making me feel like the bad guy, and I knew if I didn't get out of there, I'd say something I'd regret.

I left and took my anger out on the punching bag I'd hung from the ceiling in Sheila's bedroom.

CHAPTER THIRTY-TWO

JANE

THERE WAS nothing I hated more than leaving a discussion hanging. Jamie storming out in the middle of our disagreement was beyond frustrating. I waited for him to come back, only to hear his apartment door open and close and his footsteps fade downstairs. Hurrying over to the window, I watched him stride with that languid grace toward the Porsche. I sighed, watching him drive out of the lot and disappear down the street.

Was I pushing Jamie too hard?

Was I manipulating him?

I hoped not, but Asher had me jumpy. He wouldn't explain how he knew who Jamie was, and he wouldn't explain his reasons for keeping me at bay with his father. As much as I loved Asher and wanted to believe he wouldn't hurt us, couldn't Jamie see why I was concerned? The last thing we needed was Foster Steadman finding out Jamie was in LA looking for revenge.

Searching for distraction, I checked my emails and found a new one from Cassie. For a while, she had been a big part of my life, but neither of us liked social media or talking on the phone. We passed the occasional email. Asher, who had an abundance of acquaintances and less than a handful of close friends, once asked if I ever got lonely. Sometimes I did. However, never for a large group of friends. The only times I ever felt lonely were when I missed Jamie and what we'd had together. Or when I thought of Skye and our quiet afternoons.

Or when I had flashes of my life before my adoptive parents died.

Perhaps it was my disposition to be content with my own company, or perhaps it was just what I was used to.

I was in the middle of responding to Cassie's updates when I heard the lock on my front door catch and then turn. Assuming Jamie had returned, I pushed aside my laptop to give him my focus. I was determined to make him see my point of view, but I'd be far subtler about it.

It wasn't Jamie who stepped into my apartment.

It wasn't Jamie who closed my door and locked it.

It was Frank Kramer.

Fear chained me to the couch.

A man of medium build with broad shoulders, a paunch, and a head of thinning, pepper-speckled dark hair, Frank Kramer wasn't a particularly intimidating figure. However, one look in his eyes was enough to make me shiver.

His eyes were the coldest black I'd ever seen.

"The locks in this building are embarrassingly easy to pick," he said, taking a step toward me. His heavy boots thudded on my wooden floor, and I finally came unstuck, pushing off the couch.

"Uh-uh." Frank stepped toward me, smiling. "Just stay there. No sudden movements."

My stomach roiled as I nervously licked my dry lips. Sweat gathered under my arms, and the adrenaline spike his appearance caused made me tremble. "What are you doing here?"

He considered me. "It comes as no surprise that you recognize me. Do you know why, Jane?"

I tried not to react to the use of my real name.

"Because I'm not dumb. And neither is Mr. Steadman."

I took a step back.

"What did I say?" His voice flattened. "Stay put."

"Get out of my apartment."

Frank chortled. "Don't be brave, baby. It's not going to save you from this mess." He looked around the apartment. "You know this is a nice place for a single woman in LA. You've done well for yourself." He shrugged, squinting at me in confusion. "Why would you fuck that up?"

My heart raced out of control. I was afraid. Afraid of a man who had hospitalized his own wife. Who had framed Jamie. But I was more afraid that Jamie would come home, and Frank and Foster would take him from me again. "What do you want?"

"You think Foster didn't know who you were? You think he's dumb? As soon as his only son started spending lots of a time with you, he looked into you. Found out about the name change and the foster care ... and what should appear on a little Google search for Jane Doe, Glendale, California, but photographs of Skye McKenna's funeral. There you were, front and center, all cozy with Jamie McKenna."

Oh my God.

Frank tsked. "All you had to do was keep your nose clean. Foster was perfectly willing to believe that you were moving on with your life, and your friendship with Asher was a coincidence. But we monitored you. Not a lot. Now and then." He stepped toward me, the air around him chilly with menace. "I was lucky when I saw you with Elena Marshall. A random surveillance day to check up on you. And there you were with Elena. So, I followed you for the day, and who did you have a date with that night? Lincoln Gaines, Ethan Wright's partner. Then I see you with Elena one week later. That wasn't a coincidence. Foster doesn't think so either. Is Jamie McKenna involved in this?"

"I haven't seen Jamie in two years. Since the last time I visited him in prison."

He nodded, like that's what he expected. "He's been smart enough to get out of state. To move on. He's been smarter than you."

I glanced surreptitiously around, searching for a weapon. There was nothing useful in my immediate vicinity. The deadliest were behind me in the knife block on the kitchen counter.

"This is a warning visit, Jane." Kramer shrugged out of his leather jacket and laid it across the back of my armchair, as if he were just stopping by for tea. Then he began unbuttoning his cuffs and rolling up his sleeves.

Terror made my knees shake.

At my expression, he smirked. "I'm not going to rape you, Jane." He pointed to the gold band on his left ring finger just before he took it off and put it in his pocket. "I'm a devoted husband."

I wanted to laugh at that.

"But I am going to hurt you." He took another step toward me, talking calmly, so calmly, almost like he was soothing a frightened child. "I'm going to hurt you enough to make you reconsider whatever you're planning. You won't make Elena talk because I'll hurt her too. You won't get to Wright because he's a psychopath who could give a shit about you or your friend Skye McKenna. She's just a dead piece of pussy, and if I have to come back after this, you will be too."

I darted toward the kitchen, but I wasn't fast enough. Heart in my throat, I choked out a yelp as I felt the sharp sting of my scalp pulling. Frank yanked me by my ponytail into his chest and covered my mouth with his hand, using his weight to force me to the floor. I fought with every ounce of rage inside me, bucking and battling, grappling and crawling, trying to get away from him.

Smashing my elbow into his face, I heard his grunt of pain as his grip on me loosened. I dug my nails into the floorboards, attempting to propel myself forward into the kitchen.

He grabbed me by the calves and hauled me back down the floor toward him. I cried out, my plea for help cut off as he flipped me like I weighed nothing and slammed me into the floor. He knocked the wind right out of me and I panicked, struggling to draw a breath.

Kramer drew back his fist and smashed it into my face. Fire blazed across my cheekbone as sparks of white light flared in my vision.

He hit me again, this time near my mouth, and I felt the sharp sting of my lip splitting.

Discombobulated, I couldn't get myself together quickly enough to retreat before he hauled me up by the hair and punched me in the gut, winding me again.

Gasping for breath, I fell to my side. Fire exploded across my ribs as he kicked me as hard as he could. Another kick. Another.

And another.

Agony wrapped around me, but I tried to fight through it, tried to find my way back into my body.

"You had enough?" he asked, his voice sounding far away. "You're just a little thing. I don't want to go too far. Maybe I should break that cute little nose and we'll call it a day, huh?"

Through the blurred vision of the eye I could feel swelling up, I gauged how close he was. Then I pulled my knees to my chest, pushed through the pain, and screamed as I punched out both feet toward his shins with as much force as I could. It sent him slamming down onto my coffee table, which collapsed beneath his weight. I scrambled to my feet and shot toward the door, slipping on magazines that scattered off the table.

I was almost there, sobbing in relief, when suddenly I toppled to the hardwood, yanked down by the ankle. Roaring in fury, screaming for help, I flipped onto my back, kicking out at his grasp. He was on his knees, coming toward me, and he threw himself onto me, his fist slamming into my face again.

My face felt like a ball of swollen, burning, throbbing pain as he squeezed my chin between his hand, hellfire in his eyes. "You need more, you little bitch?" Spittle flew from his frothing mouth.

Was I in hell?

Was he a hellhound?

Yes. I thought of his wife, Juanita, and how he didn't even care about me like he'd obsessed over her. He'd cared if she died. He wouldn't if I did.

Where were my neighbors? Couldn't they hear this?

No one was coming to save me, I realized.

No.

No way had I survived the shitty cards I'd been dealt in the twenty-six years I'd spent on this planet to break at the hands of this dickless abuser!

I grabbed for Kramer's throat, trying to choke him, my nails clawing at his jugular. Kramer punched me, this time connecting with my temple.

I lost consciousness. I didn't know for how long, but when I came to, he was still there, so it couldn't have been long.

He straddled me, panting, hard. My vision was hazy; the room spun. Kramer wiped his nose and then spat on me. The wet fluid landed on my cheek, just below my eye.

The son of a bitch.

I turned away in disgust, and that's when I spotted my keys on the floor.

My arm snapped out, my hands clawing at them, and as I felt him move to stop me, I swung my arm up, keys sharp-edge out, and swiped the fucker across the face with every bit of strength in me.

He yelled, clutching at the wound, and I launched myself upward, screaming my rage as I brought the keys down with both hands—with more force than I knew I had—right into the side of his neck. They slid in after a strange, jarring, popping sensation, and Kramer slumped off me, clutching at the makeshift weapon sticking out of him. Horror and disbelief slackened his features.

Get out, Jane. Get up and get out! It was Jamie's frantic command I heard reverberating around my mind.

I wanted to scramble away. I did.

But there were black dots all over my vision.

Multiplying and multiplying until there was nothing but a starless universe pulling me into its dark depths.

CHAPTER THIRTY-THREE

JAMIE

SITTING at the coffee shop on Sunset Boulevard, near my apartment, I couldn't write. I thought if I took some time, poured all my frustration into the new novel, it might calm me down.

However, I couldn't shake my agitation.

I'd never walked out on an argument with Jane when we were younger because I hated that shit, and it only took half an hour for me to realize I still couldn't do it. I'd never be able to concentrate until she and I hashed this out.

She had to know I wasn't walking away from Foster Steadman, and *I* had to know where that left things between her and me.

No matter how concerned I was that Jane might walk away from us for real this time.

Snapping my notebook shut, I cleared my table and left the coffee place. My car was parked only a block away, but I jogged to get to it. It was thankfully only a five-minute drive back to our complex.

I felt more than a little nervous as I let myself into the building. Everything was so fragile between me and Jane. I didn't know when I'd stop expecting things to fall apart again. Hopefully, time would make things easier between us.

As I neared our floor, I thought I heard the murmur of a man's voice. Picking up my pace, I hurried upstairs. Disturbed by the sight of Jane's door lying ajar, I marched into the apartment and came to an abrupt halt.

The place was a mess.

The building manager, Ivy Martin, was kneeling next to a prone Jane.

Fear exploded through me at the sight of Jane's bloodied and swollen face, her unconscious form. I stumbled toward her.

What the hell had happened here?

A groan drew my gaze. Sitting propped against the sofa, his hands covered in blood and clutching at his neck, was Frank fucking Kramer.

My entire body felt like it had been dipped into a pot filled with molten lava.

I fell to my knees at Jane's side. What had he done? I couldn't breathe properly. My hands shook as they hovered over her. "Jane?"

"Jane?" Ivy asked.

I ignored her. "Jane, baby, wake up, yeah."

She didn't respond.

"Margot's alive, just unconscious," Ivy informed me.

I pressed my fingers to her pulse and found it strong and steady. "Jesus fuck."

I looked at Ivy and blinked in surprise when I realized she had a gun trained on Kramer.

"Ambulance is on the way. I heard a crash while I was working upstairs, and I heard Margot yell for help."

My blood turned to ice in my veins at the idea of her alone with that fucking maniac, Kramer. I could only surmise he found out what we were up to, and he'd come after Jane.

FUCK!

"Hurried to get my gun, thought I might need it. Nearly had heart failure when I heard her scream again. Had to break down the door because the chain was on. Found Margot out cold and this son of a bitch"—she nodded at Kramer—"was crawling along the floor, trying to escape, even though he's got a set of keys wedged in his neck."

"Keys," I muttered, watching Jane's chest rise and fall slowly.

"Yeah. She fought back. Boy, did she fight back. You know the kind of strength it takes to stick a set of keys in a guy's neck? But he got his licks in good before she could."

Just like that, I snapped.

Lunging at Kramer, determined to finish the asshole, I was shocked as shit by the strength in the manager as she grabbed me by the collar one-handed and threw me back on my ass.

I glared at her in disbelief and outrage, ready to take her on too, gun or no gun, when she cocked her head and said, "Police are on their way, and that sounds like them coming up the damn stairs."

The words were barely out of her mouth when the cops poured into the apartment.

JANE WOULD BE FINE.

That's what the ER doctor told me and Asher. It turned out Asher was her emergency contact, so they called him when she got rushed to the hospital.

I had never been so relieved to see someone wake up as I was when Jane's eyes fluttered open as the paramedics hurried into her apartment.

After detailing Jane's injuries, the doc told me and Asher we could see her. They were keeping her overnight for observation due to a concussion.

"Concussion," I muttered as Asher and I approached her hospital room.

"What?" Asher halted. He looked shaken. Pale.

The guy might have real feelings for Jane after all.

"Concussion," I repeated. "From trauma to her temple. Fractured ribs where the bastard kicked her. Multiple lacerations and swelling to her face from where he repeatedly hit her."

"Jamie—"

"I swung her ass out there." It felt like there were pieces of glass stuck in my throat. My words were rasping. "This is my fault."

"While I'm not happy that you involved her in this, this is no one's fault but my father's and Kramer's." Something beeped and Asher frowned. He pulled out a cell from his pocket and his expression grew taut. "I need to take this. I'll just be a few minutes."

He left me there, hesitating on the fringes of Jane's room.

I kept screwing up with her name, telling everybody it was Jane when they asked, forgetting her legal name was Margot.

Not that it mattered.

I should clean up her apartment so it didn't look like shit when she got home in the morning.

Wait, no, Ivy said she'd take care of it.

The police hadn't been too happy about the gun, but Ivy showed them her permit and they backed off. They would arrest Kramer once he was released from the hospital. The shit stain survived, despite Jane's best efforts. The cops said they'd question Jane after, but they'd need her statement soon.

What the hell would she say?

What explanation could we give?

Well, you see, the piece of scum with the keys in his neck, he helped frame me for a crime I didn't commit and then years later, I came back for revenge; he found out and took it out on my girlfriend.

Yeah, that didn't sound far-fetched at all.

Taking a shuddering breath, I pushed open the door and stepped carefully inside. It was a small, private room. I paid for it so she didn't have to share a room with a bunch of strangers. Jane would hate that.

I faltered at the sight of her lying on the bed, her eyes closed. One eye was swollen to twice its normal size, dark red and purple and angry as fuck.

There was a cleaned-up cut on her lower lip.

A massive bruise on her cheekbone, stitches where he'd split her skin open.

Imagining what she'd gone through in that apartment made my legs shake. I walked to the end of the bed and grasped the footboard. Bowing my head, I tried to pull myself together. She was alive. That was what mattered.

Was it?

Because the woman I loved was lying in a hospital bed, beaten to a pulp, because of me.

"Jamie?"

I lifted my head at the croaky voice.

Jane could only open one eye. I straightened and covered my mouth with my hand as I stared up at the ceiling, trying to get my shit together.

"Jamie, come here."

I didn't deserve to be anywhere near her, but still I went. I took hold of the hand she held out to me, pulled the chair by the bed closer, and kissed the back of her hand as I lowered down into the seat. Her fingers tickled at my cheeks, scratching against my stubble.

I couldn't speak.

There was too much to say.

"I'm going to be okay." Her voice was husky, like she'd been shouting for a long time.

"Nearly had heart failure when I heard her scream again."

Jesus fuck. I closed my eyes.

"Jamie, I'll be fine."

I forced myself to look at her.

"The bruising and swelling will go down. By some miracle, he didn't break my nose. Yay for that." She tried to smile and then winced when it pulled at the cut.

"He will pay for this, Jane."

"I don't want that." She squeezed my hand.

"Well," Asher's voice sounded loud in the room, "it's going to happen."

I glanced over at him as he came to a stop by the bed. His expression darkened with anger as he took in Jane's face.

"Jamie's right, Jane. Kramer will pay."

"Not you too, Asher."

"Not like you think." He rounded the bed to the other side, to take the empty chair there. "I just spoke to my contact at the FBI." Asher shifted his gaze from me to Jane. I tensed, my grip probably too tight on Jane's hand, at the mention of the bureau. "They arrested my father this evening and Kramer will be taken into custody once the hospital releases him."

"What?" Jane breathed.

Yeah, what?

Blood rushed in my ears.

Asher shot Jane an apologetic look. "I've been working with the FBI since before we met. Just a few weeks before we met, actually. They've been building two cases against Foster, and I helped them with both. Steadman Productions was funded with money provided by a criminal organization. An organization Foster is still actively involved with. He's been swimming in shit for a long time. They've also been working with some of my father's victims to bring serial sexual assault charges against him."

Holy shit.

Jane's nails dug into my skin as she looked at me, astonished. "Jamie."

"What does this mean?" I asked, trying to stay cooler on the outside than I felt inside.

"It means that you'll have to talk to the FBI." He gave me an apologetic smile. "I know you probably don't trust the justice system in this state very much, but I told them what I knew about your case. With Kramer attacking Jane, they want to hear about Skye and what Foster did to you. Don't get your hopes up yet, because they'll need the cashier who got shot to come forward for there to be a chance of you being cleared for the robbery.

"But whatever happens, Foster is looking at a long time in prison. No matter how the trial turns out, my father will lose everything." Satisfaction gleamed in his eyes. "His company, his reputation. The world will know what a predator he is, Jamie. I'm sorry Skye didn't live to see it, but she'll get her justice."

A sob from the bed brought my eyes to Jane.

"That's what I couldn't tell you, Jane." Asher reached for her other hand. "That's why I had to keep you out of it by lying. We couldn't have you interfering with the long game. I hope you understand."

She nodded through her tears and turned to me.

I didn't know what to feel.

I thought in that moment that I'd feel euphoric or hopeful ... or anything.

But I was numb.

Everything I'd been focusing on since getting out of prison was suddenly swept out of my control.

And Jane ...

I knew deep down that she deserved better than me. She deserved someone who wouldn't have put her in danger because of his own fucking vendetta.

The truth of that hurt so much, I went someplace else inside me. Someplace where I could feel nothing.

So that's what I felt in the end.

Numb.

Chapter Thirty-Four

JANE

I KNEW something was very wrong when Jamie didn't show at the hospital the next day to pick me up. Apparently, he'd asked Asher to do it.

Dread swam in my gut.

The pain in my face had decreased, but the pain in my ribs had only worsened. Every time Asher took a corner, I had to bite back a growl of frustration. Asher had brought me a pair of sunglasses so I didn't have to walk around looking like I'd just gone ten rounds with Tyson Fury. Truthfully, however, I was glad to be out of the hospital. Especially after the police showed up to interview me about Kramer's attack.

Reliving it wasn't pleasant, and although Asher was by my side, I resented Jamie's absence.

"The FBI might take jurisdiction over this case since it's connected to a major crime committed by Foster, so expect more interviews," Asher warned as he drove toward my apartment.

"Why didn't Jamie come?" I asked.

"He didn't say."

Fifteen minutes later, we walked into my apartment, and I drew in a deep breath as images of yesterday's attack flooded me.

No. I wouldn't be afraid of this place. I wouldn't allow that. I couldn't.

It was easy to tell myself that.

Harder to feel.

I gazed around, noting the door and table were already fixed.

"Ivy." Asher read my expression. "She's pretty impressive."

"I need to thank her." Jamie told me last night about how Ivy had come to my rescue and stopped Kramer from getting away.

"There's time for that. Why don't we get you settled in?"

My eyes caught on a huge bouquet—beautiful, expensive white roses and pale pink peonies. "Who?" I strode toward the coffee table and took the card out of the bouquet. Ivy must have placed them here for me. The card read:

Margot, we're so sorry to hear what happened. Thinking of you and wishing you a speedy recovery. Sandy, Joe, Vale, and all the team at Chimera.

"The production team." I glanced over my shoulder at Asher, wondering how they knew about the attack.

"Ah. I called in for you and explained what happened. I hope you don't mind."

The idea of fielding questions about the attack when I returned to work made me a little nauseated, but Asher had probably saved my job. "No. Thank you." I caressed the rose petals. "It was sweet of them to send these."

"More people care about you than you think, Jane."

I didn't know why. I was horrible at letting anyone in. "Asher?"

"Yeah."

"Do you forgive me?"

He took a tentative step toward me. "Baby, for what?"

"For shutting you out when I discovered you were deliberately stopping me from finding evidence that might implicate Foster."

Asher sighed. "You've been hurt a lot. And I did lie. But we're past that now, right?"

"You've been doing something so dangerous and so emotionally draining with no one to talk to about it. You amaze me. Thank you, Asher. You are one of the bravest people I know."

Emotion shimmered in his eyes as he crossed the room to hug me. Carefully.

"If you need to talk about it," I whispered, "I'm here."

"One day I will probably take you up on that. But right now, you need some sleep."

I shook my head as we pulled back from one another. "I want to see Jamie."

His presence across the hall was a pulse in the back of my head. I was so focused on him, seeing him, I could shove aside my throbbing headache and the need to sleep for a little longer.

However, when I knocked on Jamie's door, there was no answer. I knocked harder. Called his name. Receiving no response, I returned to my apartment and dug the spare key to his apartment out of my kitchen drawer.

"Jane, what are you doing?" Asher asked, following me across the hall.

"He gave me a key for a reason." I unlocked the apartment and stopped as soon as I stepped inside.

All his boxes were taped back up and piled by the door.

Next to a suitcase and the punching bag he'd hung in Sheila's bedroom without her permission.

My stomach dropped.

"It might not mean anything." Asher hovered at my back.

Each step was agony on my ribs, and I was exhausted. All I wanted to do was lie down and sleep for a decade. Now, however, adrenaline was spiking, agitating me. Seeing his laptop on his desk, I crossed the room, my gaze zeroing in on the papers folded beside it.

Not caring if I was violating his privacy, I unfolded the papers and saw the top one was the rental agreement for the Porsche and the one beneath it—

The papers fell from my hands as I stumbled back in disbelief.

"Jane?" Asher sounded far away. "Jane, what is it?"

I blinked, staring blindly out the window.

A receipt for a plane ticket.

To Boston.

"Jane?" Hands clamped down on my shoulders and I jumped, wincing as pain flared through my ribs.

"Shit, sorry." Asher held up his hands warily. "I didn't mean to scare you."

I tried to breathe normally. "No, it's fine. I'm sorry."

"What are you sorry for?"

"I don't ..." I touched my forehead. My head was throbbing. And I felt sick.

Was it the concussion or the realization that Jamie McKenna was planning to abandon me?

"We need to get you to bed."

I shook my head. "Tylenol first ... and then I need you to drive me somewhere."

JAMIE WASN'T at the rental place handing over the Porsche, and he wasn't at his favorite coffee house. For a while, I sat in

Asher's car and panicked that I should have stayed put at the apartment and waited for Jamie to come home. That I might have missed him with all my bad Sherlocking.

Then a thought occurred to me, one I couldn't shake, and soon I was directing Asher to a house on a quiet suburban street in Glendale. A house that had a back deck that looked out over the Verdugo Mountains and held within it my best and worst memories.

Somehow, I wasn't even surprised to see Jamie's Porsche parked outside it or to see him in the driver's seat staring at the house.

I'd long since given up figuring out the cosmic tie between us.

"Can you wait for me?" I asked my friend.

"Of course."

Taking a deep breath, I got out of the car and walked at a pathetic, sloth-like pace across the street.

Jamie startled as I opened the car door and eased myself into the passenger seat beside him with less speed than an octogenarian. He met my eyes with a flat, blank look. Trepidation filled me.

"How did you know where to find me?"

"I don't know," I answered. "I guess I realized after I found the receipt for the plane ticket that you might want to come here to say a final goodbye."

When he didn't answer, my anger took over my fear.

"Were you going to say goodbye to me?"

Jamie cut me a dull look. "What good would it have done?"

I felt my heart crack right down the middle, and it hurt worse than anything Frank Kramer had done to me. "You don't love me."

Just like that, his anguish overwhelmed the blankness. "Love you," he hissed. "I love you so fucking much, I can't bear the thought of what happened to you. Or that I put you in that position. You took a beating for me, Jane. And not just physically. I've hurt you so much. I've almost destroyed you." He shook his head in disbelief. "Why would you even want to be with me?"

"Jamie." I tried to reach for him, but he flinched back. "Jamie." I hardened. "You are not to blame for yesterday, and you give yourself too much credit. Kramer and Steadman were on to me when I first grew close to Asher. We're just lucky they hadn't seen me with you, or it could've turned out a lot worse for us. Especially knowing Foster has ties to a crime family.

"As for everything else, Lorna caused the bitterness between us, and I thought we'd moved past that. So if you're running away because you feel guilty, then don't. It's completely misplaced."

"It's not just that." Jamie ran a hand through his hair, resting his elbow on the steering wheel as he gazed up at the house. "I'm fucking lost, Jane. I'm so lost ... and I didn't even know how far gone I was until Asher told us that Steadman had been taken care of. I got back to the apartment and realized that what had been driving me since I got out of prison was this determination to make them all pay. And that's gone. Out of my control." He glared at me. "Who am I now?"

"You're Jamie," I replied, not afraid for him. I knew he'd find his way back to himself. His writing already gave him purpose. "Pen name Griffin Stone. The man I love, and a talented writer." I turned toward him, wincing with the movement. "I'm not saying it will be easy or that we don't have a rough road ahead of us. But I think we can do anything as long as we're together."

He was silent for a moment, processing my words.

Stupid hope rose within me.

Hope Jamie crushed when he turned to me and said, "I won't screw up your life any more than I already have."

For a moment, I didn't know whether to be angry or heartbroken or understanding or defeated.

Then it hit me. I could be all those things.

But I'd survive them.

"I love you," I told him. "I've loved you for half of my life. And I know I'll never stop loving you." Our eyes met and held, his dark with pain, mine with acceptance. "But I can't keep doing this. I know what it's like to live without you, and it was like walking around every day with this hole inside me." Tears slipped down my cheeks despite my determination to be strong. "But I survived you, Jamie. I survived you then, and I will survive you now. You know why? Because I have to believe that one day, someone will come along who loves me so much, he could never imagine a world in which he'd abandon me."

Jamie's jaw locked and he looked quickly away.

"I just need to make peace with the fact that you're not that guy."

Swiping away my tears, I reached for the door handle and pulled. "I hope you find yourself. I really do." I choked back a sob. "Goodbye."

As I crossed the street, I met Asher's concerned gaze and my face crumpled.

It felt like I couldn't breathe.

I stumbled to a stop as I gasped for air, my arms wrapped around myself as I sobbed silently through the pain. I'd only just gotten Jamie back, and now I'd lost him again. As brave as I'd sounded in the car, I didn't want someone else to come along and love me. I only wanted him. Why couldn't he let it be him?

Strong arms wrapped around me and I melted into Asher.

Then his scent registered.

It wasn't Asher.

"Doe, don't cry," Jamie pleaded in my ear. "I'm sorry, baby, don't cry. Forgive me for always making this so damn hard on you."

Anger, relief, and fear flooded me, and I grabbed onto him, my fingers curling into his shirt as I breathed him in.

"I'm so fucked up." He squeezed me closer, hurting my bruised and battered ribs, but I didn't want him to let go. "Loving me will be nowhere near as easy as it will be for me to love you. You get that, right?"

I lifted my head and he gently wiped at my cheeks, trying not to press where I was stitched and swollen and bruised. "It might not be easy now, but we'll find our way there."

"I'm a selfish bastard who can't walk away from you. The minute you said goodbye, I knew I couldn't do it. I don't want to survive without you, Jane." He bent his head toward mine, eyes blazing with emotion. "Aren't you sick of just surviving?"

I nodded, wrapping my hands around his wrists. "I vote for living instead."

His answer was a careful, loving kiss. When he lifted his head, he slid his arm around my shoulders, drawing me into his side.

Asher waved at us, giving me a relieved smile, just before he pulled from the curb and drove away. Jamie guided me back to the Porsche, and we both stopped to look up at the house.

"Let's live instead," he repeated before turning to me. "But not in Los Angeles."

I smiled a little, remembering our plans when we were kids to live somewhere quiet where he could write and I could paint. Despite the hell of the last twenty-four hours, I felt happiness soak through me like sunshine prickling my skin. I'd missed that feeling. I hadn't felt it in a very long time.

"I'll go anywhere with you, Jamie McKenna."

EPILOGUE
FIVE YEARS LATER

JANE
Colorado

THE SOUND of eighties music filtered into the lake house from the deck. Jamie liked to write chapter notes by hand while he listened to the radio out there.

While the distinctive vocals of Phil Collins sounded in the background, I took a sip of iced tea and turned the page in the sci-fi novel Asher had recommended. These days I was tired a lot more quickly and the second bedroom that had become my art studio was in the middle of being packed up.

Jamie had hired a contractor to build a separate studio for me, but it was Sunday, so our peaceful retreat was thankfully free of construction noise. Still, we were enjoying the lake house while we could because we'd be returning to Portland in a month. We split our time between a city that had a relaxed, creative vibe that fit us, and our little slice of heaven near the Rio Grande River in Colorado.

Usually we spent the entire summer in Colorado, but we

wanted to be closer to the city since I was six months pregnant with our first child.

Caressing my belly, I grew distracted, as I often did lately, and stared out of the sliding glass doors that led onto the deck and provided a beautiful view of the lake. Trees surrounded the edges of our land, and the lake glistened like a sheet of glass beneath the afternoon sun. I could see the back of Jamie's head where he sat in his chair, daydreaming about the characters currently renting space in his imagination.

Sometimes I couldn't get over how far we'd come. How the seven years that had shaped us so greatly often felt like they were a part of another life. I knew Jamie didn't quite feel that as much as I did. His years in prison were filled with memories that would stay with him forever. I had my own memories, too, that I'd never be able to let go of.

Yet, if someone had told me five years ago that Jamie and I would have the life we'd always longed for, I'd never have believed them. There were bad days when I waited for the other shoe to drop, but Jamie liked to kiss those days away. He reminded me that we had what people everywhere hoped to find and never did. That for all the bad that had happened to us, our love was the balance point.

Therapy had helped us both a lot, and although we were each reluctant to take that step, it was one of the best decisions we ever made. We'd only ever been good at letting each other in—no one else. It wasn't easy to open up to a stranger, but for the sake of our relationship, we knew we had to deal with our own issues separately to make us stronger as a couple.

It wasn't easy. There were a few bad days back then. Especially with everything else going on.

We decided to see our own therapists not long after Kramer attacked me and while we were unable to leave Los Angeles. We couldn't—we were caught in the middle of several cases brought against Foster Steadman and Frank Kramer.

It wasn't until around eight months later that we felt we could move on from LA. I'd suggested Portland after working on set production there. I'd loved the vibe. People were friendly, the food was amazing, and there was a genuine appreciation for quirkiness and creativity. There were a lot of hipsters and vegans and backyard chicken farmers, but there was just something about the place that felt right. Moreover, despite being a California girl, I liked the rain.

Only a month after moving into a house in the Northwest District, Jamie proposed. We married in a small ceremony with only Asher and Irwin Alderidge as witnesses. Alderidge was an interesting fellow. I wasn't sure I cared for a ruthless CEO being such close friends with my husband, but I knew the man had saved Jamie's life, so I couldn't begrudge him the friendship. Plus, it was obvious he genuinely cared for my husband.

My husband.

I caressed the platinum wedding band and citrine-and-diamond engagement ring on my finger.

It took awhile to get used to that. When I changed my name after the wedding, I went whole hog and returned to using Jane.

I was Jane McKenna now.

Life in Portland was exactly what we needed. While Jamie's writing career grew from strength to strength with his second runaway bestseller, *Doe* (which was a love story and not the personal attack Jamie had once hinted at), and *Brent 29* went into production, I built on my art career. It wasn't easy. But it was the life we'd always envisioned.

The only moments of real gloom were when we got pulled back to LA for the cases against Kramer and Steadman.

It took two long years, but Foster lost everything. His

production company went bankrupt, and he was sentenced to a combined thirty-three years in prison for involvement in racketeering and drug and human trafficking.

I could never have imagined the depths of his wickedness.

In the case against him for serial sexual assault, there was a long list of accusations from women against whom Foster Steadman perpetrated acts of sexual violation and coercion, in which he threatened to ruin or make their acting careers. He was sentenced to another twenty-five years for those.

He'd spend the rest of his life behind bars.

Kramer got two years for the attack on me, along with similar charges to those brought against Foster. He wasn't getting out anytime soon either.

The pièce de résistance for us was that Elena Marshall came forward and admitted to taking a bribe to lie in Jamie's case. Elena was charged for giving false evidence.

Jamie was exonerated, and since he hadn't pled guilty, he could claim compensation for wrongful conviction from the state. The State of California provided a little over $50,000 per year spent in prison as compensation in a wrongful conviction. He'd put the money toward the lake house. Since it was a private lake, the compensation was a mere deposit. Jamie had invested a fair bit of his royalties into the house.

It was worth it to see the contentment he found here.

The road had been long, but the destination was everything we'd hoped it would be.

My phone buzzed on the table beside the sectional; I picked it up to see a text from Asher. It was a photo of him in a tux, all dressed up for a New York gala he was attending in a few hours. A benefit for literacy. Rita Steadman had brought her own money to her marriage, and while it wasn't the billions she'd married into, it was enough to set up a new life in New York. Asher followed her there after the trials.

Seeing him testify against his father was heartrending. He

was one of the strongest people I'd ever met. A literacy charity now employed him, and he spent his days planning fundraising events. Despite our physical distance, our friendship didn't break down to crumbs of communication as it had with Cassie. We were too intrinsically connected for that to happen. Asher and I spoke nearly every day, and Jamie and I had already agreed to name the little boy growing in my belly after his soon-to-be godfather.

> So handsome. Have a great time! xx

Asher texted back a blowy kiss emoji, and I smiled.

A wavelike sensation in my belly made my breath hitch. I wondered if I'd ever get used to the little guy moving around in there. It was a wonder every time. The first time baby Asher kicked, it felt like gas bubbles. As the weeks wore on, I could definitely feel the thud of it more, but it wasn't painful, just wonderfully weird.

And when he moved or shifted, it was like the ocean rolling inside me.

I wondered if he'd have Jamie's ocean eyes. I hoped so.

Jamie had already told me he had his fingers crossed for my hazel-green ones.

Moving my feet off the couch, I planned to go to Jamie to let him feel the movement. I still didn't like interrupting him while he was working, but he told me he wanted to feel baby Asher's every kick and turn.

Crossing the room toward the sliding doors, however, the music coming from the radio distracted me.

I listened to the familiar notes of The Waterboys' "The Whole of the Moon" and felt a painful ache in my chest that would probably never go away.

Jamie and Lorna's relationship never mended.

Sometimes I thought maybe I should encourage him to

reach out to her, but I wasn't a perfect person, and the damage she'd done scared me. Jamie and I had talked about Lorna a lot over the years. We accepted our blame in the dissolution of our relationship with her, that our actions had driven her to hurt us. Jamie believed he could've been a more patient and understanding big brother when we were kids.

And I knew that I never should've forsaken her so easily for Jamie. So caught up in falling in love with him, I hadn't considered Lorna's feelings enough. When she gave me that ultimatum, I should've tried harder to convince her that choosing Jamie didn't mean I didn't love her.

But I didn't try hard enough. Neither of us did.

Even so, it didn't excuse what Lorna had done to us. I wasn't sure I could handle her in our lives again when we'd finally found everything we were looking for. And Jamie felt the same way.

In that moment, however, as I caught sight of my husband staring out at the lake, his body tense as the song played, my thoughts turned to Skye. The painful ache her memories caused softened as I remembered where we were, that we were together and our family was growing.

Stepping outside, I moved behind Jamie and leaned down, wrapping my arms around his chest. Resting my chin on his shoulder, my cheek pressed to his, I felt him relax.

He reached for one of my arms and gently caressed my skin with his fingertips as we gazed out at the lake, listening to the song that reminded us of Skye.

Instead of grief, I felt contentment.

It was like she was there with us, telling us she was at peace now too.

"I love you, Doe," Jamie whispered.

I nuzzled my face against his throat. "I love you too."

Bonus Scenes

Stepping into the corner townhouse in the heart of the North District, I immediately fell in love.

The street the house was on was close to cafes and pubs and quirky little boutiques. It was an amazing location.

It was an expensive location.

And the townhouse with the red-brick front façade and pale green cladding on the rear façade, with its gated two car garage, three bedrooms, three and a half baths, and open, bright living space seemed like it would be at the top end of expensiveness.

I gazed longingly at the sitting room with its beautiful gas fireplace and cursed Jamie for bringing me here.

"Now the kitchen is new but the choices are a little dated in comparison to the rest of the home so you might want to reconfigure it." The estate's agent's high-pitched voice faded along with her clacking heels as she strode toward the back of the house.

Jamie squeezed my hand. "Well, what do you think?"

"I think I've only seen one room and I want it." I glowered at him. "We can't afford this."

His lips twitched. "The second part of my advance came through for *Doe*. Even without it, we can afford this. We can afford this a lot." He tugged me through the living space toward the dining room, following the realtor.

I pulled on his hand, trying to block out the very modern but cozy house that already felt like home. "I need to contribute. You know that."

Jamie flicked a look over his shoulder to make sure the realtor was out of earshot. "You will be contributing. We talked about this. We'll split the bills. Fifty fifty."

"I thought that meant the mortgage too. I can't afford this."

"What mortgage?"

I tried to pull my hand out of his and he held on tight.

"Why would we have a mortgage when we can afford to buy a house outright?" He tugged on my hand again. "Let's go check out the kitchen. If it doesn't have an island, we'll need to put one in."

"Island. What? No mortgage?" I followed, gaping.

The last eight months had been this emotionally draining seesaw where I swung between pure euphoria at rediscovering Jamie again and extreme lows of trying to work through what we'd missed out on. There was also the long, drawn out case against Foster Steadman and Frank Kramer. That was draining too. It hadn't taken Jamie and I long to brave counselling for the sake of our relationship when the bad days started to outnumber our good days.

To my shock, counselling had helped us both hugely. It was an ongoing process but I could say that the good days now far outweighed the bad.

So much so, we'd decided finally to take the big step of moving out of Los Angeles.

I'd fallen more and more in love with Portland every time I visited so I'd suggested the location to Jamie. It didn't surprise me that he liked the vibe here a whole lot and we'd begun apartment hunting.

Two days ago, Jamie said he thought he'd *the* place.

The place turned out to be an actual house.

A house.

In the expensive Northwest District.

"It's your favorite area of Portland." Jamie had explained when I realized where the realtor was taking us.

"It's also one of the priciest." I'd reminded him.

He'd ignored me.

Like he was ignoring me now as he led me through the beautiful house that I really, really wanted. Bastard.

"So what do you think?" the realtor, Lucy, asked as we stood in the kitchen.

"It needs work." Jamie pointed to the kitchen dining space. "The kitchen is crammed into one corner and then we have this huge dining space."

"I absolutely agree."

"A new kitchen means money. Do you think they might come down in price?"

"I doubt it. This is a very sought-after neighborhood. There are already two offers on the table."

"It depends on what the rest of the house looks like."

"Well there are two master suites in this house over the three floors. The third bedroom has a guest bathroom opposite it and could be used as an office. There's also a half bath on this floor and a laundry room." She turned to the French doors that led off the kitchen. "And there's a spacious deck which is a real bonus in the city. Not to mention a two-car garage. This is a lot of property for this area."

"Let's see the—"

"Lucy," I interrupted Jamie, reminding them I was in the room. "Could you give me and Jamie some privacy for a second, please?"

She gave me a tight smile. "Absolutely. I'll meet you upstairs."

As soon as she was gone, I turned to my boyfriend.

He stared down at me with this annoying little smirk.

"How much?"

"What?"

"How much is this house?"

"Jane—"

I squeezed his hand. "We're a team, remember."

His expression softened and he pulled me toward him, releasing my hand only to wrap his arms around my waist. I bent my head back to meet his gaze. "Doe... after everything you've been through... I want you to *have* everything."

"I just want you. I don't need you to spend lavish amounts of money on me."

Jamie frowned. "And you think I don't know that?"

I shrugged. I knew he knew that.

He gave a huff of laughter at my expression. "I will not be crippling myself financially to buy this house. This house is a smart investment. And I don't know..." he glanced around, a small smile playing around his mouth. "I like its vibe. It feels..."

"Like home," I mumbled, sounding horribly ungrateful as I rested my forehead against his chest.

I could feel him shaking with laughter.

"Stop it," I grumbled.

He kissed the top of my head. "Let me do this. And I promise you can pay as many utility bills as you please. This doesn't not make us a team. We are always a team." I felt his hand on my chin and he lifted it gently. Our eyes locked. "Jane, we never keep score. Never. That's not us."

Just like that I melted against him. "No keeping score."

Jamie bent his head toward mine, brushing his lips over my lips. It was meant to be a soft, reassuring kiss but I deepened it, licking my tongue against his. I caressed his chest with my hands, smoothing them downward until they disappeared under his T-shirt and I could feel smooth skin over hard muscles. He gripped my biceps to pull me deeper into the kiss.

And then seconds later with a groan of frustration he pushed me gently away. Hunger glittered in his ocean eyes. His voice was hoarse, "That was just mean."

I laughed softly and took hold of his hand. "Sorry not sorry."

"Vixen," he muttered under his breath as he led me out of the kitchen.

"So how much is this place?"

He eyed me suspiciously.

"Hey, no keeping score, I promise. Just your teammate wanting to know what we're dealing with here."

Jamie nodded and told me the price as we started to walk upstairs.

I tripped on a step and he chuckled.

Okay then. "You do have that restitution money coming your way now that Elena has come forward to testify in your favor. That'll help."

"Even without it, we'll be fine. I have a strong investment portfolio."

"You have an investment portfolio?" I stared incredulously. "How do I not know this already? What have we been doing for the last eight months?"

He bent to whisper in my ear as we hit the second floor, "Fucking. And making love. Fucking some more. Then making more love."

My skin prickled with the memories. "We've been talking too. We're not *total* horndogs."

"Okay, baby, but I'm not the one initiating it the constant sex."

"Well I'm happy to stop if it's bothering you," I teased as we wandered into the master suite where Lucy waited for us.

"Don't you fucking dare…" he trailed off, taking in the space.

"Aw shit." I grumbled as I stared around at the spacious, airy room with its big windows and walk-in-closet. The door next to the walk-in showcased a large private bathroom. All marble. All stunning.

Jamie threw his head back in laughter, pulling me into his side. "We'll take it, Lucy."

SIX WEEKS LATER

JAMIE

Stretching my arms above my head I heard a crack in my upper back and smirked with satisfaction. Sometimes the muse hit me at the most unexpected times. Last night, I'd jolted awake around three in the morning and had slipped out of bed quietly so as not to wake Jane.

We'd moved fast on the townhouse because the owners were ready to move fast, and two weeks after seeing the place, we moved in.

It hadn't taken long for the house and Portland to begin to feel like home.

Anywhere would feel like home as long as Jane was with me.

The second master suite on the top floor had the most light, so we'd converted that into Jane's studio for now, ripping up the carpet, putting down hardwood. I was using the guest room on the second floor as my office.

Saving the four thousand words I'd written in the last five

hours, I got up out of my chair. I'd like to say I had days with word counts like that every day but it was rare. I was lucky if I wrote a thousand a day.

My latest book was a thriller, though, and the suspense scenes just flowed out of me. It was good. I was enjoying writing something different.

Opening the bedroom door, I pulled a foot back when I saw a tray sitting on the floor outside. I smirked and lowered to my haunches, picking up the folded up note beside a glass of juice and two homemade biscuits.

If you have time to pee, you have time to eat.
Love, Doe xxxx

I grinned and grabbed the glass of orange juice gulping it down. I'd been so in the zone I hadn't even taken a pee break. On that note...

After I was done in the restroom, I grabbed the tray and took it back downstairs, nibbling on a biscuit as I went.

I found my girl in the kitchen, sitting at the breakfast table with her feet up on the second chair. A newspaper was spread out before her and she was eating buttered toast.

She frowned at my appearance. "I didn't mean for you to come down with the tray. I didn't want to interrupt you."

"You didn't. I cranked out what I needed to crank out. Thanks for the juice and the biscuits." I dumped the tray on the counter and grabbed the other biscuit, heading over to her.

She lifted her feet from the second chair but as I sat down I pulled the chair closer to hers so I could lay her legs across my lap.

Her dark hair was piled on top of her head in this sexy, haphazard bun, strands trickling down around her face. We'd missed fooling around in bed this morning because of my work.

Seeing her in my T-shirt and nothing else hotly reminded me of this fact.

I wonder... I slid my free hand up the back of her leg.

"What are you doing?" Jane squirmed, smiling at me, that gorgeous dimple popping in her left cheek.

My fingers caught on the cotton of her underwear.

The discovery was disappointing.

"Panties?" I snapped the edge of them making her huff with annoyed laughter. She pushed at me with her foot, nudging my cock by accident. Heat swirled in my gut.

Jane's eyes darkened at my expression. "I'd like to finish my toast."

"You can finish your toast. I'm not stopping you." I slipped my fingers beneath her underwear and my cock throbbed at her gasp.

"Jamie," she breathed, dropping her toast as her head fell back on her shoulders.

"This is how I want to start my day." I leaned toward her, pushing my fingers into her tight, wet heat.

Jane opened her eyes to narrow little slits and widened her legs, watching me as I finger fucked her.

God, she was the sexiest woman alive.

"T-shirt off."

She did as demanded and seeing her beautiful body bare in the bright light coming through the kitchen door made what little patience I had die.

I stood up, pushing all the stuff on the table to the back of it, chuckling in anticipating as Jane followed suit and jumped onto the space I'd cleared. I kissed her, breaking away as she tugged at my T-shirt. Once it was gone, I groaned under her greedy caresses, hissing when her hand disappeared into my pajama bottoms and she gripped me tight.

I pushed them down, along with my boxer briefs, and spread Jane's thighs apart, holding her legs up off the table, her ass to the edge of it, and I sank into her.

We fucked on our kitchen table, making it one in many pieces of furniture we'd already christened since the move.

As I came inside her sweet body, my grunt of relief swallowed in her kiss, I marveled at Jane Doe's ability to make me so fucking happy I could die with it. Even with all the other shit swirling around on the edges of our lives, I was happier than I ever thought possible considering what we'd been through.

And I knew just what would make me happier.

TWO DAYS LATER

Jane

On the way back from my meeting with the nearby art gallery owner, I stopped in at a coffee house Jamie liked best and grabbed two coffees to go.

The meeting hadn't gone well.

Apparently my art didn't "speak" to the gallery owner on an emotional level so she wasn't interested in selling my work there. I knew I shouldn't be upset because I had other galleries along the west coast showing my work. But it still stung (no matter how certain of yourself you were) when someone didn't like the physical expression of your creativity and spirit.

I shouldn't have felt glum walking up the front stoop to the townhouse I shared in Portland with my loving, sexy boyfriend. I knew that. But despondency hung over me as I stepped into the house. It lifted a little at the sight of Jamie sitting on our sectional reading a book. Or he had been. He was staring at me now.

The light in his eyes dimmed when he saw my expression. He stood up, dumping his book on the couch before striding toward me. Taking the coffee out of my hands he placed them on the side table and then pulled me into his arms. I snuggled against his chest holding on tight.

"There will be other galleries."

"I know," I muttered. "It just sucks."

"I know." He kissed my hair and then eased me away from him. Something glittered in his eyes. Excitement or nervousness. I couldn't quite get a read on him, which was unusual. "I've got something that might cheer you up."

He didn't sound so sure.

"Okay?"

Taking me by the hand, and by hand, I mean squeezing it so tight it almost hurt, Jamie led me to the staircase. "Is everything okay?"

"Fine."

I raised an eyebrow at his abrupt answer but continued to follow him upstairs.

Jamie led me into our bedroom. I was about to ask him what was going on when I spotted the large gift-wrapped present on the middle of the bed.

"What is this?" I smiled, curious.

"A housewarming gift." He nudged me toward it.

"It's big." Excitement filled me, my earlier melancholy disappearing. "Ooh what could it be?" I waved my fingers over it making Jamie smile.

"Open it and find out."

Something about his tone made me take a second look at him.

There were definite shadows of anxiety in his eyes. "Baby, are you sure you're okay?"

"I will be if you open the damn present."

I laughed at his shortness and then harder when I heard him muttering, 'evil woman' under his breath.

I wondered what it could be that he'd be nervous to give me.

A thought occurred to me. "Ooh is it kinky?"

Jamie stared at me incredulously for a second and then he snort-laughed. "No! Get your mind out of the gutter and open the fucking present."

Laughing harder now, I sat on the bed and tried to pull it toward me. "Ooh it weighs a ton." Standing again, I ripped at the pretty wrapping and eventually revealed a walnut chest. Stumped, I glanced at Jamie and he was actually biting the top of his thumb as he waited impatiently for me to open the chest.

This was clearly important to him.

I stopped joking around and unclipped two brass clips on either side of the chest and pushed the weighty lid open. My breath left me as I stared inside. Pulling on the two drawers beneath the first layer, I discovered a plethora of goodies.

It was a stunning professional oil painting set. I'd never owned anything like it.

"Jamie," I breathed, feeling like a kid at Christmas. I wanted to open all the colors and test out all the brushes and—

My eyes snagged on back of the chest. Where there was a row of tubed oil paints. Except the middle tube had been replaced with a midnight blue velvet ring box.

No way.

I felt Jamie lean by me to pluck the box out of the chest. I looked up at Jamie and found his eyes bright with emotion. Then as he slowly lowered to one knee in front of me, my heart rapidly beat.

Its beat pushed at the emotion in my chest, making it swell until I could barely breathe past the feeling constricting my throat. Tears shone in my eyes making my vision somewhat blurry as Jamie flipped open the box and held it out to me.

It was a halo diamond engagement ring with an unusual yellow stone in the center.

And it was just like Jamie to choose a ring for me that I wanted badly without even knowing I wanted it.

My eyes flew to his from the beautiful ring and the tears shimmering in mine spilled over at the utter adoration on his face.

"Jane, years ago Skye realized how I felt for you before I'd even told you."

At the mention of his sister and my once pseudo-sister, and hearing the gravel of emotion in his voice, my tears fell faster.

"She wanted to know what my intentions toward you were." He grinned and my heart ached. She was one of the first people to truly love me and look out for me. "And I still remember what I said to her. Every word of it." He leaned toward me, holding the ring up higher. "I said that you deserved to be loved. That no one had ever loved you the right way except for Skye. And that when a guy came along for you that he needed to love you so fucking hard to make up for all the times people were stupid enough to forget to love you. And I told her then that I planned to be the guy to love you like that."

I could barely see him through my tears now. "Jamie..."

"I know there have been times that it seemed like I didn't love you the way you deserved... but I promise you, Doe, that since I was eighteen years old I have loved you with every piece of me. Even on the days I thought the worst of you, I loved you so much it hurt."

I nodded, knowing it was true because I felt the same way.

"I didn't think I could ever come back from what happened to Skye and me. Or from losing my chance at revenge. I didn't think anything could save me from that. But you did. *You* saved me, Jane. And now we're here and I wake up every day and I can't believe, that despite all the shit still going on in the background for us right now, that I wake up happy. That the days I forget about my time in prison are becoming fewer and fewer. I never felt free even when I got of that place. But I'm free now. I'm free with you. And I want that kind of freedom for the rest of my life. I want you for the rest of my life. No one but you.

Will you marry me, Jane?"

I fell into him, sobbing because it was the most beautiful goddamn thing anyone had ever said to me. Just when I thought I couldn't love him anymore than I already did!

His arms wrapped tight around me as I cried. "Those... those are happy tears, right?" he asked uncertainly.

I laugh-sobbed. "Its...It's... your own damn fault. Freaking writers and ... beautiful words." I sobbed harder.

And that's when I felt Jamie's body shaking.

With laughter.

"So is that a yes?"

I leaned back, his face a blur. "YE—"

My yelled "yes" was swallowed in his kiss. I wasn't complaining. In fact, I was ravenous for him now. Jamie pushed me onto my back on the floor, kissing me hungrily as I wrapped my legs around his waist. We moved against each other, my skin flushing hot with anticipation.

Jamie broke the kiss with a muttered curse and lifted his body off me but only to take the discarded ring box, pull the ring out of the velvet bed, and then slip it onto my engagement finger. He slid his fingers through mine, holding me tight as he stared at it with the kind of caveman possessiveness that caused a delicious flip low in my belly.

I whimpered.

His eyes flew to mine. Whatever he saw there made him smirk and he raised my arms over my head, pinning them above me as he rubbed himself between my legs. "I think my wife needs me to make love to her."

I grinned, shivering at the term. "I'm your fiancé."

"Technicality," he muttered before kissing me again.

And then we christened the bedroom floor.

TWO MONTHS LATER

Jamie

To say I was impatient to marry Jane was an understatement.

I had my hands clasped in front of me, squeezing them tight with anticipation as I waited for her to appear. If it had been up to me, she and I would have been married immediately. But although we knew our ceremony would most likely consist of only two witnesses and a minister, Jane wanted to wear the dress and pick the perfect location.

And I wanted to make her happy.

So I waited.

Now I was done waiting.

The sound of the ocean lapping at the shore behind us was soothing but I was impatient for the music to cue because then I'd know Jane was about to appear on the sand from the woods behind her. We'd decided to get married near Otter Rock. We were staying at inn nearby and having our wedding dinner there with our witnesses.

Asher Steadman and Irwin Alderidge were the only two guests at our wedding.

I knew Jane had her reservations about Irwin but as I met his gaze he gave me a pleased, reassuring smile. We were strange friends— never would have been friends in another life. But the man had saved my life in more ways than one while we were in prison together. And I think I'd offered him the same.

Or he wouldn't have taken time out of his. busy schedule to be here on my wedding day.

As for Asher, I respected him hugely for what he did to take his father down. And I was warming to the guy now that I knew he wasn't *in* love with my girl.

The music started.

Jane chose it.

I approved.

The Reason by Hoobastank played out of small speakers that looked like rocks. They created an aisle for Jane to walk down toward the beach.

Jane appeared out of the woods, walking carefully down a rocky stairway onto the sand.

And my breath left me.

She was an angel.

She was *my* angel.

Her long dark hair had been styled in loose silky waves and she wore a wreath of small white flowers around her head like a halo.

The dress was perfect for her. The bodice was tight but it had a high waist, the fabric flowing loose to her feet in layers of white silky material. The straps were beaded but fell off the shoulder. She held a bouquet of flowers and I glimpsed flat white sandals on her feet beneath the fabric... but my attention was immediately drawn back to Jane's face as she floated toward me, an ethereal vision in white.

I was luckiest son of a bitch in the world and I vowed never to forget it.

Her eyes were bright with emotion as she drew to a stop beside me, and as she turned ever so slightly I saw the dress had a sexy low cut back. It was perfect. She was perfect.

"You are so fucking beautiful," I told her hoarsely.

The minister cleared his throat.

I flicked him a semi-apologetic look before turning back to my bride.

"So are you." Jane beamed up at me.

I didn't care about her calling me beautiful. After all the darkness I'd brought into her life, I felt fucking grateful that she saw beauty in me.

The music dimmed in the background from the small speakers.

The reverend began to speak but I was so busy staring at awe at my girl I nearly missed my cue for the vows.

I took her hands in mine and slid a platinum gold band down her finger so it nestled against her engagement ring. I raised her hand to my lips and pressed a reverent kiss to it, making her eyes shine brighter. "Jane." Holding her hands against my heart, I stepped closer to her. "With this ring, I thee wed. And I vow to bring as much light and goodness and love to your life as you have brought to mine. I vow to make the good days outlast the bad. And I'm not saying there won't be bad days. I wish I could guarantee that but that isn't guaranteed for anyone. But I promise you now, that anytime the rain comes our way, I will be there reminding you that we're the luckiest two people in the world because we have something so few people find. We have the kind of love that rivals the greatest love stories. It's the kind of love that we *know* will see us through anything. I can get through anything with you by my side. I love you so much, Doe."

I watched Jane struggle not to cry and decided to help her fight that battle by kissing the life out of her. The minister cleared his throat again and I could hear Asher and Irwin chuckling.

Jane giggled, her eyes still bright with emotion but the tears had subsided.

"Now Jane," The minister turned to her.

Jane reached behind her to Asher who held out a wide platinum band.

I wanted it on my finger now. I wanted everyone to know I belonged to Jane.

I grinned at her as she slid the ring over my knuckle and she laughed happily. "Feels good there," I murmured.

"Good." She held my hands tight and stared up at me in wonder with those stunning hazel-green eyes. It was the wonder that killed me. In a good way. After everything we'd been through, my beautiful Doe still had the wonder. And that was fucking awesome. "It's hard to follow that," she joked, but her cheeks were stained a little red with blush. "My fault for marrying a writer who always has the perfect words."

Everyone chuckled at this.

"Jamie," Jane took a deep breath. "With this ring, I thee wed. I might not have the perfect words but I have the truth. The truth is that I have loved you since I was thirteen years old in some form or another. And I love you more than I've ever loved anyone. You are a perfect spill of light through the window, a beautiful shadow of movement, every color in my paint box, every scratch of pencil on vellum, every drop of emotion that falls on my canvas. You are my inspiration, my creativity, the end result... You're everything. You're my soul. And I vow to never forget it, to never take something so precious, so rare, for granted. I will take care of your heart for the rest of my life because not to do so would be to neglect my own."

"Fuck," I breathed out through the well of fucking tears clogging my throat. "Those words are pretty goddamn perfect, Doe." I kissed her again because I couldn't not.

"Uh, by the powers vested in me, I now announce you husband and wife. You may kiss the bride," the reverend announced loudly and quickly.

Jane and I laughed against each other's mouths and I

wrapped my arms around her as we broke apart, pressing kissing along her cheek and into her hair as I held her close.

A round of clapping behind her brought my eyes to Asher and Irwin.

Irwin was grinning big and happy.

Asher was wiping tears off his cheeks.

I thanked the minister and then feeling generous, I released my wife so she could hug her friend.

My wife.

While she and Asher hugged, Irwin and I shook hands.

"Pleased as hell for you, son." He said, covering our hands with his other. "She's one of a kind."

"She is that." I grinned, so fucking happy I thought I might burst with it.

Needing her back in my arms, I let go of Irwin's hand and reached for Jane. She turned into me immediately and I skimmed my fingers down her bare back. I was looking forward tonight. Our first time as husband and wife awaited us.

"How about we get our guests back to the inn for some food, Mrs. McKenna?"

Her eyes bright with joy she snuggled into me. "Mrs. McKenna. Now that sounds really good."

"What food or the name?"

"The name." She reached up to kiss me softly. "Mrs. Jane Jamie McKenna."

Possessiveness flooded me. "Oh yeah, that sounds fucking awesome.'

Laughing, Jane pulled back and turned toward our friends. "My husband and I invite you to dine," she announced with a fake posh accent.

Irwin and Asher gave her similar doting smiles.

"Is every sentence now going to start with my husband

and I?" Asher teased as we followed the minister off the beach. I kept Jane tucked into my side.

"Yes," she said to Asher's back as we trailed at the end of our tiny entourage. "Is that a problem?"

He laughed as he looked back at us briefly over his shoulder. "No problem here."

"Well, wife," I said a few seconds later helping her up the rock steps, "We did it."

"We did, husband. It feels good."

"Those were some vows," my voice was hoarse with emotion.

"I meant every word."

I squeezed her hand as my gaze flickered down her dress. "Have I told you how beautiful you look?"

"You have. You cursed in front of the minister."

"Oh yeah so I did."

"And I told you that you look beautiful too." She pushed into my side, her breasts crushed against my ribs. "And you do... but you also look exceptionally sexy in that suit. Like ... I'm extreme levels of turned on right now anyway because of the whole husband and wife thing... but you in that suit..."

I flushed hot at the heat in her expression. "Oh you can't look at me like that when we're in company."

"I think I need you before dinner." Her hand slid down to my backside.

My gaze flew to where Asher, Irwin and the minister were making their way through the manmade path in the woods toward our waiting cars. "Are you serious?"

"Extremely."

Asher turned to look at us. "You coming?"

"Uh..." I glanced down at my wife, saw the utter want in her gaze, and looked back at Asher. "You guys go ahead. We'll catch up."

He raised an eyebrow and then shook his head with a disbelieving grin. "Okay then."

He'd barely turned around when I grabbed Jane's hand and started leading her off the path into the thick of the woods. I didn't stop until we were well out of earshot with no one else around. That wasn't to say we might not get caught.

"We could get caught," I reminded her as I pressed her up against a tree.

Like I knew it would, her face flushed with arousal. "This is an emergency." She tugged me toward her and our mouths slammed down on one another's in hungry urgency.

As we devoured each other, I reached for the folds of her dress, the fabric light in my hand and felt Jane plucking at my suit pants. I got to my destination first, sliding my fingers beneath her lace panties.

Heat and lust flooded my dick when I discovered how wet she was.

"Fuck," I muttered against her, hurrying to take over her fumbling of my pants.

Seconds later, I was thrusting into her slick heat. "Oh fuck," I groaned against her lip, squeezing her breasts over the beaded bodice of her wedding dress.

"Jamie." Her head fell back against the tree trunk as her hands grabbed at my ass trying to pull me closer. "Harder, baby... I want it hard."

The urge to fuck her into next week was real... but, "This isn't the most romantic first time between a husband and wife."

Her eyes flew open. "It's the hottest first time. We love each other. We'll make love all the time," she gasped as I hit her g spot. "But right now your wife needs to be fucked and that's okay!"

Her words snapped what little control had I left. I felt under the layers of her dress and grabbed her thigh, spreading her wide. And then I began to fuck her against the tree. Her moans and gasps filled the woodlands, each getting higher and more frantic in pitch. "I'm addicted to your pussy," I murmured in her ear, knowing it made her hot. "Tonight, when we're alone, I'm going to—" I groaned as I felt her inner muscles ripple around me, squeezing me hard. "I'm going to lick every inch of you."

"Jamie!" she cried as she kept coming around my dick.

"I'm going devour my wife's pussy because it's my favorite fucking thing to eat."

Her hips juddered against mine, her gasps turning to little moans of satisfaction and I finally let myself go.

"Doe!"I shouted as my climax tore through me, my cum flooding inside her in throbbing pulses.

I slumped against her, my head buried in the crook of her neck. Her skin was hot and damp.

It took a minute or so for us to collect ourselves.

"Your dress," I muttered, feeling languid and satisfied beyond belief. "Did we ruin it?"

"I don't care," Jane sighed, caressing back. "It was worth it."

Chuckling, I lifted my head to press a soft, wet, long kiss to her lips. My dick throbbed inside of her again and I pulled back. If we didn't stop I'd be fucking her against the tree for a second time.

Holding the layers of her dress up out of the way, I carefully pulled out and then took the cotton handkerchief from my suit pocket out. I smiled wickedly at her as I pressed it between her legs. "Never thought this is what I'd need it for, but can't say I'm complaining."

Jane laughed, rolling her eyes as she playfully pushed my hand away.

Her dress fell back around her feet.

Except for her swollen lips, flushed cheeks, lopsided hair wreath and slightly disheveled hair, she looked untouched.

I pressed my lips together, trying not to laugh as zipped myself back up.

"I looked freshly fucked don't I?" she groaned, touching her hands to the flower wreath around her head.

"Yes." I answered honestly. "You look perfect."

And I meant it.

Jane suddenly shrugged. "Oh well. Like I said. Totally worth it."

I pulled her away from the tree and made her turn so I could check out her back. I'd forgotten the dress was backless and there were scratched from the tree bark. "Fuck. Does that hurt? You should have said." I brushed my fingers across marked skin.

"What is it?" Jane tried to peer over her shoulder.

"Your covered in scratches from the tree."

"Oh." Her lips trembled with laughter. "I didn't even feel a thing."

"It's not funny. We'll need to put salve on it when we get to the inn." I took her hand and began leading her back through the woods, annoyed at myself for screwing her against a goddamn tree.

"Jamie, I'm okay."

Jane tugged on my hand pulling me to a stop.

She scowled at me.

Not exactly the expression I wanted to see from my wife on our wedding day.

"Don't ruin a perfect first time as husband and wife. My back is fine. It's just a few scratches."

The truth was I just hated seeing anything marring her skin. I hadn't quite gotten over the beaten she'd taken from Kramer or the weeks it took for the bruising to disappear. I wouldn't ever get over it.

"You sure?"

Jane pushed into me, wrapping her arms around my waist. She tilted her head back to meet my gaze, her eyes smiling. "It was delicious and hot and everything I want from you. Never hold back with me, Jamie. You know how I like it." Her voice got low and sultry and might as well have been a stroke to my dick.

"Okay, stop talking like that. We have a dinner to get through before I can get you alone again." I slid my arm around her shoulders and started walking back to the car.

"Okay, I'll be good. A good little wife who is definitely looking forward to being eaten this evening by her husband."

I groaned. "Doe!"

She laughed happily and I warmed at her teasing, even if she was driving me crazy.

"Let's just get back to the inn with no more cute dirty talk, okay?"

"Okay. I'll try."

"Try very hard." I caressed a hand down her back. "I'm still getting some salve for your back first," I muttered.

"If it'll make you feel better we can do that." She patted my stomach. "I'll do whatever makes you happy."

I smiled down at her as we walked. "Then I guess we're going to be very busy doing whatever makes the other happy, huh?"

Jane grinned up at me. "Look at us. We're so sickeningly in love. Do you think we're irritating to be around?"

"Like I give a shit."

"Yeah I don't give a shit either." She shrugged.

The car came into view up ahead. Asher, Irwin and the minister were already gone in the other car.

"I was thinking," I said as we approached the car. "Maybe we should start looking for that place on the water we always wanted."

"I'm already blissfully happy, Jamie. You don't need to do that. I might overdose on happiness."

"Well we wouldn't that." I held the door open for her and waited until she was in, dress and all, before closing it.

When I slipped into the driver's side, we looked at each other. She reached for my hand, like she couldn't bare not to touch me. "If the house on the water would make you happy, though, I'm all for it."

"We'll see. Look around maybe." I squeezed her hand.

"We have time. We've got a lifetime, Mr. McKenna."

That aching fucking feeling filled my chest. The pleasure pain that existed within me from the moment I'd started to fall for this woman. "Not even a lifetime is enough, Mrs. McKenna. Don't you know I'm a greedy bastard when it comes to you?"

A huge smile spread slowly across her face, the dimple I adored creasing her cheek. "That works for me."

I laughed at the edge of sexy wickedness in her words and reluctantly started the car. "Here we go. We're driving into the rest of our life together."

"Drive slow," jane said softly. "Let's savor every second."

About the Author

**For free books, updates and reveals, sign up to
Samantha's newsletter:
https://geni.us/samsnewsletter**

Samantha Young is a *New York Times*, *USA Today* and *Wall
Street Journal* bestselling author from Stirlingshire, Scotland.
She's been nominated for the Goodreads Choice Award for
Best Author and Best Romance for her international bestseller
On Dublin Street. *On Dublin Street* is Samantha's first adult
contemporary romance series and has sold in thirty-one
countries.
Visit Samantha Young online at http://
authorsamanthayoung.com
Instagram @AuthorSamanthaYoung
Facebook http://www.facebook.com/authorsamanthayoung
Tiktok @AuthorSamanthaYoung

Printed in Great Britain
by Amazon

43293918R00229